Hannah and the Preacher

Hannah and the Preacher

Rebecca Lorraine Walker

Tate Publishing & *Enterprises*

Published by Tate Publishing & Enterprises, LLC
127 E. Trade Center Terrace | Mustang, Oklahoma 73064 USA
1.888.361.9473 | www.tatepublishing.com

Tate Publishing is committed to excellence in the publishing industry. The company reflects the philosophy established by the founders, based on Psalm 68:11,
"The Lord gave the word and great was the company of those who published it."

Cover design by Kandi Evans
Interior design by Lindsay B. Behrens

Published in the United States of America

ISBN: 978-1-61566-607-2
1. Fiction: Christian Romance 2. Fiction: Historical
09.12.09

Dedication

This book is dedicated to my husband's parents, Kenneth and Estelle Walker. I learned so much from you by watching your example. Your faith in God has stood the test of time and is now being passed on to the next three generations. Your example of simply believing God's promises has proved before many witnesses that he is faithful. I thank you for pouring into my life, for all I have gleaned from you. So many of your descendants are ministering to others the things you taught us. Although Kenneth is gone home, I know he is waiting, saying, "The gate is open; come on in."

On the following page is the poem I wrote for Kenneth Walker's eulogy. I will be forever grateful for the treasures both he and his wife have placed within my heart.

A special thanks to you both for giving me my very own, very special preacher man! I love you!

In Loving Memory of Kenneth Walker

The Gate Is Open, Come On In
To my friends and family waiting behind
I've enjoyed a good life and now crossed the line
To each of my loved ones, both women and men
I've left the gate open, so come on in

We'll talk of old times and cherished things
The memories we've made have not taken wings
To my dearest Estelle who shared my life
Thank you for being a wonderful wife
As my arm was extended and I pulled you to my chest
It is waiting, still extended, and I am at rest
I'll wait for you 'til we meet again
The gate is open, come on in

I've fought a good fight and the faith I've kept
And for my loved ones' souls I've wept
'Tis not in vain, for I have confidence in you
You'll make it to heaven with God's love to see you through
Some say I'm remembered as a man of faith
God promised my household would be saved

I've a great invitation to offer to you
I've left the gate open, come on through
My God will help you each step of the way
I promise he'll turn your darkness to day

To my family who wants to call, "Daddy," and have me answer, "Yep"
Come on over, and take the step
I can't come to you, but to me you can come
Bring a whole crowd, we'll have some fun
Don't weep for me because I'm gone
There's no sickness here and heartache has flown
I've left behind a legacy to you
It's a relay race; let's see it through
To each of you the baton I pass
Run swiftly and bring your loved ones at last
I'm waiting for you just past the gate
Come on in and don't be late

Acknowledgments

Special thanks to my husband, who has an editor's eye. Thank you for being excited about every book I write and for your words of encouragement. Sincere thanks to my children and their families, who are some of my biggest fans. The love of my family is the most important treasure God has given me, and within that treasure box is a priceless gem, my dear, sweet, little mother.

Thanks to my readers for your wonderful reviews of my books. You bless me and encourage me to keep on writing.

Above all, I offer thanks to my heavenly Father, the lender of the gift of writing. May I bring glory to you, offering hope and encouragement that only you can give.

Chapter 1

Dusk was settling softly like a blanket over Laurel City as the stagecoach made its way to the station. *My beloved hometown,* thought Hannah Rose Baxter, peering out the window at the early evening shadows.

Dust coming through the windows as the driver pulled up short sent Hannah into a coughing frenzy. Wiping her eyes with a handkerchief she had embroidered at finishing school, she smiled. After being away for six months, she was truly home, dust and all. Typical of the March winds blowing through Florida, this spring was proving to be dry.

The Caloosa River lay calm before her at the end of the boardwalk. The setting sun meeting the river on the horizon with a blaze of majestic colors proudly announced its departure.

"What a beautiful sight," Hannah said to her mother, who was also watching the play of colors.

Adeline Baxter smiled, breathing a tired sigh. "My daughter, the artist. There's nothing like a Florida sunset to welcome us home."

Rising from the seat of the coach, the ladies began their descent with Garrett Baxter's assistance.

"Thank you, Father."

Grandmam and Grandpappy exited, along with Hannah's twin brothers and her sister Sara. Grandmam patted Hannah's shoulder as they reached the boardwalk. "Our last girl to attend Mrs. La Peau's finishing school. I'm so glad we were there to see you graduate, but these bones need a rest."

Hannah's eldest sister and her husband, Elizabeth and Ethan, waved, turning the corner in their buggy. "Load up," Ethan called, pulling alongside the boardwalk.

Little Beth, now two years old, echoed her father's call. "Woad up," she yelled excitedly, her brown curls bouncing as her father pulled back on the reins. Carefully scooting forward on the seat, she reached out to her great-grandmother, as if in desperation. "Mam." Her little arms were waving frantically, her voice rising to a shrill pitch, now accompanied by rapidly moving legs. "Maaamm."

"I'm coming, little darling." Grandmam's smile erased the tiredness from her face as she rushed to embrace Elizabeth's daughter. Turning in circles with her great-grandchild, Hannah thought Grandmam's tired bones had suddenly been invigorated by the sweet call of the dear one.

Garrett Baxter reached for a kiss from his granddaughter. "I'll only be a minute. Need some supplies from Paxton's General Store."

Adeline was next in line for Beth's kiss. "Wait for me." After a long smooch from the little one, she rushed to join her husband.

The twins, Blaine and Blythe, were busy loading the wagon with the luggage while awaiting their parents' return.

Ethan welcomed Hannah with a warm embrace. After hugging her sister and kissing her niece, Hannah placed her reticule on the seat of the buggy and turned, chancing a look at Mrs. Eaton's Hats and Accessories for the Well Dressed Lady. A candle flickered in the window of the millinery shop, as if silently welcoming the young girl home.

I'm so glad to be home. But where is Isaac? Is he waiting in his mother's shop? She had sent a missive saying when she would arrive.

Knowing she had a few minutes before her parents finished their errand, the young girl decided to knock on the door of Mrs. Eaton's shop. She paused, changing direction when something caught her attention out of the corner of her eye. With the deepening shadows, she couldn't decide if her eyes were playing tricks on her or not. Placing her hand on her forehead, she strained to see the young couple just outside the new livery stable.

The young man seemed to be rushing the young lady in a discrete, secretive manner. Bending slightly and drawing his hat low, he turned vaguely toward Hannah. Just as quickly turning away, he shoved his companion through the open door of the stable and followed.

Was that Isaac? Who was the girl? Maybe I'm mistaken, but I'm sure going to find out. Hannah, never one to leave something to chance, rose to the occasion. Hiking her skirts ever so slightly, she crossed the road, never mentioning a word to her family who was busy discussing the trip home from St. Augustine and passing Beth from one to the other.

Easing up to the door of the stable, Hannah wondered how to approach the situation. *I could ask about hiring a wagon.* She smiled, sure the new owner and his not-so-bright assistant wouldn't recognize her from their brief encounter three months ago.

Peering into the stable, seeing no one in sight, Hannah crossed the threshold, prepared to find out the desired information.

"Isa—"

Just as she started to call out, the assistant appeared, his hands raised purposefully. Blackness engulfed her as the mucking shovel hit her head with a dull thud.

"Somebody hep me. Please somebody, won't ya hep me?"

Garrett Baxter heard the call as he and Addy exited the store with their supplies. Dropping the goods in the buggy, he ran down the road toward the stable. Abraham, the hired hand, stood distressed over a heap of skirts on the ground.

Addy was close on her husband's heels. She gasped in horror as they drew closer. "Oh my dear, that looks like Hannah's traveling suit, but how can it be?"

"Isn't she in the buggy?" her husband asked, racing a little faster to the stable.

"I don't remember seeing her when we stowed the supplies. Oh Jesus, help us."

"I dittint mean it. I dittint mean it. Dat boy done an says de outlaw was a comin', and I jus took de muckin' shovel to 'em, but dat's a girl. Don't look like no outlaw ta me, Mista Garrett." Abraham rocked back and forth, helplessly wringing his hands. The blood on the mucking shovel lying beside the girl attested to the unfolding tragedy.

Garrett Baxter quickly crossed the threshold. "What are you talking about? The outlaw was caught last week in Tinn City." Bending down, the gentle father stared into the bloody face of his youngest daughter.

His wife let out a moan, seeing the blood now making its way down the front of Hannah's suit. "No, no, no. How on earth did this happen?"

Lifting his daughter gently in his arms, Garrett Baxter began running down the road to the doctor's office. "Let them be able to help her." The prayer came to Addy on the wind.

Seized with panic, darting back to the buggy, she almost tripped over her own skirt. "She's badly hurt. We're taking her to Wyatt and

Katherine. Please pray." She turned, running back toward the doctor's office.

Looking perplexed, Elise Baxter called, "What on earth is going on, my dear? Who's hurt?"

Adeline yelled back, "Hannah's been badly hurt."

Reaching out to her grandmother, who looked as if she might swoon any minute, Elizabeth turned to her husband. "Ethan, take us to the doctor's office."

Fear radiated from the faces of Hannah's family. Ethan picked up the reins, driving the short distance to the office. "Stay calm. You can't help Hannah if you're in a dither." Though his voice was gentle, his face showed his own fear.

Blaine jumped down from the wagon as if he was in control. At fifteen, he stood tall enough to be grown but was severely lacking in wisdom. "She'll be all right. I'll wager she's fakin' it. Probably just wants some attention from Isaac. After all, she's been away for a while."

"I'll thank you to hold your tongue, young man." The look Grandmam gave her mischievous grandson stilled him.

"Hannah wouldn't do that, Blaine." Blythe looked at his brother reproachfully.

Arriving at the doctor's office, total chaos was greeted by Dr. Wyatt Baldwin and Katherine. The doctor-nurse team was always ready for an emergency. Visibly shaken, the young nurse gently called her youngest sister's name, peering into her unresponsive face.

"What can we do? What can we do?" Adeline Baxter asked of no one in particular. Wringing her hands and pacing the front office, she ran into her mother-in-law's embrace as soon as the lady entered the door.

"It will be all right, dear," Elise Baxter soothed. Her sad countenance belied her words.

"We will take good care of Hannah," Wyatt Baldwin promised, coming back into the front office. "We need to make her comfortable and begin the stitching right away. Please pray as we do our best. The rest is up to God." With that, the kind doctor exited the front office, returning to his wife's side.

"Any change?"

"No, Wyatt." Katherine gently rubbed her sister's arm. "I'm praying Hannah will wake up."

"It's time to get down to business." Reaching for the cloth, damp with an antiseptic solution, Wyatt finished cleaning the affected area.

Shaking his head, he realized the stitching would be extensive. "Thank God it is above the hairline. The scar won't show as much."

"It's just dreadful, Wyatt."

"I know, dear. We'll begin stitching the inside."

Katherine was already at his side with the supplies.

"I know what you're thinking. This is your beautiful sister, and we'll do all we can to keep her that way." The doctor kissed the falling tears of his beloved.

"Thank you, Wyatt."

"God help me," he breathed as he began stitching the long gap.

Katherine was jokingly called the Suture Queen by her husband. Her fine hand at embroidery had paid off. She was the best at suturing and had the certificate from a medical forum contest to prove it. But Wyatt hadn't given it a second thought; this was her sister, and it was too much to ask.

Finishing the internal stitches and dreading the outside work, which needed to be a work of perfection, Wyatt was relieved to feel Katherine nudging his elbow. "I'll take over from here."

"Are you sure?" Wyatt cocked an eyebrow, searching his wife's face.

"I'm better, aren't I?" The half grin spreading across her face assured him.

"Far better, my dear. I'm right here should you need to be relieved."

"I'm so glad I have you."

Katherine carefully matched the flesh, meticulously lining up every edge.

Standing at her side, Wyatt gently mopped the sweat from her brow. "You're doing a beautiful job."

With his praise, her tense jaw relaxed just a bit. "I hope so."

Finally, the last stitch was neatly set. Doctor and nurse drew deep breaths of relief.

"Will she wake up, Wyatt?"

"God willing." He removed the needle from his wife's hand, drawing her into his embrace. He held Katherine there for a few moments before releasing her. "I'll advise your folks."

Stepping into the front office, the doctor was met with looks of apprehension from the entire family. "You may come in for a moment."

Everyone crowded through the door, anxious to see Hannah. As they gathered around the bed, tears began falling at the sight of her pale and motionless form. Their vivacious Hannah appeared as still and cold as a stone statue.

"She is so full of life. I can't believe she's silent." Adeline Baxter slowly turned away, holding her hand to her face. "I can't bear to look."

"She'll be up and running in no time, Addy," Garrett Baxter comforted. "You'll see. She'll have the time of her life sketching and painting the twin foals in the pasture."

"If only she wakes up." His wife stifled a sob, burying her face in his shoulder. "What if she never gets to use the oil paints the La Peaus gave her?"

"Sure she will, my dear." Garrett pulled Addy closer, as if to shield her from the pain.

Sara stood beside the bed, moisture showing in her eyes. Blaine and Blythe stood behind Elizabeth and Ethan, their hats held with nervous hands.

Little Beth reached toward the bed from her father's arms. "Nannah, wake up, Nannah."

"That's right, baby girl, we want Hannah to wake up too. Let us pray." Grandpappy looked around the room at all the family members. "Our God is able. We will believe for a miracle."

"Yes, we will," Grandmam readily agreed, pulling a handkerchief from her sleeve in an attempt to staunch the flow of tears, which had worsened with Beth's request.

The family held hands, bowing their heads as their patriarch prayed to the one who could do abundantly more than they could think or ask.

"Our most kind heavenly Father, we come to you this evening knowing you hear our cry for help. We bring to you our dear child, hoping in that blessed hope that you have given us. We humbly ask for a miracle." His calm voice, so full of faith in his God, soothed the group in the crowded room.

Katherine moved to her mother's side. "Mother and Father, you are welcome to stay. We'll share the vigil and take turns sleeping in Wyatt's old room upstairs."

Garrett Baxter kept a protective arm around his wife. "We would be glad to take you up on that offer."

He turned to the others. "Sara, would you look after the boys? Ethan and Elizabeth will give you a ride home."

Sara nodded. "I'll be glad to." What a change the whole family had witnessed in the strong-willed child who had blossomed into a fine young lady. "Don't worry about a thing. We'll see to the chores and get Ethan's help if needed."

Ethan gave his father-in-law a pat on the shoulder. "You know you can count on me. Anything you need, just ask."

"I appreciate that, Son."

Soon the Baxters were headed back to their home at Laurel Oaks. The night journey would have been full of gloom if not for the prayer that had given them hope.

As Ethan pulled into the drive under the canopy of oaks, Grandmam quietly remarked, "Thank you, Lord, for covering us with your love." They had reached their beloved home, which welcomed them, offering refuge in this, another storm.

Chapter 2

Garrett Baxter made his way downstairs and into the sick room. “How is she? I’ve tossed and turned and can’t get my mind to shut down. If only I’d not gone into the store for supplies . . . ”

“Father, ‘if only’ wishing will not make Hannah well; faith in God is our only hope. You and Mother have taught us that all our lives.” Katherine’s gentle tone broke through the fear showing on her father’s face. She moved to stand beside him, offering a warm hug.

“I know, dear. I just wish it had never happened. I still don’t understand.”

“Just think of her well and sketching and painting again.”

“That’s a good thought.” The rumpled man ran a hand through his tousled hair.

“I’ll pour you a cup of coffee, Father.”

“Your mother just came upstairs and fell across the bed. She was asleep by the time her head hit the pillow.”

Katherine handed the strong brew to her father. “I think I’ll try to catch a nap while you and Wyatt hold watch. Call me if there is any change. Hannah has not moved all night.”

Climbing the stairs, Katherine breathed another prayer. “Please let her wake up this morning, Lord.”

"Katherine, Katherine, come quick."

Somewhere a voice was calling, trying to break through the nurse's foggy mind. *Where am I?* Slowly sitting up in bed, reality dawned with brightness, causing her to scramble from the bed. Running to the door and snatching it open, Katherine descended the stairs two at a time.

Mother was close on her heels. "What's wrong? I shouldn't have fallen asleep."

The two almost tripped over their skirts trying to get into the sick room. Wyatt's tired face reflected hope by the bedside. Hope caused Katherine's heart to lighten. "What's happening?"

"Hannah just opened her eyes. She's asking for Isaac."

Mother ran to Hannah's side. "Oh dear. For goodness' sakes, will someone please go and get Isaac?" She busied her hands, rearranging the blanket covering her daughter.

"I'm off and running." Grabbing her shawl against the early morning chill, Katherine ran down the boardwalk, hoping to find Mrs. Eaton at her shop. "I get most of my hat decorating done in the early hours when no one is around," Katherine remembered her saying. She prayed this was the case today.

Knocking on the door, the nurse stood still.

"Katherine, what can I do for you at such an early hour? Oh my, you look absolutely—"

"Horrible?" Katherine finished Mrs. Eaton's sentence.

"Well, I wouldn't say that, but you do look a little peaked."

"Yes, mam, and I'm awfully sorry to bother you, but I must see Isaac at once."

"Really, dear? Well, Isaac is sleeping in, seeing that he's home from studying law at the university, but I'll send him over once he's had his breakfast."

"Mrs. Eaton, you don't understand. My sister came home on the evening stage from finishing school and has met with a most unfortunate accident. Abraham hit her over the head with a mucking shovel, thinking she was the outlaw that has been plaguing the area."

"What on earth put that thought in his head? Heavens to Betsy, Katherine, is Hannah all right? You know Isaac is quite fond of her."

"She just woke up and is calling for your son."

"Oh dear, I'll wake him. I'm sure he won't mind. Just give me a minute or two; I'll have him in tow."

To Katherine's joy, the sophisticated lady left all decorum behind, running down the road to her house nearby. The last glimpse Katherine had of Mrs. Eaton, her perky spring hat was flying off her head, and she was fighting to keep her petticoats and bustle under submission as she high-stepped it toward home.

Returning to the doctor's office, Katherine informed her family, "Isaac will be here soon. Mrs. Eaton has gone for him." Removing her shawl, she joined her parents at Hannah's bedside.

Wyatt stepped behind his wife, bending low to whisper. "Is that the flash of red and purple I saw running past the front window?"

She could hear the chuckle in his voice. Katherine squeezed the arms surrounding her.

"Isaac!" Hannah murmured the single word, reaching out to the emptiness beside her bed. Her eyes remained closed, her head a mass of beautiful hair with a huge bandage intruding upon the tresses.

Soon Isaac was making his way through the door. "I'm here. Where is Hannah?"

Locating her in the corner of the room, he rushed to her side. "Hannah, it's Isaac. I'm here, dear." His voice was sweet as he bent low, looking at the bandage in horror.

"Isaac, you came." Hannah's voice was barely audible. "I thought you wanted to see me. I'm home now." The words came slowly and with much effort.

"I do want to see you, Hannah, I do." Isaac picked up her pale hand, laying it against his cheek. "I'm here. Everything will be all right now."

"Sure."

She sounded anything *but* sure.

Isaac sat by Hannah's bed until noon. "I'll have some dinner at the hotel and be right back." Cocking his brow, he looked Wyatt up and down before demanding, "Hold my spot."

Wyatt gave a curt nod before Isaac left the room.

Turning to his wife, the doctor whispered, "Something doesn't seem right, but if he is courting Hannah, we'll have to give him the benefit of the doubt."

Frowning, Katherine turned away.

A few minutes after Isaac left, Hannah whispered to her mother.

"Oh, glory be!" Mother exclaimed. "Our sleeping beauty is hungry. I think she needs some soup."

Katherine was already rising from her seat. "I'll go over to Miss Amy's Hotel and get some."

Running out the door in a hurry, the nurse reached the porch of the hotel and paused to catch her breath. Looking in the front window of the dining room, she saw Isaac chatting easily with a sophisticated-looking woman. *They seem cozy. The audacity of that young man,* she thought and then scolded herself for being judgmental. *Maybe he has a reason for being with her.* What could possibly be his reason when her sister had nearly died and now wanted his time and attention?

Forcing herself to walk through the front door, keeping her eyes averted, she went to the counter to place her order.

A look of concern creased Miss Amy's brow. "Isaac told us Hannah was attacked by Abraham."

"Something like that, but we're not sure what brought it on. Why would someone take a mucking shovel to my sister's head?"

"Well, you know, Katherine, Abraham is a simpleton. If he did this to Hannah, then who is next?"

"I don't think he's dangerous, just confused. Father said he mentioned something about an outlaw, but the outlaw has been captured in Tinn City."

"I'm very uneasy about this. Some of my customers frequent the livery to rent a carriage. Thinking about them being hit with a mucking shovel gives me the willies." The proprietor handed Katherine the soup.

"I know, Miss Amy. Thanks for the soup. Vegetable beef is Hannah's favorite."

"You take good care of your sister, Katherine."

"I will," the nurse replied, looking down as she passed Isaac's table.

Nearing the door, she heard Isaac's call. "Katherine."

She turned toward Isaac. "Yes?"

"Tell Hannah I'll be back soon."

Katherine realized the girl was nowhere in sight. *Was she a figment of my imagination? I wish she was.*

Anxious to leave, Katherine replied, "I-I'll tell her." Uneasiness threatened to choke her. Why was she so upset over this well-educated man who had won her sister's heart? She didn't have the answer to that disturbing question. *I'm sure he's of impeccable character. Just needs to set aside his spoiled ways and grow up.*

Stepping into the bright sunshine, Katherine tried to shake off the clammy feeling of dread. But it clung to her like a cloak. *Isaac had better not hurt my sister,* Katherine thought, opening the door to her husband's practice.

For her sister's sake, she determinedly forced a smile. Spooning the soup into Hannah's mouth, she relayed the message from Isaac. "Your friend will be here soon."

"Good. I can't quite place the events of yesterday in order. I know I wanted to see Isaac, and the next thing I remember is being surrounded by darkness." Hannah's voice was weak.

"Shh, now don't go worrying yourself about yesterday. It'll come to you soon enough."

"What will come to her?" Mother asked from her perch nearby.

"The details of the accident," Katherine explained.

"Whatever were you headed to the livery stable for, Hannah?" Her mother could not conceal her concern.

"I don't remember. I just know I wanted to see Isaac."

Katherine sent her mother a warning look. "That's enough remembering for now, Hannah. You need plenty of rest and no worrying. Doctor's orders!"

Hannah's happy-go-lucky attitude was back in place. "Yes, Nurse." She smiled, crossing her eyes at her sister.

The door to the sick room opened. "I'm back." Isaac made his way to the bed, a fixed smile in place, just as Katherine fed Hannah the last spoonful of soup.

"I'll be back to check on you in a few minutes, Hannah." The nurse and her mother quickly exited the room.

"No hurry." Isaac waved them away.

After having a cup of tea with her mother, Katherine decided to check on her patient. She stopped short at the door to the inner office, hearing Isaac's words.

"What do you remember about the accident?"

"Only that I wanted to see you. Nothing else is clear."

"What a dear." Isaac's voice dripped honey.

His voice grated Katherine's nerves. It seemed calculated and unfeeling, as if reading a cold script. Knowing it was impolite to eavesdrop, she continued standing by the door with her ear placed against it.

Isaac was continuing the questioning. "So you don't remember why you went into the livery stable?"

Katherine's indignation brought bile to her throat. *I'd think he was building a case if I didn't know better. That's enough interrogation.* She marched boldly into the room.

"I'm sorry to interrupt your visit, Isaac, but my patient needs her rest. You may come again tomorrow, but only for a few minutes."

A look of relief passed over the young man's face. Katherine's gentle heart wanted to pound out of her chest. *No wonder I am so upset with this man. He looks relieved not to have to stay with my sister. Whatever is going on sure doesn't spell love.*

"Good day." The nurse crisply dismissed the visitor.

"Yes, mam." Isaac tipped his hat as he left the room.

Wyatt entered, having just finished a bowl of soup with Dr. Windam. "Why do I get the sensation that a chill just blew through here?" he whispered to Katherine.

"So you have the same feeling of foreboding that I sense when he's around?"

"Yes, but let's keep this to ourselves. We don't want to judge too harshly. We'll just keep our eyes and ears open."

Chapter 3

After the door closed behind Isaac Eaton, Dr. Wyatt Baldwin began examining his patient.

"How are you feeling, Hannah?"

"A little confused, but I'm better since I ate the soup."

"Answer a few questions for me, Hannah. What year is it?"

"Eighteen seventy-two."

"What town are we in?"

"Laurel City, Florida."

"What made you go to the livery stable yesterday?"

"I'm confused about that, Doctor. I just know I wanted to see Isaac."

"That is a bit confusing, unless he was at the livery stable."

She slowly shook her head. "I can't remember. I'm so tired."

"That's enough questioning. You need your rest. Your mother will be right here beside you."

Joining his wife in the outer office, the doctor shook his head. "Doesn't make any sense why she would go to the livery stable."

"Maybe she'll remember soon."

"I sure hope so." Stepping behind his wife, he began rubbing her tired shoulders.

Hannah Rose Baxter awoke the following morning, having slept throughout the afternoon and all night. Her eyes were alive with a fresh sparkle, even though they showed signs of blue and purple bruising from the accident. "I'm ready to go home." She looked at her doctor and nurse defiantly.

Katherine returned her sister's bold stare. "My, aren't we feeling better? You never were one to be kept down by anything, always ready for the next adventure."

Her brother-in-law observed his patient, rubbing his chin in indecision. "Let's see how steady you are on your feet."

With her mother's assistance, Hannah walked the entire length of the room twice. Smiling brightly, she knew she had convinced the doctor to let her go. "I'm ready for Laurel Oaks."

"If I let you go home, will you promise to rest before taking off across the pasture on your horse?"

"If I must, then yes, I'll rest."

"You must, Hannah. With this type of head injury, it is imperative that you allow yourself time to heal. No new adventures for a while."

"All right," she answered too brightly. Hannah loved adventure. Her curiosity was always getting the best of her.

Katherine gave her sister a pointed look, daring her to defy the doctor's orders. Giving her a hug, she watched as her father helped her into the carriage.

"Please tell Isaac I'll be at home." Hannah waved good-bye.

Mother placed a protective arm around her youngest daughter. "It'll be so good to have you home. You've been gone so long, and I've missed your contagious joy. Besides, Sara and I need you. We've been outnumbered by your father and the twins, and I have another concern."

"What is bothering you, Mother?"

"No need to worry, Sara's just a little too quiet these days. She hasn't been herself in a long while."

Hannah's look of concern quickly brought another explanation.

"I'm sure she will be fine; she just seems to be taking life too seriously, since her conversion."

Hannah grinned. "I'll see if I can liven things up a bit."

"Now, Hannah, you must take care of yourself." Mother patted her daughter's arm.

Hannah laid her head on her mother's shoulder. It felt good to be home where she belonged, surrounded by those she loved.

The canopy of oaks on the carriage drive gave a warm welcome to the young lady returning from her grand finishing at Mrs. Fancy La Peau's Finishing School. What would life hold for her? Was Isaac a permanent part of her future? *I always thought I'd marry a preacher. I'll ask him if he's missed his calling.* A smile covered the face of the beautiful girl at peace on her mother's shoulder.

The week following Hannah's return to Laurel Oaks brought the March winds, spreading the sweet fragrance of the orange grove. Resting in the rocking chair on the back porch, Hannah welcomed spring.

Twin foals neighed in the corral, jumping and cavorting on their shaky legs. Hannah smiled, watching them. "I'll be glad when I can sketch them." Her head still complained when she attended to the fine details of drawing.

"Shouldn't be long now." Her mother turned from the clothesline, carrying a basket full of clothes. She joined Hannah on the porch. "The breeze dries the clothes so quickly." She removed a pillowcase from the hamper, holding it to her nose. "Nothing smells better than fresh laundry, dried in the Florida sun."

Hannah smiled at the sight, reaching to help her mother fold the bed sheets. Completing the task, her mother disappeared into her kitchen.

A couple of blue jays flitted from branch to branch on the nearby oak tree, dressed in its spring foliage. The male jay chased the female, as a suitor begging for attention. Up and away she cavorted, slyly turning to catch a glimpse of her pursuer. Chirping and mocking, she continued her escape, teasing her follower.

I sure don't have that problem, thought Hannah. *My suitor has not paid me the slightest attention since I've been home. He's probably sending out letters of reference, trying to secure a position in a law firm. He'll see me when time permits.* But when would time permit? The one letter Isaac had sent to her at finishing school told of how much he missed her and wanted to be with her.

Shaking off despondent thoughts like an extra garment she wished to be rid of on a warm day, Hannah rose from the chair, making her way back into the kitchen.

"How can I help with supper, Mother?"

"You can take the bread out of the oven and butter the top. Have you had any news from Isaac?"

Hannah shook her head.

"Maybe your father will bring you a message from town."

"I expect Isaac will come when he's ready. He's a busy man, Mother."

"I'm sure he is, my dear." But she didn't look convinced.

Hearing the clang of the harness, Hannah knew her father had returned with his supplies. Pretending nonchalance, she waited for him to enter the house. The twins had accompanied him and were unloading the wagon.

Slicing the bread, she looked up to greet her father.

"How's my sweet girl?"

"Just fine, Father."

"You look pale." He gave her a peck on the cheek. "I have a message for you."

"Really, Father?" Hannah stilled the knife cutting the bread.

"Your sister said to come in when you feel better and she will treat you to dinner at Miss Amy's Hotel."

Sure the disappointment was showing on her face, she smiled. "That sounds nice."

"Oh, and by the way, I saw Isaac."

Hannah's face beamed. "And?"

"He said to tell you hello." Her father looked away.

"And that's all?" It had been a week, and Isaac had not paid a visit to Laurel Oaks.

"I'm afraid so, my dear."

Trying to hide her disappointment, she changed the subject. "I think I'll go for a walk after supper."

"Now, dear, be careful not to overdo yourself."

"Mother, I've been a very good patient. It's time to move around a bit more."

Fried pork chops and yams were temptingly arranged alongside dishes of creamed corn and cowpeas. Crackling cornbread crowned the feast on the Baxter table. However, Hannah's appetite wouldn't allow a second helping. Always one to see the good in people, she was having doubts about Mr. Isaac Eaton.

Grabbing a light wrap, Hannah quickly exited out the back door. Unwilling to share this delightful evening with anyone, she made her way toward the back pasture.

Thousands of wildflowers poked their colorful heads through the blanket of delicate spring grass gracing the meadow. The cows were grazing in the east pasture, and this beautiful spot had been left unmarred.

Not having visited this spot since coming home, Hannah viewed the landscape with sincere appreciation. *Wish I had my pencil and sketchpad.*

Dim rays of the setting sun were shining through the oak trees. Sparkles of light danced across the flowers, enhancing the brightness of each color.

Hannah delighted in the feeling of peace and contentment in this special place. Removing her shoes, she sat on the tender grass, plucking a dainty flower nearby. Inhaling its sweet fragrance, she thought, *Everything will be all right, with or without Mr. Isaac Eaton. I never pursued him. He's the one who was running after me in such a huff at Christmas.*

Blocking out her gloomy thoughts, Hannah removed the tortoiseshell combs that were keeping her sun-kissed brown tresses at bay in the strong March wind. And, oh, did the wind feel ever so good blowing through her hair. All those months at finishing school, and not a day had gone by that she could enjoy a romp in a meadow with her hair blowing free.

A horse whinnied nearby. At first she thought nothing of it. Realizing there should be no horses in this area, she turned.

The accident must have affected my brain. That cannot be... Is it? She wiped her eyes.

"Hello there... is it Miss Hannah?"

Turning to make sure the visitor was who she thought, Hannah quickly hid her bare feet and ankles in the grass. Primly displaying her skirts in a more ladylike fashion, she reached for the combs to secure her hair. *Where are my combs?* She was frantic.

Realizing she had not spoken to the visitor, she tried to sound more confident than she felt. "Yes, uh, sir, uh, well, yes. And how are you this fine day?" *What a dumb thing to say, and I just graduated from finishing school.* She couldn't help but smile, thinking of how Mrs. Fancy La Peau would tutt if she could only see her now.

The visitor smiled back. As he dismounted from the beautiful black stallion, Hannah was amazed at how good looking the preacher was. Her breath caught in her throat. "Has it been two years, Preacher?" *Well that's the second dumb thing I've said to him.*

Wendell Cunningham smiled down at the beauty before him. "Yes, mam, it's been two years, and I've counted every day."

"You've counted every day?"

"Yes, mam. And, Miss Hannah, I still carry the sketch you made for me at the camp meetin'."

"You do?" She looked at him with incredulous eyes.

"Yes, mam."

Hannah laughed. The preacher's face showed embarrassment.

"I'm sorry, sir, I didn't mean to laugh. It's just that you aren't supposed to be calling me mam."

"Yes, mam ... I mean, yes, Miss Hannah." The preacher smiled. "I'm serious about carrying that sketch. It's in my Bible, and I look at it every day." His eyes took on a soft, faraway look. "Helped me through some tough times on the circuit."

"It did, sir, I mean, Preacher?"

Still unable to find her combs, Hannah brushed back the tresses blowing wildly around her face. She caught the preacher watching her.

Clearing his throat, Wendell Cunningham spoke. "I came to visit your grandpappy. Had a hankerin' to go back to the Seminole village."

"That'll make Grandpappy happy, and I'll tag along if I may."

"That'd make me real happy, Miss Hannah. I was hoping you would go like the last time."

Hannah knew that propriety called for her to return home. *But why am I so reluctant to leave?*

The preacher must have felt the same need. "I didn't mean to intrude on your evening, Miss Hannah. Just couldn't help myself when I saw you in the field. Had to come on out and say hello. I'll head on over to your grandfather's place. See you in church on Sunday."

A devilish grin crossed Hannah's face. "Yes, sir, Brother Preacher Man."

"Now, Miss Hannah, don't be callin' me sir, seein' as how I've done dropped the mam."

"Yes, sir." She gave him a salute. Suddenly it didn't matter if Isaac came for a visit or not.

Hannah watched Wendell Cunningham making his way to her grandparents' cabin. He sat tall in the saddle, lean and muscular. A finer-looking man she had never seen.

Isaac's face clouded her mind. "No, not you, Isaac. The preacher man's better looking." *Now that isn't a nice thing for a lady to think, a fine lady fresh out of finishing school, no less.* That thought was accompanied by an impish grin. Hannah reminded herself of Blaine, but she didn't mind at all.

Returning home just before the last rays of the sun were spent, her face sparkled.

Sara looked at her sister questioningly. "My, but don't you look refreshed. What on earth did you do out there, Hannah?"

Mischief danced in Hannah's eyes. "I'll never tell."

Wendell Cunningham made his way through the meadow toward the minister's cabin. How long had he sat there watching Hannah before his horse whinnied, giving his presence away? What a beautiful sight she had been with her hair blowing in the wind, a flower drawn delicately to her nose.

What I would give to have a wife like her, Lord—beautiful, graceful, fun-loving Hannah. His trip to Laurel City two years before had taught him that she was all of these things. Yet he had been dumbfounded in her presence then.

Wendell found himself speaking aloud. "Lord, did you bring me here, chasing the imposter of Rev. Finney two years ago, so that I could meet this lovely creature? I've carried her in my heart ever since. Can this be your will for her to be mine? I sure would like that, Lord, if you could arrange it."

"Hello there, young man," Grandpappy called from the front porch rocker, interrupting Wendell's thoughts.

"Well, uh, hello, to you, Reverend."

"Now, Preacher, we're past that. Just call me Grandpappy, like everyone else around here."

Throwing the horse's reins over the hitching post, Wendell made his way to the front porch.

A hearty pounding on the back was his warm reception. "Good to see ya, young man. How's the circuit?"

"Circuit's good. Just had a hankerin' to visit the Seminoles."

"Sure am glad. Elise, honey, would you bring another glass of tea out here?" he called from the open door.

Grandpappy motioned his visitor to a rocking chair on the porch.

"Sure sits comfortable."

"Yeah, Ethan made these chairs. His business took off so fast he can hardly keep up. Shows you what the Lord can do."

"Yes, sir."

"Well, my dear, what a pleasant surprise." Elise Baxter grabbed the young preacher in a warm embrace. "Son, there's been many days since you left that I wished we had you around these parts. Grandpappy could sure use your help with the Seminoles. And by the way, have you had supper?"

"Mam, I'm just fine. Had me some trail coffee and a biscuit about an hour ago."

"Just fine? I don't think so, young man. You'll eat supper at my table, or my name's not Elise Baxter. Sit and visit. I'll call you in soon."

Grandpappy gave the young man a resigned look. "We'd better do what she says. Don't want my wife riled." He smiled as he set the rocker in motion. "Had any meetings in Florida lately?"

"Yes, sir, as a matter of fact I have. Passed through the town of Rosewood; met the parson at the chapel. He asked me to stay on and preach for him. His health is failing; says he don't know how much longer his ticker's gonna do its job. He was taking some tablets for chest pain."

"Do say. Well, I heard the parson was a kind gentleman. It seems he agreed to take the ministerial position until someone else could be found."

"He's a gentle man of God. I have to say it kinda took me by surprise seeing the steeple in the distance as I rode into Rosewood. The town wasn't there two years ago, and now it's full-fledged and thriving." Wendell shook his head in disbelief.

"Yes, son, Rosewood seemed to spring up almost overnight with the coming of the railroad. Sure is bringing growth to our area; shortens the cattle drives. Garrett and his cowboys only have to drive the cattle a short distance to the rails now."

Wendell rocked in perfect rhythm with Grandpappy. "Makes it easier and less costly, I would say."

"That's right, son. And his wife, well, she's all smiles with him not being away from home so long."

"Supper's ready." Elise's sweet call brought the men from their places of repose.

The cozy dining room with candles and flowers gracing the table made Wendell long for someone to share his life with. Visions of a green-eyed beauty with tresses blowing in the March breeze turned his thoughts away from the conversation. Looking up, he realized Grandmam was asking him something.

Embarrassed, the young man stammered, "Sor-sorry."

"Did you want another glass of tea or a cup of coffee, son?"

"I'm enjoying the tea, mam. Thank you."

Conversation flowed freely around the parson's table. Grandpappy told Wendell about some squatters on the edge of town. "Word is they've been stealing and butchering the Madisons' hogs. Two of the boys were caught red-handed pulling a hog through the brush."

"Anything being done about it?"

"I'm going out to visit them tomorrow. Thought I'd take a few chickens to help them out. Addy is collecting eggs, and Elizabeth has some fresh pineapples to give. I'll check out the situation, try to discourage any more stealing."

Wendell's fork paused halfway to his mouth. "Wouldn't hurt to invite them to church."

"That's my plan, son. Would you care to come along?"

"Sure. I stopped by Ethan's home, and he asked me to stay with them. Just come by, and I'll ride out with you."

"We'll take the wagon."

Wendell finished his plate of beef steak and potatoes and rose to leave. "I'll be ready, Grandpappy."

Turning to Grandmam, he hugged her. "Thank you for the most delicious meal I've had in weeks. Sure gets lonesome on the circuit."

"The good Lord knew you were coming. I cooked too much supper for the two of us."

"Sure was good, mam."

Leaving the cabin, heading back to Ethan and Elizabeth's home, Wendell's thoughts again turned to Hannah. *She sure was a beautiful sight, sitting in the spring grass amidst the wildflowers. The sparkle in those green eyes isn't matched by the brightest sunrise. Wish I could see them every morn.*

Chapter 4

Wendell awoke in the middle of the night to the sound of frantic pounding on Ethan and Elizabeth's door. Putting on his shirt and grabbing his trousers, he opened his bedroom door to see Ethan answering the knock.

"Howdy, Son! Ya gonna let yore ole pa in, or ain't I good enough fer ya? My friend in Tinn City tole me you done an got rich offa the furniture makin' business. Guess ya made money offa what I taught ya."

"Come in, Pa, but please be quiet. My baby girl is sleeping."

"Well, what's the truth, boy? Did ya get rich offa what I taught ya?"

"Pa, you are a great carpenter. But sad to say, you never taught me anything about making furniture. The good Lord helped me learn."

"Oh, so you's givin' the Lord credit for what ya got from me? That ain't bein' very grateful, Son." Reeking of alcohol, the man swayed, nearly falling.

"Pa, did you visit your friend who makes moonshine?"

"I ain't had but a smidgen to drank, Son. You and your maw—God rest her soul—ya both the biggest naggers in the world, a never wantin' a man to have a good drank. Done an learnt how to make it my ... " He slapped his hand to his mouth, sealing his words.

"Pa, you can stay the night, but you've got to behave yourself. I won't have you acting like this around my wife and baby."

"That ain't a payin' your pa no respects. Watch your mouth, boy, or I might be a slappin' it. This here is my house, an you won't be a deefyin' me in my own house."

"Pa, this is my home. You deserted it, and I've returned and cleaned up the place like Mother wanted. You can lie on the sofa and sleep it off, but I'll have to ask you to leave if you can't mind your manners."

Wendell had been standing against the wall, watching the scene unfolding before him. His stomach clenched, nausea coming over him in waves. *This is too reminiscent of home. Reminds me of Granny's intoxication and rantings.*

Feeling as if he might smother if he stayed in that room, he quietly eased back inside the bedroom. Sitting on the bed, holding his head in his hands, Wendell willed his emotions to correct themselves. *Hope I don't have nightmares tonight.*

"Lord, help us all." The preacher continued to pray, hearing Ethan making his way back to the bedroom after his father's snores proved he wouldn't be causing any more trouble for the time being.

Easing down on the soft bed, his last thoughts were of Hannah in the field of wildflowers.

Yawning and sitting up in bed, Wendell Cunningham felt rested after sleeping on the soft down mattress at his friend's home. "Sure beats the hard ground with a saddle for a pillow."

"What beats a saddle for a pillow?" Ethan's voice came through the closed bedroom door. "I was just coming to get you."

Opening the door, the young man greeted his friend. "That bacon is callin' my name."

Trying to erase the happenings of the night, Wendell determined to face the day with confidence. This had been his practice all his life. Granny's raising of her orphaned grandson had required hope to survive.

Quickly washing up with the cool water from the pitcher on the nightstand, the preacher let the refreshing liquid wash away the last bit of the night's disturbing happenings. Had his friend expected this intrusion from his father? Had God sent him to help Ethan at this difficult time? Exiting the bedroom door, he was anxious to meet the day's unfolding.

Elizabeth smiled from her place at the wood stove. "Good morning, Preacher."

"Good morning, Elizabeth. Thank you for a good night's rest."

"You are welcome to stay as long as you like."

A loud snore from the sofa proved Ethan's father was still sleeping off his liquor.

Ethan sat his daughter in a small chair with no legs, placing her atop a kitchen chair.

"That's a nice contraption, Ethan."

"Made it special for my little girl." Ethan sent a wary look toward his father on the sofa.

Wendell received the silent message. "I'll be right here."

"Sure appreciate it, friend."

The group around the table joined hands. Elizabeth looked at her daughter. "Say grace, Bethy."

"Gwace." The child giggled, covering her mouth with her hand.

Her mother scolded. "Bethy."

"Tank woo, Jesus, foa dis food . . . Ahhhmeen."

"These biscuits are the best I've had since I ate yours two years ago."

Elizabeth smiled at Wendell's praise. "It doesn't seem like it's been that long."

Ethan's father stumbled from the couch, his hair matted, his clothes wrinkled and smelly. "What don't seem like it's been that long? Ya mean since ya done an seen me?"

"Good morning, Mr. Dodson. Well I haven't seen you in six years, since you moved away." Elizabeth scooted her chair back, as if to rise, but Ethan's look halted her movement. "Welcome home."

"You that Baxter girl, that oldest Baxter girl? You done an married my rich son?"

Elizabeth slanted a sideways look to her father-in-law, then to Ethan.

"Pa, sit down and have some breakfast. Elizabeth makes the finest biscuits in Laurel City."

"Couldn't be better an ya ma's. She had to go an catch the fever an die, leavin' me to fend for myself. Terrible thang she did, a dyin'. Leaves a man powerful thirsty."

"Pa, you were powerful thirsty when she was alive."

"Watch yer mouth, boy."

Fear and determination showed in Elizabeth's eyes. "Could I get you a cup of coffee, Mr. Dodson?" Her voice held a commanding tone.

"Guess I cain't get nuthin' stronger from the likes of my boy." Running his dirty fingers through his hair, he reached for the back of the kitchen chair, nearly falling.

"Wash up at the back door, Pa." Ethan's voice allowed no foolishness.

Ethan's father mumbled under his breath, sauntering off to the wash pan.

"Wash up, Paw." Little Beth echoed her father, covering her mouth with her hand. Everyone shared a smile before the man made it back to the table, ignoring the grandchild he had never seen.

Ethan turned to Wendell. "How's your meetings been, Preacher?"

"Doing very well. Just came from a meetin' in Georgia that lasted four weeks. Sure was satisfyin' seein' all them souls come to Jesus."

Ethan's father scowled at his eggs and bacon, digging in with a shaky hand manning the fork.

"Do you stay in homes or sleep on the ground?" Elizabeth asked Wendell.

"Well, usually a preacher or someone in the church will ask me to stay in their home. Many times I've pillowed my head on a saddle beneath the stars. Still do when I'm en route to the next meetin'; takes too much money to stay in the inns and hotels all the time. Offerings are slim but that's no bother to me. Whatever the good Lord provides I'll be content with. Just like Paul, I've learned to be content in whatever state I find myself in."

Ethan's father intruded in the conversation. "I'd be content if'n I had the money of my boy, here."

Elizabeth passed him the pan of biscuits. "Have another biscuit, Mr. Dodson."

"I've had enough. Thank I'll be a visitin' my friend." He stood abruptly.

Ethan followed his father out the door. A mule stood tied to a branch of a nearby orange tree. His father untied the scrawny thing and jumped astride.

"See ya later, Son. Need to thank about sharin' with ya pa. I started this here fine place, an now you've a takin' it without even sayin' thanks. Orta be ashamed, plum ashamed."

"Pa, you are welcome here if you behave. If you don't mind your manners around my wife and baby, I'll be asking you not to come until you can. This is my family, and I'll not have them subjected to the way I was raised."

"Lotta 'preciation I get fer all I done for ya." And with that, Ethan's father kicked his mule in the sides, heading off down the lane. "Got me a better famly." His last words floated back to Ethan on the wind.

Ethan returned to the table. "Sure was a sad sight. Pa's no doubt headed to get another bottle of moonshine. He never said why he decided to come here after all this time."

"Don't give up, Ethan. Some people make a drastic turnaround. Others never accept our Lord. That was the case with my grandmother. Never would repent; she could drink as big as any man you could put beside her."

"Did your parents raise you well, Wendell? After all, you became a man of the cloth."

"Ethan, my mother died giving birth to me. My grandmother kept me, and I've never known my father. Granny was a hard woman to live with. I had a lot of bitterness to overcome, and there are days I still have to work at forgiveness."

"Our lives sound similar, only my mother was a precious lady. She loved me and taught me right; couldn't have made it without her." Ethan's last words were but a whisper.

Wendell tapped the table with his fingers. "After fighting in the war, I decided against returning home. The battle with Granny was greater than anything I faced in the war; it was a battle of the heart, one that still hurts today. She constantly told me how bad I was and how I had ruined her life."

Shaking his head, Ethan looked thoughtful. "My father always told me how I'd ruined his life."

"Granny moved me from town to town. My education is severely lacking, but God had a plan. You remember, I was saved in Reverend Finney's meeting, and that's what led me to uncover his imposter two years ago."

"Yes, and what a time we had. I'll never forget the look on the imposter's face when the saloon girl showed up wanting her money. You did good by coming here, Wendell, and exposing him."

A knock at the door interrupted conversation. "Hello," a sweet voice called from the front door.

"Come right in, Hannah. It's good to see you up and around, Sis."

Beth's hands went in the air. "Nannah, Nannah."

"Mornin', baby girl." Hannah reached down to kiss her niece, the smell of apples and cinnamon coming from the basket she held.

"Mother sent over this apple pie for the preacher. It just came out of the oven." Hannah blushed at the sight of Wendell Cunningham.

"You tell your mother I said thank you, Miss Hannah." Looking up, Wendell saw a scar in the beautiful girl's hairline visible in the bright morning sun. *What happened?* Quickly he averted his glance.

Elizabeth noticed. "Our Hannah met with a most unfortunate welcome at her arrival back from finishing school. She didn't even make it home before the livery hand hit her in the head with a mucking shovel."

Wendell's face contorted. "That hurts just thinking about it."

"It's been over a week, now. You can't keep my sister down for long." Elizabeth beamed a radiant smile toward Hannah.

Wendell's eyes lit up with a smile as well. "I can see that."

Grandpappy's voice boomed from the doorway. Joy filled the house with his entrance. Coming to kiss Beth, he turned to Wendell. "Ready to visit the squatters, Preacher Man?"

"Yes, sir. I'm ready." Wendell said good-bye to Hannah, following Grandpappy to the wagon.

Ethan walked alongside Grandpappy. "Had a visitor during the night."

"Is that right, Ethan?"

"Yes, sir. It was my pa." The look on his face told it had not been a good visit. "Guess he's gone to Tinn City to get liquored up again."

Shaking his head, Grandpappy's eyes were downcast. "I'll call his name in prayer; and your's too, son." He patted Ethan's back, then climbed up beside Wendell on the wagon seat.

"Thank you, Grandpappy." Ethan waved good-bye as Grandpappy shook the reins.

Heading down the road past Laurel Oaks, the March wind ushered the two preachers on their way to do a good deed. Chickens, their legs tied with twine, cackled and squawked from the wagon bed. Dozens of eggs sat in a large basket atop a mound of straw. Another basket held jars of guava jam, honey, green beans, black-eyed peas, and cow peas. Sacks of flour and sugar, along with a bucket of lard, completed the gifts being offered to the squatters.

Wendell looked at the basket filled to the brim. "That basket is overflowing with good things."

"My wife is known far and wide for her blessing baskets. There's a story behind it."

"I'd like to hear it, Preacher."

"When Elise and I moved to Florida to begin our missionary endeavor to the Seminoles, we almost starved. The ground was flooded back then, and nothing would grow until we diverted some of the water. We were trusting in the Lord for his provision, living on trapped rabbit and squirrel."

Wendell chuckled. "Had my share of both."

"We had visited the Seminole village, and a few natives had been saved. One cold winter morning, Elise looked up to see an old Indian squaw dropping a basket of food at our back door. She quickly disappeared through the palmettos."

The young preacher nodded his head in agreement. "The Lord has done the same for me."

"I still remember my wife's words. 'What a blessing this basket is.' And thus, the blessing baskets were born. Anytime there is a need in our community, my wife starts a blessing basket. Other family members contribute their gifts until it is filled."

"That's a mighty nice thing to do."

"The blessing baskets have come full circle. Elise purchases these baskets from the Seminoles. The blessing she received has turned into a blessing for the natives as well."

The young preacher nodded his head, breathing deeply of the warm air. Wendell pointed to the flowers gracing the roadside. "Spring has arrived in all its glory." Lavender morning glories opened their blossoms for early display.

A robin from a nearby tree trilled a melody, announcing newness of life, her babies noisily chirping with mouths wide open, hoping for a morsel of food.

The air smelled of native flora. Orange blossoms lent their gentle perfume to the spring breeze blowing as if glad for its release.

Movement ahead drew the attention of the ministers. "Looks like Mr. Madison and his boys are rounding up hogs today. Probably ready to pen and fatten a few for slaughter."

Waving as they passed, Grandpappy continued down the road. "That's the Dawson place. I think you met the Dawsons when you were here. Obadiah had received Christ and attended the meetings."

"How's Mr. Dawson doing?"

"I'm sorry to say that he's taken up his old ways; seems worse than he was before. He's beating his wife. We've tried to help her to safety, but she keeps going back, thinking he'll change."

"What about Lee, uh, let's see, Lee Kitchen? No, I believe his name is Ketchin. How's he doing?"

"Strong as ever. Lee and Leeza have another baby. God's been blessing them. They've built up a mighty fine herd of cattle, even bought the land from the neighbor and built a new home."

"Sure am glad to hear that."

"Lee's tried to help Obadiah Dawson, but the man doesn't want any help. Elise carries blessing baskets to his wife. We pray for her, and I still visit him. That's about all we can do; a man has to make up his own mind to walk in the ways of the Lord."

"That's right. Even God himself gives man his own free will to make that choice."

A couple of straggly children ran out to the road, quickly darting behind the cover of a huge guava tree. Peeking between the branches, the boy stuck his tongue out.

"Must be the squatters' children. Haven't seen them before in these parts." Grandpappy maneuvered the wagon off the road. Stopping near the guava tree, he looked at the children. "Where's your mother and father?"

The children didn't answer. Screaming and running like a scared mule, the girl took off across the field of palmettos and sapling pines. The soothing sound of the wind blowing through the trees did nothing to stop the child's mission. Her brother followed.

Staying a short distance behind, Grandpappy followed them to their camp. Smoke spiraled above the tall trees. "You whooo. Anybody home?"

A woman, mirroring the same look of fear on her daughter's face, stepped behind a large palmetto patch. Two older boys stood beside their mother with menacing looks on their faces.

"Mam, we don't want to bother you; just thought you might need some assistance." Still no one moved. Grandpappy motioned for Wendell to help him unload the wagon.

After the unloading, Grandpappy cupped his hands. "Mam, we have church in the chapel down the road every Sunday. We'd love to have you and your family join us."

Heading back to the wagon, Wendell chanced a look at the palmetto patch. "Look, Grandpappy, she's waving." Just as quickly the woman disappeared.

Looking to the side as he made a broad turn to bring the wagon around, Grandpappy pointed to the still. "They're making moonshine right here in Laurel City. Now that's not gonna work. Better go on into town and advise Sheriff Hostetler."

"No wonder they were so frightened."

"Must be a terrible life."

"It is. My grandmother made her own wine from fermented fruit. She'd sell it to the drunks until she was caught. Then she'd frequent the moonshiner's still wherever we went. We were always moving from town to town."

"I didn't know that, Wendell."

"Yes, sir, God's been good to rescue me from such a life. I've had a lot of bitterness to work through, but God has been my helper."

"I can say that too, my boy. I was as wild as an Indian on the warpath. Maybe that's why God sent me to minister to them. Sure made a difference in my life."

Pulling up in Ethan's front yard, Grandpappy stopped as Wendell stepped down. "I'll go on into town and warn the sheriff. How about us visiting the Seminole village tomorrow?"

"Sounds good to me. And, uh, sir, I believe Miss Hannah wants to come along." Wendell didn't want to miss a chance to be with Miss Hannah.

Grandpappy's grin spread across his face like jam on fresh-baked bread. "She's already advised me, son."

The young man smiled, waving good-bye to the older minister.

Walking around back, Wendell found Ethan in the barn working on a bookcase. "I can help you sand that down, Ethan."

"Why thank you, Wendell. I'm getting an order ready for pick up. I'd appreciate your help."

The afternoon passed in warm fellowship. The cool breeze filled the barn making work easier.

Elizabeth kept glasses of sweet tea filled with Beth's assistance. "I'm the cookie gull." The little girl handed her father and the preacher a cookie. "It's a snikkadewdole."

Wendell took a bite of the treat. "A snickerdoodle? Well, I like snickerdoodles."

Ethan reached down, picking up his daughter. "Can you tell the preacher that you helped your mother make them?"

"I hep Mama."

Wendell smiled at the little one. "You're a good helper, Beth."

"I know." Tilting her head to one side, she laughed.

Pleasantly exhausted after working late into the night, Wendell washed up and fell into bed. *I get to be with the green-eyed beauty tomorrow,* he thought, turning over and plumping the pillow under his head. Morning couldn't arrive soon enough for the preacher.

Chapter 5

"Miss Hannah, how nice to see you." The look on Isaac's face didn't quite match his words. Walking out of the front door just as Isaac started to knock, Hannah knew he didn't have time to school his features. Today, it didn't matter at all. Neither did she miss the fact that his eyes went immediately to her scar. Distaste was clearly evident.

"How nice of you to finally come to call, Isaac. I'm sorry; you'll have to visit Blythe and Blaine. I'm accompanying Grandpappy to the Seminole village. Or would you like to join us?"

"No, no, I-I think not, Miss Hannah. I-I'll see you later." He had the courtesy to assist her into Grandpappy's buggy.

"Morning, Isaac. We're headed to pick up Wendell Cunningham, the young, visiting preacher." Grandpappy announced this bit of information proudly.

Is he doing what I think he's doing? Hannah wanted to hug her grandfather. *I think he's trying to make Isaac jealous. He must have his doubts too.*

A look of surprise crossed Isaac's stoic face as he beat a hasty retreat.

Hannah smiled. Suddenly she felt warm inside. Turning in her seat, she waved at the disappearing carriage of Mr. Isaac Eaton, graduate of law school.

Pulling up to the front of Elizabeth's home, Grandpappy and Hannah went in. The smell of coffee and bacon wooed them into the kitchen.

Elizabeth greeted them with hugs. "Bethy is still in bed. It's too early for her to get up."

"We'll have to make do without her," Grandpappy said with disappointment.

Throughout breakfast, Wendell and Hannah exchanged glances. Warm tingles radiating from the young girl's heart to her face took the chill out of the morning air. Wendell kept looking at her, noticeably enjoying what he saw. The pile of bacon sitting on the table was barely touched by the two; their eggs were growing cold, being pushed around by the distracted guests.

Isaac's face intruded into Hannah's thoughts like a bucking bronc kicking down a barn stall. *He sure doesn't compare to this man before me. After all, we've only shared one day of courtship during the Christmas holiday. He hasn't cared enough to show any interest in me or my well-being since I've returned from finishing school.* These excuses wiped away his visage, allowing Hannah to continue enjoying Wendell's fellowship.

Grandpappy stood up from the table, wiping his face on the cloth napkin. "I think we'll be taking off now." Looking at the two plates, he added, "Better take along a biscuit and some bacon. You're both going to be hungry before we get there."

Elizabeth quickly wrapped the biscuits and bacon in a cloth. With a sly grin, she placed the cloth in a small basket, handing it to Hannah. "Have a wonderful time."

"I plan to." Hannah's eyes danced with mischief.

"You remind me of Blaine, Hannah," Elizabeth whispered.

"I'll take that as a compliment today. It pays to have fun every now and then."

"Take care not to overdo it, Sis."

"I'll try." But the mischief dancing in Hannah's eyes became more evident.

Ethan patted Wendell on the shoulder. "Enjoy your day, Wendell. I know you'll like visiting the Indians."

"That and more." His words reached and warmed Hannah's heart, as did the sparkle in his eyes.

Arriving at the dock on the Caloosa River and stepping into the boat, Grandpappy grabbed the oars as Wendell assisted Hannah. Seating her, he held her hand longer than necessary. Rewarded with a smile, the preacher pulled the rope free from the dock, making his way to the front of the wooden vessel.

Grandpappy rowed the boat with smooth, even strokes. The surface of the river gleamed bright and beautiful, reflecting the laurel oaks majestically standing on the banks. A turtle darted away, removing itself from the path of the intruders.

The early morning air was cool. Hannah, turned her head to get the full effect of the gentle breeze. Noticing the preacher watching her from his perch at the front of the boat, she took a quick breath. "What a beautiful day!"

"Yes, and beautiful scenery." But Wendell's eyes were on her, not the scenery.

Hannah tilted her head in a teasing manner. *What has changed in him?* Two years ago he seemed unable to collect his thoughts while in her presence. The change was becoming, yes, becoming indeed.

She sent him a brilliant smile. The smile was followed by a chuckle brought on when thoughts of Isaac flitted through her mind. *Isaac who?* Laughing at her own silent joke, she turned her face toward the sunlight gently caressing her cheeks. *It feels so good to enjoy the outdoors again!*

In a few moments, Hannah reached inside her satchel. Removing her sketchpad, which had been lying on her desk since the accident, she took out her drawing pencil and began sketching Wendell, who was now taking his turn rowing the boat.

A smile lit up her already radiant face.

Wendell's strong arms were pulling the oars through the water in long, purposeful strokes. Pure joy was evident in his eyes as he performed the chore. "What are you doing?"

"I'm sketching memories." And she was. Hannah's joy matched Wendell's. The man staring back at her from the page was captivating.

By the time they reached the turn in the Caloosa River, Hannah had completed the sketch. Oak trees formed a majestic backdrop on the page, the river placidly flowing beneath the boat where her subject continued to row. As she repositioned her feet, her sketchpad slid off her lap. She noticed Wendell leaning forward and staring at the drawing. He smiled as she retrieved it. A small alligator swam by, making an appearance on her paper before she returned the pad to her satchel.

Grandpappy manned the oars once they made the turn, now gliding beneath the canopy of oaks, entering the passage that would lead them to the village.

Hannah breathed deeply. They were in the swamp, but the girl who loved the outdoors felt connected to the vibrant land around her.

Her enjoyment of the scenery was intruded upon by a hawk swooping down from a tree overhead. A small chicken, pecking the wet ground on the bank in search of a worm, became prey. Ensnared in the claws of the hawk, the chick chirped loudly as the large bird disappeared into the cover of the woods nearby.

Hannah smiled at Wendell, who returned the favor. "Grandpappy and Grandmam first introduced the Indians to chickens."

Grandpappy nodded. "The natives mostly lived off of alligator meat, birds, and venison. In the early years, deer were even more prevalent than they are today. We brought beef, which was a special treat for the natives, and chickens to furnish eggs during the tough times."

Her grandfather pulled the boat close to the bank.

"Pappy, Pappy." The call was endearing. The young brave stepped out, welcoming the group. "This way." He motioned, nodding in Hannah and Wendell's direction.

"We'll visit the chief," Grandpappy advised, securing the boat on the muddy bank.

Hannah's foot slipped just a few steps away from the boat. Wendell immediately grabbed her elbow, gently steering her around the wind-fallen brush.

"Thank you." Her eyes showed more than simple gratitude.

"You're very welcome."

Hannah was pleased when Wendell continued holding on to her all the way to the chief's hut.

Seeing the visitors, the chief rose from his spot on the floor. "Welcome, Pappy. Come share food." Motioning them to sit, Wendell assisted Hannah, taking a place beside her on the blanket.

The chief's squaw scurried about, bringing them ears of warm roasted corn.

Hannah and Wendell pulled away part of the husks, tasting the proffered food. Wendell nodded his approval.

"Good, very good." Hannah smiled at the squaw who bowed low, exiting the hut only to return with tidbits of fried meat.

Grandpappy answered the question in Wendell's eyes. "It's alligator meat."

"I'm game."

After Hannah's proclamation, Wendell accepted the meat, popping a morsel into his mouth and chewing for a while. He leaned close to Hannah's ear. "If you get past the idea, it tastes pretty good; sorta like pork, chicken, and fish all mixed up together."

"That's the first time I've had it. I think it tastes like fishy pork or porky fish." Hannah murmured with a grin.

Looking at Wendall out of the corner of her eye, she thought, *He's mighty easy on the eyes.*

Catching her slanted look, Wendell had a question of his own. "What are you thinking, Miss Hannah?"

"That's for me to know and you to find out."

Grandpappy came to their blanket. "Wendell, the chief remembers how you encouraged his people during our last visit. He would like for you to speak to them as soon as they gather on the benches in the arena."

"Yes, Grandpappy, I'd be delighted."

Returning to the boat, removing his Bible from his saddlebag, Wendell walked the short distance to the arena. Small children were sweeping the grounds with brooms made of tree limbs in preparation for the service.

Taking a seat beside Hannah, the young preacher opened the book that had been his guiding light for many years, silently asking for God's guidance in the words he should speak to these precious people.

Isaiah, yes, Isaiah, that's where I should begin. Quickly turning to the Old Testament book, Wendell could hardly contain his excitement. Isaiah was definitely the order of the day, especially for these people. Soon Grandpappy was introducing him, and he made his way to the front.

"It is so good to be with you today." The smile from Hannah, beaming from the front bench, made the visit even better. He returned her smile before continuing. "Please turn in your Bibles to Isaiah chapter 54."

Hannah turned, nodding her head and smiling at the natives behind her, amidst the sound of rustling pages. Wendell knew these Bibles had been given by the Baxters as part of their missionary outreach to the tribe.

"I will begin by reading the first part of verse 17. 'No weapon that is formed against thee shall prosper.' Now let's go to chapter 65, verse 23. I wish to share this with you today, my friends. 'They shall not labour in vain, nor bring forth for trouble; for they are the seed of the blessed of the Lord, and their offspring with them.'"

Usually stoic throughout the services, the chief raised his hands, staring into the blue expanse overhead. "My great God has answered." Standing to his feet, he bowed from the waist. Next, he lay prostrate on the ground. Soon the other natives joined him, bending their knees at the altar, making a semi-circle around the podium where Wendell stood.

"I can add nothing more to what the Lord is doing in your hearts. May we continue with prayers of thanksgiving."

Grandpappy patted Wendell's back as he came to sit beside him after the two rose from their knees. "'A word fitly spoken is like apples of gold in pictures of silver.'"

"I know the scripture, Proverbs 25:11."

"Wendell, you have no idea what has been going on in these parts for the last few months. The verses you chose were exactly what the Seminoles needed to hear."

"I was very sure it was from the Lord."

"The Indians trade deer hides for much needed items. They sell to the paddleboat captain who supplies a northern fur company."

"They seem self-sufficient. What do they trade the hides for?"

Hannah scooted closer to her grandfather as he answered Wendell's question. "They trade for coffee, salt, guns, ammunition, tools, and cloth. Seminoles trade for some things in town, but the real trading comes with the arrival of the paddleboat."

"Yes, Preacher, and the paddleboat captain travels to the Everglades to trade with the Miccosukee Indians as well. Isn't that right, Grandpappy?"

Her grandfather nodded. "The Miccosukee tribe has been hiding out in the Everglades since the 1850s to keep from being sent away. They barely missed being deported to reservations further west, as did our Seminoles. The alligators, snakes, and fear of the fever sent the soldiers packing."

Rising from his position on the floor, the chief nodded in Grandpappy's direction, giving him the floor.

"Our young minister had no idea of the need in your lives. He still is unaware that your fur trade has been greatly diminished due to herds of deer being infected with the fever."

A round of applause went up.

"God's Word is always timely. Amen?"

The crowd answered in unison. "Amen, Pappy."

Praying a prayer of dismissal, Grandpappy began greeting his friends with warm handshakes.

Wendell looked at Hannah. "I had no idea, but God did. What fever is infecting the deer?"

"The Indians began finding sick and dying deer on their hunts. Finally, they realized the one thing the ailing animals had in common was ticks in abundance."

"So their livelihood has been affected."

"Yes, they've come to depend on the fur trade. Your message brought hope today."

The couple stood up from the bench. Natives came to thank them for coming. "Much blessed," an old squaw proclaimed, bowing low in front of the preacher.

"I am the one who is blessed to be a part of this day." The humble circuit rider smiled into the lady's weathered face.

A young maiden gently touched Hannah's arm, then pointed to Wendell. "See village."

"She wants us to walk through the village." Hannah smiled up at him.

"I'll be happy to." Wendell Cunningham was only too glad for an excuse to escort Miss Hannah. Grabbing her elbow, he steered her down the path, following the Indian girl softly padding along in her moccasins.

The preacher looked in the direction Hannah was pointing. "That is a hide stretcher." There before them stood two wooden poles, placed in the ground about six feet apart. Another wooden pole was set across the top, held in place by short stubs reaching out on either side. A hide was tied to the poles and pulled taut. "They have a process called braining, where they use the brains of the animals, working it into the hide and squeezing it through, improving it," Hannah explained.

"That's quite interesting."

"Yes, and if they want a hide to be waterproof, they smoke it over a fire pit laid in the ground."

They came around a bend in the path. Wendell was curious. "What is the squaw doing?"

A woman stood over a large log, smashing something with a wide tree limb, rounded on one end and sharpened on the other. Hannah smiled. "She's grinding corn for cornmeal. That is their mill."

Stepping closer, Wendell could see the upright log, which reached waist high on the squaw, had been hollowed out about one foot deep. As the couple watched her grinding the corn into meal, the woman smiled, showing only a few teeth.

Coming into a clearing, two young braves were picking up their chisels and hammers, returning to work after the service. Straddling two logs, they continued working on their project.

"What are they making?" Wendell stood watching as wood chips began flying everywhere.

"They are making dugout canoes from logs, literally dug out by hand tools and elbow grease. The cypress logs are soft and very suitable for use in the water." Looking at the water in the swamp, the cypress trees proudly standing there, Wendell agreed with Hannah.

A palmetto patch loomed ahead. Small boys, no older than six or seven, were using hatchets, cutting down mounds of palmetto fans in wild profusion. Wild cries filled the air. Wendell didn't know whether to run or stand still.

A chuckle erupted from Hannah. "They're just having fun while they are working. The Seminoles use the tough fiber between the stems of the leaves and the bark to make twine and rope. Father purchases it for use at Laurel Oaks or he trades them beef for rope."

Continuing down the village path, an Indian squaw was salting a hide. Wendell stopped. "What is she doing?"

"The Indians use a lot of salt in the process of curing hides. First, they scrape the hide clean and then cover it with a thick layer of salt. That hide is probably from the alligator we dined on today. The Indians will sell it to Mr. Eaton, and he'll make boots out of it."

"They have quite an enterprise here. When I visited with Grandpappy before, we didn't walk through the village. This is interesting."

Hannah's eyes held mischief. "I'm sure it's more fun seeing it with me."

"I'll have to agree." Wendell's grip tightened on Hannah's elbow. This girl had a hold on him. He smiled at the thought. His smile broadened as he remembered her sketch of him in the boat. *I hope she cares for me.*

Walking throughout the village, Wendell couldn't remember a day when he had been more content. *This feels so right, Lord, doing your work with a wonderful lady alongside.*

The couple walked inside the trading post. Hannah strolled over to the wooden table covered with necklaces made by the young girls of the village. Some were made of seashells from the shores of the Gulf of Mexico. Others touted hunting trophies—bear claws or hog tusks—bearing witness to the cunning of the proud hunter. Hannah wrinkled her nose at those, turning to touch the colorful necklaces.

"These are beautiful, Morning Sky." Hannah picked up one boasting a pink seashell surrounded by beads of every color imaginable.

Morning Sky beamed with pride. "I make."

Hannah removed a coin from a hidden pocket in her dress. "I'll think of you when I wear it."

The girl nodded, lowering her head as she accepted the coin. Turning aside, she began stringing another piece of twine with beads.

Grandpappy joined them at the trading post. "Looks like you two have enjoyed your afternoon." As they exited the wooden building, rays of the setting sun peeked through the pines and willows nearby. "Time to go."

They waved to several young braves coming through the swamp with wild pigs slung over their shoulders. Two of the young men carried a pole bent with the weight of a large boar hog, its tusks gleaming in the late afternoon sun.

Grandpappy admired the brave hunters. "Those tusks will harm no one now. That's the danger of the hunt; the tusks can slice a man deep and wide. That meat will be roasting over a fire by sundown."

Wendell smiled at Hannah, helping her over the logs on their path to the riverbank. "Learned a lot more about the Seminoles today. Had a smart lady by my side."

Mud oozed up over Hannah's shoes. Assisting her now with both hands, Wendell situated her in the boat.

Pulling a hankie from her sleeve, Hannah wiped the mud from her shoes. Reaching over the side of the boat, she daintily washed the mire from the lacy scrap of cloth, laying it beside her on the wooden seat to dry.

This action was not lost on Wendell. Not one word of distaste was uttered by the girl. *She is a true lady, one that adjusts well without complaining. What an admirable trait.*

Chapter 6

The trip back to Laurel City passed with the evening breeze blowing softly as the boat made its way through the placid water. *This day could not have been better,* Hannah thought, casting a smile toward Wendell Cunningham. *I want to remember it forever.*

Hannah was lost in her own thoughts, thinking about the preacher finding her in the meadow filled with wildflowers. That had been a wonderful day. She realized Wendell Cunningham was watching her from his seat in the boat. He was smiling back at her.

Feeling the boat softly come up against the dock, she looked up to see Isaac Kline, the colored man her father had rescued from a lynching in Tinn City, rapidly making his way toward them.

"Grandpappy, Grandpappy," he called, kicking his mule in the sides. The old mule continued at the one pace she knew: slow.

Hearing the call first, Hannah stood up. She turned to her grandfather, who was throwing the rope around the dock, mooring the boat. "Grandpappy, Isaac is calling you."

"Which one? Your Isaac, I mean Isaac Eaton or Isaac Kline?"

A cloud passed over Wendell's face. She answered her grandfather quickly, hoping to cover his words about Isaac belonging to her. "Isaac Kline, the one who's sweet on Miss Hattie."

Hannah turned to Wendell. "Miss Hattie is the town seamstress. Isaac's been sweet on her for two years." The preacher nodded, but his features betrayed his concern.

"Grandpappy, I's so glad I fount you. They's said you's ortta be gettin' back 'bout sunset. I done an been out to Laurel Oaks a lookin' for ya. Miss Hattie . . . " Poor Isaac stopped to catch his breath. "Miss Hattie, she up an agreed to be my wife. Well I's prouder an a peacock wif all dat bright plumanage or plumage or what 'er it be's. I's jes mighty proud."

"Well that's wonderful, Isaac. I'm proud too."

"Oh, yeah, Grandpappy, I 'mos fergot the mos' impotant part. Will you marry us up, like real fas, as soon as I can get 'er to da altar?"

Grandpappy's soft chuckle filled the air. "I'd be mighty proud to tie the knot, Isaac. You both deserve to find happiness."

"Thanks ya, sir. I shore do thanks ya." Isaac got off of his mule, running over to shake the preacher's hand.

"It's good to see you, Miss Hanner, an dis here's de preacher done an caught dat imposter two years ago, huh?" He grabbed Wendell's hand, pumping it ferociously.

Wendell nodded. "I'm the man, guilty as charged. Sure was a good day in my life."

"Gotta go tell Miss Hattie you gonna do da onners, Preacher." And with that, Isaac straddled his mule and headed to Miss Hattie Mae Williams' sewing shop.

Grandpappy's chuckle followed Isaac Kline. "Love does strange things to people."

Hannah looked at the mule hauling the happy man down the road. "I'm glad God brought him to us."

"Mighty fine man, Hannah. And Miss Hattie's a mighty fine woman."

Wendell chimed in. "Sounds like a match made in heaven."

Grandpappy went to retrieve the wagon from the livery. Not one to be easily spooked, Hannah waited outside. The last time she entered that door, she had met with an accident. Reaching up, she touched the scar hidden beneath her hat. It was still sensitive.

The movement was not lost on Wendell. "Are you all right?"

"Yes, thank you."

Grandpappy came around with the wagon, and they made their way to Laurel Oaks. Just before reaching the drive, they stopped to let Wendell off at Ethan and Elizabeth's home. He reached for Grandpappy's hand. "Thank you, sir; was a pleasure." His eyes were on Hannah as he spoke.

She extended her hand.

"Thank you for a wonderful day, Miss Hannah."

"The pleasure was mine, Reverend." Her smile erased the worry that had creased his brow since the mention of Isaac. She patted the hand that held hers, wishing to reassure him.

Wendell held her hand until Grandpappy cleared his throat. "Tomorrow's a new day. We'll see each other at church."

"Yes, sir. I'm looking forward to it."

Sunday morning was filled with the sound of birds singing. Hannah stepped into Sara's room, looking out the bedroom window to the canopy of oaks. "The robins are having their own service this morning, it seems."

"Yes, aren't they lovely?" Sara leaned out the window, her hair blowing softly in the morning breeze.

Hannah decided to have a talk with her oddly quiet sister. "What has become of you, Sara? I miss your fun-loving ways."

"I've left my foolishness behind. I'm waiting on the Lord to see what he wants me to do."

"Oh, Sara, the Lord wants what you want. Don't you think he cares about your feelings?"

"Hannah, you don't understand. My feelings got me into a lot of trouble."

Hannah knew Sara spoke the truth. Her wild sister had caused the family much grief; going so far as to be expelled from Mrs. Fancy La Peau's Finishing School for Young Ladies due to her involvement in the suffrage movement. However, during the brush arbor meetings with Wendell Cunningham two years ago, Sara had been transformed, returning to her faith. But it seemed Sara was always overboard one way or the other. It was time for Hannah to speak candidly to her sister.

"Well, Sara, you were a bit foolish and far-fetched with some of your ideas, but you are a bore now. I don't mean to hurt your feelings, but I can't find any of my sister Sara in there." Hannah pointed to Sara's heart.

"Good, all of God and none of me. I wasn't any good."

"That's where you're wrong. We had lots of fun in this house because of you. Mother even misses you being yourself."

"Did Mother tell you that, Hannah?"

"Yes. We all miss you." Hannah reached out, touching the tresses gently blowing in the breeze. "Please come back to us from where you have gone, Sara."

"I'm afraid."

"Afraid of what? Where did my sister go? You weren't afraid of anything. Remember?"

"Hannah, I don't want to remember. I was bad to my family and bad to Tobiah. I don't want to be that way anymore."

"Well, you don't have to be bad. Just be yourself. Have fun. There's nothing wrong with that." Leaving the room to get dressed for the morning service, Hannah turned back to her sister. "God created you special, Sara. Don't let him down."

Sara turned from the window to smile.

Hannah rushed to her room to finish getting ready.

"Let's go," Garrett Baxter called up the stairs. Hannah and Sara ran down, nearly tripping over each other in their haste.

"We'll be right out, Father." Hannah ran into the kitchen, grabbing a banana muffin for her and her sister to share.

"Oh, I need a hatpin," Sara exclaimed.

Hannah pointed to the parlor. "There's one lying on the fireplace mantel." Her sister ran to retrieve it.

The girls were out the door by the time their father brought the carriage around. Down the drive they went, the twins adjusting their cowboy hats against the bright April sun.

Reaching the end of the drive, they all waved at the doctor's buggy jostling toward them. Katherine and Wyatt's home stood in the distance, tucked away in their own private meadow on the Laurel Oaks property.

"There's more flowers peeking through the roadside grass." Mother, the avid gardener, always noticed flowers.

Turning toward the chapel, Hannah could see Wendell sitting on the front stoop of Elizabeth and Ethan's house entertaining Beth. Waving, she felt a tremor jolt through her heart like a Florida thunderbolt. *He does strange things to me.*

The smile that followed brought a laugh from Sara. "Always knew you two were meant for each other."

"Now, Sara, don't be a matchmaker. What about you and Tobiah?"

"Whatever the Lord wills, Hannah." Her statement was dismissive.

"Whatever the Lord wills, Sara? It's not the Lord marrying Tobiah; it would be you."

"You marryin' up with Tobiah?" Blaine asked, a smirk turning up the corner of his mouth.

"No, Blaine." Sara sent him a despairing look.

"Why not, Sara?"

"Blaine, that is none of your concern."

Shaking his head, Blaine pulled his cowboy hat low. "You ain't what you used to be, Sara. You used to be fun."

Sara turned to look out the window. She missed the sorrowful looks coming her way from her mother and sister.

Pulling into the church yard, Hannah alighted, inhaling the sweet smell of spring. The green grass, the orange blossoms, the roses making their way up the trellis, as if striving to reach the steeple, satisfied her need to enjoy the outdoors.

Ethan had fashioned the trellis after Elizabeth planted a small rose bush by the front door of the chapel. She had cut a stem from his mother's yellow rose bush, planting and nurturing it into a full-size plant.

Hannah paused to smell the yellow bud just opening. She entered the chapel, bidding Widow Crouch and Mrs. Norseworthy a fine good morning.

"Don't know what's so good about it." Widow Crouch was in her normal Sunday go-to-meeting mood.

"Ain't that the truth." Mrs. Norseworthy echoed the grouchy lady's sentiments. Mr. Norseworthy sat quietly nearby, smiling and nodding at Hannah.

Tilly Dawson was seated in her normal place, the space beside her empty. Hannah touched her on the shoulder. "Sure miss having your husband here, Mrs. Dawson. Tell him we all miss him."

"I will, Hannah. Don't do much good no more. He was all tanked up with moonshine last night. Cain't figure out where he got it. Were'nt gone long enough to go to Tinn City."

Hannah remembered that Grandpappy and Wendell had happened upon the squatter's still. She tucked this information away to share with her family later. Laurel City was a dry city. Whoever was doing this was breaking the law.

Making her way to the pew, Hannah smiled when Susannah Frost took a seat beside her. "Good morning, Hannah."

"Mornin', Susannah. What were you doing yesterday? I went with Grandpappy to the Seminole village."

"Helping Mother make soap. She wanted to make one more batch while it's still cool. It'll be too hot to stand over a fire in a few more days. We used some lavender this time; smells real good."

Hannah sniffed the air. "It's a lovely scent." Her friend must have had a Saturday bath with the fragrant soap.

Susannah Frost was Hannah's best friend. Her family had lived in Laurel City before the war but had moved to North Florida after her father's war injury. Mr. Frost's family helped him get back on his feet, and the family had returned to Laurel City.

Hannah reached over, playfully pinching her friend's shoulder. "It's so good to have you back home."

"Mornin', Susannah." That voice belonged to Matthew Madison. Looking on, Hannah could see that his hair was perfectly combed and he was wearing a cravat; this was a new Matt Madison. A faint blush colored his cheeks as he discretely handed Susannah a note, taking a seat behind her.

The question in Hannah's eyes brought a whisper from her friend. "He's been visiting me on Friday evenings."

Squeezing Susannah's hand, Hannah couldn't help cocking an eyebrow at the second Madison child, whose face now glowed crimson red. He had pulled their braids in school and teased them unbearably. The cut on his arm that Katherine had sewn up a couple of years before was only faintly visible. Matt Madison had turned into a fine young man.

Susannah poked her friend's side. "When can we ride our horses, Hannah?"

"Tomorrow's not too soon for me."

Susannah cocked her head to the side. "Are you sure you're up to it?"

"Never felt better." Wendell Cunningham's face played across her mind's eye. Closing her eyes, relishing the vision, Hannah was abruptly interrupted by a tap on her shoulder.

"Morning, Miss Hannah." That voice caused bells of alarm to ring in her head. Suddenly feeling as if she might swoon, she turned to see Isaac Eaton, taking a seat beside her with a self-assured smile plastered across his face.

Why is he here? He never finds time to attend Sunday services. "Morning, Isaac." She couldn't think of another thing to say, for it surely was not good to see him. *Must have come because he knew Wendell Cunningham would be here.*

Hannah turned to Susannah, making a face and crossing her eyes. Susannah stifled a giggle.

Grandpappy and Wendell made their way through the back door, finding a spot on the front pew. Wendell turned in his seat. His eyes came to rest on Hannah, and he smiled warmly. The smile froze as he glanced at the sophisticated man seated beside her.

Hannah felt the color drain from her face. *He's probably figured out this is the other Isaac.* She bit her lip, moving closer to Susannah on the bench. She wanted nothing to do with the man who had studied law at the university. One day of courtship had not blossomed into romance for the adventurous girl who felt shunned by her suitor.

Isaac made her feel uncomfortable, now glancing at the scar. Hannah reached up, pulling the peacock-plumed hat a little lower. She would not be intimidated. He could go find someone else who wasn't damaged goods. She turned her face toward the front pew.

Grandpappy stood before his congregation. "Please stand with me as we lift our voices in song."

Somehow Hannah made it through two hymns. If Isaac had not been standing beside her, she would have enjoyed singing with Susannah.

"And now, my friends, it is my pleasure to have Wendell Cunningham bring us the morning message."

Applause filled the building as Wendell took the podium. His green cravat matched the color of Hannah's eyes. His dark locks lay neatly dressed around his handsome face, his black suit completing the image of a fine-looking man.

"It's good to be back in Laurel City. I've missed this kind congregation." Wendell's eyes searched out Hannah before quickly glancing away.

Hannah willed him to look back and find the warmth she so desperately wished to exude. He never made eye contact with her again. She fidgeted with her woven fan. Though it was beautifully decorated with Indian beads, the moisture filling her eyes blurred its loveliness.

She barely heard the words of Wendell's message, and then he was coming to a close. "I leave you today with a promise from our Lord." Wendell's voice held assurance. "He will never leave you nor forsake you. This rings true in my life. When no one else is there for me, Jesus is."

Hannah hung her head in dismay. *He feels betrayed and forsaken. Dear Lord, how can I fix it? I haven't tricked him. I don't want Isaac Eaton, Lord; I want that circuit-riding preacher.*

The beautiful girl stood with the congregation, her sad eyes searching the eyes of the preacher. Their gazes locked; he appeared to be remembering yesterday. Just as quickly, a veil seemed to shutter his look. "It's been good to be with you, once again. Lord willing, we will meet again this side of the pearly gates."

Panic took her breath away, just as if someone had dealt a blow to her midsection. *Is he leaving? I have to stop him; I have to talk to him. I have to get to him.*

Hannah moved toward the aisle, Isaac giving her a look as she bumped into him. Grabbing her elbow, he smiled at the young preacher coming to meet them.

"Introduce us, Miss Hannah, dear." The look Isaac gave her was sickeningly sweet.

"Wendell Cun-Cunningham, meet Isaac, Isaac Eaton." Hannah put her head down. This was not at all what she wanted to be saying.

Wendell's face held the tell-tale hurt that had to be radiating from his heart. Extending his hand, he looked away from the young girl. "So you are the other Isaac; that clears things up a bit."

The puzzled look on Isaac's face would have made Hannah's heart bubble with joy had it not been for the pain now filling it. She reached out, hoping for a moment with the preacher.

Turning away with sad eyes, Wendell Cunningham continued shaking hands with the parishioners. Following not far behind,

Hannah's heart was pounding. Feelings of desperation assailed her, threatening to take her breath faster than a tightly bound corset.

The feeling escalated when Mrs. Norseworthy stepped into the aisle, further delaying the preacher. "Come to our home and share the noon meal, Reverend. Nadine would make for fine company." She smiled as if her offer was a tantalizing treat, not to be turned down.

"I'll be taking my leave, Mrs. Norseworthy. I'm hitting the trail now."

Hannah felt as if she would surely swoon. Isaac's hand on her elbow propelled her out the door into the bright sunlight.

Hannah made her way to the family carriage. Wendell had said his good-byes while Isaac kept a tight hand on her. She barely murmured good-bye to Isaac. Her world was turning upside down.

Seated in the carriage, wiping her moist brow with her handkerchief, a deep sigh escaped Hannah's lips.

Sara reached over, touching her sister's forehead. "Are you all right?"

Breathing ragged breaths, Hannah shook her head. "No."

"Is it your head or your heart that's hurting?" Sara's words oozed sympathy.

Hannah looked down at her hands, nervously tracing a pattern on her skirt. "You know, Sara?"

"I've always known, even before you knew."

"He's leaving, Sara." The floodgate of Hannah's tears could not be held back.

"I know. He told us, said to give you his best."

"He did?"

"Yes, and he looked very sad. He's hurting as much as you, Hannah."

"I didn't set out to hurt him. I have no romantic feelings for Isaac." She dabbed at her tears.

"Hannah, you were taken with Isaac during Christmas because of his attention. He really wooed you. Anyone would be flattered."

"He sure hasn't wooed me since I returned home."

"I'm sorry to say, but I learned last week from Mrs. Eaton that Isaac found a sketch you had drawn several months back and thought you would be great for his profession, sketching court scenes for him that could be placed in prominent newspapers."

"She told you that?"

"Not per se, but I put two and two together, and it always makes four. That's why he wooed you when you were home."

"I'm so glad you told me. It confirms what I'm feeling. He didn't really care for me. And guess what; I'm really not sad. The only thing I'm sad about is the hurt Wendell Cunningham is feeling."

Arriving at Laurel Oaks, the girls went indoors, changing their clothes and donning aprons to help with Sunday dinner. As they ran downstairs, Wyatt and Katherine were just coming in the door, followed by Ethan and Elizabeth.

Little Beth ran straight to her grandmother. "Gramma, I hep, I hep."

Adeline Baxter kissed her granddaughter. "You've got to get your apron on." She lifted the miniature apron from the peg by the back door.

"Matches Gramma." Beth pointed to the sunflower on her little apron.

Elizabeth smiled proudly, stirring the pot of chicken and dumplings and sending its tantalizing aroma throughout the house.

Katherine followed Hannah to the springhouse to bring in the butter. "I noticed your dilemma this morning. I have a morsel to help you make a decision."

"Katherine, Isaac has proved to me that he does not care. I don't know why he had to show up this morning and ruin my chances with the preacher."

"I think he's selfish and spoiled. What he wants he gets. Just so you know, when you were ill, I saw him with a girl in Miss Amy's dining hall. I wanted you to know, but I didn't feel it was right to tell you while you were recovering. Since then, I've seen her in Mrs. Eaton's shop."

"Who is she?"

"They say she is a business acquaintance. Her father owns a law firm up north and wants to hire Isaac."

"That's a little suspicious. Why is she here?"

"I thought so too, especially when I saw her leaning against Isaac in a cozy way."

Hannah's eyes sparkled. "Tell me more. I'm well recovered now, and I like a good story."

"I happened in unexpectedly at Mr. Eaton's leather shop. Isaac was manning the shop while his father was away. This girl's name is Isabel Benson, and she has more than business on her mind."

"Really?"

"Yes, she was leaning against Isaac but quickly moved away when I entered. Isaac smiled, looking uncomfortable. Next, Isabel, said, 'Introduce me, darling.'"

"And so he did."

"Yes, and he looked nervous, quickly getting the new bridle Wyatt needed."

As the girls made their way to the back porch, Hannah reached out to her older sister. “Thank you, Kat. You are my sister and my friend.”

Katherine whispered as she opened the back door. “I’ll be praying for you and the preacher man.”

Hannah smiled her thanks.

Chapter 7

Wendell Cunningham made his way down the lonely road headed out of Laurel City. The pain in his heart was unprecedented. Nothing had ever hurt so badly, not his grandmother's assaults or even the atrocities he faced during the war.

The young preacher had lost his heart to Miss Hannah Baxter. A lovely vision of her sitting amidst the field of wildflowers played across his memory. Her beautiful brown curls blowing freely in the gentle breeze, enhanced with the light of the setting sun, had nearly taken his breath away. It threatened to do the same now.

Bowing his head against the brilliance of the afternoon sun, he ambled along the path taking him away from his dream of having this wonderful girl by his side. It was a dream he had clung to for two years. The sketch in his Bible attested to his attachment to Hannah.

Despondency settled around him like a heavy winter coat, too heavy to throw off. Several hours later, Wendell realized the afternoon shadows had deepened into the afterglow of evening. He was entering a small town where he had previously ministered.

Making his way to the inn, he gave his horse to the stable boy. "Two scoops of oats, son."

Flickering candles beckoned him inside. The proprietor looked up from his paperwork. "Evenin', Preacher. Gonna be stayin' fer a while?"

"Just one night." Wendell paid the nominal fee, taking the key from the kind man.

"Food's hot in the keetchen. Greta's got the best cheeken an noodles ya ever set yore jaws to."

Wendell's stomach growled, reminding him he hadn't eaten since the biscuits and sausage gravy he had enjoyed with Ethan this morning. It seemed so far away: Laurel City, home of his beloved Hannah. *His* beloved Hannah. It seemed it was not to be, not with the other Isaac hanging on to her.

He sighed, placing his saddlebags in the room and making his way to Greta's kitchen. The chicken and noodles teased his taste buds, the yeast rolls melting in his mouth, yet Wendell was hard pressed to enjoy the fare. His mind was occupied with thoughts of brown curls and green eyes, alight with promises of adventure and laughter. Closing his eyes, he savored the memories they had made in the Seminole village. A voice at the table intruded into his private thoughts.

"My noodles are that good, ain't they, Preacher?" Greta stood there, looking mighty proud of herself. Her toothless grin spread deep and wide across her face as she wiped her hands on her apron.

He couldn't tell the lady that closing his eyes had nothing to do with savoring the noodles; he was savoring something far better than noodles. "The food is delicious. Could I have another roll, Mrs. Greta?"

The woman almost tripped over her big leather shoes running to the kitchen and returning with two yeast rolls instead of one. "I don't want my guests a goin' away hongry. Can I getcha some more sweet tea?"

"Yes, mam. You make really good sweet tea."

Finishing his supper and making his way to his room at the back of the establishment, Wendell fell into bed with his boots on. A deeper sadness crept around him, wrapping him in its blanket of despair. Tears fell onto the lumpy pillow cradling his head. *Am I never to have the desire of my heart, Lord?*

His grandmother's face came to the forefront of his mind. He could hear her even after all these years. "Ya won't never amount to a hill o beans, Wenell. Ya got that bad blood o ya paw in ya. Ya know ya kilt my girl, Wenell. She died a havin' ya, and fer what? Ya ain't worth a hill o beans."

Wendell turned on his side, rearranging the pillow, trying to find a place of safety against the memories. He fell into a fitful sleep.

"Help, help. Somebody help me. Granny, I'll be a good boy. Don't hit me, Granny. Please … "

Sitting up in bed, the sweat poured from Wendell's body. His hand went to his heart. It was about to pound out of his chest. Realization dawned; the nightmares had returned.

A soft knock at the door proved he had spoken aloud. "Preacher, ya all right in there?"

Wendell opened the door. "Mr. Holmes, I'm all right. Sorry, I-I had a nightmare."

The proprietor stood in the hall, hair askew, looking at him with pity. "Just want to make sure no one's a hurtin' ya. Shore sounded bad, son." The candle he held dripped wax onto his thumb. He ignored the intrusion. "Well, go on back to bed. Ya need yore sleep."

"Thank you, sir."

Wendell sat on the side of the bed, unwilling to go back to sleep and make a fool of himself again. *How long, Lord, do I have to be troubled by these nightmares? Will Granny never lose her hold on me, even from the grave?*

Words from the Good Book rose up in Wendell's disquieted soul. "Cast all your care upon him, for he careth for you." Feeling comforted, the preacher lay, once again, to receive rest for his journey.

Green eyes danced across his closed eyes, sparkling above the placid waters of the Caloosa River. Sweet dreams took him back to the Seminole village. A smile played upon his lips as he relived his day with Hannah Baxter in paradise.

Sara burst into Hannah's room. "Get up, get up, sleepy head."

Hannah opened her eyes, unwilling to face the bright morning sun as Sara drew the curtains back. *What is going on here? Looks like the old Sara is making an entrance into my room, full of life and mischief. I must be dreaming.*

"You look as chipper as a spring bird on a limb in the sunshine. I didn't sleep much last night. How about showing some respect." Hannah smiled, sitting up in bed.

"Just wanted to make you feel better after yesterday."

"I'll be using the old prayer bones for Wendell Cunningham. Sure would like to have him for my own." Hannah's eyes danced along the sunbeams, making their way across the room. She had been taught as a child that prayer could change any circumstance. She'd be on her knees, petitioning God for his assistance.

"Get dressed, and we'll go have some fun."

"What kind of fun?"

"Just get dressed." Sara backed out of the room, a secretive look telling of her intent.

Quickly dressing, Hannah met her sister on the stairs. Heading into the kitchen, they grabbed a biscuit, slathered it with guava jam and made their way outside. Hannah followed Sara to the barn. "Are we going to milk the cows?"

"Look, Hannah, I wanted to show you the new calf."

Excitement glowing in her eyes, Hannah lifted the latch to the stall, rushing inside to pet the black wobbly animal. The calf reached up, licking her fingers. "You're so dark, we'll call you Molasses."

"I knew you'd enjoy the visit." Sara looked pleased with herself.

Finally, Molasses bedded down for a rest on the hay strewn for that reason. Big calf eyes watched Hannah as she closed the latch behind her.

"Susannah is coming this morning. We're going to run our horses in the meadow. Want to join us?"

"You go ahead, Hannah. You haven't had much time with Susannah since your return. I think I'll go for a ride in the back pasture." A familiar look crossed her face.

Hannah teased her sister. "Gonna visit Tobiah?"

"What's it to ya?"

"It's good to see you've come home, Sara. I don't know where my sister went for a while, but it's good to have you back."

"I started listening to what everyone was saying and realized God wants me to be me. I'm pretty happy with the realization."

"I am too. You have fun, Sara."

"I plan to for a change. It's been a long time." Sara looked wistful as she straddled the mare, removing the combs from her hair.

Hannah looked on with pleasure as her sister rode out of sight, a little too quickly for the old mare. "Poor old mare."

Flying up to the corral where Hannah was feeding her horse a carrot, Susannah pulled back hard on the reins, stopping her horse in a cloud of dust. "Hannah, where ... where is your father? Something ... awful ... has happened, get him ... quick."

"Father, Father, we need you."

Garrett Baxter came out of the stall where he had been checking on the new calf. "What's wrong, girls?"

The words tumbled from Susannah. "Mr. Dawson . . . blood . . . " She paused, catching her breath, while the stallion pranced as if sensing the need for a quick exit. "I passed the Dawson place on my way here. Mr. Dawson's been shot. His wife was yelling something about squatters and moonshine. Mr. Madison went to fetch Dr. Baldwin. I passed them heading back to the Dawson place."

"I'll go over there; see if I can help."

Hannah turned to her father, who was already atop his horse. "We'll fetch Grandpappy. He told the sheriff about the squatters and the still last week."

"I remember. I'll get my Colt and head over there." Dismounting and running through the back door of the house, he turned, yelling back to Hannah. "Fetch Mr. Smythe and Tobiah, Hannah."

"Yes, sir," his daughter and Susannah yelled back.

By the time everyone was rounded up, Grandmam had already prepared a basket of food from her pantry. "Mother and Elizabeth will have something to add."

With bread still warm from Elizabeth's oven and Mother's butter, freshly churned this morning, Hannah and her friend headed out to deliver the basket to Tilly Dawson. Grandmam would follow with herbs and poultices in case they were needed. She had treated many gunshot wounds before the town had a doctor.

Turning in at the Dawson place, an eerie silence filled the morning air. The girls dismounted, taking the basket up to the porch, hesitantly waiting at the door.

The twins, Jeremiah and Jedediah, came to the door, terror showing in their eyes. Each girl reached out, pulling a twin into a comforting embrace.

Hannah broke the silence. "Is your father all right?"

Jeremiah stepped back. "No, mam. Doc Wyatt don't thank he's a gonna make it, and I don't neither."

The other twin shook his head. "Me neither. He's a bleedin' like a stuck pig at a Madison butcherin'." Jedediah buried his head in Susannah's shoulder.

Jeremiah led the girls into the house.

Broken lanterns strewn around the front room told of a disturbance. Mrs. Tilly Dawson appeared from the back room, her black eyes a further testament. "Cain't tell him nothin', Miss Hanner. Since he went back to the moonshine, there ain't been a smidgen of peace in this here place." Putting her hand to her cheek, the distraught woman looked in resignation at the strewn glass.

"Grandmam sent a basket, Mrs. Dawson."

"Why, bless her soul; always thankin' 'bout someone else's troubles." The battered wife sat on the decrepit sofa, soothing a tear in her worn skirt. She murmured, "And he was a doin' so good not long ago."

"I'm so sorry, Mrs. Dawson." Susannah gave the woman a hug. "If we can do anything to help, please let us know."

"I'll be needin' someone to watch the little one." She pulled her young daughter close. "Don't want her to see her pappy like this."

Susannah took the girl's hand. "Come with me, sweetie. We'll go see the banty roosters at my house."

"Can I pet 'em?"

"Sweetheart, you can give them some mashed corn. How about that?"

"I wanna go. Pappy hit Mama. Pappy mean." At her daughter's words, Tilly Dawson broke into a sobbing frenzy.

Susannah and Hannah were about to take their leave when Grandmam entered. Going straight to the crying woman, she held her as the pent-up tears continued to flow.

"He's a dyin', Mrs. Elise, he's a dyin'."

"Now, now, Tilly. We don't know that for sure." Reaching into her reticule, the kind pastor's wife pulled out an embroidered hanky. "Here, dear, let's get you wiped up."

But Tilly Dawson refused to lay aside her fears. "I'm a sayin' he's a dyin'."

Wyatt Baldwin stepped through the curtain separating the rooms. "I'm sorry, Mrs. Dawson. Your husband didn't make it."

A wail with the ferocity of a summer storm rent the house. Sorrow gripped the faces of those gathered in the old, battered house. The twins once again clung to Hannah and Susannah, who had not been able to leave.

By this time, Mr. Madison came out of the back room, followed by Grandpappy. "He wouldn't accept that God could forgive him for what he'd done. Said he deserved to burn in the hottest pit just like his father told him." Grandpappy shook his head, going to Tilly Dawson's side.

"He's been a sayin' that since he come flyin' into the yard all bloodied up an a fallin' offa his horse." The poor wife shook her head.

"Well, I guess the Lord giveth and the Lord taketh away." Mr. Madison said.

"This time, Mr. Madison, the Lord giveth, and Satan taketh away. It was his plan all the time to destroy this man. God wanted to spare him and give him a good life."

"Guess he jes hooked up with the wrong partner, ain't that right, Preacher?"

"Yes, Mrs. Dawson, I'm afraid so."

Mr. Frost came busting through the door. "Is Mr. Dawson all right?"

"I'm sorry to say he passed on." Wyatt Baldwin's face mirrored the sorrow evident in the room.

"I was plowin' in the field and heard a shot not far from my place. Couldn't see nothin' through the woods except a spiral of smoke. I been noticin' that for quite some time, figured it was somebody passin' through just makin' camp for a few days."

Mr. Madison turned to Mr. Frost. "So you've noticed the smoke too?"

"Yes, and I heard another shot followed real fast by two more. I said to myself, 'Now, Nathaniel, that just don't seem right. If a body was a huntin', it shouldn't a taken that many shots.' That's when I figured on checkin' things out."

"What did you find, Mr. Frost?"

"I followed the smoke cross the pasture to a squatter's camp. Low and behold, there was Mr. Dodson a still holdin' onto the gun in his hand, campin' out with a woman and four children, two of them might near grown. There was a moonshine still a blazin' right there in the mornin' sun. Lookin' out front, I saw a horse leavin' at a quick pace, the rider barely stayin' in the saddle. I recognized the horse as belongin' to Obadiah Dawson."

"Well, I reckon Mr. Dodson doesn't know he's killed a man." Grandpappy moved toward the door. Hannah knew he would go to Ethan before he visited the sheriff. Patting the back of the departed's wife, Grandpappy was out the door.

Grandmam continued holding her friend's hand and offering comforting words. Hannah and Susannah headed home.

Hannah's friend waved good-bye, turning her horse in the opposite direction, the little Dawson girl riding safely in front of her. "Guess we had our ride today, not the one we wanted, but a ride nonetheless."

Hannah sadly nodded. "See you later, Susannah."

Hannah saw Mr. Smythe and Tobiah coming toward her. Tobiah pulled back on the horse's reins. "We were in the back field plowing; we came as soon as Ma gave us the message. Any word about Mr. Dawson?"

"It's not good, Tobiah." Hannah's look said the rest. The young man picked up the reins, heading toward the Dawson property.

Just before Hannah turned into Laurel Oaks, she spotted Ethan headed back down the road they had just traveled accompanied by her father and Grandpappy. "Sorry, Ethan."

Ethan turned sad eyes her way. "Please go to Elizabeth. She's with your mother and Sara."

When Hannah entered the kitchen, Katherine was there as well, holding Beth while Mother and Sara sat on either side of Elizabeth.

"I guess Ethan's father will never learn. He's always been in trouble, and it all had to do with moonshine. I never dreamed he was making it himself. For heaven's sake, now he'll more than likely spend the rest of his life in jail." Elizabeth walked away from the table. "And me in the shape I'm in, it makes it all worse."

Mother looked from Katherine to Elizabeth. "Is there something you are waiting to tell us?"

"Mother, I'm in the family way again. You know how Ethan feels about saying anything too soon. I just need someone to understand how it feels in my present state."

"I'm sure Ethan won't mind that you told us, dear."

Katherine looked from her mother to her sisters. "Can you keep another secret? I've been dying to tell it. I'm in the family way too; looks like this house is filling up with cousins."

In spite of the trouble at hand, the antebellum home rang out with congratulations and blessings as the little group celebrated the news.

Mother looked prouder than a peacock. "God is good."

Chapter 8

It was late in the night when Grandpappy's wagon rolled into Laurel Oaks. Elizabeth's ears, fine-tuned for listening out for Beth, alerted her that the men had returned. Jumping up from her pallet on the floor, she ran to greet the men of her family.

Ethan's eyes, moist and downcast, told a haunted tale. "I had no idea my father was living in the woods and running a still."

His wife stepped up beside him, placing an arm around his waist. "Did you take him in to the sheriff?"

Tears began to flow down Ethan's cheeks. He just stood there, shaking his head back and forth.

Elizabeth looked to her father, who answered softly, "He turned the gun on himself when he saw us. Must have known what was coming."

"But, Father, what of the woman and children?"

Grandpappy answered. "They were nowhere in sight; must have been scared to death and left in a hurry."

Ethan wiped his eyes, swallowing hard. "Now we've got two men to add to the cemetery. It clearly was a fight over moonshine." He looked at Grandpappy.

"Obadiah Dawson told me the story on his deathbed. Feeling powerful thirsty, he paid a friendly visit to Ethan's father. Thinking no one was there, he picked up a jug of lightning. Taking a drink, he headed toward his horse with the jug."

"So he was stealing the shine?"

"Yes, Elizabeth. Mr. Dodson stepped from behind a nearby tree, demanding that he hand over the jug or the money. That's when Obadiah made a run for it. Sorry to say he didn't get far before being shot. He kept going, and Ethan's father kept shooting."

Elizabeth reached up, wiping the trail of tears from her husband's face. "I'm so sorry, Ethan."

"I just wish he would have lived for the Lord. This never would have happened."

"You can lead a thirsty horse to water but he's got to take a drink himself, Ethan."

Ethan nodded slowly, placing his head on his wife's shoulder. She held him like a child, comforting the only way she knew how. Her lips barely moved in silent prayer. Elizabeth could not take the pain away, but she knew someone who could.

News spread like wildfire throughout Laurel City. Nearly every family made their way to Ethan's home and to the Dawson home with their condolences. Pans of food filled the tables of both houses as people came to show their concern, sitting with the families, sharing their sorrow.

On Thursday morning, April 20, 1872, the main road in Laurel City was filled with mourners, making their way westward to the town cemetery. It had been decided that a double funeral would be held.

Grandpappy led the procession with Tilly Dawson and her family in tow. Ethan and Elizabeth followed behind, sharing the doctor's carriage with Wyatt and Katherine. Garrett Baxter's carriage brought up the last of the Baxters, followed by the townspeople in their conveyances.

Grandmam was seated beside her friend, holding her trembling hand. "We'll get through this day, Tilly, the good Lord willing."

A small smile curved one side of the sad lady's mouth. "An if'n the creek don't rise." She finished the saying, turning back to look into the faces of her children. "Somehow they ain't seemin' as sad as they ortta."

"They'll be all right, Tilly. God is with them."

"Well, Obadiah weren't no good pappy. I guess they's jes glad fer some peace."

"I'm glad fer peace." Jeremiah spoke quietly, staring down at the toes of his worn-out shoes.

Seated beside him, Jedediah spoke up. "I'm glad Mama ain't a gonna get hurt no more by Paw. That's what I'm bein' glad fer."

Grandmam just patted her friend's hand.

All of a sudden the somber gray sky began to darken. Buggies made a quick entrance into the cemetery, their owners looking overhead at the ominous clouds. Gathering around the freshly dug graves, the group huddled beneath parasols against the pelting rain.

Leeza Ketchin made her way to Tilly Dawson. "I'm so sorry, my dear. If not for the mercy of God, it could be me standing in your shoes." Tears were streaming down the dear woman's face as she embraced her friend.

Stepping back, the new widow clutched Leeza Ketchin's arm. "I 'member 'bout Lee almost gettin' hisself shot by that Injun. I jes wish Obadiah woulda stayed on the Lord's path like yore man."

Once again, the women embraced, making a pitiful silhouette as lightning split the sky behind them. A nearby weeping willow bent low in the wind, adding its mournful touch.

Grandpappy spoke loud, in competition with the wind, moaning its sad tune. "We are gathered to say good-bye to our neighbors." The kind man's eyes filled with tears, yet he pressed on. "The weather today matches the turmoil in our hearts. I will offer the word of God as the only consolation I can give."

Thunder rolled, adding its rumblings to the gloomy event. A peal of lightning lent a sense of urgency to the gathering. Hurriedly reading the scripture, speaking peace to the family members, Grandpappy closed his worn Bible. Looking at the people standing around the open holes in the ground, he said, "At a time like this, God is the only one who can bring comfort."

Tilly Dawson buried her face in her hands. Grandmam patted her back.

Garrett Baxter stood with his hand on Ethan's shoulder. Elizabeth leaned on her husband. Her mother held Beth nearby.

"I will quote from Philippians 4:7 and 8: 'And the peace of God, which passeth all understanding, shall keep your hearts and minds through Christ Jesus. Finally, brethren, whatsoever things are true, whatsoever things are honest, whatsoever things are just, whatsoever things are pure, whatsoever things are lovely, whatsoever things are of good report; if there be any virture, and if there be any praise, think on these things.' And this is truly what the Lord would have you do in this situation. All of your tears will not bring these men back. Let our God be your comfort in this time of need."

The sky continued to darken, the wind blowing with fierce intensity. A mother possum, her babies in tow, scurried across nearby graves as the pine boxes were lowered into the ground. Several men quickly scooped shovelfuls of dirt into the newly dug holes, mounding the dirt. The shovels were dropped in quick abandon as lightning streaked across the sky. The mourners ran to their carriages, quickly heading toward the safety of their homes.

The Baxter carriage made its way under the canopy of oaks, swaying in the wind. A heavy downpour of rain, accompanied by lightning, spooked the horses. Thunder rolled as Garrett Baxter rushed his family indoors, quickly settling the horses after disengaging them from the carriage.

Rushing into the warmth of his home, he joined Addie and the girls around the kitchen table, sipping cups of hot chocolate. The twins were sharpening their knives on the stone in the corner of the kitchen.

Garrett looked at his boys.

Blaine sent his father a cock-eyed grin. "Good day for whittlin'."

"Shore is." Blythe affirmed.

Addie smiled up at her husband. "Want a cup of hot chocolate, dear?"

"I think I need something a little stronger. Got any coffee?" Garrett Baxter stooped over his wife's chair, planting a loud kiss on her forehead.

"Yes, it's already hot and strong like you like it."

"That's my girl. You stay seated. I'll help myself. Think I can spoon my own sugar today."

Hannah questioned her father. "Ethan and Elizabeth went home. Do you think they are all right?"

"I think they probably need some time alone to grieve properly."

Grief, that's what she felt. Hannah's heart matched the dismal weather. *I miss Wendell so. Wonder where he is? Is there a storm brewing there?* In her heart a storm of a different kind was brewing.

"Hannah, what's wrong?" Sara placed a hand on her shoulder. "Want to talk about it?"

The younger sister nodded toward the stairs. "Excuse us, Mother." And with that, the sisters were out of sight and promptly seated on Hannah's bed.

Sara smiled. "This feels different."

"What, you being the one to offer help and counsel?"

"Yes. Now tell me what's bothering you. I know it has to do with Wendell Cunningham."

"Sara, I really care for him. He has been in my thoughts since I met him, even if I wouldn't admit it."

"What about Isaac?"

"I thought I would never see the preacher again. Isaac seemed a respectable suitor and I was flattered."

Sara placed her hands on her hips in that sassy way that had been missing for a long time. "Why, Hannah, you are a beautiful, talented girl. Any man would be honored to be your suitor."

"I might say the same of you, Miss Sara." Hannah stared her sister down.

"We're talking about you right now." Sara affected her exaggerated Southern drawl. "Isaac might have studied law at the university and now be a graduate of law, but I've never trusted the man. He's a spoiled child that never grew up. "

"That's what I've felt since I've been home from finishing school: distrust. And that girl, Isabel, Isabel Benson; well, something's not right with that situation."

"Hannah, I didn't want to cause any trouble, but she's not the only one I've seen Isaac Eaton around town with. I saw him with Nadine in his buggy just yesterday. I knew it was her, but as soon as they saw me, Nadine ducked down in the seat and Isaac waved like a politician out gathering votes."

"After the way he ignored me following my return home, I got the message that he wasn't really interested. And, come to think of it, Sara, something just flashed through my mind."

Excitement sparkled in Sara's usually docile eyes. "Share the flash with me, girl."

Hannah nodded her head, understanding dawning. "The day I returned home, I remember thinking I saw Isaac with a girl. When he looked up and saw me, he quickly dashed into the livery stable. That's why I went there." With eyes flashing, Hannah rose from the bed. "That little weasel." She paced the floor, tightly clenching her fists.

"So that's why you went to the stable and got hit with the mucking shovel?"

"Yes, and I don't understand why Abraham would hit me like that. He met me once when I was home at Christmas."

"Why would he hit you?"

"I don't know, but mark my word. I will find out." Determination, accompanied by gritting teeth, showed in Hannah's eyes.

"I'll help you, Sis."

The two linked arms, turning in a circle and laughing in spite of the situation.

"It's good to have you back, Sara."

"It's good to be back. I thought of what you said about God wanting me to be myself. Just gotta keep the buggy rolling in the middle of the road, not in the ditches."

"Sara, you're so funny. What about you and Tobiah?"

"That's fodder for another day, Hannah."

"Well, we better get you fixed soon. Why you're practically an old maid now." Hannah laughed a delightful laugh. The bedroom was filled with love and companionship that only sisters can share.

Another loud clap of thunder drew the girls' attention to the window. The giant oaks were swaying in the wind, small branches falling to the ground below. "With this weather, we won't be finding out anything about Isaac today."

Sara grinned at her sister. "Won't the anticipation be worth the wait?"

A fit of giggles erupted from both the girls.

"We could be really bad together, Sara."

The next morning, Sara and Hannah accompanied Grandpappy to town. The storm of the previous day had left debris all over Laurel City, and Grandpappy was rounding up a group of men to help clean up the mess. His granddaughters kept their mission a secret, glad for the excuse to ride into town.

Excitement glowed on the girls' faces. Hannah nudged Sara. "Where should we begin?"

Sara shrugged her shoulders. "Why not be bold and go to Mrs. Eaton's first?"

"Did I hear you say you want to go to Mrs. Eaton's shop, girls?"

Hannah's heart beat a merry tune. "Yes, Grandpappy, Mrs. Eaton's will be fine."

"I'll be in town for a while. You girls have several hours to shop or visit."

"Thank you, Grandpappy." Sara alighted first, followed by Hannah, the girls quickly making their way to the millinery shop.

Pausing before going in, Hannah straightened her hat and pinched her cheeks.

"You look fine, Sis. We'll show that rascal a thing or two."

Lifting her nose just a touch, Hannah straightened her back. It was time for business.

Sara followed her sister, knowing full well she could take care of herself, but nonetheless wanting to be a part of this adventure.

Mrs. Eaton appeared from the back room at the tinkling sound of the bell above the door.

"She looks frightened, as if she's seeing a ghost." Sara's whisper matched Hannah's thoughts exactly.

"Morning, *Baxter* girls." She said Baxter a little too loudly, but not before a smiling Isabel followed close on her heels.

Hannah covered her mouth, whispering to Sara. "That is the girl Isaac was with the day I returned home. She's wearing the same red hat. I know it's her."

Sara took charge, affecting just enough of her pretentious drawl to thwart the attention of the ladies. "Well a fine morning to you, Mrs. Eaton, and is it Isabel? And word has it, Isabel, that your father owns a prominent law firm."

Isabel preened with Sara's flattery. "Why yes, he does. I'm trying to talk Isaac into joining my father's practice."

Hannah jumped right in, smiling like a true Southern belle. Two could play this game. "How's the persuasion coming?"

Mrs. Eaton's began nervously dusting a perfectly clean shelf, turning away from the confrontation. "Girls, could I show you anything?"

The question stopped Isabel from responding to Hannah's question. The young Baxter girl understood the lady's intent.

Sara mischievously saved the moment. "We're trying to choose which hat Widow Crouch will purchase for summer. I see your collection is already full of new selections."

And with that, the girls marched back to the display window at the front of the store. Finding a yellow hat covered with monkeys and bananas, Sara touched the brim, setting the monkeys in motion, as if chasing the bananas. "That is the one."

"I'll agree." The girls left the store, holding in their giggles until they were a safe distance away from Mrs. Eaton and Isabel.

"We created quite a stir," Sara said proudly.

"Sticking the broom in that rat's nest, there's no telling what will come flying out. We're bound to catch the big rat sooner or later."

"Let's go into Paxton's store and get one of those dill pickles."

Hannah nodded. "I haven't had one since I left for finishing school."

Heading straight to the pickle barrel, the girls paid Mr. Paxton, deciding to check out the new shipment of summer cloth. Trying to stay hid, as to avoid Mr. Rivers and the gossipers' bench, they quietly perused the aisles, eating the tasty pickles.

"Mother will love this print." Sara pulled out the edge of the cloth to show Hannah.

Nodding, Hannah couldn't help but overhear Mr. Rivers nearby. "Yeah, they says that there Baxter gal, she's really messed up in the head after Abram done an hit 'er with the muckin' shovel."

Mr. Norseworthy spoke up. "Well, Rivers, cain't say as I saw nothin' wrong with her head at church. Looked mighty purty to me."

"Oh, Noseworthy, what would you know? Did ya ask ya wife if'n she was purty?" Mr. Rivers chuckled and continued. "Now as I's sayin' afore I's intrupted, that girl cain't be right in the head after a lick like at."

Hannah and Sarah almost choked on their pickles. They stood dead still, listening.

Someone else spoke up. Hannah turned toward the voice, trying to place who it was. Recognition dawned. That voice belonged to the livery stable owner. *Must have come over for a cup of coffee.*

"Well, Rivers, you cain't put all the blame on Abraham. I know he's kinda tetched, but he makes for cheap help."

"I don't call that cheap, a messin' up a young gal's life. What with her bein' so young an all, an she use to be purty." He mumbled almost to himself. "Reckon she's ruint now. Hanner, that's her name, almost fergot."

Hannah's eyes blazed. She moved a foot forward. Sara's huge eyes warned her against making herself known. She clenched the dill pickle in her handkerchief until it was mush.

The stable owner was speaking again. "Anyways, Rivers, ya need to hear me out. Abraham was jes tryin' to protect hisself."

Mr. Rivers let out a chortle. "Protect hisself from what, pray tell? That lil ole gal don't weigh as much as two sacks a flour. How's she a gonna hurt him?" The old man smacked his lips over bare gums, shaking his head from side to side.

"I'm tryin' ta tell ya, but ya won't listen, Rivers. Isaac Eaton runned into the stable with that new-fangled girl what's a chasin' after him in town. Name's Isabel or Jezebel, or some kinda bell. Anyways, Isaac tole Abraham that the outlaw was a comin', and poor boy was ready fer 'im."

"Well, do tell. Now that story'll shore be worth the tellin' 'round this here potbelly stove. Betcha I can fill up this here gossipers' beanch fer two weeks a tellin' that 'un." Mr. Rivers rocked his chair back and forth, his movements increasing in momentum and speed.

The girls were peeking through a spot between bolts of summer material. Hannah whispered softly. "He's got fodder for a long time, and I'm the subject."

Grinning and joining hands as they made a swift exit, the girls ran outside and didn't stop until they were seated under an oak tree by the river. Hannah laughed until her sides and head hurt. "How would you have ever guessed we would have learned the truth in one of Mr. Rivers' gossiping sessions?"

"Doesn't that beat all? But, Hannah, aren't you upset to know the truth?"

"I've been upset, Sara. Now that I know the truth I feel much better. There's no need in spending my time pining over what happened or what might have been. The way I look at it, the good Lord spared me from the likes of Isaac Eaton." Hannah paused for a moment, a sudden thought illuminating the happenings of the fateful day of her arrival home. "Isaac must have told Abraham that the outlaw was coming in order to buy himself some time to escape with his girlfriend."

The men were busy cleaning up the boardwalk and the street. The girls shared a good laugh as Mr. Rivers and his group joined in the cleanup. Seated near the end of the boardwalk, conversation drifted over to their ears.

Mr. Rivers had cornered Lee Ketchin on the boardwalk. "Why, do tell, Mr. Kitchen, have ya heared the latest news?"

"Don't reckon I have, Mr. Rivers, but I'm sure you're about to tell me."

Mr. Rivers never missed a beat. "Yeah, they's a sayin' now that that thar faincy lawyer, name o Isaac Eaton, he was a tryin' to haf Miss Hanner kilt."

"Oh, Mr. Rivers, I wouldn't repeat such as that. It's true that Mr. Eaton is a reckless young man, but I'm sure he meant her no harm."

"No, Kitchen, I done an got it from a good source. It be the truth, I'm a downright shore on this 'un."

"You want to help me pick up this tree limb, Mr. Rivers? I think I need help."

The old man just stood there for a while, looking at the huge branch. "Well, I guess I can, but I'd shore like ya ta call on some 'un what's younger … Tobiah, Tobiah." Mr. Rivers was frantically waving at Tobiah Smythe coming down the road on his horse. "Tobiah, come an hep with this here cleanup. Mr. Kitchen cain't hannel this here tree limb. Beats all I done seen."

And with that, Mr. Rivers moved across the road, heading straight for Mr. Eaton's store. Instead of cleaning up the debris, Hannah was sure he was collecting more gossip to spread later.

Sara watched Tobiah with a smile on her face. "Sure is a strong, wonderful man." Her eyes jumped with joy.

"Why don't you marry him, Sara? I know he's been asking you for two years."

"Hannah, I just want to make sure it's God's will. I know God is interested in me choosing for myself; well, as long as he's a believer."

"That's right, Sara. God wants the best for you. I'm glad you're coming around. I'm sure Tobiah will be glad."

"Well, he hasn't asked me lately. I guess he's given up after being told no so many times."

Mischief showed in Hannah's eyes. "I could fill him in."

"You better not. I'm sure he'll come around in time."

"He's coming around right now." Hannah laughed at her timely joke.

"Hello, Sara, Hannah. What are you doing in town?"

Hannah looked at Sara. "We're getting into as much mischief as we possibly can."

Tobiah looked incredulous at Sara's remark. "Hadn't seen you enjoy yourself in a long time, Sara. I've missed my old friend. See ya later. I've gotta help with the cleanup." His eyes lingered on Sara's lips.

"He liked what he saw in you, Sara."

"What?" she asked demurely.

"He likes seeing the life back in your eyes. My guess is for a summer wedding… let's see, I could design your gown. You know I studied under Florence La Peau at finishing school. She loved my clothing designs."

"Hannah, don't count your chickens before they hatch. For goodness' sakes, the eggs haven't even been laid yet."

"Oh yes, they have, and they've been sat on far too long. It's time something good was hatched, and I'm just the one to crack the case."

"Hannah Rose Baxter, don't make me resort to my old ways. You will not interfere with me and Tobiah."

"Who says?" The devious look on Hannah's face told that she would interfere if she wanted to.

The girls rose from their seat by the river, chasing each other around the meadow. By the time they paused, out of breath, Mr. Rivers was standing at the edge of the meadow, looking on.

"Now he knows I'm daft." Hannah laughed.

"He'll add me to the gossiping. Remember I'm an old maid."

Collapsing in laughter on the soft grass, the girls began picking a handful of flowers. Plucking the petals, they both muttered, "He loves me. He loves me not."

Every petal had been plucked by the time Grandpappy's booming voice resounded from the boardwalk. "Girls, it's time to go."

"Yes, sir," they replied in unison.

Mr. Rivers had disappeared, but a small group gathered on the boardwalk was staring in Hannah's direction as the girls made their way to Grandpappy's wagon. Hannah removed her hat, bowing low for the spectators. *Let them think what they will.* She looked up to see Isabel and Mrs. Norseworthy mocking her nearby. Hannah smiled brightly, sticking her nose in the air as she walked by. *No need in wasting a perfectly good afternoon worrying about what other people think.*

Grandpappy helped them into the wagon. "Are you girls all right? Have you had too much sun today?"

"No, sir, we've had too much fun today." Hannah secured her hat with the hatpin, straightened her back, looking forward as her grandfather took the reins in hand. Glancing toward Mrs. Eaton's shop, she saw Isaac and his mother standing behind the display window. At her glance, they both backed farther into the confines of the store.

Sara's gaze followed Hannah's. "Gossip vine must have grown that far already."

"What kind of vine is growing already?"

"One from Mr. Rivers, Grandpappy." Hannah smiled at Sara as the dear man shrugged his shoulders, clucking to the horses.

After supper and dishes, it was time for bed.

Saying her prayers, Hannah remembered to pray for Wendell Cunningham. "Keep him safe," she whispered. Then she added, "For me." A smile graced her lips.

The end of April came and went. May brought the planting of the grass for hay. Father had been busy, along with the twins and Tobiah and Mr. Smythe, planting forty acres to see the stock through the winter months.

Another week passed, filled with helping Mother prepare for the summer garden planting. Weeds and grass were meticulously removed from the moist earth waiting to receive the seeds they would plant. Rich dirt turned under the girls' hands.

Mother looked at Sara and Hannah. "Doesn't it feel wonderful?" She was in her glory, the gentle rays of the morning sun casting playful shadows beneath the oak trees nearby. "We'll be ready to plant next week."

A blue jay edged closer and closer on a tree limb overhead, his eyes focused on the freshly turned dirt below. In one smooth move, he swooped into the middle of the patch, removing a long worm from its place in the soil.

"Good for you, little bird." Mother loved birds, especially *before* her garden was planted.

"Let's get washed up and go into town, girls. Miss Hattie wants to meet with us this morning. Says she's buying our dinner at Miss Amy's Hotel."

"Yum, what a treat. Wonder what she wants to discuss?" Hannah's eyes told of her suspicions.

"I think she's been waiting until the funeral was behind us before making her wedding plans. She probably wants some help with the wedding."

"Oh, Mother, that's what I thought. Oh … never mind."

"What is it, Hannah?"

"I was just thinking maybe she'll let me design her wedding gown. But I wouldn't want to intrude."

"Oh, Hannah, what a marvelous idea. I can help with the flowers. If she's getting married soon, we could use wildflowers," Sara said excitedly.

"Wildflowers are my favorite, Sara. Of course I love your roses, Mother. There's just something about wildflowers, springing up everywhere. No one plants them. They just show up right on time every year."

"The master gardener has his workers strewing the seeds from the air. His winged friends cheerfully do his work, Hannah." Mother's words made Hannah smile.

Washing up with water from the well, the girls quickly removed their sunbonnets, twisting their hair into coifs for the noon meeting. Changing into spring dresses, they tied on their bonnets, climbing into the wagon Blaine brought around.

Mother and the girls waved at Elizabeth, standing on her front porch, watching Beth trying to roll a hoop across the wooden planks. The child looked up, waving frantically, as if they might not see her.

"Such a sweetheart." Mother blew her grandchild a kiss, which was immediately returned.

A group of meadowlarks chirped along the roadside, flitting around, searching the ground for a bug or worm. Their yellow chests glowed brightly in the morning sun.

"Look, Mother." Blaine pointed up ahead, slowing the horses to a crawl. There on a low limb of a scrub oak was a black bear cub.

"Oh how sweet." Hannah and her family watched as the bear tumbled out of the tree, bouncing across the road and into the palmetto patch.

"I'm gonna give the horses their heads. A big ole mad mama bear is probably right behind that little one."

"You could be right, Blaine. Just be on the lookout." Mother carefully scanned the surroundings.

"Ya whoo." The horses took off like a bolt of lightning. With his squeaky voice, Blaine had scared them half to death.

Mother put her hand to her heart. "Blaine, we're more afraid of what you'll do than the bear. My goodness, boy, will you never grow up? Now slow down a bit."

"The grapes are out early." Sara pointed to the vines. "Guess the bears haven't been foraging in that particular spot yet."

"Give 'em time. If Widder Grouch don't come an get 'em for makin' jam, the bears'll get 'em." Blaine snickered. "Wouldn't it be somethin' if they both came at the same time? Hard pressed to see which one would win in that match."

"Blaine." Mother's smile belied her condemning voice.

Little green oranges could be seen on the trees lining both sides of the road. It would take several more months of growth and ripening before they would be ready to eat. Hannah could almost taste the delicious juice. "Can't wait until we have orange juice for breakfast."

"Betcha won't be that anxious for the guavas to ripen." Blaine teased.

Sara scrunched her nose. "Heaven forbid. I sure hope it's a late crop this year."

Blaine proudly shared the news. "Sorry to be the bearer of bad news, but Grandmam's tree done has little green guavas. When I rode by there the other day, she was pounding a broomstick in the ground. I stopped to help her. We added another stick, making a cross."

Sara laughed. "What was she doing?"

Blaine laughed. "She dressed it up with Grandpappy's long johns and an old hat. Said the crows have been comin' and eatin' the precious fruit and she weren't a sharin'. She called the thang a scarecrow, said it scares the crows away."

Hannah shook her head. "Wish she'd share with them birds. Sure would spare us some of the smell."

"Now girls, you know we love the end results. Look how much we've enjoyed our guava treats. Why we've nearly used up all the guava syrup and the jam; I just scraped the last bit out of the jar this morning."

"Yeah, girls, look how much we enjoy it."

"Blaine, you don't have to help with the making."

"Shore don't. I'd rather milk a cow five hundred mornings than stand over that smell for a day. When y'all come home, I cain't stand it till ya get a bath. Whew."

Pulling up in front of Miss Amy's Hotel, Mother waved to Miss Hattie, who was making her way down the street. "Pick us up in two hours, Blaine."

"Yes'm."

Adeline Baxter rushed to meet her friend. Hannah and Sara waited on Miss Amy's front porch.

Hannah noticed Sara's quick intake of breath, followed by her hand covering her mouth. Looking in the window, there in broad daylight sat Isaac Eaton holding hands across the table with Isabel Benson.

Hannah touched her sister's arm. "It's all right, Sara. I'll show that mister."

"No . . . Hannah . . . " Sara's warning died on her lips as she watched her sister swing the door wide, pick up her skirts ever so slightly, and walk directly to the table where the lovebirds were nesting.

"Good day, Isaac, and I believe Isabel, isn't it? So this is the lady who you ducked inside the stable with the day of my return?"

Wanting Isaac to know where she stood, she also wanted Isabel to be well informed. Placing her hand on her hip, Hannah looked down her nose at the girl whose hand Isaac had quickly dropped with her appearance. "Dear, lovely Isabel, were you aware that Isaac was my suitor while you were running all over my hometown with him?" The girl's face turned three shades of red.

Glancing out the window, Hannah ignored Sara, who was shaking her head ever so slightly.

Looking back at Isaac, squirming in his lovely chair, she meant to end this relationship once and for all. "Consider yourself a free man, Isaac Eaton. Mr. Rivers has spread the grapevine all over town that you intentionally scared Abraham, which resulted in my most unfortunate accident." Invigorated by his helpless look, Hannah reached up, removing her bonnet. "Damaged goods, I suppose. If I were you, Mr. Eaton, graduate of law at the university, I would find myself a lawyer. *If* I were you."

A sick look made its way across Isaac's face. Isabel chose that precise moment to exit the room. Hannah was close behind her. Using Sara's greatly exaggerated Southern drawl, she took the time to speak to the girl's rapidly disappearing back. "You have a lovely afternoon, now, ya hear?"

Isaac left the dining hall, beating a quick path behind Isabel, who was walking rapidly toward his mother's shop.

"Take a deep breath, Hannah."

"I'm fine, Sara." Hannah sat on the porch swing, taking long deep breaths, trying to relax before her mother noticed anything out of the ordinary. Hannah was glad her mother was still chatting with Miss Hattie on the boardwalk.

"Hannah, your face is strawberry red. Calm down."

Hannah smiled at her sister. "That's all right; Isabel's and Isaac's faces were beet red."

"I suppose you ended the relationship?"

"Yes, you could say that, Sara."

Mother came up the steps, totally absorbed in conversation with her friend. "Oh, yes, and by the way, Hannah creates the loveliest designs. You know the French designer at finishing school was very impressed with her."

"Oh, Mother."

"Now, Hannah, there's no need to blush. You are good, my dear."

Breathing a sigh of relief, Hannah cocked an eyebrow at Sara, whose eyes mirrored her own feelings.

After they were seated at a table, Mother gingerly touched a sample of cloth the seamstress withdrew from her reticule. "Oh, yes, Hattie Mae, you would look lovely in this ivory brocade. What do you think, girls?"

"Yes, Mother, it is beautiful."

"I agree," Hannah said, thinking she would agree to most anything at this point.

Miss Amy appeared. "What will it be, ladies? We have chicken and rice or chicken and rice. I'm so sorry. We are out of the beef pot pie already."

"Then we will have chicken and rice." Mother's voice was cheerful. "What's for dessert?"

"Now this will make up for the lack of choice for your entrée. We have raisin spice cake, lemon pie, apple tarts, and peach cobbler."

Mother answered for her girls. "We'll have the peach cobbler."

"And I'll have the spice cake. And, Miss Amy, could you get me the piece with the most icing?" Hattie Mae clapped her hands together like a child.

"Sure will."

Miss Amy served the chicken and rice, and the diners began eating.

"Now, Hattie, Sara is offering to help with the flowers," Mother advised.

"That'd be awful nice, Miss Sara. And by the way, me and Isaac's goin' to jump over the broom and tie that knot on May twentieth. That was my mama's birthday. She married up with my pa jest to be seprated when her master sold him fer twenty dollars and two mules. Ain't never heared from him again. He's probably dead by now. Mama died of a busted-up heart." The sad look on her face halted the conversation around the table. Forks clinked against Miss Amy's china.

Closing her eyes, clearing away the sadness, Miss Hattie put a smile on her face. "I'm sorry. This is a happy time. Had no business sharin' my woes with you fine people."

Adeline Baxter reached over, patting the hand of her friend.

"And so, what kind of flowers, Miss Sara? I thought of wildflowers, growin' wild and free, never takin' orders from anyone 'cept the master above."

Hannah smiled. "You sound like Mother. Wildflowers are my favorite."

Sara nodded her agreement. "That's what I had in mind, Miss Hattie."

"So wildflowers it is." Laughter bubbled up inside the woman who had endured much at the hand of a cruel master. Escaping slavery, Hattie Mae Williams was now a strong force in Laurel City.

"Miss Hannah, would you be so kind as to draw up my weddin' dress? I'm havin' the hardest time decidin' how to make it. Been porin' over patterns for weeks."

"Miss Hattie, are you sure? I know you could come up with something beautiful."

"Hattie's designs ain't got no French influence." Hattie tipped her nose as if to put on airs.

Hannah laughed. "I'd be happy to, Miss Hattie."

"I knows this is a rushed-up thang, but I do want ta get married on my mama's birthday. You deesign that dress quick, Miss Hannah, and I'll stitch it up jest as fast. The wildflowers are ready, and I know Isaac be ready. He has his suit I made him all washed up and jest a waitin' for the big day. Grandpappy's a standin' by, and Grandmam's gonna make that cake of hers that I like so much." Hattie's eyes closed, as if savoring her thoughts.

Mother smiled at her friend. "We'll make everything ready. You said you wanted to get married beneath the canopy of oaks at Laurel Oaks, right?"

"Yes, that's where Isaac found his peace, after Mr. Baxter saved him from the hangin' noose. Whew, that was a mighty close call. Why, I almost lost my man before I found him."

Chapter 9

With very little time to prepare, Hannah went to work sketching some of the latest styles from Paris. By the time she met with the seamstress at the end of the week, she proudly displayed several choices.

"Oh my, how will I ever make my choice? Course it seems I do keep eyein' that one with the bell skirt and the not-so-full bustle. I wonder if we can tighten my corset enough to make me look as good in that dress as you drawed it?"

Hannah laughed. "Miss Hattie, you have a very nice waist."

"Why thank ya, Miss Hannah, but I's been seein' myself in that lookin' glass." She shook her head, pointing to the favored sketch. "It'll be this one."

"You've made a perfect choice."

"I'll start sewin' right away, an we'll be gettin' married, as we planned. When you ride by that field beside the chapel, urge them wildflowers to stay purty 'til we need 'em."

"I will, Miss Hattie. I'm going to go find Grandpappy now. He's probably at the store."

Opening the door to leave the shop, Hannah met Isaac coming in. "Let me get that door fer ya, Miss Hanner."

"Miss Hattie picked out her dress pattern, Mr. Isaac."

"I sho is glad, Miss Hanner. I cain't wait to get hitched." He peeked over her shoulder, smiling at his sweetheart. "The Lawd sho is good."

"Yes, he is."

Making her way down the boardwalk, Hannah was happy that Miss Hattie Mae Williams was pleased with her design. She breathed a sigh of relief, opening the door to Paxton's General Store.

Grandpappy was leaning against the counter in deep conversation with his friend. "Well, Paxton, it looks like Grant's going to win in November."

"Yes, it appears that way. Course I don't know what to think about Greeley. Ain't sure about that man's ideals. May not make for a good president."

Hannah went to hide behind the bolts of material once again. Last time had proved quite fruitful for gathering information against Isaac. She couldn't wait to hear what might be going on today. She turned quickly before Grandpappy saw her making her way to eavesdrop. Curiosity often got her into trouble, but she was sure enjoying this adventure.

Taking care to scoot a bolt of material over just enough for a clear view of the chair by the potbelly stove, Hannah stood completely still, waiting for Mr. Rivers to begin. She saw his prey; unknowingly lurking nearby, two men from out of town wandered over to look at the pocket watches encased in glass beside the gossipers' bench.

"Come right chere, friends. Sit a bit and rest yore bones. I done saw ya ride up on them mules, know yore backsides gotta be sore."

The men looked at Mr. Rivers, seemingly indecisive.

"Come on, sit a while. Hey, I'll fix ya a cup o coffee; even put sugar 'n fresh cream in it."

The offer of coffee did the trick. Smacking his lips, Mr. Rivers handed the men a cup, showing them to their seat on the bench.

Taking his knife out and beginning to whittle, Mr. Rivers cleared his throat. "Whattcha thank 'bout this here election? From what I heared, it's a heatin' up." He paused, looking up at his listeners.

The older man looked at the younger, who just shrugged his shoulders. "Well, what do you think, sir?"

"Well, now, you done an ask a Southern-born gennelman. I'll tell yas, I been holdin' a grudge cause what ole Ulysses done in the war. Why us Southerners done an lost it cause o him, an look what he's done in the big house."

The younger man snickered. "What's he done, sir?"

"You ain't heared? Boy, you don't get no papers with the news in it? Whar you come from?"

"Don't read much."

Hannah could tell the young man was just egging Mr. Rivers on. The older man was trying to cover his grin, bringing his coffee cup to his lips.

"Well, sonny, let ole Mr. Rivers fill you in. I've heared a whole lot."

Both men nodded their heads, obviously quite entertained.

"Well, now let's see whar to start. Well, like I said, it all started clear back in the War Between the States. I'll never live to forget that he's the one what pinned down our own Genral Robert E. Lee in the war, won't never forgive him neither. Hear tell he's the one what tole ole fire blazin' Sherman to hit the trail to the South, what with ole Grant bein' the genral in chief of the war an all. He's shore got a lot o' blood on his conscience, if'n he's got one; don't reckon he does." He paused, getting up to refill his own coffee cup.

"Well, now let's see whar was I? Oh yeah, an then he went to the big house and brung all them Yanks there to work fer 'em, putting them in big offices. 'Tis a shame, if'n ya ask me; him a likin' them Yanks an not carin' a thang about the South. Why, we's part o the Union, don't you agree?"

The men nodded, even though Mr. Rivers continued without looking for their approval. "An then they say he's a takin' gifts, a whole lot o big gifts from his friends. Somethin' smells like a fish ta me, an we ain't a been fishin' 'round these here parts."

The older man held up his hand. "Well, Mr. Rivers, what do you think about Horace Greeley, his opponent?"

"Don't know what that word means, but I know Greeley's a runnin' again ole Grant."

"Some people say he'd do a better job."

"Well, I'll tell ya what I thank, seein's how I done heared 'bout Greeley too. He can't be too bad; he don't like them womern suffer gates, and I don't neither. Someone done an said he stays away from his wife as much as he can; even when he comes home from outta town, he stays in a boardin' house. Sounds like ole Norseworthy to me, a gettin' away from that ole cantankrous womern o his'n." He paused to laugh, looking around the store to see if anyone was listening.

The men grew restless on the bench. Rising and returning their coffee cups to the top of the barrel, they reached to shake Mr. Rivers' hand.

Unwilling to see the conversation come to a close, he looked away, continuing his political speech. "Well, jes thank of it this here way. Ulysses Grant's done an been in there fer four years. We need someone in there what's gonna hep the South."

"Hannah, I didn't know you were here."

Hannah jumped, knocking a bolt of material off the shelf. "Oh, I, I . . . " Another bolt of material joined the one already on the floor, landing atop Hannah's foot. "Ouch, ouch."

Mr. Rivers came around, staring at the young girl who was jumping up and down, holding on to her foot. Hannah barely heard his words. "I knew she was tetched. An to thank she use to be might near purty."

"Time to go, Hannah. Daylight's a burnin'."

"I'm a comin', Grandpappy." Hannah limped away, following her grandfather and glaring at Mr. Rivers. "That'll give him some more gossip to spread."

"What did you say, Hannah?"

"Oh, I was just saying I'd give Mr. Rivers something more to spread. And I can tell you, it won't be jam for his biscuits."

Hannah took her grandfather's arm as he helped her into the wagon. "'Tis a beautiful day in May. We shall enjoy the ride home."

When Hannah stepped onto the porch at Laurel Oaks, Grandpappy called to her. "A letter came on the stage for you. I almost forgot."

"A letter for me?" Could she dare hope it was from Wendell Cunningham? Running to retrieve it, Hannah nearly tripped on her way to her upstairs bedroom. Ripping open the envelope, she began reading the fine script.

Dear Miss Hannah Baxter,

It is with great pleasure that I write to inform you that you have been chosen to study under the fine art techniques of Jacques De Ponte, French artiste, at the highly esteemed De Ponte School of Art. The rec-

ommendation comes with sponsorship from Mr. and Mrs. La Peau, proprietors of Mrs. Fancy La Peau's Finishing School for Young Ladies.

Your course of studies will include the use of light and shadow in sketching as well as painting. You will be schooled in the use of oils and watercolor, using the latest techniques. In addition, you will learn how to choose the proper canvas for various projects. We feel it would greatly benefit your blossoming talent to accept this offer.

Please advise of your acceptance of this proposition. At such time, you will be supplied with enrollment papers. Date of commencement for your session will be June 10, 1872. This course will conclude in nine months.

Respectfully yours,
Joshua Greenleaf, Secretary to the Artiste
De Ponte School of Art

"Mother, Father, where are you?" Hannah descended the stairs, holding the rail for her own safety. Dashing into the kitchen, she stopped just short of tripping over her petticoats.

Her parents stared at her over their cups of tea. Seeing the look on their daughter's face, they both stood.

"Whatever is it, Hannah?" Glancing at the letter in her daughter's hand, Adeline Baxter made her way to Hannah's side. "Is something wrong, my dear? You can hardly breathe."

Hannah paused, catching her breath.

Sara opened the back door, smiling. Seeing her sister in such a fluster, she paused on her way to the pie safe. "What is wrong, Hannah?"

"Mother, Father, Sara, it's unbelievable; just look." She extended the letter, unable to gather her emotions.

Sara quickly grabbed the letter. Scanning the contents, her eyes opened wide. "Whooppee." Grabbing her sister, she hugged her, turning in circles until Hannah pulled back.

"What is it?" Father sounded both excited and anxious. Holding the letter for his wife, they read its contents.

"How did this happen, Hannah?"

"It has to be an act of God, Mother. People are not invited to study under Mr. Jacques De Ponte without first being highly acclaimed as an artist. I am a simple sketch artist, and he only receives one student at a time."

"I beg to differ, Hannah." Her father ran his fingers through his hair. "All things are possible. It looks like the Lord has wonderful plans for your life." He hugged his youngest daughter.

"We'll have a special supper tomorrow night. All the family will attend, and you may read your letter, dear. We'll keep it under cover until then."

"Thank you, Mother. We better not tell Blaine ahead of time. He'll pass this information on to Mr. Rivers when he goes into town today, and then all of Laurel City will know. I'd rather keep the news private until I share it."

"Yes, Hannah, that's a good idea. He does like to keep the grapevine healthy."

"Oh, I'm so excited, Hannah." Sara hugged her sister again. "Just wait until Susannah finds out."

"May I invite her and her family, Mother?"

"Yes, you may, dear. We'll celebrate with your best friend's family."

"Mother, may Tobiah and his parents join us?"

"How can I say no, Sara? The more, the merrier."

"I see the twinkle in your eye, Sara."

"Now, Hannah, don't be interfering."

Hannah looked offended. "Me, interfere? Why, I'd never interfere. I just might help out a bit."

"The Lord doesn't need your help, Hannah. Things are coming along quite nicely between Tobiah and me."

"Glad to hear it."

The twins came in the back door. "Glad to hear what?" Blaine never let an opportunity pass him by to gather information. No one answered his question.

Blythe sniffed the air. "What's for supper?"

"Lima beans, fried ham, and cornbread."

"Sounds good, Mother."

Mother reached up to hug her sons. The twins now towered above her. "I think everything that counts as food sounds good to you boys."

Sara shook her head. "Yes, and some things that are questionable sound good to them."

"We cain't help it."

Father nodded. "That's right, boys. I remember when my mother used to tell me I had hollow legs that she never could fill up. Eat all you want."

The following morning everyone went in opposite directions after breakfast. Mother walked over to invite Elizabeth's family to supper, making her way back to advise Grandmam of the invitation as well.

Sara was sent to invite the Smythes while Hannah was accompanied by Blythe to invite the Frost family. Katherine waved from her front porch where she was sweeping before her and Wyatt headed into the doctor's office. Hannah stopped for only a moment to invite her sister.

"That sounds real good. I won't have to prepare supper tonight."

Blythe turned the buggy toward the Frost residence. As they pulled up in the yard, Susannah ran out to meet them. Hannah's eyes danced as her friend asked what they were celebrating. "You'll have to wait until tonight to find out, but it's special."

"Is it about your preacher friend?"

"No." Hannah's spirits dropped just for a moment.

"I saw how you looked at him. Oh well. If it's meant to be, it will work out."

Hannah nodded. "See you tonight, Susannah."

"May we bring anything?"

"Just a hearty appetite."

"We can do that."

Hannah waved good-bye to her friend. She would miss her if she went to the art school in Savannah, Georgia. The offer was a once-in-a-lifetime opportunity.

As the buggy made its way down the road to Laurel Oaks, Hannah remembered meeting Mr. Jacques De Ponte at Mrs. La Peau's school. He had visited the finishing school for a special presentation in art class. Hannah remembered him lingering over her sketchpad, turning the pages slowly as if assessing each one. Never in a million years could she have hoped for this invitation to study under such a fine man.

The day passed quickly. Elizabeth came early to help with the meal preparation. Grandmam came bearing two blackberry pies, made from her homegrown berries, picked and jarred right there at Laurel Oaks.

By the time the Smythe and Frost families arrived, everyone had gathered on the back porch and in the kitchen. Katherine and Wyatt brought along Dr. Windam.

Fellowship flowed like a river, everyone basking in its warmth. Just before supper, Father asked their guests to gather in the great room. "We have brought you here to celebrate a most important milestone in our daughter's life." Looking at Hannah, he motioned her forward, placing his arm around her shoulders. "I'm a mighty proud father tonight. Read the letter, sweetie."

With trembling voice, Hannah made it through the emotional reading. "It still seems like a dream. I can't believe it's real."

Grandmam wiped tears of joy from her eyes. "I believe it, my dear. God has blessed you with this gift, and he is propelling you forward."

Elizabeth hugged her sister. "I'm so proud of you."

Ethan followed his wife in the congratulatory line. "I knew you had a special talent when you sketched my furniture for the store owners to view."

"Thank you, big brother." Hannah loved her brother-in-law just like a brother.

On and on the line went. Congratulations were rich and heartfelt. At the end of the line, Hannah turned toward the group, holding on to Susannah's arm. "I want you to know how much I love and appreciate you all. Thank you for sharing this special time with me."

Mother dried the tears from her eyes on the bib of her apron. "It's time to eat. Pappy, please honor us by saying grace."

"Grace."

"Pappy." Her voice held sweet reproof.

Grandpappy prayed a prayer of blessing upon his granddaughter and the food. Moist eyes were in evidence around the great room in the Baxter home. Love permeated the air as everyone went into the kitchen to make their plates.

Creamy chicken and vegetables covered with huge, fluffy biscuits sat in pans lining the buffet. Everyone ate more than their share of the pot pie, along with creamed corn and pole beans.

Grandmam stood to her feet. "Don't forget dessert."

And the guests didn't. Nothing was left that night except one sliver of blackberry pie. Sneaking back downstairs, thinking everyone was in bed, Hannah watched as Blaine carefully opened the pie safe, retrieving the small piece of pie.

"Uh huh. Got caught with your hand in the cookie jar."

"Hannah, you scared me plum to death. I kept lyin' in bed thinkin' 'bout this lonely piece of pie down here all by itself. Thought I'd come share company with it."

"You go ahead, Blaine. Help yourself." Hannah kissed her brother on the cheek, running upstairs to savor every detail of her party.

A soft knock sounded on Hannah's door. "Are you still awake?"

"Yes, come in."

Sara made her way to the dresser, removing the hairbrush from her sister's hand. "I'll finish brushing your hair."

"I'm on number fifteen, gotta finish the one hundred strokes, Sara."

"I'm sure we'll reach that number before we say good night." Lifting her sister's thick tresses with one hand, she shook her head. "What a beautiful head of hair you have. Wish mine was half as thick. Where's the shears?" Sara's eyes danced mischievously.

"You wouldn't. Did you have a particular topic you wanted to discuss? I saw you and Tobiah this evening; seems you're a little closer than you were."

Her sister smiled, biting her lip. "We are. I'm just waiting for a proposal."

"Really, Sara? Well, judging your not-so-long-ago behavior, I'll wager Tobiah is waiting for you to propose."

"I think I'll tease him a bit, like the old days. Only I never teased about that. I did pester him, begging him to elope with me."

"Well, I, for one, am glad to see my sister enjoying life again. I think Tobiah's rather happy to see you coming back to us from wherever you went."

Sara paused with the brushing, placing her hands on her hips. "After my salvation, I thought I had to be a stick in the mud. You helped to change my mind." She playfully pinched her sister's cheek. Resuming the brush strokes, Sara spoke with a crack in her voice. "I'm gonna miss you, Hannah. I'm so happy for you, but you will be missed."

Hannah reached up from her seat in front of the dresser, and the girls embraced as if the parting was at this very moment in time.

Sara wiped her eyes. "At this rate, we'll never get those one hundred strokes in."

"I miss Wendell Cunningham in the worst way. Maybe going away to art school will divert my attention. I may never see him again, Sara."

"I'll give you the advice everyone gives me: 'We'll pray about it.' God is able to work this out for you, Hannah."

"Sure wish he would. But, then again, maybe I'm not sober enough to be a minister's wife, what with my adventurous curiosity always getting the best of me. Maybe Wendell Cunningham needs a wife who wears one of those tight buns that make you slant eyed." The girls erupted in a fit of giggles.

"Somehow I can't see the circuit rider settling for a sober-faced Miss Always Prim and Proper. As much as he stared at your beautiful hairstyles, I can't imagine him enjoying a prude's company." Sara's eyes did a dangerous dance. She put her hand to her chest, affecting her exaggerated Southern drawl. "He was having love thoughts about you, Hannah."

Hannah answered back, enunciating her words more deeply than her sister. "Now, Sara, don't be talking like that. Why Wendell Cunningham is a man of the cloth."

"Ain't that right, dear sister, but I'll tell you, his heart beats out of his chest when he's around you. Why I'm quite sure I saw his cravat pulsing to the rhythm of his heart when he preached that Sunday."

"You flatter me, big sis." Hannah dropped the drawl, reaching out to straighten the doily Katherine had crocheted for her. "I sure hope you are right. My heart beats to the tune of the preacher."

Sara finished brushing her sister's hair, twisting it into a braid for the night. "Good night, Hannah. Sweet dreams."

"Sweet dreams to you, Sara. It's probably a good thing I'm going away. I think the two of us could get into trouble together."

Sara crossed her eyes. "I think you are right, and with you needing to practice being a preacher's wife, you don't need any bad influence." She smiled at Hannah, closing the door behind her.

Our lives are changing so. Sure hope we corral those men we want, thought Hannah.

Chapter 10

Wendell Cunningham turned his slicker up against the rain pounding his face. Pulling his hat low, he let his horse lead him down the coastal path he was following. Crossing to the east coast of Florida over the last few weeks, he had now made his way into Georgia, heading for Savannah.

He smiled, remembering the night spent with the parson near Palm City. This was the first time he had seen this kind man since his meeting two years ago. The parson had assisted him with information regarding Reverend Charles Finney's imposter at that time.

The pelting rain ceased to be felt by the minister traveling by moonlight and intermittent streaks of lightning. His thoughts turned to his time with the parson.

The parson had invited Wendell to minister on Sunday at his country church. Glad to have a pillow for his head and warm fellowship, the circuit rider accepted the invitation. He shook his head, remembering the predicament. *Those girls were sure obvious in their quest to find a husband.* Wendell laughed, shuddering as he thought of being joined to either female.

A stoic-looking woman stood before him after he delivered his morning sermon. "Well, how do, Revern Cunninham. We's doin' an invite to our parson to come an dine for the noonin'. Sho would be likin' it if'n you'd join us."

Not knowing what to say, Wendell nodded his head. "Well, uh, uh, if the parson is coming, I guess, I guess I'm with him." Out of the corner of his eye, the young minister could see the reverend approaching at a rapid pace, a look of apprehension on his face.

Rustling petticoats ushered in a crude-looking young woman with teeth jutting helplessly over her bottom lip. "Why, hey there, preacher. Yore a sight fer sore eyes."

She smiled at the lady who had just extended the invitation to Wendell. "Maw, are the preachers a gonna be joinin' us for the eatin'?"

"Why, yes, Matilda Irene, the circuit preacher done an axepted fer the both of 'um." The woman beamed with pride over her manipulative accomplishment.

The pastor's eyes met Wendell's, showing sympathy for the trap they had both fallen into.

"That's good, Maw. I betcha anythin' Charlotte Frances is jes now a takin' the possum an yams offa the stove." Matilda Irene licked her lips. The protruding teeth made it difficult, but she managed the task.

"Y'all hurry on over, Preachers. We be a waitin' to serve ya when ya get there." Sunbeams from the open church windows danced across the eyes staring up into the faces of the ministers, exposing their intentions.

As the women walked away, their bustles competing with each other for room in the aisle, the dear old pastor shook his head. "Mrs. Himmel always sets her sights on any minister passing through. Says her daughters are called to be wives to men of the cloth. She's had her sights set on me since my dear Abigail passed." Smiling a sad smile, the two exited the church. "Keep it under your hat, Preacher, but my dear Abigail would come up outta the grave if I married the likes of Mrs. Himmel."

Wendell laughed in spite of the queasy feeling rising in his stomach. "Was Matilda Irene teasing about the opossum and yams?"

"Not at all. The three of them have opossum roundups. They go out looking for the unsuspecting critters. One holds the bag while the other two chase the opossum into it."

"Are you kidding me, Parson?"

"God is my witness. They're mighty proud of their expert roundup abilities; they sell the opossums in town when they've got 'extry,' as they say."

I can only imagine what the afternoon will be like. "We don't have to stay long, do we, Parson?"

The old minister laughed. "Since you accepted the invitation, I'll let you decide when you've had enough." He reached over, patting Wendell on the back. Stepping up into the wagon, the ministers headed out to Mrs. Himmel's house.

"Why, howdy doody, shore be glad to meetcha." The girl who must be Charlotte Frances stood at the door of the dilapidated house, extending her hand. At the circuit rider's look, she quickly wiped part of the biscuit dough sticking to her fingers onto her apron. As she extended her hand, the preacher felt he had to accept it.

Mrs. Himmel crowded into the doorframe. "Now, Charlotte Frances, this be Wenell Cunninham; he's one o them thar sir cat ridin' preachers."

Wendell could feel the heat rising in his face. No one had ever called him Wenell except for Granny. The word hit a sore spot deep within his soul. *This day is going to be even worse than I thought.*

"Shore is a good lookin' thang." The remaining dough on Charlotte's hand was oozing onto Wendell's with the grip she still maintained.

Removing his hand, Wendell retrieved his handkerchief, discretely wiping the dough away.

"Come on in here." Mrs. Himmel turned to the side, allowing them entrance, and Charlotte Frances followed suit. A narrow path separated the two women, much too narrow to walk through comfortably.

The parson turned sideways, so as not to touch the ladies. *Looks like a good idea to me.* Wendell made a hasty sideways entrance as well.

"Sit right chere." Mrs. Himmel picked up her cat, flinging it across the room. She pointed to the sofa, which was covered in at least six months' worth of white cat hair.

Wendell thought he would be sick. "I believe I'll stand, mam. Been sitting in the saddle for days." He chanced a look at the table and saw the opossum was in attendance, surrounded by yams. Now he knew he would be sick.

The horse stumbled over a rock in the path, bringing Wendell back from his visit with the Himmels to his current location. The rain had stopped, and lightning no longer lit the sky.

The moon overhead lent its soft light. A cool breeze blew through the trees, relaxing the saddle-sore man.

"Believe I'll turn in for the night." Removing the saddle, placing it on the ground for a pillow, the preacher covered the soil with his slicker. Taking a blanket from his saddlebag, he settled down, trying to find a comfortable position.

Wendell's thoughts returned to the Himmels. He had never been so glad to escape anyone, except Granny. Matilda Irene and

Charlotte Frances had made no small play for his affections. Each tried to outdo the other. Wendell laughed aloud, the sound echoing in the woods.

He had finally made it through the meal. Carefully avoiding eating the opossum meat, he had slipped it off his plate and onto the floor when he felt the Himmels' smelly mutt lying at his feet. Hearing the dog smacking, he had spoke in a loud voice, recalling a trail story for the Himmels.

"I shore would be fond o travlin'." Matilda Irene's voice was but a whisper. "Can ya jes thank what it'd feel like, a sleepin' under them stars, Charlotte Frances?"

"I'd like to be a sleepin' there. Ya know I'd sleep better there than you, Matilda Irene. Cause o how you's always gettin' that crook in ya neck."

Matilda's voice oozed honey. "Wouldn't be a gettin' no crook in my neck if'n I's a layin' on a fine, strong shoulder." She looked over at Wendell, her eyes dropping to his shoulder. "Shore would be a fine place to rest."

"You ain't a gonna be on that thar trail a layin' on no fine shoulder. You cain't cook a lick, Matilda. A man on the trail's gotta have 'im a womern what's a gonna cook up a fine meal o possum, or rabbit, or even a snake if'n ya had to."

"Well, I cain't cook, but I can shore make a mean pot o coffee. That's more'n I can say fer you, Charlotte Frances. Why yore's is so strong, it'll hold a spoon right on top jes a floatin' an won't let it sank. A man on the trail's gotta have his coffee, ain't that right, revern?" Matilda Irene cut her eyes at Wendell and fluttered her eyelashes. The yams and butterbeans the preacher had managed to get down threatened to make their way back up.

"We better be going, Parson. I'm ready to hit the trail." Making a hasty exit, Wendell had hit the trail, glad to leave the Himmels behind.

Turning over he thought of what tomorrow would bring. He would make his way into Savannah and spend the night with his friend Ezra at the De Ponte Plantation.

Closing his eyes, Wendell Cunningham's last thoughts were of green eyes framed by brown curls blowing in the wind. The vision of Hannah atop a bed of soft spring grass, surrounded by wildflowers, eased him into blessed slumber.

"No, no, no." Wendell woke himself yelling. "No, Granny, no." Throwing the blanket aside, he rose, running from tree to tree, trying to escape his grandmother's fury.

"You ain't no count, boy. Ain't never gonna be."

Wendell trembled, hoping Granny wouldn't see him. "Come here, boy. I'm a callin' ya."

He was only five years old. He could feel his heart almost beating out of his chest. Stepping out from behind a tree, lest she get more embroiled, the child answered his drunken grandmother. "Yes'm. Over here, Granny."

"Why ain't ya done answered me, boy? Get yerself here. I'm gonna wallop the tarnation outta ya. Yer jes like yore no-good paw."

"Where is my pa, Granny?"

Wendell could remember his grandmother's laugh; a wicked sneer floated through the trees. But she never gave an answer.

Coming toward him, Granny had a leather strap raised high in the air.

"No, Granny, no." He fell to the ground at the base of a tree, curling into a tight ball. *Maybe she won't see me.*

Moving ever closer, the smell of the moonshine coming to him in revolting waves, Wendell tightened himself against the blows that would come. Just before she reached him, his grandmother tripped over a root.

The little boy released the breath he had been holding. Staying curled up in a ball, so as not to wake his sleeping grandmother, Wendell relaxed. This episode had passed without a beating. He lay still, letting sleep claim his body.

Awaking to the bright morning sun shining in his face, Wendell Cunningham looked around in confusion. *How did I end up deep in the forest? I bedded down near the edge. Where is my saddle and blanket?*

And then he remembered the nightmare. Granny had been chasing him, again. A mockingbird trilled its morning song from a nearby branch, mocking the man who had slept on the bare ground, curled into a ball.

Standing to his feet, Wendell raked his fingers through his black locks, looking overhead through the covering of tall pines. "Father, help me make it through these nightmares."

Feeling strengthened by his prayer, Wendell went to the creek singing its morning song nearby. Washing up, he walked to his saddlebags, retrieving the pot and the coffee he would brew.

Making a fire, he set the pot to boil with water from the creek. Sitting back on one heel, he squinted at the rising sun. *Must be about seven in the morning. With a hard day's ride, I could be in Savannah by nightfall.*

Wendell's stomach growled, thinking of Mama Eliza's food. No matter when he showed up for a visit, Ezra Perkins' wife always had food for him. But it was food for his soul just to be with the couple.

Taking the coffeepot in hand, he poured himself a cup. *Sure will be good to see my friends.* Finishing the warm brew, Wendell packed his saddlebags and mounted up. Making his way along the trail, the circuit-riding preacher let his mind wander back to when he had first met Ezra and Eliza.

The war was over, and he was roaming, unwilling to return to Granny's abuse. Wendell had been saved at a meeting under the Reverend Charles Finney's preaching. Happy over his new conversion, he decided to ride south.

When he stopped at the house where he and Granny had lived for two years prior to the war, a neighbor came to advise him of his grandmother's passing. Having felt the call to ministry and wishing he could have shared the gospel message with his only known relative, Wendell left the town behind, heading toward the coast of Georgia.

Reaching the outskirts of Savannah, he traveled through a deeply wooded area, thinking to bed down for the night. Singing began floating across the early evening breeze. He cocked his ear, pausing on horseback to determine the direction of the rhythmic spiritual that was causing his heart to dance. Turning his head to the south, he could barely make out a crude church building, a makeshift steeple reaching toward the sky, its ethereal appearance making him wonder if it was a figment of his imagination.

The sound of a breaking twig caused Wendell to turn in his saddle. A colored man rode up behind him out of nowhere. "Come on in. Yo welcomed ta worship wif us."

"I heard the music. Sure is a balm to my soul." Wendell looked down at the rifle the man was holding toward the ground.

Meeting the question in Wendell's eyes, the colored man extended his hand. "Name's Jonas. We's been freed wif the Emancpation

Proclonation, but we's gotta watch out for dem Ku Kux Klanz. They's after us hot an heavy, don't give a fig 'bout de law."

Wendell understood the need for the rifle. The church was secluded, and these former slaves could be in trouble real quick with the raiding and burning. The Klu Klux Klan was a force to be reckoned with. Covering themselves in sheets, wearing cone hats with only their eyes showing, they wrecked havoc on the slaves and their sympathizers. Property was burned, and people lost their lives at the hand of this group.

Following Jonas through the thicket of trees and brush, the dim light from the flickering candles in the windows of the little church warmed Wendell's heart. Throwing the reins of his horse over the hitching post, removing his Bible from the saddlebag, the preacher followed his new friend inside.

An elderly gentlemen, his curly hair speckled with gray, extended his hand in welcome. "Name's Ezra, Ezra Perkins. Glad to have ya, sir." Glancing at the Bible Wendell carried, Ezra looked deep into the younger man's eyes. "You be a man o the cloth, su?"

Wendell didn't know how to answer. "Well, yes, sir, I'm trying to be. Just received the call."

"I knowed it, and, su, we be most obliged if'n you'd take da stand tanight. I be knowin' a man o God when I sees 'um. I know you gots a word from the Lawd." He held on to Wendell's hand. Tightening his grip, he patted the young man's back soundly.

Wendell felt a warm stirring in his chest as he looked over the group of people gathered together. The singing had stopped. Men, women, and children were watching him expectantly.

"I started this here chuch well afore da war what was between da states. After we's got our freedom, we's still gonna worship right chere. Do us proud, boy; get on up an take da stand." Ezra pointed to the crude podium at the front of the church.

Wendell recalled that first sermon, the first he'd ever preached. He had opened his Bible and preached on God's grace and mercy to a world of sinners. Two young men had received their salvation that night.

He could remember their words. "We wants to have us a baptizin'. We'd be powerful grateful, su, if'n you'd do the onners." The shorter man had echoed the first man. "Yessa, we's a wantin' it powa full bad."

Wendell shuddered. He could still feel the chill of the creek water as they had waded out waist deep to do the baptizing. Jonas stood to the side while Ezra and Wendell did the honors. Before the night was over, thirteen more had joined the baptismal line stretching out from the riverbank.

Those being baptized were quickly given quilts from the wagons to wrap themselves in. The circuit-riding preacher closed his eyes, remembering the soft sound of the voices as the group stood on the riverbank, lifting their praises to their deliverer.

His ministry had been born in the woods outside of Savannah. Ezra Perkins had been God's helping hand in propelling him into the work. Ezra and Eliza had opened their home in the renovated slave quarters to the young preacher any time he was nearby. The current owner of the land, Jacques De Ponte, was a French artist who had purchased the plantation, hiring the slaves to stay on as paid workers. He was a godly man.

Picking up the pace, Wendell Cunningham knew he had to make it to the De Ponte Plantation by nightfall. He needed to satisfy the powerful hunger rising in his chest to see his friends. The remembrance of their first meeting intensified that hunger.

Chapter 11

Hannah placed the basket of wildflowers on the reception table. The front porch of the antebellum home was decorated in spring's glory for the celebration. The canopy of oaks covering the carriage drive formed an arch for the wedding ceremony about to be held.

Running upstairs to inform the bride that Isaac had arrived, Hannah gasped as she opened the bedroom door. The dress she had designed for Miss Hattie Mae surrounded her in gentle folds, the ivory color complimenting her friend's complexion. "Miss Hattie, you are so beautiful. Isaac is marrying a queen."

"Aw, Miss Hannah, y'all a makin' me cry. I'm so glad to be marryin' up with Isaac at this place. Laurel Oaks means a whole lots to Isaac and me."

Mother gave her friend a hug, careful not to wrinkle her dress.

Katherine handed the seamstress a dainty lace hanky. "Now you've got something borrowed, Miss Hattie."

Adeline Baxter was standing up with Miss Hattie. Garrett would stand up with Isaac. "Aren't the flowers lovely, Hannah?"

"Yes, Mother, Sara did a beautiful job arranging them."

"Couldn't have done it without you helping me pick them, Hannah."

"Oh, that was the fun part." Hannah reached to take Beth from Elizabeth's arms. "Give me sugars, sweetie."

The little girl's lips puckered, rewarding her aunt with a wet kiss. "Wuv woo, Nannah. Don't weave."

Hannah held the girl close. "I'm not leaving for a couple of weeks yet, dearie."

Hannah's leaving had been the talk of the town since she had signed the enrollment papers. Looking around the room, she knew she would miss her family and the friends she held dear.

Never one to worry much, Hannah set Beth down. "Be down in ten minutes, everyone. I'll tell the men you're coming."

She turned to Elizabeth. "It's time to start playing the harp."

Hannah returned to the front porch, asking everyone to take a seat at the tables. Elizabeth followed close behind. Sitting down, gracefully arranging her skirt, she began softly plucking the strings of the beautiful harp Ethan had purchased last Christmas.

The crowd was mesmerized by the romantic music gliding across the landscape. Some were swaying in their seats, others closing their eyes, as if to absorb each note wafting toward them on the gentle afternoon breeze.

Mrs. Madison touched Leeza Ketchin's arm. "Such beautiful music, I could curl up and go to sleep."

Leeza smiled her agreement, moving a little closer to her husband. "Makes me feel all warm and tingly."

Mrs. Smythe nodded from the next table. "Me too, Leeza."

The men took their places under the canopy of oaks. The front door opened, the music halted, and Elizabeth began playing the wedding march. All eyes turned toward Miss Hattie Mae Williams, walking arm-in-arm with Adeline Baxter to the edge of the carriage drive, where the men waited.

Beautiful spring bouquets testified to the time of year and the glorious day. Birds chirped from the laurel oaks nearby, joining in the celebration.

Grandpappy began the wedding ceremony. "We have gathered to join our friends Miss Hattie Mae Williams and Mr. Isaac Kline in holy matrimony. It is a day of blessing, a time of new beginnings that the state of our union has allowed what would formerly have been impossible. This couple may now live their lives according to their own plans, unhampered by submission to their former owners. It is my pleasure to tie this knot, a strong knot that will not be untied. You, my friends, have stood the trials and tests. God is blessing you today with a new blessing, one you will enjoy for the rest of your lives."

Isaac smiled at his beloved, and, reaching over, he brought her hand to his lips.

"Will you, Isaac Kline, take Miss Hattie Williams to be your wife? Will you love and protect her as long as you both shall live?"

"Sho nuff, I will, Preacher."

Laughter rang out from the porch.

"Miss Hattie, will you take Isaac to be your husband, loving and caring for him as long as you both shall live?"

"Yes, sir, I will." Tears of promise escaped the bride's eyes.

Hannah knew Miss Hattie Williams had waited a long time for true love. Her own heart warmed at the love emanating from the couple. A dull ache penetrated the warmth when she thought of the circuit-riding preacher. *Where is he, Lord? Please take good care of him.*

In her mind's eye, Hannah was remembering Sara's words about Wendell's cravat pulsing to the rhythm of his heart when he looked at her. She smiled, thinking about his eyes, so warm and inviting. *I enjoy being with him so much, Lord. And he's such a good-looking man. And that don't hurt a bit.*

"I now give to you Mr. and Mrs. Isaac Kline." Grandpappy had finished the ceremony.

Everyone stood, forming a congratulatory line and then returning to their wagons to retrieve the food they had prepared for the wedding feast. Katherine took a turn at the harp, playing softly until the food line diminished.

As soon as the men ate, several brought out their fiddles, harmonicas, and banjos. The afternoon turned into evening as the men continued playing every song they knew while the women cleaned up the tables and chatted.

Mr. and Mrs. Isaac Kline hugged everyone good-bye. "We'll be takin' our leave ta Rosewood for our honeymoon." Hattie Mae smiled at her friends.

Isaac's voice was filled with pride as he held his wife close to his side. "It's bound ta be a honey of a moon." Isaac helped his new wife into the buggy decorated with bows and flowers. The two waved their good-byes to the crowd of friends on the Baxters' front porch.

Finally, the sawhorse tables that had been laden with food were taken down and stowed in the barn by the men. Hannah found her father coming out of the barn. "Would you like some coffee for you and your friends?"

"Yes, that sounds good, dear."

Hannah filled cups of coffee, taking them to the men who had built a fire out back. The twin foals were peering over the corral fence. Picking a few carrots from the garden, Hannah fed the foals and then stood by the fence watching the fire burn to embers. The men had left, and the night was lonely.

Father poured a dipper of water from the bucket over the remaining coals. "What are you looking so pensive for?"

"I'm missing someone special, Father."

"I could have figured as much. Isaac was a real disappointment, wasn't he, dear?"

"Yes, sir. I'm just glad I found out before it was too late."

"You thinking about that young preacher, Hannah?"

Grinning, Hannah nodded her head.

"Seems like a fine young man."

"Yes, he does, Father."

And with that, father and daughter put their arms around each other and walked into the house.

The next week, Hannah decided to get some fresh air and sunshine. She wanted to draw. Picking up her sketchpad and pencils, she walked out the back door of the kitchen.

Finding a soft clump of grass just inside the corral, Hannah took a seat. Opening her sketchpad, she stopped breathing. There before her on the paper was the sketch she had drawn of Wendell on the boat. She shook her head, rubbing her eyes to make sure she wasn't seeing things. Looking closely, she was sure she could see love shining in the eyes staring back at her.

What a stunning image he makes. With the sun's rays as a backdrop, his hair gently disheveled from the breeze coming off the river, Hannah stared at the man on the paper. Feeling childish, yet helpless to refrain, she bent over the sketchpad, closing her eyes and planting a soft kiss on the face shining up at her. Feeling guilty for acting so bold, she looked around, making sure no one was watching. A mischievous smile lit up her face.

"What's yore face shinin' for?"

Hannah almost jumped out of her skin at the sound of Blaine's voice. He was headed out of the barn, walking toward her. *How long has he been watching?*

She hedged, closing the sketchpad. "Shining, why would my face be, uh, shining? Maybe from the bright morning sun?"

"I bet you got a drawin' of that preacher. He's the only one ever lit your face up like a fire. Old Isaac didn't stand a chance. I coulda told ya that."

"Oh, Blaine, you liked Isaac."

"Well, anyways, that's probably why you didn't."

"And it's a good thing."

"Well, I don't know about havin' another preacher in the famly. Grandpappy's hard enough to please."

"Don't you talk about Grandpappy like that, mister."

"Well, I can't get away with nothin'. Even get blamed for the things I don't do, an that ain't no fun."

"Oh, you have enough fun, Blaine. That's for sure."

"Anyways, let me see that sketchpad." His eyes gleamed with evil.

Hannah shook her head, holding the pad close. "Not today or tomorrow."

"Ha, ha. I knew it. Blythe, Hannah's kissin' a picture she drew of the preacher." He was still laughing as he walked toward his brother.

"Leave her alone, Blaine," Blythe said as he carried a bucket of milk to the house.

Hannah sketched the foals all morning. She sketched them as they cavorted, kicking and jumping in the corral. She sketched them eating their oats and lying down for a bit of rest.

Finally satisfied, she stood up to go back into the house. "Oh, oh my." Her legs were fast asleep.

A cowboy leaning against the corral fence, started toward her. "You all right, mam?"

"Yes, Johnny, I'm all right. Been sitting too long. My legs went to sleep."

"I saw you out here this morning. Blaine told me to come and look." The cowboy tried to cover a grin on his face.

"Were you watching me draw?"

"Just before you started to draw, mam." And with that, he walked away, tipping the front of his hat lower.

Hannah walked on wobbly legs toward the house. "Today would be a good day to tar and feather Blaine." Hannah didn't realize she had spoken the words aloud until Sara sent her a funny look from her seat on the back porch.

Her sister continued shelling the black-eyed peas in the big bowl on her lap. "What's he done now?"

"Snooping and sharing my private moments with one of the cowboys."

"Not Blaine." Sara laughed, lightening Hannah's mood. "Did you get enough sketches of the foals? You've been out there all morning."

"Yes, I've got plenty of sketches. I'm starving; I didn't stop for breakfast this morning."

"Mother's cooking a big pot of vegetable beef soup. She's frying the cornbread now."

"That's my favorite soup."

"I think that's why she made it. We are going to miss you, Hannah."

Hannah sent her sister an endearing smile. "I know." She rushed inside so Sara wouldn't see the tears trying to escape. Hannah was looking forward to studying art but knew she would miss her loved ones. Family could not be replaced or substituted.

"I'm starving, Mother."

"I'll dish you up a bowl of soup. And the cornbread, it's coming up now." Mother placed a small fried cake on a saucer and filled a bowl with soup.

Saying grace, Hannah tasted a spoonful of the delicious fare. "I'll miss your fine cooking while I'm away. I'm sure the De Ponte household eats French cuisine. We learned to cook a few French dishes in finishing school. They are quite tasty but can never take the place of our Southern food." Hannah savored another bite, closing her eyes. "Mother, you are the best cook in the world."

"Thank you, dear, but I think you are extra hungry today."

Her daughter smiled, eating the soup without looking up.

After the meal, Adeline Baxter approached her. "Now, Hannah, we simply must start packing your trunk today. This morning your father brought home the two new dresses Miss Hattie—I mean Mrs. Hattie—made for you."

"If we must, we'll start today."

"We'll start now."

Hannah followed her mother up the stairs. Opening the trunk at the foot of her bed, she took out the quilts being stored within.

Her mother had several pieces of underclothes draped over her arm. "We'll put your corset and under things in the bottom. In case the trunk gets opened during travel, you won't need to be embarrassed with your unmentionables being on top."

Hannah's armoire was full of day gowns, walking gowns, and a few evening gowns left over from finishing school. Along with her new dresses from Mrs. Hattie, she was confident she would be well dressed. Pausing a moment, Hannah quickly tucked two riding habits into her trunk for good measure.

Her sister came into the room. "Here's some sachets." Sara put one to her nose, drawing deeply. "It'll remind you of home."

"It'll remind me of you selling thousands of them to ladies of the North, my dear sister. You could build a house from your earnings." The sisters shared a knowing grin.

"Actually, I've been saving my money, and I could build a house; that's a nice thought." Sara's eyes had the old gleam back.

"This is so much fun." Mother enjoyed fussing over her daughters. "If only you weren't going away."

"Well, Mother, that is the purpose of packing." Hannah smiled at her sister behind her mother's back.

"All right, girls, don't joke at my expense. You know I've got eyes in the back of my head." Turning around, she hugged both of her daughters. "I love you so."

And so the afternoon at Laurel Oaks progressed with the finishing touches being put on the chore of packing. The only things to be added were the last-minute items, and they would be placed in Hannah's reticule.

Looking around the room, Hannah was already feeling as if she were moving out. Thinking of the new adventure teased her; she couldn't wait to begin the journey. "Just a few more days, and I'll be boarding the train for Savannah."

"At least you don't have to ride the stage to reach the train station. Sure has been handy with the railroad coming so close."

The following evening, Hannah's family gathered with the Frost family for a send-off party. The Madisons, the Ketchins, and the Smythes attended.

Halfway through the delicious meal of roast pork with all the trimmings, Hannah looked up to see Tobiah and Sara. *Seems like old times.*

After the meal, Hannah cornered her sister in the great room. "You two are so much in love. Why don't you just get married?"

Sara's eyes sparkled. "Hmm, let me see. Maybe that'll be my next project."

"What?"

"Getting Tobiah to elope."

"You wouldn't, Sara?"

"I wouldn't?"

Would she? It's hard to tell. "The old Sara would, and the new Sara is almost as enterprising. It is good to have you back. That in-between Sara needed to be fixed."

Sara reached out, touching her sister's chin. "You helped me find myself."

"It's time to cut the cake." And Hannah was off, cutting the cake and receiving her gifts.

The Ketchins gave a beautiful pair of lace gloves. "Thank you so much." Hannah hugged Leeza Ketchin.

"Well, with you going off to a French art school, I thought you'd need something fancy."

Susannah brought her gift to Hannah. "I hope you like it."

Opening the small package tied with a white ribbon, Hannah put her hand to her heart. "I love this, Susannah. I promise I'll write." She stared at the stationery embellished with a bouquet of wildflowers.

Grandmam and Grandpappy gave Hannah a set of drawing pencils and some "spending money." Hannah laughed, thinking, *All money is for spending.*

Katherine's gift was a new shawl. "Thought you could use it. The winter will be cooler in Savannah." Hannah hugged her gentle sister. She would miss their talks. Katherine was busy assisting her husband in the doctor's office, but she always took time to talk with Hannah at Sunday dinners.

The gifts kept coming until Hannah had opened them all. "I'm so glad you all came. Thank you for your wonderful gifts."

Finally, the party came to an end. Hannah was anxious to begin her adventure. Quickly slipping into her nightgown, she braided her hair.

Falling into bed, the young girl prayed that she might cross paths with the circuit-riding preacher. She could still envision him leaving the chapel yard. His posture had told of his sadness, his frame drooping forward as if bent to the task at hand.

Remembering their time at the Seminole village and the sketch lying safely within the cover of her sketchpad, Hannah fluffed up her pillows. Shutting her eyes she remembered every detail of the sketch. Wendell's hands on the oars, hands she wished to hold. His hair blowing in the wind. She had captured every detail on paper. But the best part was the love shining in his eyes. "I love you too, Wendell Cunningham," she whispered to the soft breeze blowing in her window.

Chapter 12

"Why hello, my son." Eliza Perkins opened the door to the humble abode behind the main house at the De Ponte Plantation. "It's so good to see ya, Mista Wendell. Now let me fix ya a plate."

Ezra Perkins appeared, buttoning up his nightshirt. Wiping the sleep from his eyes, he reached out, pumping the preacher's hand and patting him on the back. "Sho is mighty good ta look upon yo face."

Smells coming from the kitchen brought the two men to the big table. "Sure smells good, Mama Eliza." The endearment always brought a smile to the colored lady's face. As soon as they had befriended Wendell, she had insisted he call her that. He could still remember her words. "If'n ya don't mine a havin' a dark mammy, jes call me Mama Eliza."

The offer had set up residence in the heart of the young man who had never known a mother's love.

"Now hep yoself, son." Eliza looked on as if anticipating Wendell's joy.

"I won't be bashful. You know how I love your good cooking." The preacher said his blessing, digging into the fried pork and mustard greens. "Sure do like this corn pone." He smacked his lips in appreciation.

Handing her husband a cup of coffee, Eliza joined the men at the table. "What brangs ya ta dese parts, Mista Wendell? Ya preachin' nearby?"

"I'll be preaching for the Reverend Bristol at the Savannah Church by the River next Sunday; came up a little early. I was going to visit in Florida longer, but I cut the visit short." Sadness filled his chest. He hoped it didn't show. "Anyway, then I'll be heading out for Charleston. I'm going to hold revival meetings at the First Church of Charleston; got to be there by the middle of June."

"Did ya see dat Southern belle ya done tole us 'bout, what wid dem purty green eyes?"

"Yes, Ezra." Wendell put his fork down. He couldn't eat another bite of Mama Eliza's food. His eyes told a sad story.

"Well, we be a prayin' 'bout yore sitchyation. The good Lawd above'll hear us. He always do." Ezra sat there, coffee mug in hand, just nodding his head.

Wendell added his assent. "Yes, he does, Ezra. Yes, he does."

"Now let's get ya to yore bed, Mista Wendell. I'll jes turn da covers back an make sho da piller's plumped."

Eliza made her way down the hall where other slaves used to sleep, stopping at the last room on the left. Passing through the sheet that closed off the room, she retrieved the pitcher, filling it with water from the bucket Ezra had brought indoors.

"Now, ya be sleepin' mighty fine, Mista Wendell. Don't ya be a wakin' when dat firss rooster be a crowin'. Wait 'til da nex un crows."

"I'm sure the bacon will draw me out of bed, Mama Eliza."

The dear woman chuckled softly, making her way behind the sheet where they slept, leaving her husband to say his good night to the man of God who graced their home.

"The Lawd's got him some mighty good plans fer ya, preacher, mighty good plans."

Wendell nodded. "I believe that, Ezra." Feeling comforted by the old man's words, the young man made his way down the long hall, glad to pillow his head on a soft bed in a home filled with love.

Sunday made its way quickly. It seemed as if Wendell had just arrived, and yet it would be time to head out for Charleston on the morrow. Riding his horse to the church by the river, Ezra and Eliza followed in their wagon, the mules keeping a slow pace.

A few people of color visited the church from time to time during the young minister's visits. However, Ezra had told him that the town still frowned upon "mixin' the gospel" as they called it. Ezra and his people were much more content to worship in their old church.

Pulling up in the church yard, Wendell tied his horse to the hitching post as Ezra pulled alongside in the wagon.

"They's already a castin' eyes, Mista Wendell."

"Who's casting eyes, Ezra?"

Ezra looked ahead at the man who owned the local livery stable, and Wendell followed his gaze to the clerk from the stagecoach office. Seeing the young preacher look his way, the clerk smiled. "Why hello there, Preacher. It sure is good to have ya." Barely nodding his head in Ezra's direction, he continued to the front door of the church.

Just before they stepped up to the church steps, Ezra poked Wendell in the elbow. "See that 'un over there?" He tipped his head in the direction of a nearby oak tree, fully dressed in moss. Peaking between the moss, the young preacher noticed beady eyes, topped by a low-slung hat. "He's on da rumor list to be part of the Klan."

Glancing back, Wendell thought the hate shining in the man's eyes toward Ezra and Eliza testified to the possibility of the rumor mill being correct. The man's gaze locked with the preacher's, neither willing to break contact.

"Shore is mighty good to see you, Reverend Cunningham." The grating voice of Mrs. Hathaway caught Wendell's attention. Glancing beside her, he saw her daughter, Agatha Hathaway, casting flirtatious eyes in his direction.

"Good morning, Miss Hathaway." Agatha was pretty enough but nothing to compare with Miss Hannah Baxter. The remembrance of Hannah propelled the preacher forward without a backward glance, taking his place in the designated chair on the platform.

The sounds of the pipe organ gathered all the men folk who had been gossiping in the church yard. All at once, about fifty men made their way through the back door, finding their seats.

Aloof looks filled the sanctuary as the town's high and mighty looked down their noses at Ezra and Eliza Perkins. Two of their neighbors from the adjoining plantation were in attendance, sitting quietly on the back pew alongside their friends. Wendell could see people craning their necks to give the back pew's occupants unwelcoming looks.

Coming in the door, the preacher recognized the man who was rumored to be part of the Klan. He searched the crowd, leveling a sneering gaze at the colored people. Wendell's friends sat with their heads down.

The lady at the organ burst into a lively hymn. A man began making his way to the podium. "Join with me in singing. Please rise."

The congregation stood. Joining the leader's deep baritone voice, the parishioners sang in harmony. The music resonated through the building, but the singing was void of feeling.

This is God's house, but I don't feel him here. Wendell closed his eyes. *When will people ever learn to love one another as you have first loved us, Father?* The question went unanswered.

With much ado, the head deacon made the announcement. He was the man from the livery stable who had shunned Ezra. "We are pleased to have Reverend Wendell Cunningham return to us." A round of applause went up. "You are one of us, brother. Take your liberty in the Lord."

Strange that he would use that word, Lord, when there is no liberty here.

The young minister reached the podium, and, looking out on the congregation, he folded his hands. "I had another message prepared, but I feel led to exhort you concerning the love of God this morning."

The congregation smiled. *Must be expecting me to tell them how much God loves them.* The preacher smiled back.

"God sent his only son to die for every person that would ever be born—*every person.*" Looking over the crowd, he saw some were nodding, while others were staring blankly.

Wendell continued, gently pressing into unknown territory. "God does not esteem one person above another. We are all created in his image and likeness, and he expects us to love one another as he has loved us, without thought of station in life, wealth, or any other divisive thing."

Some of the nodding heads stopped. Mrs. Hathaway's fan halted, her cool blue eyes penetrating Wendell's.

Recognizing the artist, Jacques De Ponte, and his daughter, Wendell could see the man's broad smile. Mr. De Ponte was a kind, godly man. Ezra and Eliza testified to his goodness and his love for the Lord. Continuing his message, Wendell drew strength from him.

"Let the love of the Lord shine through you to *all* those around you. The Good Book says you will be known as Christ's disciples by the love you have for one another."

Sharing several more scriptures about God's love, Wendell noticed several men staring at the floor. The man who had sneered at the back pew stood up; turning on his heel, he nearly ran from the building.

"Let us pray." The congregation stood. "God of love and mercy, may we leave this place having searched our hearts to see if love truly abides within. Help us to be ever mindful that we are your representatives to a lost and dying world. Amen."

Mrs. Hathaway marched to the front of the church, Agatha sashaying behind. "Thought-provoking sermon, Reverend." She extended her hand. The eyes boring into him during his sermon were now soft and placating. "Would you honor us with your presence at our Sunday luncheon?"

"I'm already spoken for, Mrs. Hathaway. My friends on the back row have prepared a special meal for me."

The lady looked disdainfully toward Ezra and Eliza Perkins. Glancing at her daughter, her gaze softened. "What about tomorrow? Could you come tomorrow?"

Agatha smiled at her mother, turning her eyes on Wendell.

"I leave tomorrow by noon, mam. I have a schedule to keep."

Without another word, Mrs. Hathaway grabbed her daughter's arm and walked away. "Come, Agatha, we've been thrown to the side in place of those, those ... " Looking back, she flung over her shoulder, "Those terrible people of color. Wouldn't want a sympathizer as a suitor for you anyway, darling child."

Wendell realized Mrs. Hathaway had not taken one word of his message to heart. If it was thought provoking, he was sure it was provoking bad thoughts in her mind.

Shaking the few remaining parishioners' hands, he felt the coolness in the air. *Well, I delivered my soul.*

Making his way to the hitching post, where his horse stood patiently waiting, Wendell heard someone call. "Preacher, you who ... "

"Yes, mam?"

"I'm so glad you preached that sermon. It's needed in this place. Why most of the town looks down on people for one reason or another. You did a good job."

"Thank you, mam."

Wendell Cunningham made his way back to the De Ponte Plantation. Entering the iron gates, he rode past the mansion to the buildings behind.

Ezra met him at the door. The smell of Eliza's food caused his stomach to growl. "Mama Eliza, you're spoiling me with your good cooking. What am I going to do when I leave?"

"Ya gonna lose some o dem pounds I be packin' on ya." She laughed, obviously proud of the weight he had gained. Grabbing Wendell in a motherly hug, she whispered, "Sho do hep wid da pain o losin' my boy when I gets to be a mama to ya; fo a little while anyways." Reluctantly she let him go, turning to her other guests.

"Y'all come on." The neighbors who attended church were welcomed to the dinner table.

Joining hands, Wendell said a quick prayer. "Lord bless this food and all who partake…and the hands that prepared it, bless them real good, Lord."

Eliza Perkins smiled at the blessing, passing the biscuits and butter to her guests. A feast lay before them, a feast prepared with love.

Wendell made a grunting noise when he tasted the fried venison. "Um, um, this is good."

"It's da back strap, da best part o da deer."

Wendell picked up another morsel, savoring the taste. "It's so tender."

"That be da deer's fault, not mine." Everyone chuckled.

Not a word was heard. Forks scraping plates filled the afternoon quiet as the group enjoyed the fried corn, rice and tomato gravy, and cow peas Eliza Perkins had cooked to accompany the deer meat.

Lifting the cloth napkin to his mouth, Wendell scooted his chair back. "I'm so full, I came mighty close to sinning."

"There be fagiveness. Eat some mo, son. It's a gonna be some hongry days on dat trail what's ohead o ya; better stocks up fer da famine."

"A body can only hold so much at one sitting, Mama Eliza, but I'm sure I'll want some more come nightfall."

"It'll be a waitin' right chere fer ya." Eliza smiled, covering the food on the table with a big cloth. "Don't wanna be feedin' dem flies from da cheeken pen."

"I believe I'll go lay before the Lord, Mama Eliza, Ezra."

"Ya go rights ohead an take yore nap. I'm a gonna doze in dis here chair while I visit wif my friends. Course I'll jes be a restin' one eye at de time." Ezra's lids already looked heavy.

And with that, Wendell was off to his bed, thinking about Hannah Baxter and her soft brown curls—curls kissed by the sun. He reached out to touch her face, realizing he was dreaming. Turning on the bed, he settled down for a nap.

Tomorrow he would leave this place of comfort. By doing so, he would put more miles between him and the beauty with the sparkling green eyes.

Chapter 13

June's warmth encouraged more wildflowers to show their blooms. Laurel City was embellished, the colorful blossoms lining every roadside and strewn decoratively through every meadow.

Hannah reveled in the sunshine and beauty surrounding her. Her sketchpad was almost filled with horses running in the pasture, their manes and tails blowing in the wind; puppies, newly born, huddling close to the warmth of their mother; doe and fawn with occasionally a proud buck posing nearby; fish and turtles swimming in the stream running through Laurel Oaks; sketches of the rose garden with butterflies flitting from bud to flower.

These were happy days for Hannah. Still unable to believe her blessing was real, she sketched frantically, wishing to take as much of her beloved scenery with her to art school as possible.

"Hannah!" Mother's call brought Hannah from her seat on the rose garden bench.

"Coming, Mother."

Stuffing her sketchpad back in its satchel, she closed the garden gate behind her. Walking up the back porch steps, smelling the food coming from Mother's kitchen, she could hardly believe it was already suppertime.

Washing and drying her hands, Hannah walked over to the stove. "What can I do to help, Mother?"

"Set the table, dear. Sara is having supper with the Smythes, and I'm taking up the last pan of fried chicken."

"Smells so good."

Around the table, conversation turned to Hannah's departure.

"Only three more days, and we'll put you on the train in Rosewood."

"I know, Father. I'm looking forward to the adventure."

"You be careful, dear. I'm glad Miss Goldenmeyer is accompanying you to Savannah. Sure is timely, with you needing a traveling companion."

"I'll be careful, Mother." Hannah's eyes sparkled, just thinking about the adventures awaiting her.

"Hannah, I'm serious. Savannah is a large city. You must be very careful and properly chaperoned."

"I will be, Mother. I'm sure the De Pontes are cautious. I understand they have a daughter my age."

"That's what worries me, Hannah. You like to have a little too much fun. Having someone your age may double the danger."

"Now, Mother."

"Don't you 'Now, Mother,' me. I know how adventurous and curious you are, Hannah. You've got a scar on your head to prove it."

Hannah laughed. "Mother, I was just checking out my suitor."

"Yes, dear, and some things need to be left alone."

The young girl sighed, wishing Sara were here to take up for her.

"I'll miss you, Hannah." Blythe looked sad.

Blaine cocked a brow, slanting his sister a sideways look. "Try not to be kissin' any more sketches, Hannah. Maybe you'll find a real suitor in Savannah, and ya won't have to make believe anymore."

Hannah could feel her face pulsing. "Blaine, oh if I could get my hands on you."

"What'd you do? Huh?"

"That'll be enough, Blaine." Father's grin told of his knowledge of the episode.

Quiet settled around the table as Hannah enjoyed her mother's fried chicken, rice and milk gravy, fried green tomatoes, and yellow squash. "Mother, nobody cooks better than you. This is so good." Hannah reached for her second piece of chicken breast.

"Thank you, dear."

This is home, my home, and what a wonderful place it is, thought Hannah, looking around the table. *I'll miss them all, but I can't wait to get on the train. What an adventure!*

The young girl hugged her family good night, running upstairs, checking her packed wardrobe once again. Hannah was sure everything was in order. Closing the lid on her traveling trunk, tucking a few extra hankies in her reticule, the young girl breathed a sigh of relief. She was ready to begin her journey. Tomorrow morning she would do just that.

A soft knock sounded at her door.

"Come in."

Sara walked in, having just returned from an evening drive in Tobiah's buggy. "I've got to have one last talk with you before you leave. Thank you for all your advice, Hannah. Tobiah and I are getting along well, and part of that is your doing."

"Glad to help a sister out. Maybe you can return the favor."

"I won't stop praying for you and the preacher."

Hannah fell into her sister's embrace. "I don't know when I'll ever see him again. It'd have to be God to arrange it."

"He's big enough. Look at me and Tobiah and all we've been through."

The two sisters stood by the open window looking out into the darkness. A lantern sent its light from the cowboy quarters behind the barn. A lonely owl's call floated into the room on the night air.

"I'll miss you so."

"Dear Sara, I'll miss you just as much, but I'll be home for Christmas, and what a wonderful time we shall have." Hannah smiled up at her older sister. "Why don't you run away and get married?"

Sara's eyes took on their old gleam. "There is no telling what I have in mind. Good-bye, Hannah Banana." Squeezing her sister in a quick embrace, Sara ran from the room.

Hannah would never let her sister get away with calling her that in the past. But tonight was different. Somehow it felt right to let Sara have the last word.

Opening her sketchpad, Hannah took a long look at the preacher staring up at her. Closing the cover, she placed the pad back in its satchel. It would go with her to Savannah, Georgia. She must somehow take Wendell Cunningham with her.

"Take care of him, Father," she whispered to the wind and then blew her bedside candle out. The sketch of Wendell was vivid in her consciousness as she fell into sweet slumber.

Awaking to the sound of the rooster crowing in the barnyard, Hannah jumped out of bed, anxious to begin this most exciting day. Running downstairs, she was soon accompanied by all of her family.

Elizabeth came in the door with Ethan close behind, carrying a sleeping Beth wrapped in a summer quilt. "Well good morning, Sis. We came to see you off."

"I'm so glad you came." Hannah hugged her eldest sister.

Just as she kissed Beth's cheek, Katherine and Wyatt made their way in the front door. Katherine went straight to her sister, placing a beautiful hanky, embroidered with wildflowers in her hand. "For your trip."

"Thank you, Kat." Tears came to Hannah's eyes as she hugged her special sister, the one next to her in age. "You are such a beautiful young woman."

Katherine wiped the tears from her eyes. "I shall not be sad. You are ever so glad to leave us." She pinched her sister's cheek. "Go have fun, Hannah."

"I will."

After a breakfast of biscuits and sausage gravy, the family gathered for final hugs. Father and Mother would be the only ones accompanying Hannah to the train station in Rosewood.

Grandmam wrapped Hannah in a warm hug. "I'm so proud of you, dear. Now, don't you be forgetting to do the Lord's work in Savannah. What your hand finds to do, do with all your might."

"Yes, mam."

Grandpappy was next. "Don't be letting ole Isaac trouble you, Hannah. He's not worthy of you, my dear. You forget all about him in Savannah."

"Isaac who? Grandpappy, that young man has shown me who he is. My heart already belongs to another."

Grandpappy's eyes twinkled. "Good girl."

Father pulled the carriage around front. Blythe and Blaine loaded Hannah's trunk and art satchel.

As she waved good-bye, the carriage began its journey down the drive of canopied oaks, taking Hannah away from her familiar world. The exhilaration was almost more than she could bear.

"You're really looking forward to this, aren't you, dear?"

"Yes, Mother. I can't wait to begin studying new art techniques and improve my talent."

"Bless you, my dear. I wish you the very best."

Pulling up in front of the spinster's home, Hannah alighted, taking deep breaths of the roses growing along the path to the door.

"Hello, Miss Goldenmeyer." Father stepped down to assist the dear lady. "So glad you will be accompanying our Hannah."

The kind lady smiled. "Hello, Mrs. Baxter, Miss Hannah. I sure am glad we can ride the train together. My sister was really wantin' me to come but I didn't want to go alone."

"Well, Miss Goldenmeyer, we're pleased for the both of us."

Adeline Baxter and Miss Goldenmeyer began talking about gardening. Settling back in the carriage, the only sore spot in Hannah's life was missing Wendell Cunningham. She closed her eyes, envisioning the beautiful day spent together at the Indian village. She could feel the pencil in her hand, sketching his visage.

Slowly, wrapped in sweet remembrance, Wendell's face came alive from the sketch she had drawn. Once again, she saw and felt his love shining forth, reaching out to her. It was free for the taking. Smiling, she lifted her hand, reaching for the man whose strong arms were rowing the boat, his hair blowing in the wind.

"Hannah, dear, it's time to wake up. I believe you were dreaming."

"Don't wake me. Oh, Mother, it was a wonderful dream." Hannah spoke through the fog with her eyes still closed.

"Dear, the train station is in sight. Now straighten your hat, and you might want to tighten your combs."

Hannah reached up, checking the twist of her hair and the combs holding it in place. As she secured the hat pin, the carriage came to a halt at the station. In the distance, a train whistle blasted the morning air. The clackety-clack of the wheels rolling over the railroad track matched the rhythm beating an excited tune in her soul.

Hugging her father and mother good-bye, Hannah never took her eyes off the train as it came alongside the platform. Black smoke filled the air. "Oh my." She reached out, grabbing a cinder in her white glove, as if she had found a treasure.

"Oh, dear, you'll be a mess by the time you reach Savannah."

"It's no problem, Mother. Just the price of progress and a small price I might add."

"Whoever washes your clothes might not agree with you, my dear."

"I'm sure someone will find a way to get the cinders out."

Miss Goldenmeyer said her good-byes, heading to find a seat on the train. Father had transported the spinster and Hannah's luggage to the proper place, and it was now time to see her off on the train.

"All aboard." The engineer yelled.

Hannah hugged her parents and ran up the steps of the train, taking a seat by Miss Goldenmeyer. The engineer's last call was followed by the forward jerking motion of the train. Immediately beginning to cough, Hannah reached for the hanky Katherine had given.

"Are you gonna be all right, dearie?"

"Yes, Miss Goldenmeyer. Isn't it fun?"

"Well, yes, dear. I suppose so. At least it is funny." The kind lady started laughing.

"What's so funny?"

"You should see your face, dear. It's covered in little black cinders."

"Oh, that." Hannah waved her hand as if dismissing the bothersome specks clinging to her face, her hat, her hair. "You're covered too. Oh well, we're gonna have fun anyway."

"Yes, we are, dearie." And with that the lady reached over and patted Hannah's gloved hand, sharing a few more cinders.

Hannah looked at the town as they continued moving away from the train station. "Father said this town sprang up almost overnight. Look at all the businesses."

They rode past a blacksmith shop, a livery stable, a boarding house, and a dining hall.

"There's a hotel up ahead, and look, there's a huge mercantile." Miss Goldenmeyer pointed out.

"Oh, and look, there's a church." Its steeple was reaching to the sky near the edge of town. As they rode by, a sign boasted the name Rosewood Chapel. "What a sweet name. Reminds me of our chapel in Laurel City."

"I was thinking the same thing." The spinster smiled.

A small, white house came into view just beyond the church. The front yard was enclosed with a white fence. A birdhouse inside a flower garden was accommodating several blue jays. A trellis covered with pink roses stood by the front door.

Hannah's mind began to wander down a track all its own. What would it be like to share Wendell Cunningham's life? Perhaps he would one day pastor a church like this one. She smiled, thinking of being by his side and doing the work of the Lord. Oh how she had enjoyed sharing time with him at the Seminole village.

What a beautiful home the little parsonage would make for a young couple just starting out. The train was heading faster down the track, gaining speed as it went. Hannah's thoughts were gathering speed as well, racing toward building a family with the fine circuit rider who had stolen her heart, riding out of town, taking it with him.

Chapter 14

Wendell Cunningham arose early. Even at this hour, Mama Eliza's kitchen was sending forth a wonderful aroma. He could smell the sausage cooking. Better enjoy this last meal. Hitting the trail would mean cold biscuits and venison jerky for most of his dining. Ezra had given him the jerky last night; Eliza would supply the biscuits this morning.

Washing his face in the cool water, the circuit rider combed his hair, spending a moment in front of the looking glass on the wall. Though it was tarnished, if he stood just right he could get a pretty good view of himself. The eyes staring back at him were lonely.

Turning away, Wendell's thoughts traveled back to Laurel City. *I wonder what she is doing today.* He could see Hannah seated among the wildflowers, the wind blowing her beautiful hair to the tune it was playing. Shaking his head to gather his thoughts for the day, the preacher walked through the sheet, making his way to the kitchen table.

"Mornin', Preacher."

"Mornin', Ezra. Sure smells good in here."

"Set yoself down at Mama Eliza's table, son. I be a wantin' to sen ya off right nice. Gonna fill ya belly an ya saddlebags too. Gotcha some biscuits done an packed an some muscadine jelly fer later."

"Why thank you, Mama Eliza."

"I's jes more'n happy to be a givin' what I can to a man o de cloth. Makes Eliza mighty proud to be a heppin' ya carry that gospel to de lost."

Setting a plate of sausage, biscuits, and gravy before Wendell, the kind woman patted him on the shoulder. "I's jes mighty proud to call ya my son."

"Sho nuff." Ezra Perkins echoed his wife's sentiments.

Warmth flooded the preacher's soul. *God has his ways of showing me he cares through the hands and hearts of his servants.* Wendell Cunningham felt humbled by the love of these people.

"You mean more to me than I can say." His voice broke. "Never had love like the love you've shown me."

"At's all right, son. You goes right on ahead an say de blessin' over da food."

Wendell blessed the food, the house, and his friends. The sausage, biscuits, and gravy filled his stomach just as sure as the kind words had filled his heart.

The three friends walked into the meadow where the horses grazed. A morning breeze blew across the hillside, bringing with it a promise of a beautiful day.

"Nice day fer travelin'."

"Yes, Ezra, it will be nice. Sure do hate to leave the two of you. You're like family to me, the only family I have."

"Ya gonna be back. I'm sho somebody's a gonna be needin' to hol' revival meetin's at the river, an they be a callin' on ya, son. Jes like dey did las year."

"I'll look forward to it, Mama Eliza."

"Ya jes keep yo head held up high, son, and we gonna be a seein' ya again real soon." Eliza reached for a hug.

Ezra stepped up, patting Wendell's shoulder and keeping his hand there as the three walked back to the barn.

"I sure do thank you both for your hospitality and for letting me borrow this horse." Wendell patted the sorrel stallion that would take him to Charleston, South Carolina.

Ezra watched as Wendell walked into the barn stall for one last visit with his horse. "We gonna fix yo horse up fine. The leg on dat stallion be gettin' better. Eliza be fixin' up a poultice. Now don't ya worry yo head none."

"Been with me a long time. So glad you'll be tending him."

"I'll be sayin' my good-byes now, son, gots to go make a pick up at the railroad station."

Wendell waved good-bye to Ezra from the stall where he was currying his horse with a brush. He knew he should go, but he couldn't bear to leave just yet. Finally, he patted his stallion and rubbed him behind the ears, setting the brush on the shelf.

Saddling the borrowed sorrel, Wendell took the food Eliza brought from the kitchen. "Thank you, Mama Eliza."

"Ya sho nuff welcome, son. Now take care o yoself." Eliza brushed a tear away.

Waving good-bye, Wendell urged the stallion forward, making his way through the beautiful gates of the De Ponte Plantation. Looking into the sky, he sighed. *Almost wish I could quit travelin' and settle down, but whatever your will is for me, Lord, I'll follow that path.*

Hannah's trip came to a close as the train pulled into the Savannah Railroad Station. The large brick building with its overhanging roof offered shade to the passengers. Hannah's breath came out in exhilarated puffs, looking around at all the other trains—some picking up passengers, others disembarking. Cinders surrounded her. Pressing her hanky to her mouth, she coughed. Tired from her journey, Hannah bade Miss Goldenmeyer good-bye, putting her hand to her eyes in search of the De Ponte carriage.

"Miz Hanner Baxter?" Someone was walking toward her. "Name's Ezra, Ezra Perkins at yo service, mam." The colored man bowed low in front of Hannah.

"Glad to make your acquaintance, Mr. Perkins."

"Miz Hanner, ole Ezra's jes ole Ezra. Don't be callin' me nuthin' else, mam." A broad smile spread across the man's face. He covered his mouth when a belly laugh erupted, refusing to stop.

Hannah was confused. Why was this man laughing?

"Sorry, mam, xcuse me, mam. Jes cain't hep myself none. Dem cinders from dat train done an turnt you black as ole Ezra."

Hannah laughed. Raising her glove to her face, she tried to wipe the cinders away.

"Sorry, mam, you jes rubbed in the black mo." Shaking his head, he reached for her satchel. Hannah followed him to the elaborate De Ponte carriage. "I heps ya up, Miz Hanner."

"This is quite some carriage." Hannah rubbed the polished wood decorating the conveyance.

"It be a vis-à-vis, Miz Hanner. Jes a high-falutin' French buggy."

The carriage boasted beautiful leather seats facing each other. Depositing her satchel into the carriage, Ezra Perkins placed the wooden step on the ground for Hannah to step up into the conveyance. "Yo sho be a sight, Miz Hanner."

"I like you already, Mister . . . I mean Ezra."

"An I likes you jes fine. I'd a knowed you by dem green eyes Mr. Jacques De Ponte tole me ta look fo. Now you be a waitin' right chere whiles ole Ezra finds yo trunk."

After the trunk was loaded, she could not believe the smooth ride of the fancy carriage. And so it was that Miss Hannah Baxter, art student of the renowned artiste Jacques De Ponte rode through the streets of Savannah, Georgia, with black cinders smeared into her face.

Hannah noticed huge warehouses down a side road. Mules and horses strained, pulling wagons loaded with bales of cotton stacked high in the air. She caught a glimpse of the wagons being unloaded on a scale inside a building. A man stood nearby with a pad of paper.

Savannah had been known in antebellum times to house the Cotton Exchange, which set the price for cotton around the world. During times of Reconstruction, and with the Emancipation Proclamation, the large plantation owners had lost much of their slave help. This had led to a decline in the production and sale of the crop. Garrett Baxter had given his daughter a history lesson about the city before she embarked on her journey.

Bluebells carpeted both sides of the road they were now traveling. Lamp posts stood their guard, ready to be lit when daylight dropped beyond the horizon. Children playing on a grassy square in front of a stately home chased each other, falling on the ground, their energy spent.

"We's not far away, Miz Hanner," Ezra yelled from his seat up front, turning down a road lined with majestic oaks, heavily dressed in moss.

"These beautiful oaks make me feel right at home."

The blasts of several steamboats sounded from the Savannah River, as if welcoming her to the city. *The Belle of the South* that visited Laurel City paled in comparison to these large riverboats. Straining her eyes, Hannah could make out the name on the side of the largest one: *SS Savannah.* "That is a mighty big boat."

Ezra looked out at the river. "Its fame done spread cross de world as da firss steamboat ta cross da Atlantic Ocean, exportin' goods ta overseas ports. Made it firss crossin' in 1819 an took her eighteen days ta go from Savanny clear to Liverpool, Englan. It be famous fer da cotton shipments."

The boat rested in the harbor, proudly lending itself to the rich heritage of this place. Horse-drawn wagons made their way to the river, their flat beds loaded with bales of cotton for shipping.

Looking out the window as the carriage made its way over a brick road, Hannah saw a man on horseback passing by on the far side of the passageway. Ezra waved to the man, yelling, "Bye, son."

At that moment, someone in an open buggy raced between the carriage and the rider, cracking his whip and nearly running into the man on horseback.

For a moment, Hannah's breath caught in her throat. The buggy just missed the rider. When he turned his head, her eyes locked with his below the low slung hat he wore. *Wendell, could it be Wendell?* She strained her eyes, daring to hope. As he continued on his way, she knew she was wrong.

I must be desperate, thinking Wendell and I would cross paths in Savannah.

Hannah had almost called out to Ezra to ask if he knew the man's name, but turning to get one last look, she realized the horse he rode was a reddish brown color, not the black stallion that was Wendell's.

"Whew!" Laying her head against the padded leather seat of the carriage, Hannah was ready for a bath. However, excitement still coursed through her veins as she thought of all the adventures that awaited her.

Unwilling to miss anything, Hannah took another look out the window. A couple of young men near the river were riding bicycles. She had seen sketches of the funny contraptions in *Godey's Lady's Book*. "Sure looks like fun," she murmured to herself.

Before Hannah knew it, they were pulling up in front of a magnificent plantation with grounds stretching as far as the eye could see. She held her breath, taking in the details of this lovely place.

"Here we be, Miz Hanner. Dis here a gonna be yo home fo de nex nine months. I says welcome to ya."

"Why thank you, Ezra."

Sighting the massive, elaborate home proudly standing behind a magnificent garden, the young girl's sharp intake of breath was slowly released. Hannah Baxter's beautiful antebellum home at Laurel Oaks paled in comparison to this mansion. Barely able to remain seated, she couldn't wait to see what treasures lay inside the boundaries of this large plantation.

Ezra was opening the iron gates onto a drive beside the plantation home. "What ya be thankin', Miz Hanner? Ya reckon ya can make do in dis place?"

"I believe I can make do right nice, Ezra." Staring up at the three-story edifice, Hannah could scarcely believe this would be her home.

Ezra returned to the carriage, clucking to the horses. "Ya gonna be a likin' dem good-smellin' flowers what be strung all over da grounds." He pointed to the elaborate garden in front of the mansion. Blossoms of every color imaginable gleamed in the bright sunlight. Hannah noticed the intricate design of the flower garden. Huge oaks framing the grounds were draped heavily in moss.

"Why, Ezra, I can't believe the beauty of this place." Hannah craned her neck, turning to take in the full effect as the carriage continued on its way.

"Sho keeps da gardner mighty busy, a pleasin' Miz Bernadette. Miz Bernadette be Mr. Jacques wife." Ezra's whisper barely came to Hannah's ears as they made their way around the side of the mansion.

The elderly gardener waved from where he was trimming a hedge of hibiscus. Hannah waved in return.

Ezra nodded toward the man. "That be ole Erastus, done an trimmin' up the crimson-eyed rosemallow high biscuits."

Hannah could see why the hibiscus were so named. The full white blossoms boasted crimson centers, further decorated by feathered white stamens peeking through the red cores. "Absolutely lovely."

A long, narrow building came into view. *Might be old slave quarters,* Hannah thought. *Sure looks clean and well kept.*

As they turned the corner, reaching the back of the mansion, Hannah stuck her head out of the carriage window. Looking high into the sky, she called to Ezra. "What kind of tree is that?"

"Why, Miz Hanner, that be da glory of Miz Bernadette. Ain't nobody better be a doin' a bad thang ta that there tree. It be right by her bed chambers on da number-two floor of da house."

Hannah inhaled deeply. A mixed smell exuded from the stunning lavender blossoms. "The flowers are sort of shaped like a bell or a tulip. And the smell ... well, I can't decide if it smells like jasmine or gardenia."

Ezra laughed. "Yo got a keen nose, Miz Hanner. It be a smellin' like em both. An Miz Bernadette, she be powerful likin' dat smell.

Why, she brangs dem blossums in da house after supper, what to get da smell out, she says." Once again, the man was whispering.

It was Hannah's turn to laugh. "What's the name of this tree, Ezra?"

"Why, you's a cureus one; that be a Royal Empress Tree, sorta fits Miz Bernadette jes so."

The carriage continued traveling in back of the house as Ezra further explained the tree. "In de winter it be cover wif furry buds jes da size of a pea, mind ya. Those buds jes be a waitin' fer da firs sign o spring to ex plode in those perple flowers ya be a seein' it all dressed up in."

As they left the tree behind, Hannah could see that its lofty branches reached above the third floor of the De Ponte home. The purple blossoms fully dressed the huge tree. Hannah shook her head incredulously, looking at the stately sight.

"Jes wait'll ya see inside da big house. It sho nuff is filt wif purties, what wif the mizzus likin' her fancies an all. Sho is mighty im pressive."

Hannah touched her face with the white glove that was now almost black. "Oh dear, Ezra. How am I to enter the De Ponte home looking like this?"

Ezra laughed again, another belly laugh. "We be a fixin' ya, Miz Hanner, as bes we can. My Eliza be glad ta hep out a damsel in de stress."

Hannah relaxed a bit. "I'd be mighty thankful for any help."

"Yessum, you be a needin' to turn back to yo natchral color afore ya be meetin' da mizzus."

Hannah smiled in spite of herself. The longer she was with Ezra, the more she knew they were going to be close friends. The dear man already seemed like family.

Hannah and Ezra came to an elaborate iron cage. White with gold embellishments, the cage gleamed in the bright noonday sun. Chirping was heard, and Hannah's curiosity got the best of her. "Are those cockatiels, Ezra?"

"Yessum, and on de other side, they be pair a keets. Da mizzus be a likin' her birds now. She be able to see dem from her winders, an da big tree be castin' shade on de birds in dis hot summer."

Beautiful white cockatiels flew from perch to perch in the fancy cage. Sure enough, as they moved slowly forward, parakeets of every color peeked through the cage bars at the curious girl perusing them from the carriage. "They are beautiful, absolutely beautiful. I can't wait to sketch them." Enthusiasm caused her to rise from the carriage seat, bumping her head on the side.

"You be careful, Miz Hanner. There be mo days fo a seein' dem birds. Many mo days, fo sho."

Hannah laughed as the carriage came to a stop in front of the long, narrow white-washed building that she had thought to be slave quarters. Lavender Johnny-Jump-Ups filled the flower boxes gracing the windows, their fragile petals bending in the breeze coming off the Savannah River. Below, rows of daisies and their near twins, Woolly Sunbonnets, were flanked by pink roses.

Ezra came to help his charge alight. "Welcome to Ezra and Eliza's most umble abode."

A sweet-looking lady came running out the door of the building. "Why ya must be Miz Hanner a hidin' unda all dat black. Come on in hea, honey chile, an let Eliza scrubs ya up a bit." Eliza covered her mouth, chuckling. "Cain't emagine Miz Bernadette a seein' ya like dat. She be a thankin' Mr. Jacques done an hire him some mo kitchen hep. Come hea, chile."

Hannah put her hand out, withdrawing it quickly. Removing her blackened gloves, she extended a clean hand. "Glad to meet you, Mrs. Perkins."

"Now, Miz Hanner, I's jes Eliza, an don't ya be a addin' nothin' to it." She wrapped Hannah, cinders and all, in a welcoming hug.

Hannah knew she would be close friends with Ezra and his sweet wife. In a way, she felt she had come home.

Wendell Cunningham realized he had stayed a long while in the barn with his horse when he looked up to see Ezra in the distance, already returning from the railroad station. He had only made it a mile down the road when he waved at the passing carriage.

"Oh my goodness!" The young preacher reached up, wiping his brow. "Merciful heavens, that was close." Rearranging his hat, he turned to look at the crazy buggy driver that had come within a hair's breadth of hitting him. His gaze landed on a young girl in the De Ponte carriage. He felt dizzy. *Is that... no, it can't be.*

Getting a better grip on the reins, he also reined in his thoughts. Those eyes looked like Hannah Baxter's eyes. *But no, they couldn't be... or could they?* Wendell Cunningham shook his head, trying to clear his thoughts. Turning in the saddle for a backward glance, he realized the girl was black. She wasn't Hannah Baxter. *Must be someone the De Pontes are hiring as a maid.* For some reason, although he knew it was not Hannah, he couldn't get those green eyes out of his mind.

"Lord, it's a long way to Charleston. If I'm already this scatter-brained and I haven't left town yet, how will I make it all that way to do your work?" When no answer came, Wendell asked for his creator's assistance. Settling in for the long ride, the preacher began humming a tune. The green eyes teased his mind.

Chapter 15

Looping her arm through Hannah's, Eliza Perkins stepped through the door her husband had opened. "We's a gonna get cha warshed up, Miz Hanner. Now ya be a sittin' down right chere." Pulling out a chair at the kitchen table, Eliza reached for the tea kettle, pouring a cup and setting it in front of Hannah. "Now ya drank up while I get da soaps."

Spooning in sugar, Hannah added cream to her tea and took a long sip, quenching her thirst. By the time Eliza returned, Hannah had emptied the cup. "I'll jes fill er up again an brang ya a elderberry muffin from da pie safe. Now ya jes sit still, Miz Hanner."

Tasting the muffin, she closed her eyes. "I know where I'll be sneaking out for a visit. You're a good cook, Eliza."

"Why, I thanks ya, Miz Hanner. Now you jes sit still an I'll be a usin' dis here soap. Made it myself a usin' da mucilage from da high biscuits plants; it be a soothin' da skin while I be a scrubbin' it clean."

"You use the hibiscus plant to make soap? I never heard of that. My grandmother uses rose petals."

"Yessum, dem juices what be in de high biscuits plant be plum good fo yo skin. We's fount it out a pickin' cotton. Oh, mercy full heavens, dem ole cotton plants be a scratchin' da tarnation outta us what be a pickin' dat cotton." Eliza shook her head with the remembrance. "Why, we be a rubbin' da high biscuits flowers on us ta make it feel better. See, Miz Hanner, I done an got me a idea ta put it in my soap. Now evrybody done an wants Eliza's soaps." She laughed, rubbing Hannah's face a little harder.

"Thank you, Eliza."

"You's mo an welcome. Now we's gots to do somethin' wid yo hair." Eliza removed Hannah's hat, reaching for the combs securing her hair. Pulling a comb through the tresses, Eliza shook out the cinders, making quick work of fashioning the young girl's hair into a complimentary style. Bringing the looking glass, she smiled at Hannah's reaction.

"I know where to come for my hairstyles too. I'm quite impressed with your talent." Hannah was also impressed with the clean face staring back at her. Her cheeks shone a bright pink without a trace of a cinder anywhere.

"Now, Miz Hanner, yo hair so purty, it done an all but fixes itself. Now, off to da back room an getcha a fresh dress. Ezra done an brought in yo trunk."

Hannah went into the last room on the left, partitioned off by a sheet. Removing her dress, she sat on the side of the bed to rest for just a moment. A nightstand beside the bed held a Bible. Picking it up, her brow creased. A folded piece of paper looking much like one from her sketchpad lay on the table where the Bible had been. Curiosity won out. Hannah picked up the paper. Opening it, she fell back on the bed, calling out to her new friend. "Eliza, Eliza, where did you get this?"

"What, Miz Hanner? Where did I get what?" Running through the sheet, finding Hannah in her camisole and petticoats, Eliza ran right back out of the room. "Oh, Miz Hanner, what be happenin'?"

Standing up, Hannah quickly threw on her dress, nearly displacing a comb. "Come in, Eliza."

"Are ya decent?"

"Why, yes, I'm decent."

Eliza tentatively pulled back the sheet. Hannah was still fastening the buttons of her dress. "Now what be wrong?"

Hannah pointed to the sketch she had drawn for Wendell two years earlier. It was a sketch he had requested, one showing her in his brush arbor meeting. "Where did you get this?"

"Why, da preacher what be a stayin' wif us on his travels. Had a be him. He de only one whats been in dis room."

"What is his name, Eliza?"

"Name be Wendell Cunningham."

Hannah fell back on the bed. "Eliza, oh, Eliza."

"What, honey chile?"

"Eliza, I thought I saw Wendell on the road about a mile from here. I thought it just couldn't happen, and he was riding a sorrel horse instead of his black stallion."

"His stallion be in da barn. Gots him a hurt leg. Ezra an me be doctorin' it."

"Well, knock me over with a feather. Where did he go?"

"He done gone to Charleston. Gotta preach at a church up dat way, Hanner. Glory be, I cain't believe dis. Why de good Lord done an brought ya to us an us be a prayin' fer ya."

"Praying for me?"

"Yes, Miz Hanner. Mista Wendell done loss his heart." Eliza took a step back, crossing her arms over her chest and shaking her head from side to side. "So you da reason fer da preacher's sad eyes. I'da never figuret it in my born days. Why, the good Lord done an has his ways; my, my."

"Well, now he thinks I have a suitor."

"Well, do you, Miz Hanner?"

"Not anymore, Eliza."

"Well good. Now we gots ta get cha ready ta meet Miz Bernadette. She be 'spectin' us to brang ya over right away."

"Do I look all right?"

"Why yessum, ya sho nuff do."

Eliza went to the front door. "Ezra, you can be a takin' Miz Hanner nex door ta meet da mizzus."

Ezra appeared momentarily. "We be a loadin' ya back up in da carriage, Miz Hanner. Heavun ferbid dat we walk up to da back door. Gots to be propa like an brang you aroun' in style." The old man laughed in spite of his words.

Bringing Hannah around front, Ezra helped her alight, escorting her to the front door. Answering his knock, the housemaid opened the door, her crisp uniform spotless in the afternoon sun. "Hilder, this here be Miz Hanner, done an come up from Flarda ta study de arts."

The maid looked Hannah up and down. Seeing the kindness in the young girl's eyes, her face lit up with a smile. "Welcomes ta Jawgia, Miz Hanner. Jes come right in an make yoself at home. Miz Gabrielle sho nuff gonna be proud to have yo fine compny." With the blank look on Hannah's face, she explained. "Miz Gabrielle be 'bout yo age. She be da artees' daughter."

Hannah smiled at the maid's pronunciation of Jacques De Ponte's title. "I'm sure I'll be glad to meet her."

"You come on into da parlor, an I be a gettin' um alls ta come an meetcha."

The efficient maid escorted her charge past a marble top commode in the entrance hall. A gilded mirror above the chest topped with floral embellishments spoke of affluence as the young girl glided by.

Ezra had said good-bye and taken his leave. Hannah was on her own now. Feeling excitement coursing through her body, she followed Hilda into the parlor. She was amazed at the "purties" and "fancies" all in one room. The maid left unnoticed as Hannah perused the elaborate parlor. She was surrounded by exquisite furniture, boasting rich floral upholstery in shades of rose, powder blue, and cream. Intricate carvings embellished the wood of the furniture.

A pale pink sofa in the shape of an *s* caught Hannah's attention. Walking over, touching the fine fabric, Hannah knew it was silk. Draperies covering the huge front window were of the same lovely silk. The softness of the sofa beckoned her to sit.

On a table beside the sofa, Hannah touched the bronze angels holding a candelabra at the base of a pedestal. Below the fancy piece sat a box of chocolate Cadbury candies. "La ti da," Hannah whispered, touching the box that had been advertised in *Godey's Lady's Book.* Her mouth watered at the thought of tasting one of the morsels.

"I see you have found my tête-à-tête sofa to your liking." The lady had come into the room, quietly taking Hannah by surprise. "Bernadette De Ponte, my dear, and my daughter, Gabrielle."

Hannah rose, extending her hand to mother and daughter in turn. *Mrs. De Ponte seems fake, but her daughter has mischief dancing in her eyes.* Hannah smiled politely at Bernadette De Ponte, returning Gabrielle's mischievous look.

Gabrielle took a seat beside Hannah on the *s*-shaped sofa. The young girl found herself face-to-face with the artist's daughter. This sofa was made for private conversations.

Gabrielle lifted the box of chocolates, removing the top. "Have one, Hannah."

"Thank you, Gabrielle." Hannah savored the rich taste of sweet chocolate melting in her mouth. She liked her new friend and her surroundings already.

Mrs. De Ponte retrieved two of the chocolates before turning toward the parlor door. "Relax a few, my dearies. Hannah, rest your feet on the tabouret."

With the young girl's look of confusion, Bernadette pointed to the tufted foot stool nearby. "We'll meet again for the evening meal. Then you shall be shown your accommodations. I understand you have met the artiste at the finishing school. He shall dine with us." With a fluttering of her hands, the pretentious lady breezed out of the room, taking the chill with her.

"Do rest yourself, Hannah. Prop your feet up on that stool; it won't break." Gabrielle put her feet up, setting the precedence. Hannah obligingly followed suit, feeling rather spoiled to be propped up in the middle of the day on such fine furniture.

"Your mother is quite sophisticated."

Gabrielle waved her hand. "Pay her no mind, Hannah. She puts on airs. My father is half French. Mother wants to be French." The girl put her hand to her face, glancing toward the door. Her voice came out in a whisper. "She changed her name after she married Father."

"Really?"

Gabrielle broke into a fit of giggles. "She will send me to the guillotine if she finds out I told you, but her name was Mary May Slossum—quite a change to become Bernadette De Ponte." The girl raised her nose in the air and mimicked her mother's fluttering hands.

Hannah tried to cover her grin. "I met your father at Mrs. Fancy La Peau's Finishing School. He seemed very nice, working with us in our art class."

"My father is the most unpretentious man you will ever meet. He loves his God and his family. Mother loves herself."

This bit of information took a moment for Hannah to digest. She enjoyed the fact that Gabrielle was so willing to share secrets with her. It appeared she would have a nice time in Savannah, a right nice time indeed.

"Gabrielle, oh dearie . . . "

"Yes, Mother?"

"Please show our guest to the dining room."

"Yes, Mother."

"Come, dear." Gabrielle motioned Hannah to follow, exuding an air of superiority. The girls barely sobered before entering the huge dining room.

Bernadette De Ponte immediately gestured toward her husband. "Hannah, the artiste, Jacques De Ponte, at your service."

It was hard for the young girl to believe the lady was not of French descent, her accent was so heavy. Extending her hand, Hannah was greeted warmly by the artist.

"We are so glad to have you here, Miss Hannah. I remember perusing your sketchbook at the finishing school—quite impressive."

"Thank you, sir." Hannah was humbled by the praise of this man.

"Take a few days to settle in. We will begin your lessons soon enough." His warm smile told of his gentle nature.

Jacques De Ponte reached to either side, clasping the hands of his wife and daughter. Gabrielle reached for her new friend's hand as her father began praying. "Our gracious heavenly Father, giver of all things good, we thank thee for thy bountiful blessings. Bless this home and all who enter and the food, which you have so graciously given. Amen."

Snapping her fingers, Bernadette turned toward the kitchen. "Come, come, darlings." Hilda appeared with a younger look-alike at her side. "Hannah, meet our chef, Phoebe."

"Evenin', Miz Hanner. I's please ta meetcha."

"Good evening, Phoebe. The food smells delicious."

Phoebe stepped behind Bernadette De Ponte, efficiently placing a serving of roast beef on her plate, then moved on to the artist.

Are these people served by their help? Her silent question was answered as Hilda appeared with a bowl of creamy mashed potatoes. The serving continued with the addition of carrots and asparagus.

Gabrielle dropped a carrot on her dress.

"Now Gabrielle, tut, tut, my dearie. You must learn to mind your manners." Bernadette looked personally offended, as if her daughter had committed an atrocity.

One look from the offender, and the girls averted their eyes, paying close attention to their plates. Hannah bit her tongue to keep from smiling.

Looking around the dining room, Hannah studied a blue-and-white plate sitting in a holder atop the buffet nearby. She recognized the mansion and the name on the plate: The Hermitage. Seeing Bernadette proudly watching, she spoke. "The plate, it's Andrew Jackson's home, correct?"

Her host lifted her nose a little higher. "Yes, dearie, it was a gift to me from Rachel Jackson, the president's wife. Actually, it is a Hermitage Collector's Plate made in Staffordshire, England."

"Jes a bit o puddin' ta finish off a good meal." Hilda and Phoebe brought out small dessert dishes filled with vanilla pudding, topped with raspberries.

"I'll not have dessert tonight; must pay attention to my curves." Bernadette rose to leave. "Later, dearies. As soon as you are finished, we will get you settled, Hannah."

"Thank you, mam."

"She's watching her curves tonight because she ate a whole box of Cadbury chocolates yesterday."

"Gabrielle, dear, be nice." The smile on her father's face showed his amusement.

"This is a beautiful place, Mr. De Ponte."

"Hope you'll enjoy being here, Miss Hannah. We will study three mornings per week. You are free to roam the property and sketch as much as you like."

"Thank you, sir."

"The plantation has special meaning to me. My father was French, my mother American. After my wife and I married, we moved to Paris, where I could study art and be with my parents. My love of Georgia made me long to return."

"I can see why you would love it here."

"After Father died, I returned with my mother and family. I chose Savannah because I wished to purchase a working plantation. I paid the slaves for their labor and set them free, allowing them to sharecrop the land. I chose this plantation because of its close proximity to the Savannah River. A few years later we lost my mother and the war started."

The artist paused, as if remembering the war, before continuing. "The Savannah River is famous for the camp meetings held here. The La Peaus suggested this area so I could enjoy these meetings."

The art student could tell her teacher's spiritual commitment ran deep.

Bernadette beckoned from the door, just as they finished their dessert. "Enough about the camp meetings. It's time to settle our guest. This way, dearie."

Gabrielle rose and Hannah followed. Reaching the bottom of a spiraling staircase, the girls climbed the stairs to the third floor. Hannah remembered that the couple's bed chambers were on the second floor.

Turning left at the top of the stairs, Gabrielle pointed to the first door. "This is my room. Yours is at the front of the house. You'll have a perfect view of the gardens on the front lawn."

"I'll love that. I'll enjoy waking up to the sound of the birds in the trees and the beautiful sight below."

They had reached the end of the hall. "This is your room." Bernadette stood to the side while the girls entered.

Hannah put her hand to her cheek. "Oh my, oh my … " Her eyes darted around the room, hardly able to take it all in. "It is so beautiful, and the furniture … I've never seen anything so wonderful."

Bernadette De Ponte looked quite pleased that Hannah was so impressed. "Oh, it's nothing, really, dearie. These pieces are old. They are the French style of Louis XV, matching the rest of the house furniture."

Hannah stroked the silk bedspread lying atop the mahogany bed. The bed was shaped different from anything the country girl had seen.

Gabrielle smiled at her friend's perusal. "It's a sleigh bed, Hannah."

She moved to the armoire, gingerly touching the roses carved into the wood. A writing table stood nearby, clearly the Louis XV style with its curved legs and gold detail.

Bernadette De Ponte pointed to the front window. "A window seat for times of private contemplation, dearie."

The window seat was backless, boasting curved sides gilded in gold. Walking over, Hannah touched the floral fabric of the seat. "This is beautiful."

"It's your room, dearie, and the copper tub in the corner can be filled with warm water at any time. Phoebe and Hilda attend to our baths. Now I'll leave you to put your clothes away and rest."

Gabrielle and Hannah shared a chuckle as soon as the door closed. Once again, Gabrielle mocked her mother's upturned nose and fluttering hands. "Now, dearie, take a rest."

"We shall have the most fun, Gabrielle."

"Yes, Hannah, I've needed a cohort in mischief for a long time."

Unable to resist the birds calling from the trees, Hannah walked over to the window. Placing her hands on the sill, she leaned forward, breathing deeply of the breeze blowing through the stately branches. "What a magnificent view. I think I shall faint from the beauty."

"Save the swooning for the fainting couch in the great room. Mother would enjoy the drama. She wears her corset so tight she often ends up on that couch."

"I haven't enjoyed myself this much since Susannah and I jumped off the hay wagon."

"Who is Susannah?"

"She is my best friend back in Laurel City. In second grade, two of the Madison brothers kept pulling our braids when we were out Christmas caroling, so we jumped out the back of the wagon to get away. We ran behind for the rest of the night; that is until Grandmam realized we weren't on the wagon."

"Sounds like fun. I lived in Paris in second grade and went to a strict school of my mother's choosing. She wanted her daughter to be the most sophisticated child in France." A mischievous grin spread across Gabrielle's face. "So sorry to disappoint her."

"Gabrielle, you've got to stop this. I do believe we will turn our livers over if we keep laughing."

"Laughter doeth good like a medicine."

"So you quote the Good Book too. Are you born again, Gabrielle?"

"Well, of course, much to my mother's chagrin."

"Your mother doesn't approve?"

"Absolutely not. She feels it makes one much too serious and unable to enjoy the finer things in life."

Hannah could tell Gabrielle wasn't teasing. "It's hard to imagine that."

"It's true. My father has been distressed over Mother's lack of spirituality since their wedding day."

"Really?"

"I know I shouldn't be telling private details, but I can't help myself. Mother attended church, pretending to be a believer until after the marriage."

"How sad for your father."

"Yes, God is an important part of his life. He never gives up hope that my mother will come to her senses."

"I shall help you pray for that."

"Thank you, Hannah. I already feel like you are my best friend."

"We shall have lots of fun."

"Now, I really must leave, or Mother will lecture me for not letting you rest. I'll see you tomorrow."

With the closing of the door, Hannah looked around her room, taking in the beauty. Shades of blue and lavender with hints of pale pink made up the color scheme. Gold embellishments on the furniture added to the elegance. Removing her shoes, Hannah felt the softness of the rug beside her bed through stockinged feet.

Opening the beautiful armoire, she began filling it with her clothes from the trunk Ezra had delivered.

Removing her dress, Hannah thought to take the sketch from her pocket that Wendell Cunningham had left behind. Washing up a bit at the washstand, she put on her yellow summer gown.

Going to the side window of her room, she looked toward the long, narrow building that lay behind the house. Wendell had stayed in the room at the end; she could see the window from her upstairs perch. Hannah could almost imagine him staring back at her through the flour sack curtains. A smile parted her lips. Breathlessly, she whispered, "Wherever you are, sleep well, my love." A breeze blowing through the window seemed to answer. She took one last look at the night sky.

Lying across the bed, she opened the folded sketch. It was the one the preacher had requested at the brush arbor meeting in Laurel City. He was ministering up front while Hannah was seated in the audience. "Where is Wendell Cunningham, Lord? Did he leave this sketch behind on purpose? He said he carried it in his Bible for two years. Has he given up hope?"

No answer came. Hannah sleepily read a passage from her Bible, placing the sketch safely within. The last thing she remembered was murmuring a prayer for *her* circuit-riding preacher. She could dream anything she wanted to dream.

Chapter 16

Wendell Cunningham stepped down from his saddle, moving closer inland, away from the humidity of the coastline. Safely within the forest, he chose a spot to bed down for the night, tethering the sorrel nearby.

The sound of a breaking twig alerted the preacher to check out his surroundings. A dark image moved toward him in the moonlight. He reached for his gun. One could be none too careful with thieves and carpetbaggers on the loose. "Who goes there?"

"Just lookin' for someone ta share a fire with. Ya got any grub, mister?"

"Got a few cold biscuits and some jerky. Could boil up a pot of coffee." Wendell watched closely as the man walked toward him.

"I's powerful hungry, an the coffee be a soundin' good. Ain't had me no coffee in a month o Sundys."

Wendell kept his eye on the stranger, who was yet to introduce himself. Starting a fire, he set the coffee pot to boil with water from the nearby creek.

"What brings you this way, sir?"

"Nuthin' much. Jes travelin'."

The man was disheveled, and his eyes kept darting about. An owl sent its eerie hoot from the branches above. The man jumped at the sound.

Wendell extended his hand. "Name's Wendell Cunningham, circuit-riding preacher, sir."

The man shifted uncomfortably, quickly shaking hands and removing his from Wendell's. As the man pulled away, the preacher noticed a deep gash just above his wrist. "Name's, uh, name's, uh, Daniel Cochran."

Wendell knew this man was no more Daniel Cochran than he was. He was running from something. Heaven forbid, the man might be a criminal running from the law.

After feeding his guest, Wendell offered a blanket for a pallet. *It's gonna be a long night, Lord. Keep your angels camping nearby.*

Early the next morning, Wendell finally dozed off to sleep. Waking to the sound of a mockingbird, the spot where the man had spent the night was empty. *Thank you, Lord.*

Looking toward the fire, he noticed the coffee pot was missing. *Should have expected that,* he thought.

Taking his Bible from the saddlebag, he reached in the front to retrieve the sketch Hannah had drawn. That sketch had kept him from feeling altogether alone for more than two years now. His heart skipped a beat. *It can't be. Oh no, where… where is the sketch?*

After searching the pages of the Bible and the saddlebags, Wendell realized he must have left the sketch at Ezra's home on the nightstand. That's the last time he could remember having it. *Oh, Lord, how will I make it through? I've come to depend on those beautiful eyes in that sketch to bring me comfort and companionship.* This sketch had been his personal request. It had kept the memories of the brush arbor meeting and the girl who had captivated his attention alive for these two years.

A scripture came to mind. *"I will never leave thee nor forsake thee."*

"Thank you, Lord." Wendell Cunningham opened his Bible, receiving strength for the new day stretching out before him.

After washing up at the creek, he filled his cup with the cool, refreshing water and ate a cold biscuit. Saddling the borrowed horse, he knew it was going to be a long day. Traveling held less interest for the man than it had before he met Hannah Baxter. Nevertheless, he put his foot in the stirrup and climbed up.

The sun rose high in the sky, and by noon, Wendell stopped, picking some ripe muscadines growing on an old fence in front of an abandoned home. The state of disrepair told the preacher that the plantation had most likely not been able to continue after slave labor had come to an end. Some plantation owners kept their slaves as sharecroppers, while others kept them just as before. Many slaves were too afraid to leave or claim their freedom. "That'll make for a good sermon. The old devil does the same to those bound up in sin. When God offers them freedom and a profitable life, they stay in their sins, not knowing the glorious life that awaits them if they will accept their freedom."

Tasting the sweetness of the muscadines, Wendell put the rest in his saddlebags, mounted the sorrel, and took off. He was anxious to reach Charleston and share this revelation with the congregation he would minister to. A few more days and he would do just that.

By late afternoon, a drizzling rain slowed the preacher's progress to a crawl. Mud made travel difficult for the horse. The farther north they traveled, the more the rain came down. Finally, Wendell decided to stop at an inn. The stable boy took the sorrel. Wendell placed a coin in his hand. "Cup of oats and a rub down."

"Sho nuff, mista."

The dining room was nearly full, and the food smelled delicious. *I think even a tomato sandwich would taste good right now.* Wendell's granny had just about raised him on tomato sandwiches.

The preacher took a seat by a window, half raised to let the cool breeze in. Nodding to the man seated at a table nearby, Wendell noticed he wore a badge. "Evening, officer."

"Evening, sir. You headin' north?"

"Yes sir, I'm headed to Charleston. I'm a circuit-riding preacher."

"Do tell. You been travelin' along the coast?"

"Yes sir, ever since I left Savannah."

"You didn't happen to run into a scruffy outlaw, did ya? Usually keeps to the coastal areas when he's on the run."

"Yes, sir, I did see a scruffy man. Came into my camp and shared my coffee."

The officer leaned closer. "Been in a scuffle with the mercantile owner. Had a pretty bad gash on his wrist."

"That's your man. Spent the night beside me last night and was gone early this morning, just before sunrise. Said his name was Daniel Cochran, but I didn't believe him for a minute. Even took off with my coffee pot."

Rising from his seat, the officer went to another table, tapping two men on the shoulder. "Gotta head out, boys. My friend here said our outlaw spent the night in his camp. He's travelin' the coastal path. Let's go."

They headed out the door, leaving behind the sound of horses' hooves on the cobblestone road.

"You gonna have the chicken and dumplins or the squirrel brain soup?"

Wendell looked up at the sour-faced waiter. "The chicken and dumplings will be fine."

The man walked away without a backward glance, returning with a cup of coffee without asking if Wendell preferred tea. The preacher added sugar and cream, which he did without on the trail, settling back in the seat to enjoy the brew.

"You from around these here parts, mister?"

"Just a circuit-riding preacher, making the circuit through the Carolinas, Georgia, and Florida. Used to preach up in Virginia, even made it as far as Maryland. I've preached in Alabama as well."

"Well now, that's where I hail from. We's really hit hard in the war. Why, it was so cold, they done an took up the carpet out of the State House to cover us soldiers up with, what with not a bein' able to get no blankets."

"Is that so? My, my. I saw my share of discomfort in the war. Sure was bad when the food couldn't get through. Got worse when our socks and boots wore out. If it hadn't been for the Ladies Knitting Society, we might have lost our toes in the winter."

"I be a knowin' that. Why, some of our men done an walked 'til they had bloody feet. We weren't near to no knittin' ladies, and worse an that some of our soldiers done an took ta eatin' cockroaches, a roastin' em over a fire."

Wendell shook his head. "Yeah, we were mighty happy to be in Georgia during the peach harvest. We ate peaches 'til we nearly turned into one."

The waiter set down the plate in front of Wendell. Pole beans and cornbread accompanied the chicken and dumplings. Bowing his head, the preacher gave thanks for this meal. He could have been eating muscadines from his saddlebag.

The next several days proved much more conducive to making good time. Wendell arrived on Saturday, one day ahead of his ministry schedule. The pastor of the First Church of Charleston had a full house. His family of six filled every room in the church parsonage.

Wendell was always put up in the fine establishment of the Edward Rutledge House. The proprietors attended the church where he would be ministering and always welcomed him with open arms. It would feel so good to lie in a fine bed and have good meals.

The circuit rider rode his borrowed horse into the stable. A uniformed gentleman took the sorrel from the preacher. "Welcome, sir."

"Thank you, Mr. Atkins. It's a pleasure to stay at this fine place again."

"We glad to have ya, sir."

Knocking on the front door, a maid in a starched uniform curtsied her welcome, opening the door wide for the preacher's entrance. "Third floor, room number six, sir. We've been spectin' ya, and it's scrubbed from piller to post."

"Thank you, Miss Martha."

"We's mighty proud to house ya. The mister and the mizzus say they see you at supper, sir."

"Thank you."

Wendell made his way to the third floor. Opening the door to his room, he felt peace envelope him as he peered out the window, seeing the steeple of St. Michael's Church. This steeple had been a lookout tower during the war.

Just looking at the steeple brought a sense of God's promise to never leave nor forsake his dear ones. It seemed to Wendell that the old church had always been there. After the war, when many homes and buildings were burned by General Sherman, it was a comfort to see St. Michael's still standing as a place of worship.

St. Michael's was the oldest church in the city of Charleston. The cornerstone was laid in 1752. With its steeple reaching 186 feet into the air, it lifted Wendall's spirits to the heavens. *I'll visit the church before I leave town. Always gives me a sense of well-being.*

Washing up at the nightstand, the young man lay atop the bed, thinking of the history these walls held. Edward Rutledge, at age twenty-six, was the youngest signer of the Declaration of Independence. Rutledge governed South Carolina from 1789–1800.

In the spring of 1791, Rutledge had escorted George Washington around Charleston. The Washington administration had relied heavily upon Rutledge's family when considering appointments to office from South Carolina.

And I am so very blessed to stay in a place so rich in history. Wendell lay dozing.

All of a sudden, green eyes wandered through the preacher's thoughts. A soft knock sounded from somewhere nearby. He sat upright in bed, shaking his head, thinking Hannah was in front of him. *It's only my imagination.*

"Mista Preacha, it be time ta come ta suppa."

"I'll be right down, Miss Martha."

The young man grabbed a clean shirt from his bag, dusted off his trousers with a brush, and, pausing at the looking glass by the door, combed his dark locks into place. Pulling on his boots and dusting them off with a polishing cloth, Wendell ran down the stairs, two at a time.

"Welcome, welcome, Preacher Cunningham. We're so glad to have you."

"I'm happy to be here, Mr. O'Toole, Mrs. O'Toole."

"Have a seat, and we'll fill up that hollow spot."

"Smells good."

"Ask the blessing for us, Preacher."

After the prayer, food was brought out by the cook, Miss Viv, and the dishes were passed around. Mrs. O'Toole swatted at a fly. "Martha, Martha, I can't bear for this fly to share our meal. Please come and fan the food."

"Yessum, I's a comin'." Martha took up her station, pulling the rope, the contraption above the table moving back and forth.

"I see we have coddle tonight. Haven't had it since I was here last year." Wendell helped himself to a generous portion of the Irish dish consisting of layers of pork sausage, bacon, sliced potatoes, and onions.

"My compliments to the cook."

Miss Viv stuck her head around the corner of the kitchen door. "Sho is glad you likes it, Mista Preacher. The recipe came from Mrs. O'Toole."

"You did a good job cooking it, Miss Viv."

"I thanks ya, sir." The smiling woman's face disappeared.

"Sure do enjoy this good Irish food, Mrs. O'Toole."

The lady smiled her appreciation for the compliment.

"How are things in Charleston, Mr. O'Toole? Are the freed slaves blending into society any better?"

"It's a slow process, Preacher. We have been going through the process for many years. Anybody different has to prove their ways to those who think they are better."

"Yes, I've seen that in my travels; shouldn't be that way, but it is."

"When we came over from Ireland, some of the plantation owners sneered at our ways. Their children poked fun at the accent our children spoke with. The resistance for the slaves is many times magnified. There's much to be overcome."

"In my travels, it seems that freed slaves are not really free. They are still bound, not being able to secure jobs or property. I hear that the sharecroppers are being cheated by the plantation owners."

"That's the news up here in the Carolinas as well. Guess it takes time for people to change."

"Yes, time and a willingness to accept others for who they are."

Mr. O'Toole wiped the last bit of coddle from his plate with a piece of his potato bread. "Thing is, Preacher, some may never be willing to accept others for who they are."

"That's the truth, sir." Wendell shook his head. "And God help them all." Wiping his mouth with a napkin, the young man rose from his seat. "I'll be saying good night. I need to put the finishing touches on my sermon; got to start this revival with a fiery message." He grinned, rubbing his hands in anticipation of the services.

Mrs. O'Toole stood. "Get us a good one, Preacher. We always enjoy your messages."

"Good evening, then."

Wendell went up the stairs, lighting the lantern in his room, sure he would be burning the midnight oil. Lifting the top on the rolltop desk, he seated himself with his Bible. Opening the front cover, he once again missed Hannah's sketch that he had left behind. Closing his eyes for just a moment, he tried to remember every detail of the drawing. Soothed by the remembrance, he turned to the passage of Scripture he wished to study for tomorrow.

Chapter 17

The first week at the De Ponte Plantation was delightful. Hannah enjoyed Gabrielle's companionship. The two young ladies, dressed in their Sunday best, descended the stairs together.

When they entered the kitchen, Hilda lifted a lid, placing bread dough to rise inside a box. At Hannah's look of surprise, Hilda proudly explained. "Dis here be a French Dough Box. It be set under da panatiere." She lifted her hand in the air as if copying Mrs. Bernadette, then smiled at the girls. "Dat be jes a faincy name fer da bread box, Miss Hanner, an it be a Louis XV, at that." As an afterthought, she added, "One a Miz Bernadette's prize possessions."

She then ran toward the pie safe. "Sweet rolls fer you gals this mornin', if'n Miz Bernadette lef y'all any." Pulling the last two rolls from the shelf, she set them on saucers, waving the girls to the breakfast nook.

Washing the rolls down with glasses of cool milk from the springhouse, the girls ran out the door to the awaiting carriage. Mr. De Ponte was in the driver's seat. "Morning, ladies. Don't we look pretty today?"

Smiling, the girls settled themselves on the carriage seat, ready for the short ride to church. Hannah could just imagine that the building would be filled with high society folk from the surrounding area. Riding by the church on previous occasions, the very structure spoke of wealth, with its imposing columns and huge stained glass windows. As they neared, the sounds of the pipe organ filled the morning air.

The girls were escorted into the church on Mr. De Ponte's arms. The older ladies greeted Hannah with aloof politeness and even snooty looks.

Once seated, Gabrielle turned to her friend. "Pay them no mind. They wouldn't know God if he tapped them on the shoulder."

Hannah covered her face delicately with a fan.

"Please rise for the opening prayer," the man behind the podium asked. He seemed to peer just over their heads, as if they were not in attendance. Hannah thought he fit in with this congregation quite well. "Our Father, forgive our iniquities this great and dreadful day of the Lord. Amen."

Hannah felt a chill run up her spine even though the weather was warm.

"Open your hymnbooks to page twenty-seven. Our lovely Agatha Hathaway will lead us in song."

Agatha Hathaway *was* lovely. She looked down her nose at the congregation. "Sing your best this morning please. If you do not know the songs, kindly refrain." Hannah watched the girl's beauty dissipate with her unkind words.

Hannah could not believe the audacity of the young lady. Her beautiful voice rang out loud and clear, yet the message of the hymn was lost with her upturned nose.

Gabrielle touched her arm, pointing to the words in the hymn book. Hannah began singing, but her heart was back home. Closing her eyes, she could imagine singing with her family in their little chapel by the stream. Warmth flooded her body, chasing away the chill.

"You may be seated. We will share today's message regarding tithe and offerings." The aloof Reverend Bristol spoke for twenty minutes on giving to the church. "You are not giving until it hurts. God wants the best you have, not your leftovers. This church needs money to upkeep the sanctuary as befitting the wealth in this town. We do not want to look like the meager chapel on the other side of the tracks. I exhort you to give. We will take up the second offering as Mrs. Redburn returns to the organ."

And with that, the lady pompously marched to the organ, beginning her mournful tune.

The offering plate passed for the second time. Mr. De Ponte obediently placed several dollars in the plate, smiling at the stern usher. The man moved on, standing in front of the next parishioner until he gave another offering.

Gabrielle put her hand to her face, whispering to her friend. "You are a bit surprised, aren't you?"

"It is different here in Savannah." If this was the way rich, affluent people worshiped God, Hannah was glad her family was neither rich nor affluent.

Exiting the church, Agatha Hathaway swished by with a rush of petticoats. "Hello, Gabrielle. Weren't you going to speak?"

"Yes, Agatha. How are you today?"

"Just fine. By the way, have you seen the circuit-riding preacher? Sure do miss him." She looked at Hannah smugly, fluttering her eyelashes. Casting her eyes up and down Hannah, she continued. "Who is this?"

"Meet my new friend, Hannah Baxter. She is an art student, studying under my father."

Unimpressed, Agatha ignored the introduction. "Well, have you seen Preacher Cunningham?"

Hannah wanted to reach out and wipe the smile right off Agatha's face. Instead, she walked away, following the artist to the carriage.

Gabrielle caught up with Hannah. "What do you think of Agatha?"

"Can't say for sure."

"That matches my opinion of her perfectly."

The second week of art school had begun, and this morning the young scholar was sitting under the fine tutelage of Jacques De Ponte. Hannah felt privileged to have the man's undivided attention, as she was his only student.

"We will study the effect of light and shadow this month. Learning and achieving the maximum use of these in sketching and painting brings a depth to the finished piece of art that cannot be achieved by any other means."

Hannah listened attentively to the artist. Intent on learning and making the most of her time here, she wished to seek and follow instruction well. Watching the demonstration on the easel, she gasped as landscape came to life, showing the time of day and details or lack thereof depending on the subject's availability to light.

"Your turn. Place any subject in the brilliance of the noonday sun. Next, surround the subject with landscape or objects showing more or less of the light, depending on the position of them in respect to the light source."

Hannah stood before the easel. Another adventure awaited her. In spite of the artist's presence and his extraordinary abilities, she felt up to the occasion. Wishing to press forward into the unknown, she put her pencil to the pad on the easel in front of her.

From memory, she sketched her father's stallion, reared on his hind feet with a snake nearby. The stallion seemed ready to pounce, his nostrils flaring in the sunlight, the hind legs shadowed by a tree nearby, falling between the sun and the horse. Details of the snake were glaring in the brightness of the sun, unshadowed. Pointed fangs loomed menacingly, ready to strike. The coil of the snake's body, taunt and poised, spoke of the damage to be inflicted in just a moment's time. Under the shadow of the nearby tree, a bird blurred into the trunk, details covered by the darkness there.

Time passed quickly for the girl standing before the easel, obviously transferred in her mind back to her home in Laurel City. The lesson had made its way deep into her heart. The response to that lesson was obvious as the shadow and light techniques made their way onto the paper.

Jacques De Ponte stood back in amazement, watching the scene unfolding in front of him. "You have a gift, dear."

Hannah's pencil paused in midair. "Sir?"

"You are definitely gifted. Never before has someone learned these techniques so quickly. While I can show you a few places where you need to lighten or darken the sketch, you have certainly grasped the technique." Putting his hand to his jaw, the artist shook his head in amazement.

Hannah's back was to the artist as she finished shading the frog sitting just below the corral fence, watching the stallion and staying away from the menacing hooves. "Thank you, sir." Her words were a bare whisper; her mouth curved determinedly as she shadowed the frog to perfection.

Patting his student on the back, Mr. De Ponte turned to exit the room. "Practice sketching out of doors, Hannah, with the varying degrees of sunlight. Choose any subject, keeping the effect of light and shadows at the forefront of your sketching. 'Til we meet again, my dear."

"Thank you, sir."

Gabrielle was waiting outside the art studio in the hall. "I heard what my father said to you. He came out of that room looking amazed."

"At me?"

"Yes, Hannah, amazed at your work. You must be very talented."

"Oh, it's nothing I do myself; it's God's gift to me. It's really his gift *loaned* to me."

"What do you mean by that?"

"It's nothing I possess, Gabrielle, just something he allows me to use for his glory."

"Okay, that makes sense."

"Were you saying your gift is for the glory of God, Hannah?" Bernadette had joined them at the top of the stairs.

"Yes, mam."

"Now, now, dearie, you should take credit for what you do."

"I can't take credit when it is a gift from God."

"Tut, tut, dahling." The lady waved her hand, dismissing the conversation. The accent, which had been missing, returned with full force. "Come, dearies, have a sandwich with me."

The girls followed her to the kitchen. Soft rolls stuffed with chicken salad stood on the sideboard next to a crystal compote filled with mixed fruit. "Help yourselves, dearies."

After their simple noon meal, Bernadette De Ponte handed a list to Gabrielle. "You girls may accompany Ezra to Two Mules Junction."

Retrieving their bonnets from upstairs, Gabrielle grabbed Hannah's hand, running downstairs and out the back door toward Ezra and Eliza's place. "We're gonna have some fun today."

"What is Two Mules Junction?"

"It's the most fun place you'll ever see."

"Why?"

"'Cause you never can tell just what might happen in Two Mules Junction."

"It sounds like fun, but it doesn't seem like the kind of place your mother would approve us going."

"Oh, she trusts Ezra, and she doesn't know all that happens in Two Mules Junction. It's our best-kept secret. You see, Hannah, my mother sends Ezra there to get flour from a special mill, Chisolm's Mill."

"What's so special about Chisolm's Mill?"

"Mother says they have the finest flour for making French pastries. She declares there's a secret ingredient in the flour."

"Is there?"

"No, Ezra asked old Mr. Chisolm. He said the flour is extra fine because they run it through the mill twice."

"Well, that makes sense, I guess."

"Yes, but don't tell Mother. She may ask the Savannah Mill to do the same and stop our trips to Two Mules Junction." Gabrielle affected an exaggerated Southern drawl. "'Twould be a shame."

Ezra opened the front door of his home before the girls had a chance to knock. "What's all that gigglin' 'bout, Miz Gabrielle?"

"I was telling Hannah our secret." At Ezra's confused look, she further explained. "About the *fine* flour at Chisolm's Mill."

Laughter erupted from the jovial man. "It's a well-kep secret, sho nuff. Kinda keeps us a makin' dem trips we likes so much." Calling good-bye to Eliza, Ezra brought the wagon and mules around. The three settled on the hard board seats of the rickety wagon, just as happy as if they were riding in the elaborate De Ponte carriage.

Excitement welled up in Hannah's chest, making it difficult to draw a full breath. Gabrielle reached over, grabbing her friend's hand. "We're gonna have the mostest fun, you and me."

She turned to Ezra. "We might just get to see another chapter play out in the Totem Chronicles."

"Yessum, Miz Gabrielle, that sho would be fun." As if in anticipation, he clucked to the mules. "Dese hea mules be a havin' two paces: slow an slower."

Making their way out onto the tree-lined road, the Savannah River begged their attention.

The early afternoon sun glistened off small waves making their way to shore. A couple near the river's edge was just returning from an outing, the small boat tossing about precariously. The young man jumped over the side, pulling the boat to shore. The girl in the boat held on to her hat, which was doing its best to fly away. Seeing the couple made Hannah remember the nice day spent with the preacher on the Caloosa River.

A pot hole in the cobblestone caused the older mule to almost lose her footing. "Come on, Blossom. Don't ya be a lettin' us down now. We gots places ta go an thangs ta tend to."

Riverboats up and down the river blew their whistles in passing. At a nearby dock, cotton was being loaded on a huge boat bearing the name *Liverpool Enterprise. Must be a boat from England.* Another boat, marked *Charleston Timber Mills,* was being loaded with logs floating downstream.

"Sure is a busy river."

"Sho nuff is, Miz Hanner. We does exports an imports in this river an a mighty large number of em if I do say so myseff. Dat cotton on its own makes fer loadin many a ship from da ex change. It goes ta ports all roun de world. Yessum, da Savanny River, she be a impotent river at dat."

The girls laughed quietly behind Ezra's back.

Under the bluff at the river, Hannah noticed piles and piles of bricks. "What are those bricks for?"

"Dat's da brickmakin' yard. Brickmakin' been goin' on under dat bluff more'n a hunderd years."

A block from the Savannah River, Ezra pointed at an old inn. "Dat be de Pirate's House and de Herb House be a joinin' onto da inn. It be da oldest house in da state, and it be made o bricks from under dat bluff."

"The old inn looks spooky."

"Yes, Miz Hanner, an rightly so. Rumor says dat many a man done an drunk his grog an past out cold only ta wakes up on a ship a goin' somewheres an he don't be a knowin' how he got on da ship."

Gabrielle nodded. "That's right, Hannah, they say there's a tunnel that runs under the inn to the river where the drunken sailors were carried to ships waiting to sail the high seas. The sailors woke up, realizing they were shanghaied as unwilling crew members."

"Dat place could sho tell some stories if'n dem walls could be a sayin' their piece. Drinkin' and fightin' an tellin' tall tales, dat what dem sailors an pirates be a doin' there fer more'n a hunderd years."

Hannah was glad when they left the Pirate's House behind.

Dogwoods lining the road they were now traveling sent their gentle fragrance on the afternoon breeze. Their white and pink blossoms dressed the area in formal attire. Hannah drank in the view, enjoying the delicate scent.

Turning again, the mules plodded along through mud puddles left behind after the morning showers. "Roads ain't so nice out dis a way."

Hannah was enjoying the adventure in spite of the hard wagon seat. Wild grapes hung in clusters on an arbor fashioned in the yard of a family. Children reached for the ripe, purple clusters, filling their mouths with the fruit.

A puppy barked as if guarding the house they were passing. A woman waved from her spot in the garden as the old wagon rattled by. Thoughts of her mother filled Hannah's mind as she waved back to the lady filling a basket with ripe tomatoes.

Before an hour had passed, Hannah saw the wooden sign that read *Two Mules Junction.* She thought she heard music. "Is the church choir practicing this early in the day?"

Ezra looked sideways at Gabrielle. "That's not church music you hear, Hannah."

"Where's it coming from?" She strained to hear while searching the countryside. Nothing was in sight.

"You'll see real soon."

A sharp turn to the right gave Hannah a completely new view. A large, wooden building stood about a hundred yards in the distance. This was the location of the music. But Hannah was confused. Who was playing music in the middle of the day?

Drawing closer, Hannah could barely make out the sign up ahead; it read *The Watering Trough.*

"The Watering Trough? What is that?"

Once again, Ezra and Gabrielle exchanged looks. As they drew near the weathered building, Hannah was surprised to see a man being tossed out into the muddy street.

"Oh my." She was shocked when a buxom woman came running out of the saloon door, her hair tightly bound in a bun.

"Now, Elijah, what shame you be a brangin' to the Lord's name. I've done an tried all I knowed, an you just cain't leave the whiskey alone."

A scared-looking young woman with smudges of color above her eyes peered out from the upper window of the building. "You all right, Lijah?"

Hannah noticed that Ezra had pulled the mules and wagon to the other side of the road and stopped.

Elijah got up out of the mud, rubbing his head. "I'll be all right after I sleep it off, sweet thang."

The big woman headed toward the drunken man. "Don't ya be a sweet thangin' her. I'm yore sweet thang, an ya don't even know it. Glory be, what am I ta do with ya, Elijah Totem?" Her hands balled into fists, the woman looked into the heavens.

Putting her hand to her mouth, Hannah suppressed a laugh. "It is well worth the ride on this hard wagon seat to see all this excitement."

Gabrielle returned the whisper. "Oh, it gets better than this. You haven't seen the best show yet. Maybe the Totems will be at it again next time we come into town."

Mrs. Totem walked out in the mud, retrieving her husband. He could barely walk. "I ain't had me no dealin's wif that womern; jest wanted me a drank," Mr. Totem said.

Holding his arm, she proudly walked down the middle of the muddy road, her dress dragging behind her. She seemed not to notice the people lined up in front of the mercantile, watching the latest unfolding episode of the Totem Chronicles.

Getting a closer look, Hannah could see the bun on the back of Mrs. Totem's head was pulled so tight her eyes took on a slanted look. She remembered her conversation with her sister about tight-bunned women.

Gabrielle looked at the pious woman. "She's a church-going woman, but everyone in town knows how mean she is. Her husband can't seem to stay away from temptation; says he has to drink to live with her. I'd say she needs to loosen that tight bun a bit."

"Seems to me she's a bit strong a tryin' to make a convert outta ol Lijah. Throwin' him outta the saloon ain't a showin' too much o the love o da Lawd, fer's I's concernt, anyways." Ezra shook his head as if surely there was a better way. "He done come a flyin' outta dat door like a sack o taters."

Hannah and Gabrielle chuckled.

"Catch yo breath, girls. Dey be another Totem Chroncle to be a laughin' at nex week, sho nuff."

"I sure hope so." And Hannah meant it. "I would give a shiny nickel to see that show again."

"Me too."

"If'n I had me a shiny nickel, I jes might pay fer de show, too."

Ezra pulled up in front of the Chisolm Mill. The girls jumped down, racing up the steps to get the first view of the grinding of the old mill. The wheel was being turned by water diverted from the river nearby.

"How 'bout you ladies sittin' for a cup o cool cider?"

Cool cider sounded good to Hannah. The ride in the July sun had been quite warm, in spite of the sunbonnet shading her face.

Gabrielle smiled at the lady. "Yes, mam, Mrs. Chisolm, we'd love a cup of cider. Meet my friend, Hannah Baxter."

Hannah extended her hand. "Good afternoon, Mrs. Chisolm, I'm pleased to meet you."

"Pleasure's all mine, Miss Hannah. What beautiful green eyes you have." The woman handed her a cup of the sweet drink.

"Thank you, mam."

The girls enjoyed their cider while watching the wheel just outside the window. At the back of the room, the flour was being scooped into sacks, which Gabrielle said Eliza would use for making her dresses.

Ezra finished his cup of cider and paid for the flour. "Time ta go, girls. We gotta stop at da mercantile."

Saying their good-byes to the Chisolms, the girls raced to the wagon.

"All right girls, we's loaded and ready to go." Ezra unhitched the mules from the hitching post under the tree.

Turning back to the mercantile, there was no sign that the Totems had visited the saloon. The music, which had halted when Elijah came flying out the door, was playing again. A couple of bow-legged cowboys were headed that way, their spurs clanking on the boardwalk.

Pulling up in front of the mercantile, the girls alighted, following Ezra up the porch steps. Immediately one of the men, sitting in a rocking chair nearby, nodded. "Did ya see the show, Ezra? Ol Elijah done an lost his rudder."

A man smoking a pipe slapped his knee. "He's dizzy as a goose after the mizzus throwed him out on his ear. Don't know if'n it was from the whiskey or the lick to his head, but he won't likely get straight fer a while."

"Now not too much of that from you, Jesse, you's out on yer back last week. Did you so soon ferget?"

Ezra rushed the girls through the door, away from the antics of those carrying on outside.

Once inside, Hannah's eyes adjusted to the dim light. The mercantile was full of all kinds of things. The girls went over to the china cabinet.

"Look at those beautiful cups and saucers. Grandmam would love them."

"Are you missing home, Hannah?"

"Yes, at times, but I'm having too much fun to want to go back just yet."

Moving over to look at the shoes, Hannah tried on a pair of indigo blue slippers. The plant grew extensively in these parts. Gabrielle grabbed a pair, and the two paraded around the store, swishing their skirts and drawing attention from a tight-bunned lady. "Oh, for heaven's sake." She turned, huffing and sticking her pious nose in the air.

The girls joined Ezra at the counter after putting the shoes back on the shelf. The clerk smiled. "No indigo slippers today, ladies?"

"Not today." Gabrielle rewarded him with a flirtatious smile.

"Come along." Hannah grabbed her friend.

"Da mizzus o de big house gots ta have dem sweeties." Ezra paid for the Cadbury chocolates.

"It takes two boxes of chocolates a week to keep Mother happy."

"How does she keep such a nice shape?"

Gabrielle laughed. "She just keeps wearing the corset tighter. She yells at Hilda to pull the strings harder."

By the time the girls had situated their skirts in the wagon, they were ready for the ride home. "Well, it's been fun visiting Two Mules Junction. I can't wait to come again."

"I knew you'd like it, Hannah."

Ezra climbed up on the seat, clucking to his mules. "We's gonna take anuther way home. Gonna take ya through da apple orchard. We'll get us some o dem early apples. Most of em be ready next month, but dey's plenty fer us right now."

"Sounds good to me." Hannah perked up at the idea of seeing an apple orchard. She was used to the orange groves back home, but the thought of tasting a fresh apple made her mouth water.

Just a few minutes into the ride, the air was filled with the sweet smell of the orchard. Lining both sides of the road were rows and rows of apple trees.

Swallow-tail kites and sparrows darted from tree to tree, enjoying their romp in the late afternoon sun. The colorful sky made a beautiful backdrop, enhancing the apple orchard. "Wish I had my sketchpad. Sure could practice light and shadows in this place."

"You ortta be sketchin' out in da peach orchard at home, Miz Hanner. It be right there jes a waitin'. 'Tis a purty sight fer sho. All dem peaches a hangin' on dem trees wif da sun slippin' down pass dem hills."

"What are y'all hiding from me? I didn't know there was a peach orchard on the plantation."

"I'm sorry, Hannah. I didn't think to tell you. It's on the back side of the plantation. I'll take you there."

Ezra stopped the wagon, and, standing up on the seat, he reached up, retrieving two perfect apples and handing them to the girls. Next, he chose a smaller one for himself.

"You're always putting others first, aren't you, Ezra?"

"Dats what de Good Book says, Miz Gabrielle."

Ezra pulled a few more apples. "My friend owns dis orchard. Jes bought it plum out from his master las month. He been a share croppin' an makin' a bundle on da cotton what dat land produce dis year."

"That's wonderful, Ezra."

"It sho nuff is. The Lawd made da way, an my friend says me an Eliza can get all da apples we be a wantin'. Eliza done an been up here wif me ta pick a wagon full. She be a makin' apple butter an apple cider. We's gonna enjoy dem apples dried fer pies in de winter an ground up to make apple pancakes right now." Ezra licked his lips.

"You're making me hungry, Ezra."

Hannah squirmed on the wagon seat. "Me too. That apple hit bottom real quick."

"I be tellin' ya girls. Ya gots ta come for breakfas an try dem apple pancakes."

"We will," Gabrielle answered.

Ezra pointed to a group of flowers growing in wild profusion along a wooden fence they were passing. "Dat be the red buckeye flowers what da Cherokee Injuns use ta catch fish."

"To catch fish, Ezra?"

"Yes, Miz Hanner." Spotting a group of lilies on the other side of the fence, he pointed. "And dose yellow trout lilies out by dat pond, da root o dat plant be a makin' da fish ta bite. Mus be a feesherman a livin' in dat house."

He pointed to the dilapidated wooden structure they were now passing. A young man sat on the porch, whittling and whistling a tune, a pile of wood shavings at his feet. Nodding his head at the man, Ezra turned to look at the girls. "Might ortta fix up da place a bit."

As they came back into Savannah, the evening shadows were falling, turning the landscape into beautiful silhouettes against the sky.

Wonder where Wendell is? Could he be staring into the sky, thinking of me? How I wish I could be with him.

Hannah closed her eyes, relaxing to the movement of the wagon, which felt like a boat gliding through the water. Looking up, the old oak trees draped in moss could have been the same ones lining the Caloosa River. Hannah's thoughts were filled with the man with dark locks, rowing the boat on the seat in front of her. She could feel the pencil in her hand, sketching the man. The eyes filled with love for her stared back. From somewhere far away, she could hear someone calling her name. Unwilling to be drawn from her dream, she didn't care to answer.

"Hannah, Hannah, are you asleep? We're home; it's time to go inside."

Chapter 18

Revival services continued into the third week. Wendell Cunningham spent time each day, praying and preparing his sermons. It had been a fruitful time for the First Church of Charleston. There were many conversions. There would be a baptismal service following the Sunday morning service. This would be his final meeting. Rising from his desk on Saturday afternoon, the young preacher went to the window looking out at St. Michael's Church. *Think I'll go for a visit.*

Combing his hair, he descended the stairs, walking the short distance to the church.

Opening the door, Wendell was overcome by the deep sense of historical significance this church held. Pew number forty-three held a special place in his heart. Walking up the aisle, he slid into it. George Washington had worshiped in this very pew in 1791, and seventy years later, Robert E. Lee had worshiped here.

Awe filled Wendell's heart as he sat, worshiping his God, offering silent praise. This pew was an original, made from native cedar.

His eyes rose to the ceiling, where the chandelier, ordered from London in 1803, was lit with candles in the late afternoon shadows. His eyes moved to the pulpit, standing high and supported by two Corinthian columns. During the Federal Bombardment of 1865, a shell had burst into the house of worship, leaving a scar at the base of the pulpit.

Wendell rose from the pew and walked to the altar. Bowing to his creator, he brought his petition before his God. "Father, guide my steps. If it is possible, please allow Hannah Baxter to be my wife. And, Father, take the nightmares away. I pray for your peace. Amen."

The church bells began ringing. Wendell found his way into the room where Washington Gadsden was orchestrating the ringing of the bells. He had previously met the man, who had been at this job since 1837.

"Afternoon, Mr. Gadsden."

"Good day to ya, Preacher. I took a peek inside the sanctuary. Thought that was you a prayin' at the altar."

While he talked, Mr. Gadsden and his helpers pulled the ringer ropes, one at a time, each attached to a wheel and giving its own special tone. They worked the ropes smoothly, a different tone sounding with the ringing of each bell. Each pull was spaced evenly, the effect being a perfect rhythm to the sounding of the bells.

Leaving the church, Wendell walked across the road to the Rutledge House. He had enjoyed the comforts of this home and his time of fellowship with the O'Tooles.

Mr. O'Toole greeted Wendell at the door. "Come join us for stew."

"I love Irish stew."

Seated at the table, the small group enjoyed the delectable lamb with tasty vegetables cooked into a hearty potage.

"We'll surely miss your fine companionship at our table, Preacher."

"And I will miss your fine Irish dishes and your fellowship, Mrs. O'Toole."

"We will look forward to next time, Preacher. Stop in for any reason if you are up this way. We have a new bridal suite." The woman averted her eyes, blushing.

Wendell understood the offer. His heart was touched. This simple woman wanted him to be able to enjoy the companionship of a wife. She raised her eyes to his. In them he saw kindness and someone who understood his loneliness.

"Thank you, Mrs. O'Toole."

The slight nod of her head spoke volumes.

Wendell rose from his supper. "Good night, friends."

"Good night." The word spoken in unison by the Irish couple fell on Wendell's ears as a blessing. Tomorrow he would leave the church, conduct the baptismal service, and hit the trail.

"No, no, no." Wendell thrashed his head from side to side, desperately trying to get air into his deprived lungs. "No, Granny." He could feel the pillow pressing down on his face, covering his nose. Granny's eyes taunted him, as he peeked over the top of the pillow. In the moonlight, those eyes were even more menacing. He felt the bed trembling beneath him. A quick intake of breath wasn't enough to calm his starved lungs. Granny's wicked laugh resounded in his ears as he struggled to breathe.

"Preacher, Preacher ... open the door. Who's in there? Open the door, or I'm coming in."

Wendell Cunningham shook his head, trying to distinguish why Mr. O'Toole would be calling out to him when Granny was standing over him. Sitting up in bed, holding his chest, he could hear the pounding on the door. Opening his eyes, Granny was not to be seen. Once again, the nightmares had brought his grandmother back into his life.

"I'm all right, Mr. O'Toole." Wendell opened the door, sheepishly looking out at the man holding a lantern. "I'm right sorry to wake you." Running his fingers through his hair, Wendell turned to look out the window.

"Preacher, no never mind to waking me. I'm just glad you're all right. It sounded real bad below. Sounded like you was thrashing around in a powerful bad fight. I's coming to help you."

"I guess I was fighting my granny."

"Sorry, son. So sorry." Bowing his head, the man turned away.

Wendell closed the door as Mr. O'Toole made his way down the stairs.

"How long, oh Lord?"

Going to the desk, he opened it and sat reviewing his sermon. "How can I preach your Word when I have so many unanswered questions?"

The walls of the room held no answers.

Green eyes and sun-kissed tresses floated across his vision. *Lord, how could I ever ask her to share my life with these nightmares between us? She doesn't deserve this.* Then his mind went to Isaac. *Guess she'd be better off with him; he'll be able to provide for her.*

Holding his head in his hands, Wendell's eyes landed on a verse of Scripture: "The just shall live by faith."

"I do have faith in your Word, Father. Please deliver me from this agony."

Believing the battle with his grandmother would end, Wendell thought of the verse from the Bible that said, "When God closes a door, man cannot open it."

"I will believe you to do just that. There will come an end to this." With renewed faith in his Lord, the preacher pillowed his head until morning light streamed in the window, bringing the steeple of St. Michael's Church into view.

Hannah awoke to Gabrielle pounding on her door. "Hurry up, sleepyhead. We're burnin' daylight."

Sitting up in bed, rubbing her eyes, Hannah threw the sheet back and padded to the door. "It's barely the crack of dawn. What are you up to, Gabrielle?"

"Come on, throw your clothes on, and let's go have some fun."

Hannah was still unconvinced. "What about your parents?"

"My parents are long gone. Father is taking Mother to Atlanta to watch some plays. We've got the house to ourselves for two weeks." Her words tumbled forth, excitement dancing in her eyes.

"It sounds like fun to me," Hannah said. Out the back door they ran, their hair barely pinned up in combs.

"First stop is Eliza's kitchen."

"Gabrielle, what if Ezra and Eliza aren't awake yet?"

"You silly girl, can't you smell the bacon?"

Hannah sniffed the air and grinned. Pounding on the door, the girls were let in by Ezra. "Kinda been a figurin' on you twos a comin', what with yo mama an papa bein' gone. Come on in. Eliza's cookin' enuff fer all o us ta eat twice."

"Morning, Eliza." Hannah echoed Gabrielle's greeting. She felt uneasy, bursting into the kind lady's kitchen.

The big smile from Eliza was contagious. "Yo sho nuff does fill a body wif joy, a comin' fer brake fass. Have yoselfs a seat at Eliza's table. I'll take da biskits out, an we be a eatin' fo yo know it."

Seated around the table, it almost felt like home. "This apple butter is wonderful, Eliza."

"Why thanks ya, Miz Hanner. Ya eat alls ya be a wantin'; they's plenty mo where dat come from."

"I want to help you make it."

"I'll yell fer ya nex time I gets da jars out."

Ezra spread marmalade over a second biscuit. "What ya girls be a plannin' fer dis fine summer day?"

"Well, Ezra, we're going exploring. Hannah hasn't seen the peach orchard yet. Thought we'd ride the horses back there."

"Good way ta spen a day. Take de ol mares. Dey be easy ta ride. I gets um saddled up, Miz Gabrielle."

"Thank you, Ezra."

Finishing their breakfast, and bidding Eliza good-bye, the girls ran out of doors. "You aren't planning on riding in that good dress, are you, Gabrielle?"

"Why, yes, I suppose. What else am I to ride in?"

It was Hannah's turn to look mischievous. "Come up to my room. I'll show you."

Running through the house, which the girls would have never done in the presence of Bernadette De Ponte, they quickly made their way to the third floor.

Out of breath, Hannah stood in front of the armoire. Reaching to the back, she pulled out two suits of clothing. "Riding habits for both of us."

Gabrielle blushed. "My mother would swoon for sure if she saw me in this." She reached for the split skirt and matching chemise. Clothing flew across Hannah's bed as the girls redressed. Running downstairs, they met Ezra at the barn.

Ezra did a double take when he saw their attire. "Yo mama knows 'bout ya wearin' dis, Miz Gabrielle?"

"Now Ezra, you know my mother is away, and what she don't know won't hurt her a bit."

"Well, I's a guessin' you's right, but see dat y'all don't be a leavin' dis here property."

"Now, Ezra, why would we do a thing like that?"

"Miz Gabrielle, is ya fergettin' you's a talkin' to ol Ezra? Ezra be a knowin' 'bout yo galavantin' ways. Done an pullt you outta a whole mudbog full o trouble, an don't you be a fergettin' it; ol Ezra ain't."

Gabrielle gave the man her brightest smile as the girls accepted the horses. Both swung their legs over the saddles, straddling the old mares.

"Heaven hep us all." Ezra covered his eyes, turning back to the barn. They heard him mumble as he walked away. "Keep em outta trouble as bes you can, Lawd up on high."

The girls laughed, digging their feet into the mares' sides. "Get up." Gabrielle clucked to the old horse without any improvement in speed.

Hannah laughed at her friend. Ezra had given them two slow horses. "He must be trying to teach us patience."

Gabrielle threw her head back, the combs slipping out of place, falling to the ground. Hannah removed her combs, stuffing them into the pocket of her riding habit. "It feels so good to be free today."

"Just wait until you see the peach orchard."

"I can't wait."

It took a while to plod their way through the woods, around a pond, and over a few rolling hills. When the orchard came into view, Hannah gasped. There before her were thousands of ripe peaches just waiting to be taken. Reaching out, she plucked the succulent fruit, savoring its sweetness. "Never had a peach that tasted so good."

"They are delicious." Gabrielle reached up, picking her own peach. Riding along in the orchard, Hannah thought she had never before visited such a delightful place. Row after row of peach trees embraced the early morning light. Dew was still on the trees, glistening in the sunlight.

"This is a beautiful place." Hannah let the old mare have her head. Gabrielle joined her in her race across the hills. The going was slow but invigorating nonetheless.

Gabrielle pointed to a group of birds nearby. "It's a family of wrens. They've made their home in the peach orchard."

"I love this place."

"You would love it even more when it's in full bloom. Pink blossoms fill the branches."

"I can only imagine. It must look like the hills are dressed in lace."

"Something like that."

After cavorting in the orchard until nearly noon, Gabrielle pointed to the land joining the right side of the peach orchard. "That's the Quantrail Plantation."

At the edge of the plantation, a large pond glistened in the sunlight, its placid waters still except for a group of ducks playfully leading their ducklings on a morning adventure. Dog fennels growing near the edge of the pond were being explored by some of the ducklings, a few becoming entangled among the mesh of stems and leaves.

Movement beyond the plants caught the girls' attention. Giggles could be heard floating across the pond. Reining their horses to the right, the girls caught sight of two colored boys, stooped low with Mason jars in hand.

Gabrielle urged the old mare forward. "What are you doing, Adam Moses and Noah Aaron?"

The boys jumped as if they'd been caught with their hands in the cookie jar. Seeing Gabrielle, the fear on their faces broke into warm smiles.

"What ya doin' yoself, Miss Gabby?" The older boy smirked, as if deliberately trying to rile her.

"Adam Moses, does your mama know you two are out here at the pond by yourselves?"

"We's a pollywog huntin', Miss Gabby. We's a tryin' ta fine da bestest pollywog what'll make fer a gran champyun in da frog races."

Noah Aaron jumped in. "We's a gonna take dem home in deez Mason jarz and a gonna grow em up real big like."

"Adam Moses, don't bypass my question. And what about you, Noah Aaron? Can you answer me?"

The boy threw his Mason jar to the ground, as if to release himself from any connection to the unchaperoned outing. He ducked his head. "Naws, mam. Mammy don't be a knowin'."

"Cain't have no fun."

"Adam Moses, how many times have you been told by your mama to stay away from the pond unless someone is with you?"

A big tear rolled down the boy's cheek. "Don't tell er, Miss Gabby."

Gabrielle's stern look relaxed. "I won't tell this time, but you boys cannot come to the pond alone."

Both boys smiled brightly. The older of the two, Adam Moses, looked to be about eight years old; his brother couldn't be more than six.

"Miss Gabby, I tells ya a secret if'n ya can keep it to yoseff." Adam Moses cut his eyes toward Hannah, distrust showing in them.

Hannah got down off her horse and extended her hand. "Howdy, Adam Moses. I'm Hannah Baxter. Pleased to meet you."

The boy noticeably relaxed. "Awright, I guess she can hear too."

Gabrielle came close, holding the horse's reins in hand.

The boy thrust his hands deep into his bib overalls. "Well, we's appose to be gettin' eggs from da cheeken pen."

"Well, why aren't you?"

"We's scaret, Miss Gabby." Noah Aaron stooped down. Picking up a stone at the water's edge, he skipped it across the pond.

"Why are you afraid?"

Noah Aaron looked at the ground. Raising and dropping his shoulders, the boy looked to his brother to continue.

Looking older than his few years, Adam Moses thrust his hands deeper into his pockets. "Deys bean a fox in da cheeken pen a thievin' from dem cheekens. Bean a gettin' all dem eggs an one o da roosters be a missin'. Mammy's powerful mad."

"Are you boys scared of a little ole fox?"

"Naw, Miss Gabby. Thang is, we ain't a be thankin' it's a fox a tall."

"Why would you say that, Adam Moses?"

"'Cause we done an seen footprints, Miss Gabby, big uns. Done an seen um taday." The boys' eyes grew larger with the telling.

"So we's jes runned away an go a huntin' pollywogs."

"Is that right, Noah Aaron?"

"Yessum, dat's right."

"All right. You boys go on back to your mama."

"Yessum."

The girls watched the children until they ducked into the barn behind the slave quarters. Gabrielle explained their situation. "The Quantrail Plantation is quite large, producing several crops. Most of the slaves stayed on as sharecroppers after the Emancipation Proclamation."

"That has happened on some of the larger Florida plantations as well."

"Mr. Quantrail is not as fair with his ex-slaves as he should be. The boys' parents, Marcus and Nettie Brown, barely get by on the meager money they earn. Nettie's chickens and eggs help the family survive. She sells them on market day at one of the town squares."

"What kind of chickens does she have?"

"Banties are her favorite. People come from all around to purchase her colorful, strutting fowl."

Hannah tried to think of a way to help Nettie. "Maybe we should try to catch the thief. Nettie needs her eggs and her chickens."

The girls mounted their horses, meandering through the edge of the peach orchard.

Gabrielle's face lit up. "Now would be the time to try to help Nettie. Mother is gone, and no one would know if we slip out tonight."

"Sounds good to me." Hannah's excitement glowed on her face. She felt a stab of warning from her conscience but pressed it down. *We must help Nettie,* she defended. *She really needs us.* That seemed to soothe her raw feelings of guilt. If someone was in need, her family had always been the first to help. Renewed excitement for this grand adventure now filled her.

Stopping to let the horses drink from a stream, Gabrielle motioned for Hannah to pull alongside. Whispering, as if someone might overhear, the girl explained. "Rumor has it that the

Underground Railroad had a stop right here at this very stream." Pointing ahead, she continued. "This stream connects to a larger one, which meanders through the back country for many miles."

Hannah's eyes grew wide, imagining slaves making their way in the dark, meeting those who would take the risk to help them to freedom. "Tell me more."

"I'll let Ezra tell you. Let's go." And with that, Gabrielle headed back to the barn with Hannah following close behind.

Ezra met the girls, as if he had been awaiting their return. Taking the horses in hand, he started into the barn.

"Ezra, tell Hannah about the Underground Railroad."

The old man's eyes lit up. Nevertheless, he looked around as if making sure no one was listening.

The girls followed Ezra into the barn, waiting patiently as he watered and fed the old mares. He picked up his currying brush and began to brush them down. "Dem was the days, Miz Hanner." His eyes took on a faraway look. "Dem was the days, fo sho. Always figgert I's gonna leave after settin' jes one mo slave on de path ta freedom. Thang is, dey was always one mo a needin' to be set on dat path." He stood still, the brush in hand, as if looking back across the years before the war.

"Dat peach orchard holds many a memry fer ol Ezra. At da back, near da stream, dere be a copse o thick maple trees, an da stream be a runnin' on out through um. Dat be where we be a havin' da slaves meet up wif us. Me an Eliza done be a leadin' em wif a lantern likes a fire by night, a leadin' um to freedom, all a dem what's come ta us fer hep."

"Tell Hannah why you never left, Ezra."

"Well, befo da war, da owner of dis here plantation, Mr. Raybern, he done an sold my boy, done an sold em." Ezra stopped, noticeably overcome with sadness. Brushing a tear from his eye, he continued. "After dat, I says ta Eliza, 'Eliza, we cain't be a leavin' now. Dey done an sold our boy, and if'n he tries ta come back, dis here be de only place he be a lookin' ta find us.' So dats why we jes stayed on here. Glory be, sho was a fine day when de artist done an bought dis place."

Hannah could barely hold the tears back. "When did he buy it, Ezra?"

"'A few years afore da war brake out. Been better fo sho. Been a share a croppin' an a makin' a better way o it."

"I'm glad, Ezra."

"I thanks de good Lawd evry day." As an afterthought, Hannah barely heard his whisper. "Sho do miss my boy."

"God can bring him back." Hannah said the words before she thought.

"Yessum, I's 'bout given up, but I's a thankin' he can still be a doin' it."

"Don't give up hope, Ezra. Keep believing. All things are possible with God."

"I knows, Miz Hanner."

The girls said good-bye, running the short distance to their rooms to clean up.

Hannah met Gabrielle in the hall, and the girls dashed down to the kitchen to find some food.

Hilda greeted them. "Ready for some turkey sandwiches, girls?"

Both girls nodded.

Sliced tomatoes and boiled eggs accompanied the sandwiches. With their palates satisfied, the girls left the kitchen, ready for an afternoon adventure.

"Let's go down to the river, Hannah."

"Should we ask Ezra to go with us, Gabrielle?"

"It'd be more fun by ourselves."

"It would, wouldn't it? Let's go."

Sneaking out the front door, the girls made their way through the beautiful flowers. Opening the iron gate, they quickly walked the short distance to the Savannah River.

Gabrielle motioned to the ships being loaded in the harbor. "Must be a good day for the cotton trade."

"Are there usually this many wagonloads being transported to the ships?"

"Not quite this many, Hannah."

The girls took a seat on a bench overlooking the river. Watching the procession of mules and horses pulling wagons loaded high with cotton, they counted 240 bales waiting to be unloaded onto the ships.

"Fire, fire!" The high-pitched scream reached the girls' ears. Turning in the direction of the yell, they saw a small colored boy running away from the wagon that was burning into a bright blaze. Keeping low, the boy hid behind a nearby oak. As the girls watched, he quickly climbed into the full branches, taking cover there.

"This happens every summer."

"Why, Gabrielle?"

"Some plantation owners offer sharecropping to their ex-slaves as a way to keep them and get their crops harvested. The slaves are to get their percentage when the cotton sells. Many are cheated and end up burning the cotton before it makes its way onto the ships."

"Who is the boy?"

"Probably a son of a sharecropper or just a child willing to burn the cotton for a few coins. We better get back before Ezra misses us. Got to plan our escapade for tonight."

Hannah could hardly contain herself. "Shouldn't we disguise ourselves, maybe find something to turn our skin black so we won't shine so bright in the moonlight?"

"That's a good idea, Hannah. We could get some soot from under Eliza's washpot. We'll have to be careful that no one sees us. We'll wait until after dark."

Hannah shivered in anticipation. "Hey, we could maybe borrow some of your father's trousers too."

Gabrielle reached out to hug Hannah as they mounted the front steps of the mansion. "What did I ever do for fun before I met you?"

Running upstairs to the De Pontes' bedroom suite, Gabrielle quickly handed her friend a pair of her father's pants and an old shirt. Before leaving the room, she retrieved two straw hats from the hat rack. "Father loves to plow the field now and then. He calls these his plowing hats. They'll do just fine."

Although they had the house to themselves, the girls ran up the second flight of stairs as if pursued by an intruder. Tossing the clothes across the window seat in Hannah's room, they collapsed on the sleigh bed.

Gabrielle laid out the plan. "We'll get all gussied up around dark. We'll wait until the moon is up to light our way. Then we'll sneak out to Eliza's washpot and rub the soot into our faces and arms."

"Maybe we should take a weapon."

"A weapon, Hannah?" Fear showed on Gabrielle's face. "What would we need a weapon for?"

"One never knows when one might have to defend oneself."

"Do you really think we will need to defend ourselves?"

"Shouldn't take unnecessary chances."

"Hannah, I think we threw that to the wind when we planned this adventure."

"Well, maybe we should take a big stick... just in case we have to use it."

The girls began looking around. Gabrielle lifted the poker from the hearth of the fireplace in the upstairs drawing room. "This should do just fine." Laughing, she wielded the poker like a sword. "Do I make a good pirate, Hannah?"

The girls continued their search. Opening the top desk drawer in the library, Gabrielle pulled a Colt revolver from her father's secretary. "This has been here since the war."

Hannah raised her hand. "I don't think we'll need a gun, Gabrielle."

"Oh, fooey, we'll take it just in case we need it."

"Well, hold that thing down, girl, and don't be touching the trigger. Wouldn't want you to be shootin' yourself in the foot."

Returning to Hannah's room, placing the revolver and poker alongside the clothes on the window seat, the girls looked out the front window, perusing the activities of the Savannah River.

The fire from the cotton bales had been extinguished, and the last ships were being loaded for the day. As they watched, the boy who had been hiding in the tree shimmied down, quickly disappearing in the nearby cargo area.

The sun began setting over the Savannah River, the large oaks nearby framing the master's artwork. "Such a beautiful sunset painted by our Father."

"Yes, 'tis a beautiful sight." Gabrielle turned pensive. "Hannah, do you suppose we should be doing this tonight?"

Hannah's eyes set in a determined look. "Now, Gabrielle, the good Lord wants us to help our neighbor."

Chuckling softly, Gabrielle answered in Ezra's vernacular. "He sho nuff do."

With the last rays of the setting sun quickly disappearing, the girls lit a lantern, making their way to the kitchen. "It may be a long night. Better have something to eat before we leave."

Hannah answered, "Sho nuff."

Rummaging around in the kitchen, the girls set out bread, strawberries, and cheese.

Hannah tasted the creamy tidbit. "This cheese is good, Gabrielle."

"Nettie makes it. Has her own cows. The boys milk them, and she makes curds and cheese to sell on market day."

"Who would buy curds?"

"Hannah, people line up for Nettie's curds. She fries them on a cast iron griddle over an open fire in the marketplace. She says many a time the sale of the curds has kept her family in suitable clothes for the winter."

Hannah raised a finger. "That's why we've got to help her tonight. Nettie really needs us."

"Yes, she does."

The girls could not stop laughing. Gabrielle finally got control of herself. "We must not giggle tonight. It will give us away if the thief comes."

"I'll bite my tongue, like Mrs. La Peau taught us to do in finishing school when we needed to appear sober."

Washing down their meager supper with a glass of apple cider, the girls raced upstairs to prepare for the evening. After they had dressed, laughing and teasing all the while, they quietly exited the house, as if the walls might shout their story at a later time.

When they opened the back door, its creaking sound nearly caused the two disguised cohorts to swoon. Pressing into the darkness, a cockatiel called nearby. The girls nearly jumped out of their skin.

Bending low, they slowly made their way behind the barn to the washpot. The moonlight barely lit their way. A twig snapped beneath Gabrielle's feet. Hannah pitched forward, tripping over the unseen branch.

Laughing and biting their tongues, the girls crept nearer the washpot. Reaching the pot, they began covering their faces and arms with the soot from the burned logs below.

Unable to recognize each other in the dim moonlight, it was all they could do to keep from laughing at the disguise they had created for themselves. Their hair stuffed under the straw hats, the girls looked like gypsies.

"Time to head out." Gabrielle picked up the revolver from the ground.

Hannah saluted her friend, reaching to retrieve the poker. As if in need of an explanation, she whispered in the moonlight, "We're just helping one of the Lord's children."

Gabrielle nodded her head. "Amen, sister."

The girls stopped dead still when a candle shone through the curtains of Ezra and Eliza's home. Dropping behind a hibiscus bush, Hannah peeked around, hoping they were not already caught.

"Who be's about?"

They dared not answer Eliza. She'd probably swoon seeing the likes of them.

An armadillo scurried past the girls, causing them to gasp. The animal ran toward the candlelight in the window. Eliza peered closely at the approaching animal. "Is you what I heared, little feller? Well, have a sho nuff good night." And with that Eliza walked away from the window, snuffing out the candle as she went.

"Whew, that was close."

"Yeah, let's hurry." Gabrielle rose, leading the way toward the back of the De Ponte property.

The walk would take a while. The girls pressed forward, the evening dew causing the soot to run from their faces to their shirts. Catching a glimpse of each other in an open spot where the moonlight beamed down, it was all they could do to keep trudging ahead.

After about a half hour, Gabrielle was almost out of breath. "Should have brought the horses."

"Too much noise. We never could have made it."

"You're right, of course."

"Of course."

The girls paused for a moment to laugh at themselves.

Gabrielle grabbed Hannah's hand. "Let's go."

With renewed vigor, the girls moved quickly through the peach orchard, following the outside row. Passing the pond, Gabrielle stopped, pointing in the distance. Hannah could barely make out a wooden structure. She nodded her head, and the girls sat behind a huge oak tree, beginning their vigil of Nettie's hen house.

Sitting in the shadow of the old oak tree, the girls were a scary sight. Dressed in Jacques De Ponte's clothing, with soot running down their faces and arms, Hannah thought they would have scared any intruder—fox or human.

All the excitement leading up to the evening adventure had kept the girls vibrant. Sitting beneath the tree, still and sleepy, they began nodding off.

A flutter of chicken wings and a wild round of clucking roused the girls from their sluggish repose. Reaching for the poker, lying on the ground at her feet, Hannah arose, ready for action.

Gabrielle jumped up, pulling the Colt from her front pocket. She was having trouble removing it. Once removed, she pointed it in front of her. The loud report of the gun broke the silence of the dark moonlit night.

Hannah just about jumped out of her sooty skin. "Heavens to Betsy, Gabrielle, put that thing down. You're gonna get us killed."

"Shh . . . "

"You just shot the gun, and you're trying to get me to be quiet?"

"Shh . . . " Gabrielle pointed to the silhouette of a man crawling out of the hen house with his hands raised.

Hannah covered her mouth. "Oh no, what do we do with him now that we've caught him?"

The gun was shaking in Gabrielle's hand. "I . . . I . . . I don't rightly know."

The man continued walking toward them. "Hold it right there, mister." Hannah spoke in the deepest voice she could muster.

Stepping out into the open, the girls continued toward the man who had now stopped. All of a sudden, he collapsed in laughter, rolling on the ground.

The girls moved closer, Gabrielle's hand shaking even worse. Hannah figured she needed some help. Raising the poker high over her head, she remembered the mucking shovel as it connected to her head at the livery stable. Shutting her eyes against the thought, she paused when the man spoke.

"Y'alls jes two girls. Why I ain't a gonna be caught by da likes o y'all."

"You are already caught, mister. Don't try nothing stupid. You're going to see the sheriff. Get those hands in the air." Hannah's voice was commanding.

The man seemed to be weighing his decision. "I's wif da Klan. Ain't no likes a y'all gonna harm me."

"You ain't with the Klan, big man. Tell that to someone else. You're a colored man; ain't no colored part of the Klan." Although Gabrielle's hand still shook, she sounded ominous. With the gun pointing at the man's chest, he must have had second thoughts.

Hannah moved close, whispering in her friend's ear. "What do we do with him now?"

At that very moment, Ezra came riding out of the peach orchard, his rifle cocked and aimed at the group of three near the chicken pen. "What be a happnin'? Somebody better be a givin' me da right ainser."

The girls kept the gun aimed and the poker raised. Hannah turned toward Ezra. "We've caught us a chicken thief, Ezra. This man is stealing Nettie's banties."

"Dat you, Miz Hanner?" Ezra moved his gun in the direction of the biggest man. "Sho don't look like ya, Miz Hanner." Peering through the darkness, Ezra brought his horse up behind the group.

"Ezra, it's us. We've come to do the Lord's work in helping Nettie."

"Don't be a blamin' dis on da Lawd, Miz Gabrielle. I'll be a dealin' wif you a lil later, girls. Big boy, you a comin' wif me."

The chicken thief was slowly edging toward the trees. "Nope, ain't a goin' nowheres but home."

"I know who you is. You be dat caintankrous William Crews from de Cotton Exchange. You be a loadin' da wagons what's headin' fo da ships a deepartin' round da world."

The man turned. "Ain't so. Don't know no William Crews."

"You's on da wanted poster. You's wanted fer stealin' in Two Mules Junction, done an stole Mr. Totem's cheekens."

"Ain't so. I be's a leavin' now." William struck a trail behind the chicken pen. Five seconds later, Ezra's gun went off, followed by another gunshot.

"Gabrielle, don't be shooting that thing again. You'll surely kill us all before the night's over."

"It wasn't me, Hannah."

Before Hannah could ask who shot the second time, a man stepped out from behind an outbuilding. "Evening, Ezra. Been a listenin' since ya got chere. Jes bidin' my time til ya needed some hep."

Gabrielle whispered to Hannah. "That's Marcus Brown, Nettie's husband."

Although unscathed, William Crews fell to the ground, pleading. "Please, I's a beggin' ya, let ole William go, an I never be a settin' foot after Nettie's banties again."

Marcus Brown was a big man, towering a foot above William. Stepping inside the outbuilding, he brought out a rope.

"Nawsir, nawsir, don't be needin' a lynchin', sir."

"Ain't gonna be no lynchin'. You's goin' to da sheriff tied up jes right. We's deliverin' a present to da law."

The men tied his hands, his feet, and then joined them together. "Laced up likes a bird ready fer da cookin' Thanksgivin' morn."

Marcus Brown seemed quite pleased with their work. "I'll take em from here, Ezra. Won't be needin' no hep. Sho do preciate all y'all did." Marcus Brown chuckled at the sight of the girls covered in wet soot and men's clothing. "Sho is a sight." Shaking his head, he went to retrieve his wagon for the delivery to the sheriff's office.

A woman with a slight build stepped out from the shadows of the outbuilding. "Did ya catch that fox? Did ya, Marcus?"

"We caught da fox, Miz Nettie, but he be lots bigger an we done an thought." Ezra pointed to the trussed-up thief.

"Heaven ferbid, Ezra." The little woman covered her mouth at the sight. "I'm a guessin' that be a mighty big fox fer sho."

Gabrielle stepped close to Nettie. "Miss Nettie, meet my friend, Hannah Baxter."

Hannah followed Gabrielle's lead. But Nettie just stood there, peering into their faces. "Sounds like Miss Gabby, but sho don't be a lookin' like Miss Gabby." The woman stepped closer. "Well I'll be… well I'll be… Why, Miss Gabby, don't ya be a knowin' what ya maw a gonna do if'n she fines you lookin' like dat?" Grabbing Gabrielle, she wrapped her in a tight embrace. "Now, Miss Gabby, I'm sure dis be yo doin'."

"Miss Nettie, I can only take half the credit. My friend here helped with every detail, and then Ezra saved us from ourselves."

Nettie stepped closer to Hannah, offering her hand. "Welcomes to Savanny, Miss Hanner. I'm sho I won't know ya by mornin', but if you's a friend of Miss Gabby's, you's a friend of mine."

"I'm glad to meet you, Miss Nettie."

Marcus rounded the corner with the buggy, ready to load up his trussed bird.

"We be a seein' ya, Marcus. Sho ya don't be needin' no hep?"

"Ezra, I can hannel this here bird wif my hans tied hine my back." Hauling the thief into the back of the buggy, he looked at the girls. "Borry two horses fer da girls, Ezra. Dey done enuff fer da night, much less a walkin' all dat way back to da house."

"I thanks ya, Marcus. I'll brang um back on da morrow."

The girls rode bareback on the horses loaned by Marcus Brown. Ezra led the way back to his house in silence.

Reaching the barn, the girls dismounted, wishing to return to the house without a confrontation.

"Don't be so soon ta take yo leave. Jes go have a seat in Eliza's kitchen. We'll get ya both some hot tea."

Gabrielle shook her head. "We can make some at our house, Ezra. Don't trouble Eliza."

"Ain't no trouble. She be a waitin'."

The girls made their way into the kitchen, dreading the talk that was bound to come from Ezra and Eliza.

After her initial gasp at the girls' appearance, Eliza did not pry but busied herself making tea and slicing bread. She was just retrieving a jar of peach marmalade when Ezra came in the door.

Quietly sipping tea, the girls left the telling to Ezra. The man schooled his features, trying to look stern but failing miserably. "Now girls, I know you 'bout fully growed up. But ya cain't be a takin' matters o da law into ya own hands."

The girls stared into their tea, hugging the cups tightly.

"Can ya even thank what yo mama an papa would do if'n they'd a knowed what ya be a doin' dis here night?"

Neither girl raised their eyes from scrutinizing their teacups. They both shook their heads in response.

"Now I cain't have yas in danger. Yous couldda been kilt. I needs to extrack a promise that y'all won't do dis no mo."

Both girls took one hand from their cup, placing it in their lap, below the table. Hannah crossed her fingers. It was a childish thing to do, but the habit from her childhood was hard to break. When she didn't want to tell a lie, she crossed her fingers. Looking at Gabrielle, they shared a knowing grin. Her friend must be doing the same thing.

Smiling, the girls raised their heads. Looking slightly ashamed, they both nodded.

This seemed to satisfy Ezra. Bursting into laughter, he explained the story to Eliza.

"Eliza, ya shouldda seen dese two girls. Dey put many a man ta shame, a shootin' a gun an raisin' a poker at da thief."

"Do tell?"

The girls joined in the telling. "We were just doing the Lord's work."

Gabrielle added her two cents' worth. "Poor Nettie, the thief was taking her chicken eggs, and she needs them to support her family. It just wasn't right."

"An y'all set yoselfs as judge an jewry ta fix dat problem."

"Yes, mam, we did." Hannah was proud.

"We better get y'all cleaned up." Eliza went for the soap.

An hour later, dressed in Eliza's house dresses, the girls left Jacques De Ponte's clothing behind for Eliza to wash.

"I'll get da soot outta Mr. Jacques clothes, don't ya worry yoselfs none."

"Thank you, Eliza."

The girls ran into the house and upstairs. "I'm glad my parents aren't here." Gabrielle placed the gun in the top desk drawer of the secretary. Hannah replaced the poker on the fireplace hearth.

Gabrielle grabbed her friend's hand. "All is well that ends well."

However, by the end of the week, the story was in the *Savannah News.* Gabrielle read aloud. "'Mr. Marcus Brown, of the Quantrail Plantation, brought in William Crews, notable chicken thief of Savannah and the surrounding areas.'" Her eyes quickly scanned the article. "No mention of our names."

"Thanks be to the Lord. Now, Gabrielle, you better hide that newspaper. Heaven forbid if your parents were to read the article and question us."

"Good idea, Hannah. Don't know that I could keep a straight face, and I know Ezra and Eliza won't lie about the incident."

"Hide it in the bottom of my trunk." Hannah went to open the large wooden chest.

Placing the newspaper safely inside, Gabrielle wiped her brow. "Mother would swoon for sure if she knew what we did."

The girls ran down the stairs to the kitchen, laughing all the way. A knock at the back door interrupted their evening rummage for a snack.

Gabrielle opened the door. "Come on in, Ezra."

"Eliza tole me ta brang you girls some o her fresh-bake cookies."

"Thanks, Ezra. We were just looking for something to nibble on."

"I needs ta talk ta you bofe."

Ezra looked serious. The girls became sober, as well. "Marcus Brown done an says days a storey in da newspaper 'bout dat cheeken thief."

Gabrielle nodded. "Yes, Ezra, we read it."

"Well, he brangs me a part o da reeward moneys an says fer me ta be a sharin' it with bofe of y'all."

"Ezra, I don't know about Gabrielle, but I want you to give my share to Nettie."

"Mine too, Ezra. It'll help her buy some more banties."

The man looked quite pleased. "If'n ya be sure, dat's what ole Ezra be a doin'."

"We're sure." They both smiled at their friend as he took his leave.

Finishing their cookies, the girls ran back upstairs. Breathing a sigh of relief, they looked out over the Savannah River from Hannah's room.

Hannah was in a playful mood. "How about a game of charades?"

"Sounds like fun to me, Hannah."

The girls acted out, entertaining each other with dramatic reenactments from stories they were familiar with. They laughed until their sides hurt, Eliza's dresses adding to the silliness of the evening.

Gabrielle fell across Hannah's bed. "I've had all the fun I can take for one night."

"Me too." Hannah joined her friend.

When things quieted down and Gabrielle went to her room, Hannah remembered Ezra's telling of helping the slaves escape on the Underground Railroad. *That would make a wonderful sketch.*

In her mind's eye, Hannah could see the shadows in the woods, cast by a faint sliver of a moon overhead. She could hear the slaves, walking along the stream, quiet as field mice during harvest. The smell of the stream bed and the swamp filled her senses.

Removing her sketchpad from the desk drawer, she sketched as if going back in time and carrying the knapsack of a slave. She felt the intensity of the fear of the small band of captives, moving forward into the unknown, desperately hoping that their efforts would gain them freedom. The mud oozing over her feet impeded the progress, making her feel anxious.

Putting herself in the slaves' place, she sketched the group as they saw Ezra's faint, flickering light from a lantern far away. This was their only sign. It was quickly extinguished, full darkness claiming the landscape, except for the moonlight. Cypress knees stood ominously in the swamp, silently bearing witness to the fugitives' escape.

Hannah sketched Ezra helping the group into an awaiting boat and the boat disappearing into the darkness. A screeching hawk flew overhead, spreading the message of the slaves' whereabouts. Fear closed in on her, making it hard to breathe. Shadowing her sketch meticulously, Hannah drew back, happy with the depiction.

Flipping back through the pages, Hannah stared into the face of Wendell Cunningham rowing the boat. Touching his face, she prayed. "Please keep Wendell Cunningham safe, Father."

Placing her sketchpad in its drawer, she quickly dressed for bed. The sketch of the circuit rider refused to leave her mind as sleep claimed her tired body.

Chapter 19

The July heat was intense, beating down on Wendell's back as he made his way over rough terrain. Crossing a stream, he decided to stop. Letting his horse drink deeply, the circuit rider knelt beside the brook. Cupping his hands, he brought the water to his face, enjoying the cool refreshment.

"You from aroun' these here parts, mister?"

Wendell looked up to see a scruffy-looking man peering down at him. The man had soundlessly appeared behind him.

"No, sir, I'm just passing through."

"Well, ya'd do good ta pass on through without stoppin'. There's a charge fer usin' this here water."

"A charge for using the water, sir?"

The man spat a dark stream of tobacco. "That's what I said, don't recollect stutterin' none."

"I'll be moving on. Never heard of charging for water."

"I'll be a takin' a dollar afore you be leavin', mister." A menacing look crossed the man's face as he spat another stream of tobacco. The cock of a gun pulled from its sheath assured that he meant what he said.

Retrieving one of the few dollars he had been given as an offering for his revival, Wendell handed it to the man. "This money is God's money, mister. If you can hold up a preacher and take the money provided by the heavenly Father, then go in peace. But you will answer to God one day for your actions."

Taking the money, at the mention of God, the man dropped it as if he had touched a hot coal. "Ain't that jes the luck, a holdin' up a preacher man. Ain't got me no biznezz with no preacher man." The man ran away, leaving the dollar on the ground.

Wendell smiled to himself, retrieving the money. "Thank you, Father." He looked into the wide expanse of the sky.

Mounting up, he spurred the horse on. He had been on the trail for two weeks, preaching at churches north of Charleston. By next week, he wished to visit the parson in Virginia. He would speak for him on a Sunday and begin his circuit back to Savannah to make plans for the camp meeting.

The De Pontes would arrive home in a few days. Jacques De Ponte had left a note for Hannah, instructing her to sketch as many scenes as possible, using the shadow and light techniques they had been perfecting.

Sitting on a seat of soft hay in the barn, Hannah peered through the slats of the stall holding Wendell's stallion. The leg was healed, thanks to the fine care of Ezra and Eliza.

The young girl visited the stallion daily, developing a warm relationship. Sweet carrots from Eliza's garden had been just the trick, coaxing the spirited horse to the door of the stall.

"You's sketchin', Miz Hanner?" Ezra's voice stilled her pencil.

"Yes, Ezra. I'm sketching the stallion in the shadows of the barn. The sunlight peeking in from the door adds just enough brilliance."

"Good, Miz Hanner." Ezra went to the last stall, and, throwing a few scoops of sweet feed in the trough, he situated his wooden milking stool and pail beside the cow.

"All right, Miz Daisy, give ol Ezra a full bucket o milk." The cow mooed her response.

Rising from the hay, Hannah brushed her calico dress off, heading back to the milking stall. Flipping the page, she began sketching the man and the cow.

By the time Hannah had finished, Ezra set the milk inside the kitchen, returning to the garden to gather some vegetables.

"I'll help, Ezra."

"All right, Miz Hanner."

Hannah began filling a basket with summer squash, eggplant, pole beans, and ripe tomatoes. Ezra was busy cutting pod after pod of okra. As he worked, he spoke of the old days.

"Time was, Miz Hanner, we's had a whole passel o slaves a workin' in dem fields out back a here. Why, we's workin' from afore dawn to pas' dark a pickin' cotton."

"That was a tough job, wasn't it, Ezra?"

"Yes, Miz Hanner, was tough. Fondess memry ol Ezra has was my boy a pullin' a croaker sack behind him, a pickin' cotton longside his pa. Sho did make me mighty proud." Ezra paused in his cutting of the okra, wiping a tear from his eye.

"I'm sorry, Ezra."

"De good Lawd be a bearin' ol Ezra's burdens, Miz Hanner."

"That's right, Ezra, and don't forget it. He can still bring your son back. I'm believing with you."

"Thanks ya, Miz Hanner." The man seemed to get his second wind. "Anyhows, I member dem women, my Eliza a bein' one o dem, dey be a fillin' a basket wif da cotton an carryin' it atop dey head." He laughed at the remembrance. "We's called 'em cottonheads."

"Cottonheads?"

"Yes, Miz Hanner. Dem was da days. We's didn't haf much, but we's a sangin' to the good Lawd all da whilst we's a workin' in da field."

Slowly, quietly, Hannah set her basket of vegetables down on the ground. Retrieving her sketchpad from the satchel nearby, she began sketching the scene Ezra was painting with his words.

The scene came to life on the page. Men and women alike bent over cotton plants, pulling the white fluff from the bushes. Women, heads topped with full baskets, made their way to the mule-drawn wagon, depositing their loads. Little children dragging croaker sacks behind them dotted the fields.

Hannah sketched women singing, their eyes raised to the heavens as they worked the large field. A young boy had dropped his croaker sack at his feet and was doing a dance behind his mother.

The young girl was lost in her musings. Ezra's voice came to her ears on a sad note. Hannah quickly turned the page, inspired to do yet another sketch.

"Yes, Miz Hanner, ole Mr. Raybern, he be a bad master. When we's a finishin' up a pickin' dat cotton, he be a countin' da wagon loads. He always be a sayin' we gots ta pick mo cotton."

Hannah dreaded what might happen next.

"He be a brangin' out his whip. I's member feelin' dat whip, cause I's appose ta be da leader."

"He beat you, Ezra?" Hannah cringed at the thought.

Ezra nodded his head, still cutting okra. "Yessum, sho nuff. But da werstest part was him a beatin' da womenfolk what been a workin' hard through da livelong day."

"What did you do, Ezra?"

"We jes learnt ta work harder da nex day and da nex. It weren't many days we didn't feel da whip."

Hannah's pencil flew across the page, the look of fear showing in the women crouching behind the wagon, knowing they would be the next to receive the master's wrath. Young children hid behind their mothers' skirts, as if to avoid being seen. The girl added ominous clouds shadowing the sky, lending to the atmosphere of the fearful depiction.

"Well, I's thanks ya fer a heppin' wif da veggie tables. Ol Ezra be a seein' ya on da morrow. Say, let ol Ezra be a lookin' at yo sketchin'."

Quickly finishing the sketch, Hannah offered Ezra a look.

"Um huh, Miz Hanner. Dat be jes about da way it was hea. Only thang missin' be my boy's dawg." Pausing he scratched his head, a distant look in his eyes. "Yeah, ain't thought 'bout that little black dawg fer many a moon. Name was Scallywag, cause o all da trouble he gots into." Ezra's smile told of his fondness. Scallywag would be added to the sketch depicting Ezra's son.

Hannah waved good-bye to her dear friend. She moved to the front of the house, wishing to sit in the garden and draw a beautiful scene to remove the former sketches from her memory.

Her pencil now made beautiful lines on the page, bringing to life a young suitor coming to call on his lady friend. Seated on a bench in the garden, the lady hid her face behind a fan. The suitor leaned toward the girl, as if whispering an endearment in her ear.

The garden flowers lent their charm to the sketch, as did the old oak trees framing the area.

Gabrielle's voice startled Hannah. "That looks like you and the preacher who stays with Ezra."

Hannah looked closely, surprised at the correctness of Gabrielle's statement. "I didn't set out for it to be this way."

"You look like you are having a wonderful time in the garden. Maybe it can be so."

"Oh how I wish." Hannah whispered the words aloud, then covered her mouth with her hand.

"I saw your sketch of the preacher in the boat, Hannah. It's obvious you have a connection with him."

"Well, yes I do, Gabrielle, but he thinks I have another suitor."

"Do you?"

"No. I was carried away by a young law student who wooed me over the Christmas holiday. He wanted to be my suitor."

"Well, what happened?"

"He apparently was a suitor to many girls."

"A real lady's man, huh?"

"Yes, a man for all the ladies."

"Oh no, Hannah. I'm sorry."

"It's all right. I'm glad I found out before I lost my heart to him."

Putting the finishing touches on the sketch, Hannah closed the pad, tucking it away in her satchel.

"My parents will be coming home tomorrow."

"I've got plenty of new sketches to show your father."

"That's great. Miss Mary Telfair will be holding an art exhibition on her lawn at the Telfair mansion soon. I'm sure Father will wish to take your sketches there."

"Oh no, not really, Gabrielle?"

"Yes, really, Hannah. People from Savannah and the surrounding areas come to the lawn party to peruse the art exhibits. It will be quite interesting. Father always sells several oil paintings there."

"I can understand that, but I'm just a simple sketch artist."

"Not from what my father says. He says you do the best sketching he has ever seen in an apprentice."

"He really says that about me?"

"Yes, Hanner." Gabrielle crossed her eyes.

Wendell Cunningham traversed the low area, staying away from the mountains of Virginia as best he could. His stallion would have taken the challenge of climbing in stride, even enjoying the test of his endurance. The sorrel he rode was timid; he was doing his best to keep the horse on comfortable ground.

Going the long way around the mountain, the preacher was relieved when the pastor's cottage finally came into view. Tossing his hat in the air, he stopped at the well to refresh himself before stepping up on the porch of the minister's home.

Looking in the distance, the mountains seem to spring up in the pastor's backyard. The beauty of the distant hills filled his soul with gladness.

"Well hello, Wendell Cunningham. How on earth are ya?"

Wendell wiped the water from his chin. "Just admiring the hills, Parson." Walking over, he shook the man's hand.

"Shore will be good to hear you preach. Been needing some encouragement, son. Kind of gets lonely out here."

"Still having problems in your congregation, Pastor?"

"Sorry to say that I am. Them sheep herders been fighting mighty bad with the cattlemen. Can't seem to find no middle ground."

"I'm right sorry about that. We'll see what the good Lord can do about it."

"I'm hopin' for a breakthrough, Wendell. Shore do need the good Lord's help. Been carryin' the burden far too long."

"Well, Parson, we're not supposed be carrying them burdens; supposed to be casting them all on him."

"I know, son. I guess sometimes we forget and need to be reminded."

The parson opened his door wide, the smell of coffee greeting the younger man as they made their way to the kitchen.

"Why hello there, Wendell. Sure is good to see you." The parson's wife wiped her hands on her apron, extending one to shake her guest's hand. The woman looked as worn out as her husband.

"Good to see you, mam."

"Now sit down and have a bowl of mutton stew."

Wendell pulled out a rickety wooden chair from the table. "Thank you, mam."

After asking the blessing, the parson's face broke into a grin. "One good thing comes from the fuedin'."

"What's that?"

The parson pointed to the stew tureen. "The sheepherders keep us with plenty of mutton, and the cattlemen keep us in beef. There's plenty of meat on our table."

Wendell reached for the bowl of stew the parson's wife was handing him. "The Lord will provide, Parson."

"Yeah, Wendell, it seems as if they try to outdo each other, both sides vying for our favor."

The circuit rider shook his head, taking a large bite of a soft roll covered in creamy butter. "Don't even realize the Lord doesn't have favorites, do they, Parson?"

"No, I reckon they think the good Lord can be persuaded to see their side."

"Yes, and all the time, he's just wanting them to get along."

The parson's wife reached for Wendell's bowl, refilling it. "Maybe the good Lord sent you our way to help us, Preacher."

"That just may be."

The stew hit the right spot to satisfy Wendell's hunger. Showing him to his room, the parson said good night.

The young preacher sat by candlelight at the crude desk in the back room. Long into the night, he searched the Scriptures. "Love thy neighbor as thyself" would be his main theme. He would also expound on living a life of peace.

Closing his Bible, Wendell Cunningham eased himself down on the mattress filled with straw. His long legs hung off the end of the bed.

"Thank you, God, for friends and an opportunity to share your Word. Father, don't let the nightmares come tonight." The words barely escaped the young preacher's lips before he fell asleep.

The invitation to Miss Mary Telfair's Art Exhibition and Lawn Party came as expected. Jacques De Ponte brought the invitation into the art studio to show Hannah.

"Miss Hannah, we will be exhibiting your sketches. How are you coming on making the necessary improvements I have pointed out?"

"I'm finished, sir; that is, if they meet with your approval."

Taking the sketches from her satchel, Hannah placed them along the drawing table for the artist's consideration.

"Very good; very good, indeed." Jacques De Ponte seemed well pleased with all of the slavery scenes. Stopping at the sketch of Wendell in the rowboat, he pointed to his right shoulder. "Now this could use a bit more shadowing. Notice the position of the sun; it would be falling less on the right shoulder."

Shadowing more, Hannah turned to the artist. "How is this?"

"Just a bit more. You've almost captured the light to perfection."

Adding the last stroke for shadowing, Hannah stood back to get the full effect. Pleased, she looked to the artist.

"Perfect, my dear." Jacques De Ponte gathered all the sketches. "I shall have Joshua Greenleaf see to their proper framing. You are finished, Miss Hannah. We shall attend the exhibition on Saturday."

Hannah breathed a sigh of relief, smiling as she exited the room. She had completed her assignments, and her instructor was pleased. What more could she ask for? And to have her work exhibited . . . she felt like jumping for joy. She could hardly wait the three days until the exhibition.

Saturday dawned bright and beautiful. "Such a wonderful day, dahlings, for the art exhibition." Bernadette De Ponte was in her element, the long feathers of her flamboyant hat reaching high into the air.

Gabrielle smiled at Hannah behind her mother's back. "The French accent is extremely heavy today."

"What is heavy today, dahling?"

"Oh, uh, breakfast is heavy . . . eggs, bacon, grits . . . it's a heavy breakfast, Mother."

"You could have eaten a sweet roll, tut, tut."

Finishing their breakfast, Gabrielle and Hannah ran out to the family carriage. Situating their skirts just so, they both tilted their noses in the air, making light of Bernadette's high and mighty attitude.

"We will visit the mansion today, dahlings. It was built in 1819. Miss Telfair's father was governor of the state in the 1700s. The Telfairs were a very affluent family." Bernadette was in high spirits.

Traveling down the road in the carriage, Bernadette had instructions for the girls. "Now, dahlings, be sure to keep your parasols up against the sun. Wouldn't want to harm the skin." The girls shared a grin, as the feathers of her hat touched the roof of the carriage.

"Yes, Mother." Hannah could tell Gabrielle was fighting to keep from laughing. In doing so, her face became very sober.

"No pouting, dearie, and be on your best behaviour."

"Mother, I am not twelve."

Bernadette gave her daughter a scathing look. "That would be hard to prove, dahling."

Remembering their escapade to catch the chicken thief, a broad smile made its way across Hannah's face.

The carriage rolled past several of the town squares, stopping in front of St. James Square.

All of a sudden, Bernadette was quite flustered. People were milling around on the lawn of the mansion. "Here we are, dahlings. Can you believe it?" Bernadette stepped out, pulling her husband along at a rapid pace. She nearly tripped in her haste to join the crowd perusing the artwork.

From their seats in the carriage, the girls could hear Bernadette prattling. "Hurry along, Jacques. We might miss something. Please, dahling, can't you go any faster?"

Hannah and Gabrielle alighted, joining Ezra in laughter. Raising their parasols against the sun, they stepped onto the lawn, as far away from Mrs. Bernadette as possible.

"My, what beautiful drawings." Turning to look, the girls saw a prominent-looking man touching the frame of one of Hannah's slavery sketches. Peering close at the signature, his eyes held a question. "And who is the artist?"

Before Hannah could answer, Gabrielle stepped closer to the gentleman. "Mr. Rozier, I would like you to meet the sketch artist, Miss Hannah Baxter. She is a student at my father's school of art."

Hannah extended her hand.

"Pleased to meet you, mam. Are these sketches available for purchase?"

Hannah was taken aback by the question. "Well, uh . . . "

Gabrielle took over. "Yes, Mr. Rozier, they are available."

Hannah looked at her friend, who stared back. When Mr. Rozier stepped closer, perusing the sketch of the master whipping the slave, Gabrielle put her hand to her face, turning ever so slightly. "The exhibition is for selling your artwork, if you're lucky enough to find a buyer."

Realization dawned on the girl from the small town of Laurel City.

"Mr. Rozier is a top official for the city of Savannah."

Hannah's eyes grew large as she realized the magnitude of this man's attention.

The man turned, giving her his full attention. "I would like to display your sketches as part of the history of the city of Savannah, my dear. Never have I seen finer depictions of days gone by."

Hannah courtsied. "Thank you, sir." Out of the corner of her eye, she saw Bernadette De Ponte approaching.

"Oh, Mr. Rozier, sir, how nice to see you." Bernadette extended her hand, bent at the wrist and held in a most sophisticated manner.

"Mam." Mr. Rozier nodded, taking the proffered hand, then returning to his perusal of Hannah's sketches.

"Are you interested in our student's sketches, Mr. Rozier?"

Irritation showing on his distinguished face, the man responded, "Yes, mam." He turned, continuing his inspection.

Bernadette was not to be denied the glory of the prints being somehow connected to her. "They are quite lovely, aren't they, sir? And from such a novice artist, nonetheless."

"Mother." Gabrielle's one word was silenced by a sharp look from her pretentious parent.

"And as I was saying, sir ..."

Mr. Rozier's words stopped her in midsentence. "Yes, mam, they are quite lovely; one would never guess they were the work of a novice."

Bernadette looked as if she had been reprimanded.

Turning back to Hannah, Mr. Rozier smiled broadly. "We will see to having these sketches placed on the walls of city hall, my dear. However, they will be left in place for the remainder of the exhibition. Others may only wish they could take possession." He stood back, crossing his hands over the cane he held, and nodding at the collection.

"Thank you, sir." Again Hannah curtsied, deeply honored and humbled by the prominent man's praise.

Bernadette was preening as if the sketches were her own work. Hannah could hear her nearby, telling the news that Mr. Rozier had set his sights on purchasing them.

Gabrielle pulled her along. "Pay no mind to Mother, Hannah. You should be proud. Father knew your work was impressive."

"Thank you, Gabrielle."

"You're welcome."

"Where, where is she?" An elderly lady sitting on a sofa on the porch was looking around, her eyes making contact with Hannah after someone pointed her out. "Come here, my dear."

The refined lady motioned Hannah to sit beside her. "So you are the sketch artist, my dear?"

"Yes, mam."

"How lovely you are. What beautiful green eyes. And your name is Miss Hannah Baxter?"

"Yes, mam."

Reaching for Hannah's hand, she squeezed it. Hannah could feel genuine appreciation exuding from the lady.

"I am Miss Mary Telfair, the coordinator of this event."

Hannah's breath caught in her throat. "I'm so glad to meet you, Miss Telfair."

"I should say the same, my dear. I have an appreciation for beauty, and your sketches have captured my heart. The depictions of slave life will grace our city's halls, telling our history as words alone could never portray." She was so excited she squeezed Hannah's hand once again.

"Thank you, mam. You are kind."

"I am captivated by the sketches of the man in the rowboat. I believe I met the gentleman at last year's camp meeting. Could that be so?"

"Yes, mam, he's a circuit-riding preacher."

"Wendell Cunningham, I believe?"

"Yes, mam."

Turning her head to the side, surreptitiously, Mary Telfair asked a shocking question. "Your garden sketch, my dear, was that of you and the preacher?"

Hannah didn't know how to respond. "You could surmise that."

"I thought so, dear. I will purchase the rowboat and the garden sketches." A blush blossomed on the elderly lady's cheeks.

Hannah patted her hand. "Must be a romantic at heart, mam."

"Yes, dear, and I never married in all these years." She looked wistful, but promptly schooled her features.

Bernadette was standing nearby. Miss Telfair spoke in hushed tones. "I understand you are studying under Mr. Jacques De Ponte."

"Yes, mam."

Looking at Bernadette, she whispered, "Heaven help you with that one, dear."

Hannah laughed aloud, covering her mouth when the object of their attention sashayed onto the porch.

"Dear Miss Telfair, how nice of you to host this beautiful lawn party and exhibition."

"Thank you, Mrs. De Ponte."

Bernadette curtsied, her French accent heavier than Hannah had previously heard. However, Miss Telfair appeared to have already dismissed Mrs. Bernadette De Ponte.

She left the porch, walking over to a nearby lady flaunting large jewels. "Mrs. Damon, my dear, have you heard the news? Our own art student's sketches are being purchased by the city of Savannah."

"How nice, Mrs. De Ponte." Mrs. Damon looked genuinely impressed.

Mary Telfair continued her conversation with Hannah. "Never could stand pretense, Miss Hannah. Just be who you are."

The two shared a chuckle.

"Now tell me, dear, where did you learn to draw in such a fascinating manner?"

The young art student enjoyed sharing Miss Telfair's company. The afternoon passed with Hannah being introduced to some of Savannah's upper echelon. Wendell's stallion print was sold to the owner of a large plantation. Hannah was commissioned to sketch stallions of four of Savannah's elite families.

Back at the De Ponte mansion, Hannah sat down at the desk to share all the good news with her family. "I would have never dreamed that my sketches would grace city hall," she wrote. Sharing every detail of the fine afternoon she had spent sipping punch and carrying a parasol, Hannah acquainted her family with every person she had met on Miss Telfair's lawn in St. James Square.

The young artist curled up in her bed, glad for the wonderful day she had enjoyed and the new friends she had made. When she reflected on all of her prints being sold, she whispered a prayer, thankful she had thought to make two of each. Nothing would be missing in her collection.

Chapter 20

Laurel Oaks bustled with August activity. Calves were being branded, horses readied for the group of men coming from Miami, Florida, to look at the purebred beauties.

"Slick 'em down, boys." The head cowboy gave orders to Blaine and Blythe, who were busy with the currying brush. "The men'll be here tomorrow." Patting a buckskin mare on her rump, he moved forward to trim her front feet. "Gotta have 'em lookin' top notch. Word has it these here horses are bound fer Cuba with a load o' cattle them Miami cowpunchers are readyin' fer shipment."

"Sure do hate to lose these horses."

"You always say that when Father sells a batch, Blaine."

"Yeah, but these are right special, done got 'em tame as rabbits."

"You always say that too." Blythe brushed the mane of a fine black stallion.

Blaine looked uncomfortable. Wishing to change the conversation, he turned to the head cowboy. "Hey, did ya hear the news about my sister?"

"Which one?"

"Hannah."

The cowboy shook his head, resting his arms on the barn stall. "Don't reckon I did, Blaine."

"She's done an got her sketches bought by the city hall of Savannah."

A low whistle drifted across the barn. "Do tell. Now ain't that somethin'? I betcha yore mama and papa's done prouder'n a struttin' peacock."

"Yeah, you could say that." Smiling, Blaine turned away, his eyes suddenly dancing with mischief.

"What are you plannin' now, Blaine? I know that look, and somebody's gonna be gettin' the brunt end of yore tricks."

"Now, Brother, why would you think that?"

Blythe shook his head, waiting to hear his brother's plans.

"I's jes thinkin'." A cocky grin split Blaine's face.

"Yeah, and that's enough to scare anybody half outta their wits."

"Aw, Blythe, I'm jes gonna have a little bit o fun. Gonna try to cinch that love match between Hannah and Isaac."

"Now, Blaine, you leave Hannah's love life to her. I never did trust Isaac."

"Me neither, but I'm gonna make him sorry he cain't have her."

"How's that?"

Blaine grinned wickedly. "You'll see, Brother. We'll go into town today. Mother needs some ginger from Paxton's store."

Quickly washing up, the boys bade their mother farewell, riding into town bareback.

"What are you going to do, Blaine?"

"We'll go look at the hats in Mrs. Eaton's store. Isaac should be there."

Pulling up in front of the store, the boys ran up the steps. The overhead bell announced their arrival.

"He's here." Blaine pointed to the back of the store. "That girl's with him."

"Hello, boys. What can I help you with?" It was Isabel Benson acting as if she owned the millinery shop.

"Oh, we's jes lookin' at summer hats. Wonderin' if you's runnin' a special."

Isabel looked at Blaine as if he had two heads.

Blaine must have felt the need to explain. "Just feelin' mighty neighborly taday. If'n ya had a hat cheap enough, we's gonna surprise Widder Grouch with a present."

Isaac came from the back, amusement showing on his face. "Now why would you be so generous to your enemy, Blaine?"

"The Good Book says to do good to yore enemies."

Blythe took up the conversation. "Well, do you have any hats at a good price?"

Blaine jumped in, ready with the bait he had prepared for Isaac. Looking rather nonchalant, he casually mentioned the real reason he had entered the hat store. "You do know that my sister is real famous now, don't you, Isaac?"

Isaac's attention was immediately captivated. "Isabel, dear, could you check out back and see if the kittens need to be fed?"

"I just fed them this morning, Isaac."

"Well, feed them again."

As soon as the back door closed, Isaac Eaton sidled up to Blaine. "And how is your sister famous, Blaine?"

Grinning, Blaine continued. "You shore you haven't already heard?"

"No, Blaine, now what is it?"

"Well, she's so good at drawing that the city of Savannah has bought her sketches."

"Whatever for?"

"Said they like her drawings of the days of slavery. Gonna hang um in city hall."

Isaac rubbed his chin. "Is that so? You ain't lying to me, are you, Blaine?"

"If I'm a lyin', I'm a dyin'. Had a daughter of a governor buyin' her sketches too."

"Blythe?" Isaac looked to the truthful twin to affirm his brother's story.

"He's tellin' the truth this time, Isaac."

Isaac pulled his trousers up, although they were already in place. The boys heard him whisper as they turned to leave Mrs. Eaton's shop. "Sure changes things. Would be mighty good for my vocation."

Just as the twins were walking down the steps, Isaac ran to the door. "Hey, boys, where exactly is your sister located in Savannah?"

Blaine's eyes twinkled; his information had administered the desired effect. "Well, now let's see, Isaac… " He paused, tapping his forehead. "Oh yeah, it's the De Ponte Plantation; it's right across from the Savannah River."

The boys mounted their horses, Blaine taking off down the road at the speed of lightning.

"Hey, Blaine, don't forget the ginger for Mother."

Blaine's stallion slid to a stop as he turned the horse around. "Well, I'm glad you's thinking for the both of us, Blythe. I's jes thinkin' about how Isaac's gonna go after our sister."

"Hannah won't be none too happy with you, Blaine."

Throwing back his head, Blaine laughed as they pulled up in front of the general store. "I know she won't be happy, but I'd give a purty penny to see ole Isaac beggin' for her hand in marriage so's she can sketch his court scenes."

"You ortta be ashamed, Blaine."

"Ortta, but ain't."

Throwing the reins of their horses over the hitching post, the boys dashed inside Paxton's General Store.

Ordering the ginger, Blaine took a few coins out of his pocket to pay Mr. Paxton.

"Come 'ere, boys." It was old Mr. Rivers yelling from beside the pot-belly stove. "Come on an rest yore haunches."

Blaine was anxious to feed the grapevine, and Blythe obligingly followed.

"How's that youngess sister o yore'n?"

"She's all right, I reckon. Ain't seen her in a while." Blaine was fueling the gossip fire in Mr. River's bones.

"Well, cain't say as that's a bad thang, boys. I heared that Hanner done an got sent away to Savanny to one o' them thar schools fer the infirm, a seein' how's she got addled when that Abram done an hit her in the head with the muckin' shovel." The old man chomped down on nothing, smacking his lips and shaking his head as if it was a real pity.

Blaine chuckled, adding more fuel to the fire. "Well she's a drawin' up in Savanny. Leastwise she can do that." His alligator vernacular always worsened in Mr. River's company.

Blythe kicked his brother's shoe, which only won him a glare.

"Yeah, I done an heared yore parents are a sayin' she's at a faincy art school, but I know the truth. Done an seen that girl a runnin' 'bout in yonder field like she's jes a babe. Her sister done an chased her down; she's plum addle-brain. 'Tis a shame, fer shore."

"Guess it is at that. But you don't be a sayin' I said it, Mr. Rivers, ya hear? Would brang a powerful shame on the famly."

"I can see that, boy. Don't you worry none. I'll keep yore secret safe right chere within these here walls."

"Thank you, Mr. Rivers. Yore a good friend." Blaine stood, shaking the old man's hand.

Blythe stepped up, shaking the old man's hand, as well. "Good-bye, Mr. Rivers."

"Good-bye, boy. Now you don't haveta be shamed a yore sister. It happens in the best a famlies."

Blythe shook his head. "I'm mighty proud of my sister, Mr. Rivers. She's a famous artist."

"Shore she is, sonny. Now you jes keep a believin' that." Mr. Rivers sounded like a parson. He reached up, patting Blythe on the back.

A young couple nearby was looking at the cast-iron cookware.

"Come here, younguns. Sit right chere." The boys heard Mr. Rivers lower his voice as they pushed the door open. "Ya'll knowed Hanner Baxter afore she got tetched?"

Blaine laughed aloud as they mounted the horses, leaving the town behind. "It's been quite a profitable day, Blythe."

"Aw, Blaine. That ain't funny."

"Shore nuff is. I'll race you home." And the race to Laurel Oaks was on.

Wendell Cunningham carefully chose his path, leaving the mountains of Virginia behind. Traversing the wooded hills, breathing deeply of the sweet smell of summer, the circuit rider felt renewed.

Looking around, he took in all the wonders of God's world. The mountains hugged the man without a home, as if saying he belonged to the maker of the universe. That was comforting to the traveler who knew loneliness as a constant companion. More and more, Wendell yearned to settle down.

His heart lurched at the thought of Hannah Baxter. "Where is she now, Father?" The wind in the trees blew a soft melody across his soul, a melody with no words and no answer to his question.

Paying close attention to the hill he was now descending, Wendell spoke his prayer aloud. "Father, the maker of the universe, it is but a small thing for you to fill my loneliness with companionship. Oh what I would give to have the love of Hannah Baxter."

The preacher's mind transversed time, going back to the meadow budding with wildflowers. The beautiful girl seated on the spring grass floated across his mind until he realized he had descended the heights and was now on level ground.

Darkness settled around the preacher, darkness that matched his lonely soul. "If I can't have Hannah, maybe you'll provide another girl for me, Father." Although he felt no one could ever measure up to the Baxter girl, the loneliness engulfed him, threatening to choke the very life out of him. "If only she was not being courted by Isaac, I might stand a chance. I'm sure he will never let her go. He's a man of means. He can provide for her so much better than I could."

Tossing all these ideas around and saying them aloud made the prospect of ever courting Miss Hannah seem very dim. "Your will, Father." Lighting a campfire, the preacher made a cup of trail coffee, sitting back to stare into the night sky. "Yes, Lord, your will be done. I have nothing to offer a fine girl."

The remembrance of Isaac possessively escorting Hannah out of the chapel sent a fresh pain through Wendell's heart. Falling asleep on the hard ground, he had a fitful night filled with Granny chasing him once again. He awoke in the morning, relieved to see the sun peeking over the horizon.

Several more days on the trail brought Wendell Cunningham to the outskirts of Two Mules Junction. Noticing a ruckus up ahead, he spurred the horse on.

In front of the Watering Trough Saloon, a group of women gathered, hymn books in hand. Pausing in front of the building, the preacher watched the temperance group.

"Miz Totem, you be a leadin' us."

"I'd be glad to, Margaret. Now sees ta how y'all keep up with the echo on this song." The stout lady cleared her throat. "Hmmm…" She was getting her key.

Mrs. Totem gave Wendell a stern look, bellowing out the song in a voice that was almost bass. The women surrounding her, their hair pulled back in tight buns, looked down their noses at the man watching from his horse.

Must think I'm about to enter the saloon. Guess I do look a little rough from the trail. Sure glad the good Lord don't judge on the outward. Wendell turned his head, hiding his smile. The song caused him to jerk his head forward, listening to the words of the singers.

> "Ain't a no sin a gonna be up thar"
> "Amen"
> "Ain't a no sin a gonna be up thar"
> "Amen"
> "It's a gonna be a sad day
> When yore soul be laid
> In the cold, dark grave below"
> "Beeellooww"
> "Tho whiskey be thou God"
> "Thou God"

"On earth whar thou doest trod"
"Doest trod"
"God'll send you away
On that great judgement day
Ta burn forevermore"
"Evermore"

Wendell sat in the saddle transfixed. He had seen groups from the temperance movement in several of the towns he had ridden through. It never ceased to amaze him that their message was always bad. *And the Word of God is supposed to be the good news.*

The singing had stopped, and the lady leading the group was making her way toward him as fast as her large girth would allow. She peered up into his eyes, accusingly. "You a drankin' man, mister?"

"No, mam."

"Well, mister, ya be in the wrong place. This here is no place to be a hangin' aroun."

Wendell crossed his hands over the saddle horn, looking into the woman's pinched face. "That so, mam? What would you be doing here then?"

"We're a doin' the Lord's work, mister. Callin' the unrighteous to repent afore that dreadful day of the Lawd comes and shuts in on them like a trap." The lady slapped her hands together so hard it made both Wendell and the horse jump.

"Well, mam, I do believe there is a better way. Afterall, the Good Book says that it is by the goodness of the Lord that men come to repentance."

"I ain't never read that. Don't know what kinda Bible you been reading. We gotta warn the sinner of his ways." Mrs. Totem started pounding her fist into her hand.

Wendell began easing his horse backward. The lady could prove quite dangerous. Her face was turning purple. *If this lady was selling religion, I don't think I'd be buying, much less the poor sinner.*

Tying the horse to the hitching post at the mercantile, the preacher heard the woman yelling. "Elijah Totem, I see you a sneakin' in the back door. Get yore good-fer-nothin' hide out here right now, er I'm a comin' in after ya."

A scrawny little man walked out the front door of the saloon. Grabbing him by the shoulders, the large woman pushed him along the boardwalk in front of her. The group of singing ladies followed her, their noses raised high in the air.

A man on the front porch of the mercantile laughed, taking a puff from his pipe. "Jest another day in the life of the Totems. Keeps this town entertained."

Looking around, Wendell noticed people peering out of windows in the businesses nearby. He went inside to buy some cheese and crackers for supper.

A stooped-over man was standing at the counter, feebly reaching into his pocket for a coin to pay for his sack of coffee. Picking up his cane, he pointed across the street to the saloon. "John B, did ya get a look at the Totems' live play taday?"

John B looked over the spectacles riding low on his nose, handing the old man his change. "No, I's too busy, jes heard that scruffy singin' of those meddlin' women." He shook his head in disgust.

The old man tapped his cane on the floor. "That sangin' does play bad on the ears, but I reckon as how watchin' the Totems be good fer bizness."

The clerk smiled from behind the counter. "Reckon it is good fer bizness. People come from all around to see the show."

"Sorry ya missed it John B." The old man shuffled out of the store.

Looking up, the clerk smiled at Wendell Cunningham. "I'm shore I didn't miss nothin' what won't happen nex time. Ol Elijah comes in here twice a week with his butchered cheekens. Goes to the saloon evry time."

"Is that so?"

"Yes, sir, I'm afeared it is. What can I hep you with?"

"Slice me off a chunk of that cheese, please, sir." Wendell pointed to the big wheel of cheese standing atop a barrel nearby. Reaching for some crackers, he laid them on the counter, pulling out some coins.

Walking out of the store, Wendell sat on the front porch, rocking in the chair next to the man with the pipe. "We'll be having a camp meeting at the mouth of the Savannah River at the end of September. Sure do wish you would join us."

Squinting, the man looked out of the corner of his eye at Wendell. "You a man a the cloth?"

Wendell nodded, biting off a piece of cheese and crunching on a cracker.

"I'd a never a guessed it. Guess you don't be looking … uh … "

Wendell finished his sentence. "Don't look dignified enough?"

"Pious … that's the word … You jes look, well … jes ordnary, I reckon. Don't be seemin' like there be a mean bone in yore body."

"The Lord Jesus was not pious, sir. He was a servant to all. And his anger was not stirred by the sinner, but by those religious leaders who thought they were better than others."

"Why, preacher, I ain't never heared no man a the cloth talk like that. I jes might come an hear ya. Jes might … "

Wendell stood to leave. "We'd be mighty glad to have you. Nice sitting with you, sharing such a fine evening." Shaking the man's hand, Wendell descended the porch steps.

Just as he mounted the horse, the man called from the porch. "Oh, and preacher, you'll be shore ta have them tempernce women thar." He hung his head and laughed aloud.

Smiling, Wendell waved to the man, who was rocking and puffing on his pipe.

The circuit rider would bed down in the woods in Two Mules Junction. Tomorrow he would make his way into Savannah and meet with the presbytery to discuss plans for the camp meeting.

Finding a spot in the woods, Wendell made camp. Placing a blanket on the ground, he started a fire and slowly drank his coffee.

As the last rays of the setting sun filtered through the trees overhead, an owl called out, announcing the end of day. The lonely sound reminded Wendell that he too was alone with no one to share his life.

Thoughts of Hannah filled his mind, bringing joy. He remembered her sketching the revival scenes, bent over her sketchpad intently. His memories of her had helped him make it through many rough times. The joy they shared made him feel whole, as if there was a purpose for his existence.

Sleeping under the trees, pillowing his head on the cold, hard saddle, Wendell wished for a home to call his own. But more than that, he wished for the sweet companionship mirrored in the eyes of his friends, Ethan and Elizabeth Dodson.

Easing into slumber, he dreamed of a girl with brown, sun-kissed tresses blowing in the wind. He stared deep into her green eyes, finding solace there.

Chapter 21

Hannah Baxter had taken many more lessons from Jacques De Ponte in preparation for drawing the stallions commissioned at Miss Telfair's lawn party. Ezra had kindly taken her to the various locations around Savannah to complete the task of observing and sketching each magnificent horse.

This morning, standing in the studio with the light poring in the large windows, she took a step back as the artist critiqued her work one last time.

"Just one additional fine line of shading, curving along the flank, and this will be perfect, my dear." The artist pointed to the final area for correction.

Perusing the other sketches proudly standing on their easels, Jacques De Ponte nodded his head in approval. "I couldn't have shown more personality exuding from each horse myself."

Hannah was stunned at this praise from such an acclaimed artist. She was nearly speechless, trying to form a response. "Why . . . why, thank you, sir."

"'Tis a pleasure having you for a student, dear." And with that, the artist made his way to the door of the studio. "Make the minor correction, and we will deliver these prints this morning."

Hannah was ecstatic. Jacques De Ponte, artiste extraordinaire, would be accompanying her to deliver her sketches. As soon as the door closed behind him, she jumped up and down, barely able to contain her excitement long enough to make the final correction on the sketch.

Seated inside the carriage, Hannah and the artist waved good-bye to Gabrielle. Ezra clucked the horses into a fine trot as they made their way into the countryside. It was near the end of August. Although the sun was shining brightly, the cover of the carriage and the breeze blowing off the Savannah River made traveling tolerable. Hannah's excitement chased away any thoughts of the summer heat.

Pulling up in front of the Meriweathers' antebellum home, the artists were received by the butler. "Right this way." Ushering them into a magnificent parlor, the man swept out of the room, his coat tails crisply swishing, matching his purposeful stride.

Comfortably seated in the parlor, with Ezra waiting outside, Hannah's excitement could not be kept at bay. "I hope they'll be pleased with the sketch, Mr. De Ponte."

"They would have to be blind not to be pleased, my dear." Reaching over, the artist patted his student's hand.

Mr. and Mrs. Meriweather promptly appeared at the parlor door. The artist and his protégé stood. Stepping forward, Mr. Meriweather extended his hand, his wife following suit. "So glad you could come. Aren't we excited, my dear?"

Jacques De Ponte placed the covered sketch on the easel he had brought. With great pomp, he reached forward, slowly removing the soft cloth covering. "And now, Mr. and Mrs. Meriweather, I present you with your commissioned sketch." And with that, the artist fully removed the covering.

Mrs. Meriweather gasped. "And to think, our own dear Lucifer posed for his own drawing." She moved to the other side of the room, taking in the full effect. "It looks as if dear Lucifer will come tearing right out of the sketch at any moment." Endearment showing in her eyes, she wiped away the mist with a lace handkerchief.

Suddenly she turned to Hannah. "Oh my, you are a dear, sweet girl to capture our Lucifer's pompous attitude on paper. Looks as if he rules the world." Opening her arms wide, the lady squeezed Hannah.

Hannah well remembered the days she had spent in the lavish barn, sketching *dear* Lucifer. The horse had kicked three wooden slats from his pen.

"George." The lady glared at her husband.

He wore a blank look. "Yes, dear?"

"George ... " The lady nodded toward Hannah.

"Oh, yes, dear." Reaching into his front pocket, the man removed a roll of bills fastened with a gold clip. Casually removing a few, he tried placing them in Hannah's hand.

"Oh, no, sir, you've already paid." Hannah hid her hands behind her back.

"Nonsense, my dear. We paid not nearly enough. This will be ... shall we say ... a gratuity for a job well done." The man forced the money into Hannah's hand.

"Why, thank you, sir."

"You will be long remembered, dearie, in this household. And just might be that Lucifer will pose for another sketching in the future." Mrs. Meriweather's face beamed her approval.

Leaving the plantation behind, Hannah was relieved the first stop on their route had met with approval.

"That be's what use ta be da Mulberry Grove Plantation, Miz Hanner." Ezra was pointing to a large area of land along the Savannah River. A steamboat belched its way through the water, behind a stand of mulberry and oak trees.

Jacques De Ponte looked out the window of the carriage. "It really is a shame, Miss Hannah."

"I don't see much of anything. What happened?"

The artist shook his head before answering. "It was a beautiful place, Mulberry Grove. Named for the mulberry trees cultivated for producing silk in early colonial days, these grounds were home to many slaves. In later years, the state of Georgia gave this place to Nathaniel Greene for his military service during the Revolutionary War."

"It must have been a very old plantation."

"One of the oldest along the Savannah River. It has other historical significance. Nathaniel's widow, Catharine Greene, hired Eli Whitney to tutor her children here when the teaching job he had secured in Savannah turned out to pay only half of the promised wage."

"Eli Whitney, inventor of the cotton gin?"

Jacques De Ponte grinned. "Yes, Miss Hannah, while he was living at Mulberry Grove, he designed the machine that would separate the seed from the cotton. Would you like to guess how he was inspired?"

"I can't imagine."

"He is said to have been inspired after watching a cat trying to pull a chicken through the fence. Only some of the feathers came through with the poor creature; thus the inspiration." Mr. De Ponte paused, noticing Hannah's look of unbelief.

Jacques De Ponte looked out the window at the uncultivated land, land now untended, overgrown with weeds. "There's not a sliver of the plantation's magnificence left." Shaking his head, he continued. "You've heard of Sherman's March to the Sea?"

"Yes." Fear almost choked Hannah. Looking out on the desolate land, her heart melted, thinking of the wonderful place that had been in the path of the general.

"General Sherman burned his way from Atlanta on his fiery march. This once beautiful plantation was an object of his wrath—the mansion and all remembrances of historical moments are gone, save for in the memory of those who knew this wonderful place."

"Did anyone think to sketch it?"

"Yes, Hannah, there are a few sketches. We can thank the good Lord for that. We can also thank the Lord that our dear city of Savannah was spared."

Hannah shuddered. "I can't bear to think of the beauty that would have been destroyed at the general's hand."

"Sherman, seeing the beauty of our city, sent a telegram to President Lincoln on Christmas Day 1865, offering him Savannah as a Christmas present." The artist wiped his brow. Hannah believed it was more than the heat of the day that prompted his gesture.

Just before leaving the plantation behind, Hannah noticed a partial wooden fence from long ago, covered with pink and white foxglove blossoms, which seemed a lasting testament to the former glory of the place. The flowers and the remaining railing spoke of perseverance and beauty still thriving long after all hope was seemingly lost.

Quiet covered the carriage like a heavy quilt. Both of the occupants were lost in their own thoughts as Ezra turned down a side road, heading toward their next stop to deliver Hannah's artwork.

Thinking of what might have been on the plantation, had it survived Sherman's wrath, Hannah could imagine the grounds planted with thriving crops by the river. She pulled herself from the dark thoughts as she felt the carriage turning.

The artist broke the silence. "I'm sure the Gladstons will be happy with your work. Your sketch of their stallion is my personal favorite. The pose is depicted in excellence."

"Why thank you, sir."

Once again Hannah was met with a kind reception and extreme approval. The other sketches were received as graciously as the first, the proud owners insisting upon placing extra money in her hand.

Hannah came home with a bundle of cash to add to the commissioned money she had stored in her trunk. Just as she had finished stowing her funds, Gabrielle burst into her room. Hannah smiled at her friend, thinking they would settle in for a nice chat.

"Hannah, oh, Hannah, you won't believe it. You've got to get freshened up."

"For what, Gabrielle? What is happening? Are we entertaining dinner guests?"

"Oh no, Hannah. *We're* not entertaining anyone; you are."

"What do you mean?"

Gabrielle produced a calling card. Her eyes took on a dreamy look. "A fine-looking gentleman left this for you."

Hannah's mind went immediately to Wendell. Then she remembered Wendell was nowhere around. Feeling disappointed, she looked down at the calling card. "Isaac Eaton, at your pleasure. I will call for you in the front garden at dusk."

Gabrielle watched, obviously anticipating Hannah's words. "He's absolutely gorgeous, Hannah."

Hannah's hands went to her hips, her eyes taking on a menacing look that Gabrielle had never seen. "So he is meeting me in the garden, huh? Well, I'll meet him all right."

Gabrielle looked puzzled. "You don't want to meet him?"

"Gabrielle, let me fill you in. This is the young man that is responsible for me getting hit in the head with the mucking shovel."

"Oh no." The young girl put her hand to her mouth. Hannah had told her about this man but had failed to mention his name. "How dare he come here?"

"Yes, how dare he?"

It didn't take Gabrielle long to come up with a plan. "Why don't we fix him up real good, Hannah?"

Hannah's eyes lit up at her friend's suggestion. "What do you have in mind?"

"Why not meet him in the garden, be ever so sweet, even take some of Mother's Cadbury chocolates to share, and hear him out. Obviously he wants something from you, if he is the user that you say he is."

"And then what?"

"Well, the garden bench is right below your window. When you point up to the window, I could pour a bucket of water on his head at just the right moment."

"Oh, Gabrielle, I only had half as much fun before I met you. That's a grand idea. I'm sure I'll know when he needs a good soaking."

"Yes, and you could play along and let him think he's pulling you into his plans, and then we'll fix him up for sure."

"Well, if he is supposed to be here at dusk, we'll have to hurry with supper. We will need plenty of time to get me all gussied up for this divine, romantic evening."

Gabrielle's eyes danced with the same mischief playing in Hannah's. She hugged her friend. "I can't wait."

Descending the stairs to the kitchen, the girls were served by Hilda and Phoebe. "Yo mama an papa says dey gone out fer de evenin'. Be back afore midnight."

"All right, Hilda." Gabrielle winked at Hannah. Their plan would be even more fun with no parents around to intrude. Finishing the meal, the girls ran upstairs to Hannah's room.

Wendell took the route through the orchards, making his way into Savannah. A few peaches were still hanging on the trees. The owner had previously offered his fruit to the preacher. Stopping to partake of the sweet treat, Wendell let the horse wander nearby.

Three peaches later, wiping his lips, the preacher mounted the horse. He was ready to meet the area ministers and finalize the plans for the camp meeting.

A breeze coming off the Savannah River made the ride quite pleasurable. Urging the horse along, the circuit rider made his way to the pastor's house on the south side of town. The group would meet in the parlor.

"Howdy, howdy, Revern Cunninham." The country pastor grabbed Wendell in a bear hug.

"Good to see you, Reverend." The staunch minister from the wealthy, elite church on the rich side of Savannah extended his hand and, with a curt nod of his head, dismissed Wendell.

Several other pastors gathered around, men who counted on the circuit rider's visits to this area. Each had different doctrines, all with a common goal to serve the Lord Jesus.

Wendell was expected to address his fellow ministers. "I'm looking forward to the camp meeting next month. It is an honor that you have chosen me to minister each night."

"Jes wouldn't be right with nobody else."

"Thank you, Pastor Hunter."

A well-educated minister had a suggestion. "I do believe it would be in our best interest to hold down the noise this year."

Several others nodded their heads. "We've been told there's an uprising against this meetin'. Gonna haf to wear our guns again this year." The country preacher looked concerned.

"I understand trying to keep down trouble, and there will always be resistance to the Lord's work, but I believe God will help us in this endeavor. We should not make it known that we are armed."

"I agree, Brother Cunningham. That is only using wisdom."

"Yes, I believe jes what y'all are a sayin'. But we do need to be mighty watchful 'cause I got it from a good source that the Klan ain't none too happy 'bout coloreds comin' to the meetin's."

"Well, who is happy about the coloreds coming? Maybe we should send them away if they show up." This was from the pastor of the Church of the Frozen Chosen. The town had given the church its facetious name because of their lack of Christian warmth.

Wendell knew things could get out of hand real quick. Many in the South harbored ill will toward the freed slaves. "Brethren, I'll go back to the Word of God. 'Be kindly affectioned one toward another.'" And with that, the talk of banning the ex-slaves from the meetings halted.

Sharing supper with the ministers, the final plans were in place. Camp meeting would begin the last day of September. The air would be cooler and the mosquitoes less by that time.

Making his way to the De Ponte Plantation, Wendell's thoughts were filled with plans for the meetings by the river. His heart warmed, thinking of those who would receive salvation. "Lord, give me the messages you would have for your people."

Turning down the road near the river, the preacher anticipated seeing Ezra and Eliza Perkins. He would spend a few days with his friends. The clip clop of the horse's hooves soothed his mind. Soft rays of the sun filtered through the magnificent oaks standing guard around the front lawn of the De Ponte Plantation.

Wendell's attention was caught by a young girl standing in the third-story window. Squinting his eyes, he thought it must be the daughter of the artist.

Dropping his gaze to the garden below, his heart picked up its beat. "I cannot believe my eyes." There before him, in the early evening light sat the most beautiful sight he had seen since leaving Laurel City. Urging the horse toward the gate, he suddenly pulled back on the reins. "It cannot be. This is Savannah. It cannot be… Can it be?" It looked like Hannah sitting on the garden bench below the window where the artist's daughter stood.

Deciding anything was possible with God, Wendell remembered Hannah's artistic abilities and the fact that the De Ponte Plantation was indeed home to the artiste Jacques De Ponte. His heart quickened. He gave the horse its head, rushing toward the gate. Fumbling, he tried to open it, but the latch would not move beneath his nervous hands.

"Miss Hannah… Miss Hannah Baxter… "

The loud whistle of the steamboat on the Savannah River drowned his words. Peering through the iron bars of the gate, he got a clearer view of the girl on the bench. *This is indeed my Hannah, I'm sure of it.*

Jerking the gate open, Wendell mounted the horse and began flying toward the beautiful girl surrounded by flowers. Just as he opened his mouth to call out to her, his words froze. Pulling back on the reins of the horse, he stopped the animal's progress before it reached halfway down the drive. Dismounting and moving stealthily toward the hedge that separated him from the garden, he peered through the flowered branches.

It was indeed Hannah. His heart almost stopped beating as disappointment flooded the preacher's soul. "No, God, no. Don't let it be so."

There before his beloved Hannah, on bended knee in the garden, was none other than Isaac Eaton. Beside her on the bench, a huge bouquet of crimson roses stood in a vase, a gift from her suitor. Wendell could see the man's winsome face covered in a happy smile of confidence.

Hannah's soft laugh came to his ears, the most beautiful melody in the world. He watched painfully as she picked up a chocolate from a box, placing it in Isaac's waiting mouth. The young preacher's stomach lurched.

Wendell did not know how long he had paused, watching the garden scene play out. He quietly stepped away from the hedge, mounting the horse he had left on the other side of the drive. His last glimpse was of Isaac holding out a small box for Hannah's inspection and the huge smile covering her face. He couldn't bear watching the romancing of the only girl his heart longed for.

Tears sprang to his eyes. Pausing to get a hold on his emotions, Wendell quietly made his way past the house of comfort behind the large De Ponte mansion.

"She's too far above me, Lord. I guess this is your way of showing me." The sad man put the borrowed sorrel in the barn stall, joining his own stallion in the next. Sitting against the wooden slats, he sobbed, letting his sorrow run down his face in streams of tears.

The door of the barn creaked open, a light shining in the dark confines of the barn. *How long have I been here?* It was very dark.

"Who's in da barn?" Ezra held the lantern overhead, a club held in his other hand.

Wendell grinned at the sight. "It's just me, Ezra."

"Wendell, that you?"

"Yes, Ezra." Wendell stood to his feet, brushing the hay from his trousers.

One look at the preacher in the lantern's light, and Ezra's eyes took on a very concerned look. "What's a matter, son? You's been cryin'."

Wendell shook his head. Ezra grabbed his arm, walking with him into the comfort of Eliza's kitchen.

"Good evenin', Wendell." Eliza came to wrap the preacher in a comforting hug. "Somethin' be wrong, son?"

Wendell nodded his head, sitting down at the table. "Pardon me, please."

"It don't be no matter, what with you a cryin', son. Cryin' be good fer da soul. Jes let it all out." Eliza patted her guest's hand.

He looked up at them through his tears. "Is Miss Hannah Baxter an art student here?"

"Yes, Wendell, an she foun the sketch you lef behind."

The young man shook his head. "She was out in the garden with her suitor from Laurel City. He was giving her a ring."

"Aw naw, Wendell, I's a thankin' yore mis taken. Miz Hanner shorely don't be havin' no suitor. She sound real fond o you."

"Eliza, she does have a suitor. He is Isaac Eaton, and he just gave her a ring."

Eliza placed her hands on her hips. "Well, if he's here den dey musta mended fences."

"I reckon so. He is here." Wendell held his head in his hands.

Eliza shook her head and brought hot tea to Wendell. Small talk was made about the camp meeting, and everyone went to bed, sharing the sadness of the young guest in the back room.

Hannah came running up the stairs, laughing all the way to her room. Gabrielle met her at the door. "We pulled the wool over his eyes, didn't we?" Grabbing Hannah in a hug, they danced in circles like two little girls sharing a delightful secret.

"I'd give all my money from the commissioned sketches to see the look on Isaac's face again when you poured the water over his head."

"Was he proposing? I saw the ring box."

"Yes, can you believe he would have the audacity to propose to me after all the problems he has caused? I'd say we gave him what he deserved."

"We sure did!" Gabrielle plopped down on the bed. "Tell me all about it."

"He told me that Blaine had informed him of my fame as a sketch artist and how the city of Savannah had purchased my drawings. I know he just wants me because of my talent."

"What did he say after you pointed up and I dumped the water on him?"

"Actually, he started cursing and calling me addle-brained. I'd say we got the last laugh."

"I'd say." Gabrielle grabbed Hannah's hand and ran to the window. Isaac Eaton was nowhere in sight.

The girls talked, laughing and celebrating their successful prank until late into the night. Gabrielle tiptoed to her room after hearing her parents coming in downstairs.

Chapter 22

The next morning, feeling the need to connect with Wendell Cunningham, Hannah made her way to Eliza's garden. A few carrots were still available. Picking them from the ground, she wiped off the dirt, heading toward Ezra's barn. Making her way to Wendell's stallion's stall, she stopped short, seeing the sorrel nearby.

Hurriedly she continued on toward the stallion, but the door was open. The stall was empty. "Oh no." Panic beat a steady drum in her heart. Had the horse been stolen? Surely Wendell had not come back in the night only to leave before she had a chance to see him.

Running to the front of the old house, Hannah found Ezra sitting on a bench, sharpening a knife with a stone. He wore a sad look. "Ezra, Ezra … the stallion, he's gone." Her words tumbled out. Ezra continued sharpening the knife. "Ezra?"

"Yessum, Miz Hanner. The preacher done an be gone."

"What do you mean, Ezra? What … how … when?" Hannah could feel the air going out of her.

"Well now, Miz Hanner. You be knowin' how fond I am of ya an all. But now, Miz Hanner, ya shouldna be a playin' wif a man's heart, specially a good man's heart, Miz Hanner."

"What do you mean, Ezra? I'm not playing with anyone's heart."

"But ain't cha, Miz Hanner?" Ezra looked disappointed with her.

She threw her hand in the air, shaking her head. "Ezra, just come out and say it. Don't beat around the bush. What do you think I have done?"

"It ain't what I thanks, Miz Hanner. It be what da preacher done an tole me."

"What?" Confusion reigned in her mind.

Ezra looked up, his brow cocked and his eyes boring into hers. "Miz Hanner, was dat you in da garden lass night a feedin' dem Cadbury chocolates o Miz Bernadette into da mouth o dat suitor what come a callin'?"

A puzzled look crossed Hannah's face, followed by a blush. She covered a chuckle.

"Ain't no laughin' matter, Miz Hanner. Dat preacher done an loss his heart to ya."

Seeing the seriousness of the situation, Hannah put her head down, biting her bottom lip.

"Didn't dat suitor give ya a rang, Miz Hanner, lass night on dis front lawn?" Ezra paused his sharpening of the knife, pointing the object to the front of the De Ponte home.

She shook her head. "Ezra, oh dear Ezra. What a mistake I have made. It seems in trying to teach an old suitor a lesson, I have lost the man of my dreams. How can I fix it, Ezra?"

Now it was Ezra's turn to look confused. "Miz Hanner, ol Ezra can't fix everythin' what broke."

"I think you can." She rewarded him with a smile.

"What you meanin', Miz Hanner?"

"Where exactly did the preacher go? You see, this is all a mistake. I was visited by an unwanted suitor from Laurel City. Thinking to teach him a lesson, Gabrielle and I planned a romantic evening for him that would end with sweet revenge."

"Sounds cornfusing, jes like da two o ya girls."

"Well, just as he proposed, I pointed above the garden bench to my bedroom window. That was the signal for Gabrielle to drench him with a bucket of water." Collapsing at the old man's feet in laughter, Hannah looked up, finding Eliza.

Eliza joined Hannah and Ezra in laughing. "How we gonna fix what ya done an messed up, Miz Hanner?"

"We'll have to find a way. Where is the preacher, Ezra?"

"He done an gone; couldn't bear ta look on da love scene no mo, he says." Ezra's eyes still reproached Hannah.

Eliza shook her head in dismay. "We's jes gots ta pray 'im back, Miz Hanner. Won't be here 'til late September ta get ready fer da meetin' by da river."

Hannah's heart plummeted. "How can I wait so long to see him?"

"I guess you be a blamin' yoself fer dis one, Miz Hanner." Ezra nodded with a knowing smile.

"I guess so, Ezra."

Wendell couldn't get Hannah out of his mind. Looking down the long road ahead, he was making his way back to Rosewood. "Lord, just take her from my mind. I can't bear this burden."

The parson at Rosewood was indisposed and had sent a missive to the Savannah Post Office requesting Wendell's services. It would prove to be a good diversion from his present situation. He could have spent a few days in Savannah before leaving, but staying with Ezra and Eliza would have been unbearable with Hannah nearby. He was glad for an excuse to leave the city behind, at least until the camp meeting. "Heal my heart, Lord."

Wendell Cunningham made a quick trip of traveling to Rosewood. His stallion's leg had healed, and the horse was champing at the bit. Reaching the Florida countryside, he allowed his horse to run free.

The delightful strides of the horse allowed horse and rider to reach the parsonage in Rosewood in record time. Arriving just before noon, less than a week after leaving Savannah, Wendell knocked on the door.

"Well, howdy, Wendell. Come right on in and bring your saddlebags. Put um in the back room."

Making his way into the kitchen, after depositing his bags, Wendell joined the minister at his table. "How are you feeling, Parson?"

"Not so good, son. Sure was hopin' you'd get here in time."

"In time for what?" Wendell looked at the pale man seated before him. His hand trembled, pouring his guest a cup of coffee.

"Wendell, I can't be long fer this world. I got one foot here and one foot there, and I'm ready ta go."

"Oh, now, Parson, you've got more work to do for the Lord right here in Rosewood. Why, you're doing a mighty fine job."

The parson shook his head. "A younger man could do much better, Wendell. I'm asking ya to take this church. You don't have to answer right away, but I believe I heard from God on this one."

The young circuit rider was honored and humbled by the man's offer. *Can this be the Lord's doing? I've been wanting to settle down, stay in one place.* Not knowing how to answer, Wendell nodded his head. "I'll think about it. When do you need to know, Parson?"

"Well, I'd like you to stay here 'til you have to leave; preach to the people, get the feel of the congregation. At the end of your stay, I'd like to know what your answer is and when you can take over."

Once again, Wendell just nodded. "I'll think this over and pray. We'll see what the Lord thinks about the situation."

"Wouldn't have it no other way, son."

Wendell settled in, preaching each service, mixing with the congregation and getting to know them.

"You've got a right nice group of people here, Parson." The two were sharing an evening meal of rabbit stew and corn pone, furnished by one of the parishioners.

"They sure do like you, Wendell. There's new excitement in the church, just with you being here."

The young preacher had felt that excitement. "One member of your congregation is from Laurel City; I met him there."

"Yes, Matthew Madison. Took a job with the railroad depot, checkin' bags and sellin' tickets. Says he's tired of butcherin' hogs and wanted to do something else with his life."

"Says he's gonna get married at Christmas and bring his wife here. His wife to be is my beloved's best friend."

The parson seemed puzzled. "Your beloved's best friend?"

Wendell's slip of the tongue was unintentional. "I guess I shouldn't have said that."

"Why, son?"

"The young lady I love has another suitor."

A grin split the old minister's face. "Fight for her, son. 'All's fair in love and war,' they say."

"Yes, Parson, they say. But I'm afraid it's a little more complicated than that."

"I'm here if you want to share your burden."

"Well, sir, I've been wanting to settle down. I sure was hoping to win the heart of Miss Hannah Baxter."

The pastor perked up. "Is she the daughter of Garrett Baxter?"

"Yes, sir."

"Mighty fine people, the Baxters."

"I agree. Only problem is that I saw her suitor from Laurel City giving her a ring in Savannah where she is attending art school."

Shaking his head, the parson looked at Wendell with pity. "We'll pray for the Lord's will, son. Who is this suitor from Laurel City?"

"Isaac Eaton. He's a fancy lawyer. I know he could take better care of her and give her finer things than I could."

"Son, it ain't the finer things that count. It's the love in the heart that matters." The parson looked across the room at a sampler hanging on the wall. Wendell guessed it was a piece of his deceased wife's handiwork. The man's eyes glazed over. Wendell touched his arm.

A smile crossed the old minister's face. "I fought for my sweetheart, and I won." The smile was replaced by a look of longing. "I'm wanting the other world more than this one all the time, son." The parson of Rosewood stood to his feet and, patting the young preacher on the shoulder, softly padded to his bedroom.

Wendell moved to the rocking chair in the front room. Closing his eyes, he envisioned Hannah in this setting. He could hear her laughter ringing throughout the rooms, enlivening the quiet little cottage with her fun-loving ways. He smiled, enjoying the vision. "I'd love to take this pastorate, Lord, if it be your will. And could you add Hannah Baxter as an additional benefit? Guess I haven't totally lost hope, Lord."

Hannah's days were filled with longing for the preacher who had come and gone. Never one to let her burdens get her down, she continued sketching and learning everything she could from Jacques De Ponte.

Now becoming proficient in the use of oils, Hannah was enjoying the added pleasure of painting her scenes in vivid or muted colors.

Miss Mary Telfair had come for a visit and insisted on buying her first oil on canvas before it was finished. It was titled *Romance in Savannah.* Based on the sketch of Hannah and Wendell in the garden, the young artist had embellished the scene, letting her imagination run wild. Her feelings for Wendell had deepened. Somehow she had managed to convey this onto the canvas. Oh how she wished to be a part of his life.

This morning Hannah was putting the finishing touches on the oil painting. "And where are you, Wendell Cunningham?" The man on the canvas gave no answer, but his eyes were full of love. The love there could sustain Hannah until he returned. September was half over, and she was counting the days until the preacher returned.

Determined to learn everything possible during the six months left of her studies, Hannah practiced her brush strokes every day. Feathering with less paint and globbing for a fuller look kept her busy with her studies while Wendell was somewhere else in the world.

Taking a break from her lessons, Hannah arose one morning, dressing quickly and tucking an apple tart in her dress pocket. She wanted to breathe in the outdoors. Staying in the studio had fueled her hunger to be outside.

Always one to carry along a pencil and a few pieces of paper, the young girl wanted to be ready if she had an idea for a poem or a story. She sat on a small bench beside a hibiscus bush in front of Ezra's barn, enjoying the sun and the apple tart. Pink blossoms decorated the bush. Reaching out, she plucked a flower, placing it behind her ear.

Coming out the front door of her house, Eliza was laden with a stack of trousers and shirts. Almost calling out to her, Hannah wished for a few moments more to be alone with her own thoughts.

The young girl watched the woman draw water from the well. Looking into the heavens, the older woman said, "Thank you, Lord." Eliza began humming a tune as she lit the fire under her washpot, pouring the water in. Next, she scraped small pieces of lye soap from the bar with a knife.

Putting the clothes into the soapy water, Eliza began stirring the pot with her paddle. Watching Eliza from the cover of the hibiscus bush, Hannah strained her ear to hear the words coming from the woman's lips.

In just a few minutes, Hannah realized her need for the pencil and paper. Reaching into her pocket, she was glad she was prepared. Eliza's song was quickly transformed into a poem on paper, the young girl making the necessary substitutions for the rhyme. She titled the poem, "Eliza's Song."

Eliza's Song
Hung my harp on de willer tree
Ain't no song inside o me
Dey sole my boy on de auction block
Highest bidder bought em fer stock
Cried my heart out at his feet
Dey haul him off; he was a lookin' at me
Me an Ezra done an stay in dis shack
Hopin' our boy is a gonna come back
Lef my harp on de willer tree
Ain't no song inside o me

Eliza stilled the movement of the paddle. Reaching up, she brushed a tear from her eye. Peeking around the hibiscus bush,

Hannah saw the woman looking into the sky. A smile spread across Eliza's face. The paddle began to move, the song on her lips picking up its tempo, as she lifted her voice victoriously to the heavens, continuing her song.

> Den one day I saw da light
> Jesus came down ta me at night
> Says everythang's gonna be jes fine
> Pick up yo harp, gal, an don't you pine
> Took my harp from da willer dat day
> Picked it up an started to play
> Got me a song an I'm a gonna sing
> Praise an glory to my king
> Praise an glory to my king

Again, the paddle stopped its motion in the washpot. Eliza stood there, looking into the sky as if finding her hope there. A smile broke out on her face, a smile to rival the brightness of the noonday sun. Hannah could barely hear Eliza murmur, "It'll be better in da by an by." Pulling the paddle from the washpot, she added, "Yes, it sho nuff will." She looked into the sky, once again. "Thanks ya, good Lawd above."

Still watching from her cover behind the bush, Hannah was inspired. *Now that is real faith. It's as if Eliza can see what she is hoping for.*

Scribbling the words, and changing a few, Hannah had never worked faster. Finishing the poem, she tucked the paper back into her pocket. Looking up, she saw Ezra coming to the barn to do the chores.

"What ya be doin' out so early, Miz Hanner?"

"I've been listening to Eliza sing. 'Twas a beautiful sound, Ezra." Hannah's eyes misted.

"Well, Miz Hanner, Eliza sings early in da mornin', a givin' her burdens to da Lawd. It be da only way she makes it through dis life, what wif our boy bein' gone an all."

"I understand, Ezra." And Hannah did understand. The love she had seen between Eliza and her heavenly Father had stirred her deeply. She only hoped she had conveyed the depth of that love on paper. She touched her pocket, making sure it was there.

Later that evening, Hannah took the scrap of paper from her pocket, writing the lines fresh on a new sheet of paper. Sitting in the kitchen, talking with Gabrielle, she copied it in ink.

Taking the fresh copy upstairs to dry, she forgot the old copy on the kitchen table.

Remembering the following morning, she went to the kitchen to retrieve it. "Hilda, have you seen my poem? It was right here on the table."

"No, Miss Hanner. Miz Bernadette came down fer a pastry 'bout midnight. I heared her tiptoein' to da pie safe." A wide grin split Hilda's face.

Hannah shrugged her shoulders. "It's all right. I've got a fresh copy; just didn't want to leave it in your way."

Bernadette heard Hannah inquiring about the poem from her place on the stairs. She stopped midstride. Smiling at her secret, she waited to enter the kitchen until after the young girl had left the house for the morning.

"Miz Bernadette, you be a seein' Miss Hanner's poem?"

"No, Hilda." She grinned, picking up another sweet roll from the pie safe. She could hardly contain the excitement of what she would do today.

Savoring the pastry brought back her feelings of glee from the night before when she had made the remarkable discovery. Bernadette De Ponte could not believe her luck. The poem was wonderful. She knew just what to do with it.

This morning she had copied the poem, adding Hannah's name to it. She would put it in the mail to *Godey's Lady's Book* in care of the editor, Sara Josepha Hale.

Her lips tingled with the anticipation that the poem may be published. "Think of the recognition it could bring us." Bernadette closed her eyes, savoring the moment and licking her lips.

"Is the pastry dat good, Miz Bernadette?"

"Yes, it is, dahling."

Chapter 23

Hannah awoke to the sound of a child's laughter. Looking out her window, she saw a little boy kicking something just outside the gate. Peering closer, she saw it was a tin can.

As soon as the boy was out of sight, she saw Adam Moses and Noah Aaron creeping along, trying to hide behind the cover of the oak trees. *What on earth are those boys doing? I'm sure Nettie doesn't know they're away from the plantation.*

Blaine and Blythe came to mind. Her twin brothers were always trying to get away with something when they were that young. Blaine was the leader and Blythe the follower. Blaine was the troublemaker, and his brother was keeper of the peace.

Hannah knew she could not stand by and see the boys come to harm. "Adam Moses," she called from the window. "Noah Aaron, you boys better stop right there."

She had got their attention. Both boys stood behind the oak tree across the road, waiting for what would come next.

Dressing in a hurry, Hannah ran down the winding staircase and out the front door. Crossing the road, she grabbed each boy by the arm.

"What are you doing out here?"

"Aw, Miss Hanner, we's jes lizard huntin'."

"Well, it seems everytime I see you, you're hunting."

"Yessum, it do," Noah Aaron readily agreed with a grin.

Adam Moses turned his head. Hannah stepped back, laughing. Hanging from his ear was a brown lizard, holding the boy's earlobe in its mouth.

Noah Aaron looked as if he was being left out. "I gots ta fine me a lizard. I want one ta hang offa my ear too."

"Now listen, boys, you go back home. You'll have better luck looking in your mama's flower garden than you will trying to sneak down to the river."

"Ya thank so, Miss Hanner?"

"I thank so, Noah Aaron." The boy looked pleased that she had copied his vernacular.

"Aw right, I reckon."

Both boys kicked at a rock with their bare feet, racing back across the road toward the Quantrail Plantation.

A horse whinnied nearby. Looking up, Hannah could not believe what she saw. Well, it *was* almost the end of September. Oh and what a feast for the eyes this young man was. He had grown a beard, trimmed very close to his face, but the dark eyes shining down at her from the man sitting atop the black stallion melted her heart.

"Hello, Miss Hannah."

"Hello yourself, Preacher Man. Why'd you go off in such a huff? I didn't get to see you at all."

A veil shuttered the warmth in his eyes. "Guess I had good reason." Wendell Cunningham averted his eyes to the river.

"Welcome back to Savannah, Wendell Cunningham." Hannah was determined to be friendly to this man who held her heart.

"Thank you, mam."

"Don't call me mam, *sir.*"

"I'll try not to." He seemed uncomfortable in her presence, giving her a half smile.

How can I put him at ease? Hannah wanted to repair the damage caused by the garden scene with Isaac, but she felt this was neither the time nor place. "How has life on the trail been treating you?"

"I left the sketch you drew for me at Ezra's, so I've been extra lonely." Once again, he averted his eyes to the river.

"I suppose you're anxious to get some rest. Come on in. I'll open the gate for you."

"Thank you, Miss Hannah."

"No bother, Preacher."

Wendell went through the open gate, waving at Hannah as he continued toward Ezra's home.

Going back inside the house, Hannah laughed at herself in the hall mirror. No wonder Wendell had hurried away from her. Her hair was sticking out of its combs in every direction. She had hurriedly pinned up the tresses in her rush to rescue the boys from themselves. Her scar was showing, but not once had Wendell paid it any attention. The thought warmed her.

Gabrielle met her in the hall. "What are you in such a rush over?"

"Wendell Cunningham is here."

"Do tell." Gabrielle curtsied low to the ground, following Hannah into her room.

"What do I do to win his affections, Gabrielle?"

"Well, first, you need to do something with your hair. I don't think he'll appreciate your present hairstyle."

"Don't you like it, Gabrielle? I just jerked it up in a hurry to rescue Nettie's sons."

"They're always needing to be rescued. Anyway, I was going to say you would pass for one of those tight-bunned women in the temperance movement with your hair like that and looking the way you do in that dress. What have you done? I've never seen that dress before."

Hannah looked down. "Oh no. I think I'll just drop through a crack in the floor. In my haste I've put my dress on inside out."

"I was wondering, with all those strings hanging. Wendell Cunningham's gonna be wondering what has happened to you on this plantation. He's probably going to think we hired you as a wash woman."

"Gabrielle, you silly girl."

"Well, get spruced up, and we'll go visit Eliza."

"You think we should be so bold?"

"I should think so. Our ploy worked on Isaac, didn't it? I should think we can do better for the preacher."

The girls primped and preened in front of the looking glass in Hannah's room. Twisting her hair into a beautiful new style, the girls chose a smartly tailored dress for the visit.

Hannah stroked the fine fabric of her skirt. "Don't you think we're overdoing it a bit, Gabrielle? We're just going to Ezra and Eliza's house."

"Yes, but there's a very special young man as their guest, right?"

"Yes, but I still think . . . "

"Don't be thinking, Hannah. We do our best work when we aren't thinking."

They shared a chuckle.

Hilda looked up, smiling a greeting, as the girls walked through the kitchen and out the back door.

The cockatiels called out from their cage, heralding the girls' visit.

Hannah smoothed her dress as Gabrielle knocked on the door. "Eliza, we've come to call."

Eliza opened the door, her look of shock turning into laughter. "What are you gals up to?" she whispered.

Gabrielle answered, returning the whisper. "We have business to attend to, Eliza." Stepping past the woman, she grabbed Hannah's hand, prancing in the door as if she owned the place.

Noticing the girls were all dressed up and putting on a show, Ezra stood, heading for the door.

"Where you goin', Ezra?"

Ezra grinned, shaking his head. "I ain't got no dog in dat fight. I's be a takin' my leave."

His wife whispered to his disappearing back, "Ya might be a needin' ta stay an hep yo friend. I ain't so sho he's up to dem two."

Eliza joined the girls. "Have a seat, girls."

In a few moments, Wendell Cunningham came from the back of the house. Barefoot and disheveled, he made his way into Eliza's kitchen without looking into the front room. It was quite obvious he had just woke up from a nap.

"Mama Eliza, could I make a cup of tea?"

"Sho nuff, son. You set right down at da table. I'll get yo tea."

Wendell sat down, his head in his hands. The girls did not make a sound. He was seated with his back to them. "Oh, Mama Eliza, what am I to do with these feelings in my heart?"

Eliza cleared her throat. "What feelin's, son?"

"My heart hurts so bad, and now I've been offered a church to pastor."

"Sho nuff? We sho be a takin' it all to da Lawd in prayer." Eliza's hand shook as she poured Wendell a cup of the warm brew.

"I'll be needing your prayers. I don't want to be alone when I take a pastorate. The parson wanted an answer now, but I told him I'd give him an answer by Christmas."

Eliza acted nervous, as if she didn't know what to do. "Well, well, son, we sho be a prayin' 'bout dat. Here... here, son, here's some sugar an, an... some cream."

"Thank you, Mama Eliza. Are you all right? You act a bit nervous."

"I's all right, son. I's jes fine. Mista Wendell, uh, uh, we's got compny." Eliza pointed to the front room, where the girls were sitting on the sofa.

"Hello, ladies." Wendell turned back around, finished his tea, and headed to his room, noticeably embarrassed.

"We're going to be leaving now, Eliza."

"All right, girls." Eliza seemed relieved.

Gabrielle hooked her arm through Hannah's, walking back to the house. "Back to the drawing board."

"What do you mean, Gabrielle?"

"When one plan doesn't work, we'll draw out another one."

"All right. I'm game. I feel absolutely horrible that the preacher is suffering. I thought maybe I could let him know today that I'm not betrothed, but it wasn't meant to be." Hannah's heart was heavy.

The next few days were filled with plans for the camp meeting. Men from several churches lent their muscles to putting up the huge tent. Excitement coursed through Hannah as she watched the work from her upstairs perch.

Wendell Cunningham was busy from morning until night. Hannah watched from her bedroom window as the tired man came in on his horse every evening. Her admiration for him grew by leaps and bounds, her heart warming each time he paused, looking up to give her a tired grin as he passed by.

This evening as she watched, she shared the window seat with her friend. "I want to help him so bad, Gabrielle. I just know the work would be easier with me laboring beside him."

"I'm praying with you, Hannah."

Tears showed in Hannah's eyes. "Thank you. He's thinking that I'm betrothed to Isaac, and there's been no occasion to explain what really happened that day in the garden. When he smiles at me, it is a sad smile."

"God can fix it, Hannah."

"Yes, he can." Hannah turned away from the window. "Thank you, Gabrielle." She hugged her friend.

Chapter 24

"Hannah, wake up you sleepyhead. Someone is here to see you."

Gabrielle's knocking broke through Hannah's dream. "What? What… who is here?" Rubbing the sleep from her eyes, the young girl made her way to the door. Opening it just a little, Gabrielle's head moved to one side.

I must be dreaming. "How'd you get here, Sara?" Shaking her head to make sure she was awake, she pulled her sister into her room as Gabrielle left the two alone. "Come on in. It's so good to see you."

"I've missed you so much, Hannah. I have a surprise for you."

The sleepy girl opened her eyes, now wide awake. "A surprise?"

"Yes, oh Hannah, I am a married woman."

"Married… you are married, Sara?" Realization dawned when Sara put her hand forth, the little band of gold gleaming in the early morning sunlight coming in at the window. "Oh, Sara, I'm … I'm so happy for you and Tobiah. It is Tobiah, isn't it?" She looked at her sister for affirmation.

"Well, of course, it's Tobiah." Sara twisted her wedding ring on her finger, smiling at her sister. "We eloped, just like I always wanted. It has been so much fun, Hannah. You should elope."

"Well, I'll have to find a suitor before there'll be a wedding at all." Suddenly remembering Wendell, she ran to look out the front window. "Wendell Cunningham is in town and already at work putting the finishing touches on the tent and meeting grounds down by the river." She pointed into the distance. Squinting to get her eyes accustomed to the brightness of the sun, she whirled back into her room. "That little weasel."

"Who? Wendell?"

Hannah was already reaching for her clothes and starting to dress. "No, Sara, why that is none other than Agatha Hathaway down by the river. I saw her handing Wendell a cup of water. I'll dowse her with a whole bucket of water, or, better yet, I'll do the baptizing, and it won't be because she just got born again."

"What are you talking about?" Sara laughed at her sister. "Is Agatha another Nadine?"

"Pretty good comparison, Sara. Come with me to the river."

"Tobiah's downstairs waiting."

"That's good. He can keep Wendell company while I take care of Agatha."

"Now, Hannah, you must mind your manners if you are looking toward a future as wife to a man of the cloth."

"Sara Baxter, don't you preach to me. I learned what I know from watching you all my life." The girls collapsed in laughter.

Running downstairs, Hannah was wrapped in a hug by Tobiah. "Good to see you, Sister-in-law." His smile was huge, a new twinkle sparkling in his eyes.

"I'm so glad for you and my sister."

"Me too." Tobiah pulled Sara close.

"Let's go." Hannah motioned for her sister and Tobiah to follow. Grabbing Gabrielle's arm, she ushered her outside. "We've got business to attend to."

Gabrielle's smile twitched with mischief. "I'm always ready."

Hannah picked up her skirts and ran toward the river with everyone following. She would break up Agatha's morning visitation with Wendell, or her name was not Hannah Baxter.

Hurrying on through the dirt near the tent, Hannah almost tripped on a rope anchoring the makeshift meeting place. Righting herself, she walked straight toward the flirtatious female cooing and making eyes at Wendell.

"Hello, Agatha. Don't you think you've held the preacher up long enough?"

"Why, Miss Hannah, I do declare, you seem to be in a huff this fine morning. And as far as holding the preacher up, well, I like to think I've been a most refreshing diversion to this hard work." Reaching out, she touched the upper arm muscle bulging beneath Wendell's shirt.

"Unhand him, you Broad Street trollop."

Gabrielle placed a restraining hand on Hannah's arm. Sara appeared on her other side.

"Well, I do declare, Miss Hannah, you are acting most un-Christian this morning; must not have said your prayers last night." Agatha opened her fan, prettily swishing the air back and forth.

Wendell had been standing dumbfounded, watching the performance playing out in front of him. Hannah couldn't help but believe he was enjoying it. "Sorry to interrupt your repartee, ladies, but the Lord's work is calling." Smiling at Hannah, he moved twenty feet away and began pounding another anchor into the ground.

Hannah moved forward, placing her hands on her hips. "You'd be wise to take your leave, Agatha."

"I was leaving anyway, but I'll be back." The girl raised an eyebrow, casting a furtive glance in Wendell's direction before sashaying along the riverbank, parasol held high and hips swaying.

Tobiah laughed aloud at Hannah. "You're just about as spunky as my wife." He sounded proud and pleased. "Think I'll visit the preacher."

Hannah turned on her heel walking toward the plantation, followed by Gabrielle.

"We'll be right along." Sara joined her husband, already deep in conversation with Wendell.

Wendell's grin told of his amusement. "Can't tell about that girl. If I didn't know better, I'd think Hannah was jealous of Agatha Hathaway."

"I know my sister, and she *is* jealous."

Wendell lifted an eyebrow. "Sara, I might be able to believe you if I hadn't seen different with my own eyes."

Tobiah rubbed his chin. "What do you mean, Preacher?"

"Why, she's betrothed to Isaac Eaton. He proposed right on the front lawn of the De Ponte Plantation." It pained Wendell to say the words.

Sara shook her head. "What am I missing? Hannah has lost her mind, or you have the wrong information, Reverend."

"I saw it myself."

"When?"

Wendell wiped the sweat from his brow, pausing to lean on his shovel. "Just a short while ago."

Sara was visibly perplexed with this information. "I'll have the answer to this, but I'm sure there is some mistake. My sister has cared for you since the day you came to Laurel City."

Wendell looked astonished. "I wish that were true."

Sara grabbed her husband's arm. "We'll see you later, Preacher."

"Sure was good to see you both again."

Tobiah and Wendell shook hands before the young couple made their way back to the De Ponte Plantation.

Sara found her sister in the front garden. "Hannah Baxter, you will answer to me on this one."

"What are you talking about?"

Sara stomped her foot. "Is Isaac Eaton still your suitor? Are you betrothed? You better answer me quick."

Hannah could not help bursting out in laughter. "Let me tell you a story, big sis." By the time Hannah had finished, Sara and Tobiah were laughing so hard their sides hurt.

When she could speak, Sara wiped the tears from her eyes. "How wonderful, my dear sister. And to think, you did all of this without my help." She looked put out at the idea.

"Oh, I had help all right." With the question in Sara's eyes, Hannah answered. "Gabrielle helped me execute the plan to perfection." She smacked her lips smugly.

Gabrielle joined in the conversation. "Oh, I couldn't wait to dump that bucket of cold water on the scoundrel."

"I would give a newborn calf to have seen the look on Isaac's face when he got doused. Never did like that one." Tobiah smiled, thoroughly enjoying the predicament Isaac had found himself in.

The conversation continued, and Sara brought Hannah up to date with all the happenings around Laurel City. "Hannah, you'll be getting a letter soon, which will hold another surprise, but I'm not saying another word."

Hannah looked at Tobiah. "What is it?"

"My lips are sealed. You'll find out soon."

"The De Pontes invited us to stay for supper and overnight, Hannah, but we're honeymooning." Sara gently stroked Tobiah's cheek, which immediately turned a deep shade of red.

Smiling, Tobiah cleared his throat. "We'll be leaving right after dinner. The Perkins' have asked us to share the noon meal with you and Gabrielle at their home."

"Oh, it'll be delicious. I just wish you could stay longer." Hannah hugged her sister, whisperng in Sara's ear, "I'd be in a hurry to leave too if it were my honeymoon. You've waited a long time for this."

"Uh ... huh." Sara's eyes danced mischievously. She planted a quick kiss on her husband's cheek.

"Eliza will have the food ready promptly at noon. I can smell it from here. We'd best not keep her waiting." The group headed out back to the homey comfort of Eliza's kitchen.

"Y'all come right on in. I's jes heatin' up da water fer some tea, an we'll be ready."

Tobiah looked at the food spread across the table. "You outdid yourself, mam."

"Nothin' ta be spared fer Miz Hanner's famly. Y'all's da bes, da very bes."

Conversation stopped as everyone enjoyed the delicious meal Eliza had prepared. Fried cornbread, full of jalapeños, had Tobiah rejoicing and Sara begging for another jar of tea.

Tender pot roast was passed around the table for the second time. "I's made da preacher a sanwich fer his noon meal today. Says he'd be a stayin' on through da noonin', a tryin' ta get ready fer da camp meetin'."

Hannah's lips curved up at one side. "He'd be further along if Agatha hadn't held him up this morning."

"Why, Miz Hanner, ol Eliza thinks I be notin' a tone o jealousy in dat sweet voice o yours. You be knowin' what da Good Book be sayin'. 'Jealousy be as cruel as da grave.'"

"Agatha's grave sounds pretty good right now." Hannah covered her mouth as if to bite back the words. "I wouldn't go quite that far."

"Of course not." Gabrielle met her friend's eyes with a challenge.

Sara pushed back from the table. "I can't eat another bite. That's the best food I've had since we've been on our honeymoon."

"Why thanks ya, Miz Sara."

Tobiah quickly scooped up the last bit of roast and gravy with his cornbread. "Most delicious, mam."

Everyone seemed too full to walk the short distance to the front room, yet somehow they managed.

Retiring to the well-worn sofa and chairs, the group enjoyed Ezra's tales of trials of the war. "Dem Union soldiers done an took up residence right chere in Savanny. Why dey moved in nex door at da Quantrail Plantation."

"They moved in and stayed?" Tobiah asked.

"Uh huh, an da mizzus nex door done an took up wif one o da soldiers. Mr. Quantrail done an sail out ta fight da war. She use ta be a walkin' atop her house on da widder's walk, lookin fer her man ta come home."

Sara looked anxious. "Did her husband return from the war?"

"Not 'til two years later. By dat time, da mizzus didn't care cauz she had her a Union soldier an his babe."

Hannah gasped. "Oh no. Maybe that's why Nettie says Mr. Quantrail is so mean."

Eliza put in. "Sho nuff, the mista come home meaner an ever, an don't ya know dat nex summer, da babe died in da mizzus' arms." She shook her head from side to side, her eyes filled with sorrow. "Hurts pow'rful bad ta lose a chile."

Hannah reached over and patted her friend's hand.

Eliza looked up with a sad smile. "Well, it be time fer deesert now. Y'all gots ta try my apple dumplins." No one in the room dared refuse her.

Sara closed her eyes in delight after one taste. "Oh, Eliza, how heavenly. And I thought I couldn't hold another bite."

Eliza smiled her thanks.

Tobiah shook hands with the couple, followed by Sara, who hugged the kind woman who had opened her humble home to them. "Thank you so much. I shall remember your hospitality and how special you made our time in Savannah visiting my sister."

Sara turned to Hannah. The two walked out the door to say their good-byes. "I'm going to miss you so much."

"I'll miss you too, Sara, but I couldn't be happier for you." The sisters held on to each other for a long time.

Tobiah patted his wife on the back. "We'll see her at Christmas, Sara."

Sara pulled away, wiping a tear from her eye. As Tobiah assisted her into the carriage, Hannah stood there thinking what a great life they would have together. "Have a wonderful honeymoon. I love you both."

Sara waved until the carriage was out of sight.

Hannah looked to the sky. "Will I ever have a honeymoon, Lord?"

The young girl heard the door shut just as she uttered the words. "Sure you will, Hannah. And that time might be closer than you think."

Gabrielle and Hannah spent the afternoon roaming the plantation. Walking through the fields of freshly harvested squash and tomatoes, the girls each picked a ripe tomato. Just as they were taking a seat on a fallen tree branch, a call interrupted their respite.

"Hep, somebody ... Mr. Ezra, hep." The voice was pleading and pitiful.

"That sounds like Adam Moses, Hannah." Throwing her tomato to the ground, Gabrielle hiked her skirts, flying in the direction of the call.

"I believe you're right." Hannah was close on the heels of her friend.

"Hep, hep."

Stepping through the thicket of trees, the girls saw a sorrowful sight. Adam Moses was bent over, panting, and calling out in a voice almost gone silent.

"What is it, Adam Moses?"

"O, Miss Gabby ... O, Miss Gabby ... " The boy gulped for air. "It's Noah Aaron ... It's Noah Aaron." The boy's crazed eyes were pleading for help.

Shaking the boy's shoulder, Hannah asked, "What is it, Adam Moses? You have to tell us before we can help you."

Her words seemed to cause him to focus on the matter at hand. "We's, we's ... O Miss Hanner, we's at da pond again ... " The boy let out a wail.

"Oh no!" Gabrielle's terror was evident as she flew in the direction of the pond. Adam Moses's screams followed the girls as they came upon the dreadful scene.

"No, no, no. Not my baby boy. Cain't live wifout my baby boy." Nettie sat on the bank of the pond, holding a lifeless Noah Aaron, rocking him back and forth in her arms.

"Let me help." Gabrielle reached for the boy as if she could reverse the tragedy. "I should have told on the boys."

"Don't go blaming yourself." Hannah knew it wasn't her friend's fault.

Nettie clung to her son. Gabrielle gave up trying to do something to save the boy. The futility of the moment squeezed their hearts.

"He's done an gone, Miss Gabby." Upon uttering the words, Nettie's demeanor suddenly changed. Dropping the boy to the ground, she appeared to have lost her wits. "Ya cain't leave me, Noah Aaron. Ya cain't leave yo mama." She began pounding him in the chest.

"Oh no, Miss Nettie, don't beat the child." Gabrielle looked helplessly at Hannah. Both girls tried to pull the mother back from the punishment she was inflicting. In one final attempt, Nettie wailed, firmly hitting her child in the chest. The girls grabbed her hands, pulling her away from the pond.

A sound caused the three to look back at the bank. Noah Aaron, sputtering like a belching riverboat, was spitting up water as if he had drank the whole pond.

"Lawd above, I's cain't believe my eyes." Looking into the skies, Nettie spoke with conviction. "I be a servin' ya fer da res o my born days, an that be a promise to ya, Lawd." Running to her son, Nettie hugged him to her as if he was the most precious gift she could have received. And he was.

Hannah and Gabrielle joined in the celebration as they encircled the two with hugs. By that time, Ezra and Eliza could be seen in the distance, a wailing Adam Moses on the buggy seat between them.

"It's all right, Son. Yo brother ain't gone. He still wif us, Adam Moses. Come an look hea what da Lawd's done." The woman rocked her son back and forth, suddenly raising her hand overhead. "Praise be ta Jesus; ain't a gonna be doubtin' him no mo. I be in church all da Sundys o da month; evry one, ya be a hearin' me, Eliza? Ain't no ox in no ditch a gonna be a keepin' ol Nettie from a worshipin' da good Lawd."

"Glory be, Nettie. We been prayin' fer dis day fer a long time. Praise Jesus."

"Praise his good name, yessum, Eliza. I sho nuff is a believer now. Gonna come to da camp meetin' too. I needs all o Jesus I can get."

Nettie's husband appeared on the drive. "Come on over here, Marcus. Hurry, man."

Bewildered, Marcus Brown listened to his wife's tale of losing their son. At the end, he agreed that they would worship God for the rest of their days.

Leaving the Browns to themselves, the girls returned home with Eliza and Ezra. As they were alighting from the buggy, Eliza whispered, "Sho am glad Nettie didn't lose her son. Sho is a bad thang." Looking into the bright colors of the evening sky, she whispered, "Thank you, Lord."

Hannah was touched by the woman's gratitude that another woman wouldn't be suffering as she had suffered.

Later, standing in her bedroom, looking into the quickly disappearing sunset, she raised her own petition to the Lord. "Please return Eliza's son to her, Lord."

The wind rustled a few fallen leaves on the ground below. Looking down, Hannah saw the preacher returning from the camp grounds. His shoulders told of the weariness he felt. His head tilted upward as he neared, searching her window. The gesture made her smile.

"Hello, Preacher."

Raising his shoulders, a smile crossed his tired face. "Hello, Miss Hannah." She thought she heard him murmur in passing, "You sure are a beautiful sight." But the soft breeze blew the words away so quickly, she wasn't sure they had ever been uttered.

Turning away from the window, Hannah began her nightly prayer. "Father, thank you for sparing Noah Aaron and bringing his family to the knowledge of your goodness. Please help the preacher man and let him be mine if you can, and I know you can. Help us, Father, to do your will and help others. Amen."

The last words of the prayer sparked an idea. *We should make a blessing basket for Nettie. Oh, just wait 'til I tell Gabrielle and Eliza. And wouldn't Grandmam be proud to know the idea of her blessing baskets has made it all the way to Savannah.*

Contentment settled around Hannah like a shawl. She couldn't wait to present the blessing basket to Nettie. Adding to her contentment was the knowledge that a certain preacher was sleeping nearby.

"No, no, no." Loud screams pierced the air. Hannah awoke feeling as if she were watching Nettie on the bank of the pond, screaming over her drowned child.

Sitting up in bed, she realized the painful cries were coming in her window. A soft breeze gently blew the curtains. Climbing out of bed, she heard the torturous, pleading call. "No, Granny, no. I'll be good. I'll do . . . "

Peering out her window, Hannah could see the silhouette of a man writhing on his bed. The moonlit sky cast soft light into the room at the end of Ezra's home. *That's the room Wendell stays in. Oh no... what can the matter be?*

"I can't breathe, Granny. I can't... breathe." The yelling intensified as Hannah stood helplessly watching. Wendell sat up in bed, his head turning from side to side. "When will these nightmares cease?" he groaned.

Knowing she had witnessed something very painful and personal, the young girl returned to her bed, quite shaken. It made her love the preacher all the more. "Oh Lord, please help the one I love."

Hannah lay in bed, softly praying and musing over Wendell's situation. She had not realized the depth of the loneliness he must feel. She wanted to remove that loneliness, filling every moment of the preacher's life with love and companionship. *Oh that it might be so.*

Chapter 25

The brightness of the sun aroused the girl still abed at midmorning. Its warmth flooded the room, causing Hannah to stir. Just then she turned over. Something was on the floor by her bedroom door. Wiping the sleep from her eyes, she retrieved the magazine.

Must be the latest copy of Godey's Lady's Book. Perusing the front, she found it was indeed the current issue. Taking the publication back to bed, she began thumbing through the pages, in no hurry to arise. She remembered this was the day the De Pontes went shopping as a family.

A sketch of a new pattern for a day dress caught her attention. The simple gown would do well in Savannah's summer heat. She'd have to get Gabrielle's opinion.

Turning the page, she began reading the poem titled, "Eliza's Song." "'Eliza's Song'? How could someone use my same title?" She spoke aloud. Reading a little further, she exclaimed, "It is my poem!"

Jumping from the bed, Hannah dressed quickly. She must see how this had come to be. Opening the magazine, she scanned the poem, her eyes landing on the poet's name. Indeed, her name was in print. Now she was even more confused. She had not sent this poem in.

Running downstairs, taking the steps two at a time, Hannah ran right into Bernadette De Ponte at the bottom of the stairs. One look into the woman's eyes, and the young girl knew she had found the answer to her question, but how did this happen?

"Wondering how you became a published poet, dearie?"

"Yes, you could say that." The excitement Hannah felt could not be stilled. She swayed from side to side, hoping the woman wouldn't draw this out.

"Well now, dahling, do you remember the scrap of paper you left in Hilda's kitchen?"

"Yes, mam."

"Let's just say I borrowed it and sent it to Sara Josepha Hale, the editor of *Godey's,* my dear."

Hannah couldn't restrain herself from hugging the woman. "Why, thank you, Mrs. De Ponte, I never thought to enter the poem for publication."

"It speaks from the heart, dear, and this is what the editor is looking for. It also is a part of our undeniable history." And with that, Bernadette De Ponte handed an envelope to Hannah, as she walked into the kitchen toward the pie safe.

Hannah was still bewildered. The envelope trembled in her hand. She must share her news with someone. Up the stairs she went, knocking on her friend's door. No answer. Where was Gabrielle? Just as she walked out the back door, she saw the entire De Ponte family leaving in the vis-à-vis carriage. All three smiled, yelling, "Congratulations!"

"We're running late for an appointment at the tailor's," Mr. De Ponte explained. And then they were gone.

Running the short distance to Ezra and Eliza's home, Hannah could not contain her joy. Pounding on the door, Hannah grabbed Eliza in a hug as she answered her knock. "I'm sorry, Eliza. I just have some news that can't keep."

"What it be's chile? Sit down an tell ol Eliza."

Hannah barely felt the kitchen chair beneath her dress as she began spilling out her news. "Look right here, Eliza, it's a poem I wrote about you. Actually I wrote it while you sang."

"What chile, ya be a losin' yo marbles? Ya ain't makin' no sense, chile."

"Eliza, it's all right here. Read it, read it." Hannah pointed to *Godey's Lady's Book.*

"Ya be a tellin' ol Liza dat ya done an got pub leeshed by dat faincy magazeen? Dis be too much fer ol Liza ta take in. We best call in Ezra ta hep make some sense o dis sitchyachion." The lady headed for her door. "Ezra, Ezra, come on in hea. An, Ezra, I's a meanin' right now."

Ezra appeared momentarily. "I's raking the backyard, Eliza. What's so impotent it cain't be a waitin'?"

"Why you tell 'im, Miz Hanner. Go on ahead, tell 'im."

"Ezra, that day I was listening to Eliza sing, I wrote a poem from her song." Raising the magazine in the air, she continued. "Mrs. Bernadette sent it to *Godey's Lady's Book,* and the editor published it. It's all right here. Look, Ezra."

"Read it to us, Miz Hanner. We ain't had much learnin'. It'll be fasser if ya do it."

"All right, then." As Hannah read, the older couple embraced each other. Tears made sad trails down their faces.

"We thanks ya, Miz Hanner. Sho does tell a storey, jes like it happent. Ya makes us mighty proud. Kinda keeps our boy a livin' in our hearts a wee bit more, hearin' it put down on paper."

"Yessum, an it do a mama's heart good ta know so many people, even faincy people, a gonna share dat poem an feel somethin' right chere." The kind lady touched her heart. "Sho is a fine poem ya wrote."

"You were my inspiration, Eliza." Hannah went to embrace the couple.

Thinking to open the envelope, Hannah read that the editor had been looking for something both inspirational and historical to publish. She finished by saying the poem had really touched her heart. Placing the letter back into its envelope, Hannah noticed a crisp one-hundred-dollar bill.

"Oh my, oh my." Waving the currency overhead, she proudly proclaimed, "Half of this goes to the two of you."

"No mam, Miz Hanner, we couldn't take it."

"Sorry, Eliza, you can and you will. I mean you no disrespect, but you were my inspiration, and I will see that you get half of this money."

Ezra smiled his appreciation. "Thanks ya, Miz Hanner. It sho nuff will be an ainser ta what we's been a prayin' fer. We's a needin' a new wagon an don't have enuff fer it all. Sho will be a blessin'."

"Ezra, the Lord has provided."

Hannah turned to Eliza, smiling and wagging a finger in her face. "And, you, my friend, must learn to accept the way he provides the blessing."

"I's jes gonna say thanks ya, Miz Hanner."

"And speaking about blessings, my grandmother makes blessing baskets for people who need encouragement or some other assistance. I was thinking last night how we could put together a basket for Nettie."

"That sounds mighty good ta me, Miz Hanner. Ya jes need ta tell me what ta do."

"We take a basket and fill it with items that will bless the recipient. Grandmam always adds a small box of handwritten scriptures for encouragement."

Eliza clasped her hands together. "I got some jars of apple butta an peach mammalade jes waitin' ta go in dat blessin' basket fer Nettie."

"I brought some extra bars of Grandmam's rose petal soap, and oh, yes, I have an extra, beautifully embroidered handkerchief from my sister Katherine. And I could add one of Sara's sachets." Hannah was deep into planning how to fill the blessing basket.

Time passed with Eliza and Hannah collecting items for Nettie. Doing this simple task made the young girl feel closer to home.

Gabrielle called from the door. "Yoohoo . . . "

"Come in, Miz Gabrielle." Ezra went to the door. "These women jes a plannin' ta be a blessin' ta Nettie."

"I want to help."

Hannah became more animated, explaining the blessing basket to Gabrielle. Sitting down to a simple meal of smoked turkey, cheese, and bread, the ladies continued their planning.

Gabrielle thought for a moment. "Oh, I've got a brand-new sunbonnet, all decorated with fancy lace. I think it would be a nice gift for Nettie. There's an apron that Hilda refuses to wear, says it's too beautiful. I'll take that for the basket too."

Hannah tapped her temple. "Where will we get a basket? Grandmam buys hers from the Seminole village."

"No problem, Miz Hanner. I jes bought one lass market day. Didn't know when I'd need it, but da good Lawd sho nuff did." Eliza looked plum pleased with herself.

"I'll get a big ribbon for it."

"Dat be good, Miz Gabrielle."

"It's all set, then. We'll gather the rest of the items and arrange them just so tomorrow afternoon. That will give Gabrielle and me time to write the scriptures for the scripture box."

Saying their good-byes, Gabrielle and Hannah made their way back to the big house.

"Gabrielle, did you know about the money the editor paid for my poem?"

"Yes, my mother bargained with the editor until she paid that amount."

"I'll have to give her a hug for that."

"Just make sure she's not wearing that hat with the tall feathers. You might get lost in them and never come out."

The girls laughed, heading up to Hannah's room, where they spent the rest of the day penning the scriptures, blotting, and waiting for the ink to dry before folding and placing them in the box.

Coming down for supper, the girls dined alone. The De Pontes had been invited to a dinner party and were not expected until late.

Saying good night to Gabrielle, Hannah sat at the window seat, looking out toward the camp meeting site. It looked to be in order. Meetings would commence very soon. Watching the sun's descent, the front gate opened. The preacher slowly made his way down the drive on his stallion.

Jumping up from the window seat, Hannah ran to the side window. "Hello, Preacher."

When he barely lifted his head in recognition, the girl suddenly remembered the nightmares of the previous night. Even from this distance, Wendell seemed embarrassed.

"Hey, Preacher, are you looking forward to the meetings?" She would say anything to get his attention off himself.

Pulling back on the reins, Wendell looked up at the window. "I sure am, Miss Hannah. How about you?" Spoken as a friendly response, Hannah could tell he was nervous about conversing with her.

"I'm real excited. I just want you to know you can count on me for anything you need to help out with the meetings."

"Thank you, Miss Hannah. I appreciate that." And then he was gone, turning in his saddle, giving her that slight smile that she loved so much.

Seeing the sadness still showing in his face made her want to erase his sorrow, yet her heart rejoiced at the sight of him, doing a dance all its own.

Hannah listened to the song of the chickadee. A cool breeze blew in from the river, soothing her troubled thoughts about the preacher's nightmares. Slipping beneath the covers, she petitioned the Father on his behalf.

The next day, Gabrielle and Hannah rushed to Eliza's to prepare the blessing basket. Putting the bow in place, the three ladies headed out to deliver Nettie's gift.

Sunday finally arrived. Hannah was taking her time dressing for the first camp meeting service when Gabrielle knocked softly on her door.

"Come in."

"Thought I might be able to assist you with your hair."

"Please do. I've been trying to decide on a style for the past thirty minutes. Nothing seems right."

"Well, you could always play it safe and wear a tight bun." Standing back, tilting her head to the side, Gabrielle smirked. "You might look real good with slant eyes."

"Gabrielle, you know I'd never make it down to the river with my hair pulled that tight, much less sit through a church service."

"Well, you know, you're trying to win the heart of a man of the cloth." Gabrielle wore a stoic look, placing a hand on her hip for emphasis.

Laughter erupted from both girls. Setting to work, Hannah's friend twisted her hair into a beautiful style, accenting it with embellished combs. Stepping back, Gabrielle nodded her head. "You are gorgeous, Hannah Baxter."

"You are gorgeous yourself."

"Nothing can outshine those sparkling green eyes."

"Well, let's hope the preacher feels the same."

"I'm sure he does."

Hannah looked doubtful. In her heart, she was unsure of the preacher's feelings. "I hope so."

The girls descended the stairs, meeting Gabrielle's father in the kitchen. "We'll head on over to the meeting when you girls are ready."

After muffins and milk, Hannah and Gabrielle followed Jacques De Ponte out the back door. The carriage was ready and waiting.

Arriving at the river, the girls alighted, making their way into the tent. Finding a bench near the front, they took their seats.

Hannah immediately searched for Wendell. "Where is he, Gabrielle?"

"He's here. I saw him riding down the drive early this morning." Looking around, she nudged Hannah's elbow. "There he is."

Following her friend's gaze, she spotted Wendell Cunningham listening attentively to a young girl. Turning and lowering the fan from her face, Hannah could tell this was none other than Agatha Hathaway.

Indignation rose within Hannah. Rising from the bench, she ignored Gabrielle's warning to keep quiet. Marching over to the other side of the tent, she stood with her hands on her hips, looking from Agatha to Wendell.

A grin threatening to make its way onto the preacher's face was caught before it could make a full appearance.

Agatha ignored Hannah's presence, looking deeply into Wendell's eyes. "Like I was saying, Reverend, I would be more than happy to sing for you each night. I know you'll want only the best, and I can offer that."

"Thank you, Miss Agatha. I'll remember your offer."

"Don't forget my other offer, Reverend." Casting flirtatious eyes his way, she sent Hannah a challenging look.

The Baxter girl's face throbbed, her emotions rising to the challenge. "Reverend, don't forget *my* offer. I'm sure I have first dibs on any need you may have for your church services."

Agatha sent one more coy smile to the preacher before taking a seat on the front bench.

Wendell's eyes widened at Hannah's reference to her earlier promise to help in any way she could. When he turned away and chuckled, she followed him to the front of the tent.

"Do say, Miss Hannah. I would think you a jealous person if I didn't know you were already spoken for."

"I'm not spoken for, Wendell Cunningham, and don't you forget it."

Wendell cocked an eyebrow in disbelief.

Finding her way back to her seat by Gabrielle, Hannah looked to the side where a group of tight-bunned ladies had seated themselves. With an inward groan, she turned to her friend, whispering.

"How'd we manage to be so lucky to have them sit beside us, looking down their noses?"

Gabrielle covered her mouth. "Probably got mad that you were speaking to the preacher."

"Well they can get glad in the same petticoats they got mad in." Knowing she should mind her manners but already having her dander aroused by Agatha Hathaway, Hannah looked at the group of self-righteous women and crossed her eyes.

Gabrielle pinched her arm. "Better start practicing to be a preacher's wife. Gonna have to love every one of them ladies," she taunted her friend.

Music poured from the organ sitting on the makeshift stage. The congregation stood as Wendell's voice began the opening hymn. The place was charged with a special feeling, washing away Hannah's acts of impropriety. "Forgive me, Lord. You take care of Agatha Hathaway and those self-righteous biddies to my right."

Closing her eyes, Hannah let the Lord warm her soul and then she saw the error of her ways and sincerely asked forgiveness for her actions. She realized that she must be long suffering toward the self-righteous ladies who were always busy judging others, for even Jesus tired of their ways but loved them nonetheless.

Turning her full attention to Wendell Cunningham, Hannah noticed the peace written on his face, his deep baritone ringing throughout the tent. The light of the Lord shone through him, enthralling her.

"You may be seated."

The congregation seated themselves, reaching for their fans. Turning to take her seat, Hannah waved at Nettie, who was on the back row with her family. A smile flitted across Hannah's face as she remembered the joy shining in Nettie's eyes the day she received the blessing basket. Grandmam would have been proud.

All eyes were on the young minister standing behind the wooden pulpit. "My message today is titled, Faith to Receive. The Bible is God's Word. We need to read the Word until it is hidden in our hearts, where the devil can't steal it. The more time we spend in the Bible, the more confidence we have that God's promises are true. Whatever our needs may be, he has promised to meet them. I have a battle going on in my own life, and this message is for me as much as you. God is able to perfect that which concerns me, and I am believing him to do just that. We must bring our burdens to the Lord and leave them with him. He is able to do abundantly more than we can think or ask."

"Amen." Moving to the edge of the bench, a sweet little lady on the front bench was engrossed in Wendell's sermon.

Hannah made the mistake of turning to look at the scowling women to her right. One of them whispered a little too loudly. "Why ain't he a preachin' on sin? Should be hell, fire, and brimstone a comin' from that man. How's he gonna save these wicked people?"

Gabrielle turned to Hannah. "I thought Jesus was the only one who saves."

"I've got to ignore those women, or I might lose my religion." Hannah turned back toward the front, but not before she heard another loud whisper.

"Should be a preachin' on drankin' and womernizin'. Lawd knows them sinners are here and part of um are coloreds."

Closing her eyes, Hannah bit her tongue, determined to hear Wendell's sermon.

"Satan does not want us to receive these precious promises from our Lord. He brings fear, doubt, and any other thing that will take our eyes off the Lord. When we listen to his voice, our faith plummets, and we lose the battle. We must focus on the Word of God and believe his promises. It is then that we will receive. In all our ways, we are to acknowledge God, and he will direct our paths. He has promised not to withhold any good thing from those who obey him."

Hannah drank in the message as fresh rain to her soul. Looking into Wendell's eyes, she felt he had received peace from his message as well. Love, emanating from her heart, went out to the man now saying the benediction.

She couldn't help but overhear another lady from the group to her right making her feelings known. "Shore expected a much more fiery sermon. They don't preach like they used to."

"Maybe they don't need to preach like they used to, lady. Maybe God wants to say something good to his people and give them hope, like the preacher did today." Gabrielle's response was true, but Hannah felt these ladies were set in their ways and couldn't be changed.

"Well, I'll tell you, prissy missy, God'll cast the sinner into a devil's hell, and that's the truth."

Gabrielle was not to be so easily dismissed. "If a sinner goes to hell, it makes the Lord very sad, lady. You act as if he takes pleasure in sending them there. And furthermore, if we go to hell, we go against his will. He said that he is not willing that any should perish but that all come to repentance. Don't sound like he wants us to go."

"Them ol sinners need to bust hell wide open."

"I'm sorry to disappoint you, mam, but Jesus died for them ol sinners."

"Well, I say, missy, you shore don't have no respect."

"Begging your pardon, mam, it's mighty hard to respect such hatefulness. God is a God of love, mam." And with that, Gabrielle grabbed Hannah's arm and marched outside to the carriage.

"You know the Word, Gabrielle."

"My father taught me most of what I know. I just couldn't bear any more of the self-righteous talk from that group of ladies. Guess I'll be asking forgiveness for the rest of the afternoon."

Jacques De Ponte joined in the conversation. "Those ladies are the Savannah Teetotalers, my dear. Their reputation precedes them. They're known to stand outside the local saloons badgering and mocking the patrons. There's got to be a better way to show the love of God to those poor, drunken men."

Hannah caught a glimpse of Wendell trying to leave on his horse. Agatha stood beside the stallion, her hand on the reins. The sight made the girl sick to her stomach. Turning toward Gabrielle, she nodded in Wendell's direction. "I want to go and snatch that twirling parasol from her hand and use it on her backside." Putting her hand to her head, she shook it vehemently. "But of course I shan't."

Gabrielle patted her friend's arm. "She's no competition for you, Hannah. The preacher's heart belongs to you. I saw the way he looked at you during his sermon."

"Really, Gabrielle?"

"Really, Hannah."

The young girl settled back, her jealousy slightly appeased. Turning around, she saw that Wendell had freed himself from the clutches of the flirt.

Chapter 26

The next week Jacques De Ponte handed Hannah a letter at breakfast. "Came for you yesterday, my dear."

Remembering Sara's words, Hannah could not wait to open the missive. Deciding to take a walk around the property, she found a nice place of repose under an oak tree.

Tearing the envelope open, she quickly read the letter from her best friend. Susannah was getting married! Hannah jumped up, turning in circles at this good news. She would be the maid of honor in her friend's Christmas wedding.

And there was more. Dropping once again to the soft spot of grass under the oak, she continued reading. Matthew had moved to Rosewood, that beautiful town Hannah had fallen in love with on her train ride to Savannah. Now Susannah would live in that picturesque place. Another thought ran through Hannah's mind; Susannah would be attending the church she had passed.

Several sparrows hopped about, clearly enjoying each other's company. Leaning against the old oak, staring into the sky, Hannah missed her friend.

Hannah's musing turned to the camp meeting and the preacher. Just suppose Wendell was asked to pastor Rosewood. Daydreams filled her mind of the little parsonage she had passed on the train. *What would it be like to share a pastor's life?* She imagined Susannah sitting at the Rosewood parsonage table, sharing a cup of tea as they chatted about Matthew and Wendell. A loud blast from a boat on the river interrupted Hannah's reverie.

Picking up the missive, the young girl exclaimed, "Now ain't that just something?" She smiled, reminding herself of Blaine.

Susannah wanted her to stand up at her wedding and wear the beautiful jade dress she had worn to Isaac and Hattie Mae's wedding. Jumping up from her place of repose, Hannah hiked her skirts, running back toward the De Ponte mansion. Nearing Ezra's barn, she realized Wendell was standing there enjoying the view of her unshod ankles.

Unlike her sister Katherine, Hannah rarely blushed. But this was different. She felt herself go red in the face. *I'm sure he's thinking I would make a fine pastor's wife, running around in my unstockinged feet like a child.*

Wendell's grin could not be hid. Averting his eyes from her ankles *after* she dropped her skirt, he pulled the brim of his hat low with a nod in her direction. "Mornin', Miss Hannah."

"Good morning, Preacher." She would not take all the blame for his lack of self-control in ogling her ankles. *Guess men of the cloth are just men after all.*

Walking her way, the preacher surprised Hannah. "How would you like to accompany me into town, Miss Hannah? Need to go by the feed and tack store and pick up some molasses for my horse."

"Without a chaperone, Mr. Cunningham?" She looked at him accusingly.

"But of course not. Ezra will be driving his new buggy."

"Then I shall come."

Hurrying into the house, taking the time to put on her shoes and checking her appearance in the gilded mirror in the hall, Hannah reached for a warm French pastry. Hilda was just placing the cinnamon dainties on a cooling rack. Obviously proud of her culinary talents, she smiled at the young girl exiting through the back door.

"Good morning, Miz Hanner."

"Morning, Ezra."

Wendell stood beside the buggy, assisting Hannah as she climbed into the new conveyance. He squeezed her left hand, and she saw him paying close attention to her ring finger on that hand. He even rubbed the spot where a ring would have been. The question in his eyes was met by a question in her own as he seated himself beside her.

Ezra turned the buggy down a road Hannah had not traversed. Both sides of the road were lined with crape myrtles, their bright feathery blossoms decorating the path in shades of white, lavender, and pink. Hannah inhaled the fragrance of the outdoors, the breeze off the river cooling her warm skin.

Blue birds scrambled for insects under the crape myrtles, pecking the ground, chasing the elusive morsels. A woodpecker, drilling his beak into a nearby tree, paused to look at the group enjoying their morning outing. Cocking his head to the side, he returned to his pecking, his curiosity appeased.

"Beautiful birds out today."

Hannah smiled at Wendell's words. "You're a bird watcher too?"

"Love them; brought me a lot of pleasure on the trail."

"Must be a lonely life out there."

"Yes, Miss Hannah. It is a lonely life. I've had a lot of rewarding times, seeing souls brought into the kingdom and others encouraged in their walk with the Lord."

"Sure is a great calling. I love ministry. Always been a part of my life." Hannah remembered her wicked thoughts toward the self-righteous women of Savannah. "Have to keep asking for forgiveness."

"You, Miss Hannah?" Wendell feigned surprise.

Ezra's back shook.

"Don't laugh at me, Ezra."

She turned to Wendell. "I don't know when to keep my mouth shut sometimes, much less control my wicked thoughts toward better-than-thou people."

"You might want to add jealousy to your list of sins." Wendell laughed aloud.

"If we're making a list, you can start yours with lasciviousness."

"Would thou be speaking of mine admiration of thy shapely ankles, mam?" he whispered.

"Thou speakest correctly, oh high and mighty one. Remove the beam from thy eye before thou removest the speck from mine."

Now entering a business district on the outskirts of town, the preacher nodded to the Savannah Saloon just ahead. "Speaking of removing the beam ... " Wendell's voice trailed off.

Clucking to the mules, Ezra seemed in a hurry to pass the ramshackled building. Just as they came to the front of the saloon, a group of women stepped up onto the boardwalk out front. One held a placard.

"Teetotalers of Savannah. I'm sure we're in for a show. Seen these temperance groups during my travels, but I've yet to see one showing the love of God."

"Preacher, that's what I battle with all the time. How do we show the love of God to such hateful people; people clearly destroying others lives by their self-righteous attitudes?" Taking a breath,

Hannah continued. "I know in my head that we've got to love them, but my heart's not in line with my head yet."

Wendell shook his head. "Just try to remember, they are ignorant of God's true nature; God is love. Somehow they're missing it in their zeal to bring sinners to repentance."

"Yes, they are. The Bible says it's by the Lord's goodness that men come to repentance."

"You know the Word, Hannah." Wendell smiled, gently patting her shoulder. Hannah almost missed his whisper. "Sure would make a good pastor's wife."

She turned her head, smiling broadly.

Ezra slowed the buggy, pulling over to the side. Evidently this would be a show akin to the Totem Chronicles in Two Mules Junction. What would they behold this day?

"Humm … Humm … " The lady's voice rose two more octaves, trying to find the right key. Finally she struck a chord.

Hannah, Wendell, and Ezra turned their faces, squelching the chuckles rising in their chests as the most awful song they had ever heard rang out on the boardwalk in front of the old saloon.

"I can't believe it."

"It's pretty much the same with all these groups. They sing songs about going around drunkard's curve." Pausing to listen, recognition dawned on the preacher's face. "Now they're singing 'Comrades Fill No Glass for Me.' That's a Stephen Foster tune."

"You seem well versed in the temperance movement, Preacher."

"Ol Ezra done an heared some o dem songs too. One dey sang here lots is 'Touch Not da Cup.'"

The singing stopped, one of the ladies crossing the street to propagate the temperance message. Handing a book to Wendell, she looked him in the eye with condemnation. "Read this book, ya poor man. Looks like you's one o the imbibing kind. God wants ta save ya from the burnin' fire o his wrath." She looked quite pleased with herself.

Hannah couldn't restrain herself. "Why do you think this man is in need of your persuasion, mam?"

Looking the preacher up and down, she responded, tapping her finger to her temple. "Well, he's young and fine lookin', an they's usually *that* kind." She reached out, tapping the book she had just given Wendell. "This here book is *Ten Nights in a Bar Room.* Ain't been outsold by nothin' 'cept *Uncle Tom's Cabin* back in the fifties."

Hannah wanted to have some fun. "Well, how do you expect to save this man, mam?"

The woman stuttered, her bun bouncing on the back of her bobbing head. "Why, why, if'n he reads this here book, it'll scare the wits outta him for sure. It tells about drunks bein' banished to the poor house and bein' killed in bar room brawls." Confidence glowed in her condescending look.

"Well, mam, don't you think it would be better to tell the poor souls that Jesus loves them so much he died for them?"

"Well, well... uh, we get to that later down the road. Ya see, it's our plan. First we scare um, and then they get ready for the gospel." The quick jerk of the woman's head seemed to settle it, at least in her own mind.

"Is God's love ever a part of the plan, mam?"

The woman appeared confused. "Well, well... "

Hannah gestured to Wendell as if introducing royalty. "Mam, you're speaking to the preacher who is conducting the camp meeting at the Savannah River. We'd like to invite you to our services so you can learn about the love of God."

Wendell smiled at the way Hannah handled herself with the pious woman.

The woman backed across the street, pointing and saying something to the ladies of her group.

Clucking to the mules, Ezra's leaving was halted by yet another lady stepping off the boardwalk, running in their direction. "Hey, hey, there. You the reverend?" Pushing her spectacles up on her nose, recognition dawned. "Reckon you are at that. Now why ain't ya joined us on the boardwalk? You should be a preachin' fire and damnation to the lot of them sinners in that den of debauchry." She sounded ready to drop them all into the hot place.

"Mam, I believe in winning people to the Lord in a different way."

Perplexed, the woman pushed the spectacles back up her nose, peering deep into his eyes. "What different way is there?"

"The way of love, mam, the way of love."

"'Xcuse us, mam, we be a takin' our leave. Got some errans to run afore da evenin' service." Ezra was determined to escape. Turning in the seat, he held his hand to his face. "Ain't a gonna change her mind taday."

The woman raised her hand to them. "I'll be to the service tonight, Preacher. Been sittin' on the right side with my group of women. Need ta getcha a hot sermon fer those vermin a comin' to the meetin'."

"See you tonight, mam." Wendell waved, relief showing on his face as Ezra put more distance between the buggy and the Teetotalers of Savannah.

"Looks like we got mo than molasses, taday, folks." They shared a laugh.

Wendell edged closer to Hannah on the seat. "I've seen some sights with those temperance movements. In Charleston I witnessed a woman coming out of a saloon brandishing an ax. Said it was her job to tear up the devil's work any way she could. Seemed she was literally tearing up saloons with her ax."

Hannah laughed. "Must have scared a few patrons in the process."

"From the looks of her, she could have put down the ax and been just as frightening."

The two laughed in sweet camaraderie. Hannah loved feeling this way.

Ezra turned the wagon in at the Savannah Feed and Tack Supply. Wendell jumped down, quickly returning with the molasses.

Ezra turned the buggy back toward the river. They passed Sam's Barber Shop, advertising haircuts for five cents, shaves for two cents, and shoe shines for a penny.

At the end of the row of buildings, a millinery shop window advertised fall hats. Seeing a broad-brimmed obnoxious-looking creation, Hannah started laughing. "That purple and red hat with flowers and ladybugs reminds me of someone back home."

Wendell chuckled. "Let me guess, Widow Crouch."

"How did you know?"

"Let's just say I spent enough time with Blaine to understand the widow's fetish." The two shared more laughter.

Passing several squares, Ezra stopped at the produce stand. "Miz Betsy, my Eliza's jes about dyin' fer one o yo jars o chow chow relish. She be a cookin' a pot a beans wif salt pork all day. Gots enuff ta feed half a square a Savanians. She a sayin', 'Jes won't taste right wif no chow chow relish from Miz Betsy.'"

Pulling a jar from a shelf below her counter, Miz Betsy smiled at Ezra's praise. "Go right ahead an tell Eliza I's still gonna be a comin' fer a visit, real soon like."

"I tell 'er." Placing a few coins on the counter, Ezra waved goodbye, climbing onto the wagon seat.

Wendell and Hannah had been watching three boys racing their frogs beside Miz Betsy's stand.

"Reminds me of the book by Mark Twain, *The Celebrated Jumping Frog of Calaveras County.*"

"Me too, Preacher." Hannah waved to the boys as they headed down the road.

Ezra was pointing to the tree in the next square they were coming to. "Dis be Franklin Square, name after Mr. Benjmin Franklin. Dat Chinese tallow tree been here fo a mighty long time. Da seeds done sent here by Mr. Franklin hisself. Dis here town done plum full o histry, Miz Hanner." Hannah listened intently to Ezra's explanation of several of the town squares. "Savannah done dee zined in squares by James Oglethrope."

Wendell shared his knowledge of the town. Pointing ahead, he gave tidbits of information about some of the squares. "Johnson's Square held a reception for President James Monroe in 1819. And here's one you will connect with. Telfair Square, named after the governor. It houses the Methodist Church."

"Yessa, an it be made o fine Gawgia pine, from da trees right here in Gawgia."

"Washington Square is named after who?" Wendell's eyes held a teasing glint.

"George Washington, I'm sure."

"There's the Hampton Lillibridge House with its widow's walk. It dates back to 1796."

"How interesting, Preacher."

"How'd I do, Ezra?"

"Mos excellent, Preacha, mos excellent."

"Well, I had a good teacher."

Ezra smiled at the preacher's compliment.

Turning the wagon, they took another route. Soon the United States Custom House came into view. "James Oglethorpe lived there for a time, and many cases of law have been tried in the Custom House." Pointing to a building on the rear lot, Wendell explained. "John Wesley preached his first sermon in Savannah in that building in 1736."

Chatham Artillery boasted a display of the Washington Guns on wheels. "Those were captured at Yorktown and given to Savannah in 1791 by George Washington himself."

"My, we are the epitome of the educated Savannah historian, aren't we?" Hannah teased the preacher.

Wendell seemed to gain impetus. "Did you know that Savannah is located on Yamacraw Bluff, eighteen miles inland from the Atlantic Ocean? And did you know that the bluff was given to James Oglethorpe as a gift by an Indian he had befriended? Mr. Oglethorpe laid out the city of Savannah as a grid of streets surrounding squares."

"My, my, sir, do I hear pride resonating in one's voice?"

"No, mam, just pure knowledge, plain and simple." Raising his chin, Wendell smirked.

Ezra joined Hannah in laughter from his perch on the front seat of the buggy. "We's betta get y'alls home an dress fer church meetin' afore y'all both has ta repent."

Ezra turned onto a back road. Wendell placed his arm around Hannah's waist. The young girl's senses came fully alive with his touch.

Cardinals chirping on a cherry tree beside the road had never looked so red as they did today. The smell of jasmine reaching her nose gave her a heady feeling. Closing her eyes, Hannah imagined the smooth rocking of Ezra's new buggy as the gentle boat ride she had shared with Wendell going to the Seminole village.

A jolt from a pot hole disturbed Hannah's daydream, but today reality was as good as the daydream. Still feeling Wendell's hand about her waist, she leaned into his side.

They were alone in their own world for a few moments, just a young lady with her beloved by her side. Ezra's back was ramrod straight. He hummed an old spiritual, never looking back.

Wendell's breath was warm against her ear, his whisper a reminder of his nearness. "My dear Miss Hannah, *are* you spoken for?"

"What if I am?" Her words were but a whisper.

"Then methinks the one who has spoken for you will be disappointed that we are sharing this tryst."

"I am not spoken for. Let's say that I was asked but the answer was quite an enlightening experience."

At Wendell's look of confusion, Hannah related the whole story of the unwanted suitor. She retold all the situations in Laurel City, even including the tales of Mr. Rivers around the potbelly stove. Ezra continued humming, but Hannah was sure he had one ear cocked toward her quiet voice.

"So when I saw you feeding the chocolates to Isaac, you were just setting him up for the dousing?"

"Yes. I couldn't wait to pay him back for his shenanigans. Sadness set in the following day when I heard you had witnessed the first part of the rendezvous without waiting for the end."

"It caused me many hours of pain, to be sure." His arm tightened around her waist.

"Might we share a future together, Miss Hannah?"

"Might we, Preacher? Don't you think you should be asking my father for his permission first?"

Touching his shirt pocket, he pulled out an envelope. "Methinks I should fill ye in, madam."

Wendell intercepted Hannah's hand as she reached for the paper.

"Sir, thou shouldest not lead me into temptation."

"Temptation, madam?"

"I shall not rest until I know you will be my suitor, sir."

"Thou shalt rest this night indeed, madam."

Handing her the envelope, Hannah opened the note from her father to her beloved. Garrett Baxter had given his blessing on their courtship.

Hannah sent Wendell a coy look. "Perhaps you need someone less outgoing and adventurous. Won't your reputation be ruined if we should marry and people think you don't have your wife under control? What about all those tight-bunned biddies?"

"Hannah Baxter, I love you, with all of your ornery ways. Matter of fact, I think I love you more because of your spunk. Let the tight-bunned biddies decide their own fate. We'll just keep letting the love of God shine through."

A mischievous twinkle lit Hannah's green eyes. "I love you, Wendell Cunningham."

"I love you more," he whispered back.

Contentment filled the second seat of Ezra's new buggy that day—love and contentment.

"Stop, Ezra, stop."

"Why ya be wantin' me to stop, Preacher?" Ezra pulled back on the reins, and Hannah watched as Wendell jumped out of the buggy and walked just past the edge of the roadway.

Returning with his hands behind his back, the young man came up to the wagon, laying a huge bouquet of wild roses in Hannah's lap. Climbing into the buggy, he sat closer to Hannah, wrapping her in a warm embrace after Ezra smiled and clucked to his mules.

"For you, my love. Why are you crying?"

"It's just the joy spilling over. Thank you, Wendell Cunningham."

"You're welcome, Hannah Rose Baxter."

Late that night a candle burned in the front third-story bedroom of the De Ponte mansion. Bending over her sketchpad, Hannah drew the scene of the temperance woman preaching her message to Wendell, titling it, *Mo than Molasses.*

Unable to put the pencil down just yet, she sketched her and Wendell on Ezra's new buggy seat, the freshly picked roses lying beside her, her beloved's arm circling her waist. *What should I title this?* Tapping her pencil, it took only a few seconds to decide what this sketch would be named. Slowly she penciled Wendell's words of endearment at the bottom of the sketch: *I Love You More.*

Chapter 27

By the second week of the camp meeting, small tents had multiplied on the bank of the river. Although the men wore their guns, it seemed all was well. The only worry had been the self-righteous actions of the Savannah Teetotalers, which had been multiplied when Mrs. Totem showed up with her crowd of bitter old ladies.

Wendell Cunningham just kept preaching the love, grace, and mercy of Jesus Christ. Looking toward Hannah during the services, he seemed to gain momentum each night. Hannah knew her smiles warmed him to the core.

After the service on Friday evening, Mrs. Totem came to put her two cents' worth in. "Preacher, ya gonna preach on sin afore this meetin's over?"

"Well, mam, I'll preach what the good Lord gives me. Can't add anything to his message."

Her face turned three shades of red. Hannah whispered to Gabrielle, "She looks madder than a wet setting hen."

Gabrielle turned aside to cover the giggles trying to escape.

"I'll be a tellin' you, Preacher, ya ain't doin' no good just a preachin' all that love an grace when these here men need to be dangled over the hot pit. Yessir, the way I see it, they need their britches warmed by the fires o Hades."

"Mam, God gives everyone a choice. Each person has to make their own decision to serve or reject God; just as each person has to decide whether to show lovingkindness toward sinners or show them more hate than they already know."

Now Mrs. Totem was turning purple. Her friend nudged her elbow. "You tell 'im, Myrtle, you tell 'im." Her face was nearly as dark as Myrtle Totem's face.

"I'm a tellin' the man, Celia. Hold yer horses." And then she turned back to the preacher.

"Alls I'm a sayin', Preacher, is that yore gonna give an account ta God fer what you preach here, an I say these men need a good hide tannin'."

Wendell remained calm. "And all I'm saying, mam, is that I will listen to God's voice, which is his Word. I will not try fear tactics and hateful words to bring these men to repentance. Our Father draws his children with loving kindness. I feel it is our duty to follow his example."

Mrs. Totem harrumphed loudly, and, turning on her heel, she almost tripped over a bench. The tight bun at the nape of her neck bounced to the vehement rhythm of her shaking head.

As soon as Myrtle Totem stomped out of the tent with her ladies huffing and puffing behind, Wendell stepped alongside Hannah. Placing her hand in the safety of his elbow, he whispered in her ear. "That woman looks dangerous."

"She may blow up any minute."

Gabrielle added her thoughts. "Reverend Cunningham, are you sure we've got to love that group?"

"Very sure, Miss Gabrielle." The three friends shared a soft chuckle.

Now well into October, the third week of camp meeting started with a bang, quite literally. As soon as the service began, a loud report rang out behind the tent. Wendell left the stage in a hurry to find the reason for the gunshot. Jacques De Ponte was close behind. Several other men joined them.

The smell of smoke seemed very close. Slowly the women made their way toward the back of the tent. There before them was a large cross, blazing in the dark sky; its image reflected in the Savannah River.

Gabrielle grabbed her friend's arm. "Oh my, Hannah, that's the sign of the Klan."

Women huddled together, fear radiating in their faces. Several held a handkerchief to the tears pooling in their frightened eyes.

Hannah had heard of the activities of the Klansmen. Homes and plantations were burned in opposition to the freed slaves and their sympathizers. Lynching parties were formed, and many found their fate at the end of a noose.

Fear started the young girl's head spinning. Gabrielle must have felt the same; they both sat down at once.

If the first two weeks of the camp meeting had gone peacefully, the last one was already making up for the quiet. Wendell preached a fine message after the fire was doused, and the congregation dispersed quietly.

The next night, Mrs. Totem and her ladies started harassing any man in the tent who looked worthy of their persecution.

Tonight a scrawny looking man became their first target. "You there, I'm sure you tip that bottle mighty high. Repent, I say repent, or you'll make yer bed in Hades," Mrs. Totem warned with her finger in his face.

The poor man's eyes widened, and he beat a quick path out of the tent.

Gabrielle nudged Hannah. "That's the saddest part of all."

Hannah followed her gaze to the children of the temperance women. Two beautiful little girls sat on the bench watching their mothers' antics. Catching Hannah and Gabrielle's attention, they stuck their tongues out at them. One of the girls sent Hannah a scornful look.

"Training them right, aren't they?" Hannah could hardly bear the thought.

"Seems they're already filled with hate. One belongs to Mrs. Shaggerty, whose husband was killed driving his wagon home from a drunken night in the saloon."

"I can understand the hurt the woman must feel, but bitterness won't help her situation. Matter of fact, it is hurting her child."

"I've heard that Mrs. Shaggerty drags the child to the neighboring farm often, leaving her so that she can go propagate her message with the temperance women."

Rising from the bench, walking over to a man nearby, the little girl punched him in the leg. "Bad man." She wagged her finger at him.

"Oh no, Hannah. This has got to stop." Gabrielle and Hannah looked to the front of the church.

"Ladies of the temperance movement, be seated." Wendell's voice held a sharp edge, one Hannah had never heard before. A few of the women sat down, looking to their leader, who was still carrying on.

"Ladies, I said, 'Be seated.'"

"Sit down, Myrtle. You've made your point." At least one of the ladies in the group had a bit of sense left.

"God is not the author of confusion. I'll not have you good people bombarded with fear or with the harassment of the temperance movement."

A woman from the Savannah Teetotalers group gasped, pushing her spectacles back up on her nose. "I do declare."

Wendell remained undaunted. "Ladies, you are welcome here. However, if you cannot leave your antics outside, you will be escorted out by the sheriff and his deputies." Wendell pointed to the front row where the men stood at attention.

Myrtle Totem seemed to wilt ever so slightly at the sight of the large group of men looking menacingly in the direction of her group of ladies.

The service continued without incident. Wendell's sermon found a resting place in Hannah's heart.

"You may stand for the benediction. Gracious Father, of heaven and earth, we ask that you grant peace to your people. Fill us with your wisdom and love, in Christ's name. Amen."

The following two services were filled with the warmth of the Lord. Everyone gathered around the front altar, lifting their voices in praise before the benediction.

One night, at the closing of the service, Hannah reached Wendell's side. "That was such a wonderful, timely message, Reverend Cunningham."

"Don't you reverend me, *Sister* Hannah."

Her green eyes twinkled. "We're both beyond that, I hope."

"Surely, I should hope."

Riding back to the plantation in the De Ponte carriage, the artist gave his words of praise. "Wendell Cunningham makes the Word of God so clear that even a child can understand and receive God's love."

Eliza invited everyone over for a piece of apple pie. "Y'all takes a seat, an I have dat pie dished up in no time atall."

Finishing the pie, Wendell and Hannah excused themselves for a private walk. A half moon lit their path as they walked toward the stream.

Wendell reached out, taking her hand in his. "Hannah, I know we have just begun our courtship, but I need to talk with you about some things, serious things."

"All right, Wendell."

"First, you need to know that sometimes I have nightmares from my past. They are very frightening. I feel I'm back living with Granny, and I even scream at times."

"I know, Wendell."

"You do?"

"Yes, I've heard your screams from my bedroom window."

The hand holding hers grew slack. Even in the moonlight, Hannah could tell he was sad that she knew. "How do you feel about that, Hannah? I must know." His feet came to a halt, and he stood before her staring at the ground.

Releasing his hand, Hannah reached out, lifting his chin and forcing him to look into her eyes. She knew he would find love there, all the love he needed for the rest of his life.

"I want you to see the love I have for you, Wendell Cunningham. Do you see it?"

His feet shifted, his eyes returning to the ground. "Yes, I do. But I'm so ashamed, Hannah."

She lifted his chin, once again. "Ashamed of what? Would it bother you if I had been so deeply hurt in my past that these nightmares were a part of my life? What would you do, Wendell?"

When he lifted his eyes to hers, she could see unshed tears. "I'd, I'd… Well, I'd love you more, I reckon."

"That's exactly how I feel. I love you more for those things you have suffered, and I want to make the bad memories go away, replaced by new and happy ones."

Wendell pulled her close, the fragrance of the peach orchard coming to them on the wind. "I shall have you as my own, Hannah Baxter. Mark my word."

His lips claimed hers, and she relished the warmth of his admission. Her heart would never be empty or lonely again.

"We better get back before I have to change professions. A man of the cloth still has temptations."

She cocked an eyebrow, straightening his cravat. "Oh really, sir?"

"Yes, mam. Now you listen to me, Hannah. My intentions are honorable, and I would never do you any harm."

Raising the other eyebrow, she answered. "I know you are an honorable man." Standing on tiptoe, she placed a quick peck on his cheek before running back to Eliza's house to bid everyone good night.

The cockatiels sang a lovely melody as she walked by their elaborate home. "You must be in love too," she said, passing by.

Camp meeting services were coming to an end. Tonight would mark the last of this year's meetings. Mrs. Totem and her temperance ladies complained the whole night, as did the Savannah Teetotalers. Even through the complaints, there were underlying smiles on the ladies' usually stoic faces.

Gabrielle and Hannah wondered what the reason might be for their happiness. "Maybe the camp meeting did them some good."

"I doubt it, Hannah. They look like the cat that swallowed the canary."

The opening hymn brought the girls to their feet. Three songs later, everyone returned to their place on the benches—everyone except Myrtle Totem. "Jest have a quick testimony ta the goodness of God, Revern."

Hannah could see Wendell perk up, as if his messages had hit home and found a landing in the lady's hardened heart. "Tell us about his goodness, Mrs. Totem."

"Thank ya, Preacher. I believe I will. Jest want ta tell all y'all that we's been a prayin' 'bout all the saloons what be in or near Savanny. Got word tonight that our prayers got answered over this a way. The Savanny Saloon done an burnt ta the ground, a taking the barkeep an a few drunks ta their place where the fire is not quenched and the worm dieth not." Myrtle Totem raised her hand in the air, pointing her finger and shaking her head back and forth. She became so animated, she could barely keep her feet on the ground. "Jest wanted ta praise him fer a brangin' down his wrath." And with that the lady abruptly sat down.

"We're sorry to hear about those who were consumed in the fire. Please be praying for their families." Wendell turned to his first passage of scripture in the Bible.

Before he announced the chapter and verse, Hannah heard Mrs. Totem say, "Believe me, them famlies shore are better off without um. No-good drunks."

Turning to her friend, she said in a loud voice, "Matilda, where'd he say he's a gonna read from?"

"He ain't said as yet, Myrtle."

Looking toward the front, Hannah saw Wendell shake his head before announcing the scripture.

The preacher ministered on God's promise to give us the desires of our hearts. With shining eyes, he read the scripture, then gazed lovingly at Hannah. "God has granted me my heart's desire. He has filled a longing. All emptiness is gone, and in its place is every good thing he has for my future."

Matilda turned toward Myrtle Totem. "I think he's gone mushy on us."

"Oh, no bother, Matilda. He's been mushy the whole time."

Finishing the sermon, Wendell's eyes seemed to be on something at the back of the tent. After dismissal, Hannah followed him outside.

"Could I help you, sir? Seems as if you were trying to find someone."

"Yes, Preacher. I'm Ezra Perkins, Jr., and I'm lookin' for my pa."

"Ezra… Ezra Perkins, Jr.? Oh, what joy you're gonna bring tonight." Wendell pumped the man's arm nearly off his shoulder.

Hannah gasped seeing the *Godey's Lady's Book* in the hand of the young woman standing at his side. "Can it be?"

"Can what be, Hannah?" Wendell asked.

"Can it be that the magazine has something to do with you coming?"

The lady answered. "Yes, mam, it has everything to do with our coming. I read the poem, and, knowing of my husband's search for his family, we figured out that they were still here in Savannah. And all because of this poem; this one right here, 'Eliza's Song.'"

Wendell grabbed Hannah, all thoughts of finding Ezra set aside for the moment. "Oh my dear, sweet Hannah. God used you as an answer to Eliza and Ezra's prayer."

Hannah's tears were flowing like the Savannah River. "Oh my, oh my." Coming out of her stupor, she took off down the riverbank. "I see Eliza up ahead. I'll go get them."

"I'm right with you, sweetheart. Isn't that just like God?" Wendell was by her side, gripping her arm so she couldn't get away.

Hannah frantically waved her other arm. "Eliza, Ezra, your prayers have been answered. Your prayers have been answered."

"What you mean, Miz Hanner?" Eliza asked, making her way to Hannah's side.

"Ezra, Jr., your son, he's here." Hannah took hold of Eliza's trembling shoulder. The message didn't seem to be getting through. Hannah gave her friend's shoulder a gentle shake. "Your son is here, Eliza."

"Yes, I'm here, Mama." The voice behind them was followed by the son running into his mother's embrace.

"Oh, my boy, my boy, dear Father in heaven, you's so good ta ol Eliza." Hugging her son with tears streaming down her face, Eliza was overcome. She collapsed on the ground, and Ezra came to pick her up after hearing the commotion. He had been walking with his friend and had failed to hear Hannah's call.

Eliza's voice was dazed. "Ezra, our boy's come home. Our boy's come home."

"What, Eliza? You swoonin' and talkin' outta yo head, honey?"

"No, Ezra, that's why I'm 'bout ta swoon. Da good Lawd done an brought our boy back to us. Thank ya, blessed Jesus."

Reaching for her hanky, she wiped the tears from her eyes as Ezra turned, and spotting his son, fell into his outstretched arms.

Ezra pulled back, looking at his son in amazement. There were no words coming from his mouth. He grabbed his son again, weeping and thanking the Lord. Next he held him at arm's length, letting his eyes drink in the sight. "How'd ya find us, Son?"

He looked at the lady standing by Ezra, Jr. She was waving a magazine. "We read the poem in *Godey's Lady's Book* and knew you were still in Savannah, sir."

"Pa, meet my wife, Miriam."

Ezra grabbed the young lady, wrapping her in a welcoming hug. "Ol Ezra can't believe da good thangs da Lawd be doin' dis night." He shook his head from side to side, holding on to Miriam and his son at the same time. "Fill ya papa in, Ezra. Ya be a readin' 'Eliza's Song' what Miz Hanner wrote?"

"Yes, sir. It was Hannah Baxter, and I'm guessin' we just met her."

"That's me; I failed to introduce myself through the tears." Hannah was standing in Wendell's embrace.

Myrtle and Matilda walked by, casting reproachful eyes at the preacher and Hannah. She returned their looks with a sweet smile. Gabrielle came up just in time to catch the exchange. "I'm practicing for the role of pastor's wife," Hannah explained to her friend.

"You did good."

And then Hannah filled her friend in on what was happening with Ezra's family.

She walked with Gabrielle back toward the plantation. "Where were you anyway?"

"Agatha pulled me to the side, asking questions about the preacher."

"Well, what did you tell her?"

"I told her y'all were getting married." She enunciated her words with an exaggerated Southern drawl.

Hannah put her hand to her face and laughed. "Good girl."

Gabrielle gave her a petty, accusing look. "Now you should not rejoice in another's displeasure as a pastor's wife, dearie." This time, she used her mother's best French accent.

"I shall have to practice much on that one; especially if it involves someone like Agatha Hathaway."

"Don't let her get you riled, dearie."

"I'm just thinking, teeth, hair, and eyeballs all over the cotton patch."

"What?"

Hannah was remembering a story Eliza had shared about her and Ezra's romancing and how a slave girl from a neighboring plantation had tried to woo Ezra. Hannah shared the story with Gabrielle as the rest of the crowd dispersed. "Eliza said, 'I tolt dat girl, if'n ya don't leave my man alone, there be teeth, hair, an eyeballs strewn all over dis here cotton plantation, an it sho nuff won't be mine.' I saw fire in Eliza's eyes, even after so many years had passed. I remember asking Eliza what happened the next time the girl saw Ezra. She said, 'She reached up touchin' her hair; guess she wanted ta keep it. She struck a path cross dat cotton patch, not even a worryin' 'bout da thorns. She jes ran right on; ain't looked back yet.'"

"Teeth, hair, and eyeballs? You should be ashamed, dearie." Gabrielle and Hannah laughed as they caught up with the procession to the De Ponte Plantation. Everyone had decided to walk tonight, except Wendell, who was retrieving his stallion.

There was much rejoicing in the old slave quarters that night as the young couple described how they found Ezra's parents.

"The man who bought me tole me my mama and papa moved all the way out West. He tole me this plantation was burned to the groun by Sherman. Guess he was afraid I'd run away."

Miriam spoke up. "When I read the poem, it told how Eliza felt and how they had stayed in the same place in case their son returned. Only God could have given you the words to write, Miss Hannah. My Ezra was so sad over being separated from his family."

Ezra, Jr. nodded his head. "I asked a few slaves who used the Underground Railroad, and they told me papa and mama left years ago. I believed them."

"I's plannin' ta leave, Son, but after ya leff, we decided ta stay put so's you'd know where ta fine us."

Eliza wiped fresh tears from her eyes. "I jes cain't hardly comprahen how God brought Miz Hanner ta us ta study da arts on dis hea plantation. An then she be hearin' my song an makin' it better an makin' it rhyme. Nex Miz Berndette fines da ole scrap o paper an senz it off an it gets put in dat faincy magazine. Ol Eliza's burden become ol Eliza's deelivrance. Glory be."

Old Ezra shook his head. "Sho nuff."

The kind woman continued. "Jes goes ta show how God be a workin' all thangs fer our good no matter how it be seemin'. Ol Eliza's jes thankful, so thankful."

Reaching out to Hannah, she whispered, "An you's sech a big part a dat plan."

Hannah wiped fresh tears, rising to leave with Gabrielle. "We'll leave you to yourselves. Enjoy God's goodness."

"Yessum, we gonna do jes dat."

Hannah and Gabrielle hugged father, son, and the ladies good night.

"I would say that the camp meeting ended on a perfect note. God is good."

"Amen, Preacher."

Wendell walked the girls to the back door of the mansion. Gabrielle left the two alone.

"Good night, my sweet."

"Good night, Wendell Cunningham."

Hannah Baxter climbed two flights of stairs, feeling as though she could climb a dozen more. Wendell's sweet good-night kiss still warmed her lips. "Thank you, Lord, for fulfilling our deepest desires."

The smell of lavender emanating from her bed sheets wooed her into sweet slumber. But not before she sketched the homecoming with her and Wendell taking Ezra to his mother and father. The sketch showed the tears and the joy of the reunion. Wendell and Hannah stood alongside Miriam, her *Godey's Lady's Book* in hand, proudly looking on.

Chapter 28

"Hannah, wake up. We've got a full day ahead of us. I've got a plan, Hannah, wake up."

Slowly making her way to the door, she let her friend in. "What is so important this early in the morning?"

Gabrielle's smile was contagious. "Mother and Father are visiting Atlanta for art supplies. They'll be away for a week. Come on, I've got an idea."

"Sounds like fun, Gabrielle." Hannah washed her face with the water from her pitcher, drying it on the embellished towel. Quickly pulling her braid loose, she turned to her friend. "Since you have plans, how shall I dress for the day?"

"Where are the riding habits?"

"At the back of the armoire. Why?"

"We're gonna go for a ride on a bicycle, Hannah."

"I've wanted to do that since I first saw one at the river, but I have to admit, I'm just a little afraid."

"You, afraid? Just think how grand it will be."

"I don't know, Gabrielle. It sounds like fun, but I've seen many a young man hit his head when he goes flying over the front. From what I've observed, the least little bump in the road or a rock or anything, makes the contraption tip forward."

Gabrielle burst out in laughter.

"What are you laughing at?"

"Just picturing you with a big bump on your head, answering the door as a pastor's wife."

"I guess I should be practicing." One look at her friend and she shook her head. "No, I'll settle down later. Got to have fun while we can."

"With my parents gone and Eliza and Ezra spending time with their son and his wife, we only have to sneak away before the preacher catches us."

"He's meeting with the area ministers to discuss disassembling the camp ground. He'll be gone all morning."

"Good. We're having an afternoon picnic with the Perkins family and the preacher. We'll have our fun and be back in time for the picnic."

"Let's get moving then. Are you sure the man is at the river who offers the bicycle rides?"

Gabrielle pointed to the front window. "See for yourself."

Buttoning the chemise of the riding habit, Hannah walked to the window. The cool breeze tickled her senses. Perusing the riverbank, she noticed the bicycle. "Let's go."

Descending the stairs, the girls stopped long enough to gulp down a cinnamon cookie and a glass of milk.

Running the short distance to the river, Gabrielle and Hannah approached the bicycle owner. "Sir, sir, could we pay for a ride?"

The man laughed at Gabrielle's question. "You girlies go on back home and churn some butter. You got no business out here. These are toys for the boys." He seemed proud of himself, talking down to the young ladies.

"Sir, we have the money, and we want a ride."

"The answer's still no, girlies."

"Well, how about if we pay a dollar instead of the nickel you are charging?"

Gabrielle nudged Hannah, whispering, "That's too much, Hannah."

"I'm paying."

Gabrielle joined Hannah's plea. "Yeah, how about one dollar, mister?"

The man seemed amazed, unable to believe the offer of making two dollars from the girls who stood before him. Hannah could tell he was tempted to accept their money.

Ready to get on with the adventure, she upped the ante. "I'll pay three dollars for the two of us."

That cinched the deal. "All right, but I'll not be responsible for what happens, you bein' girls and all."

Both Hannah and Gabrielle smiled brightly.

"All right, you first." The man pointed to Gabrielle.

"Sure, mister." The man helped her get her seat, nervously walking beside the bicycle. Gabrielle managed to pedal the wheel, staying upright to the very end. Just as she completed the final turn of the pedal, the contraption tipped precariously to the right. Pulling with all his might, the man saved her from falling.

The man wiped his brow, then turned to Hannah. "That was close. Don't know if I want you up there, missy."

Hannah placed her hands on her hips. "You've been paid, mister; now help me up."

"You fall, I ain't gonna take the blame."

At that moment, the spectacled woman from the Savannah Teetotalers appeared, disdainfully watching Hannah trying to climb up on the bicycle. Her gaze fell to Hannah's ankle, showing beneath the riding habit. "Oh my, you a wearin' one o them devil skirts," she muttered, covering her mouth with her hand.

Hannah spoke to the owner of the bicycle. "You don't worry about me falling; you worry about helping me stay up."

Getting settled atop the seat was a laughing matter. For some reason, Hannah kept sliding from one side of the seat to the other. Finally reaching the pedal, she pushed it forward. Just before it came full circle, she saw the rock in front of her.

"Oh no." But it was too late. Pitching headlong over the huge front wheel, she felt something on the wheel biting into her leg. Her body got hung up in the handlebars before her head connected with the huge boulder to the side of the bicycle. Blackness engulfed her just as she heard Gabrielle's scream and the temperance woman mutter, "Serves ya right."

From somewhere, Hannah heard her friend calling her name. Slowly opening her eyes, she saw fear in Gabrielle's face. "I'm sorry, Hannah. We shouldn't have done this. Oh, what am I to do? It's all my fault."

"That's right, mam; it's all your fault." The man who owned the bicycle hurriedly scooted his toy into the copse of trees at the bend of the river, immediately disappearing.

"I'll be all right, Gabrielle. Don't worry." The darkness was closing in on her again.

"Hannah. Hannah, dear, please wake up."

Opening her eyes, it took a moment for the injured girl to realize she was lying on the sofa in Eliza's home.

"Girl, ya sho did give us a scare."

Hannah tried to sit up, but the pounding in her head made her lie back.

Wendell was rubbing her arm, worry and fear apparent in his eyes.

The events leading up to this moment came flooding back. "I'm sorry, Wendell."

"I'm sorry too, Hannah. And you should know better than to try such a daring feat."

"I know."

Bringing her fingers to his lips, he whispered. "It's all right. You've got an egg on your head and a bad scrape on your ankle, but you're gonna live to be a pastor's wife in spite of yourself."

"I don't look much like a pastor's wife. Guess I should practice more." Her smile was devious.

"I like you just the way you are. That's why I fell in love with you."

Eliza continued cleaning the blood from Hannah's ankle. "Don't ya be in couragin' her in her antics, Preacher." But Eliza smiled in spite of her worries.

"Where's Gabrielle?"

"I'm right here, Hannah. I'm so sorry."

"I'm just fine. Why don't you go home, and I'll just rest here."

"Go on, Miz Gabrielle. Hanner be jes fine right chere." Ezra walked Gabrielle to the door.

Hannah tried to sit up. "When are we going on our picnic?"

"That will have to wait fo anutha day, Miz Hanner. You done had too much excitement fo one day."

Finally sitting up, she realized darkness had set in.

"Ya been out stone cole for a while, honey chile. Now you rest. Mama Eliza's gonna watch out fo ya."

Hannah's eyes were closing of their own accord.

"Good night." She barely felt Wendell's lips softly caressing her fingers.

Cold November winds blew across the Savannah River, reaching deep inland. The De Ponte mansion's chimneys were puffing smoke rivaling that of the big riverboats sitting in port.

Hannah's body was mending from the fall. During her time of recovery, she had sketched many scenes. The egg on her head was only a small bump now.

She stepped out of the warm house into the cold morning air, hoping to catch a few private moments with the preacher. It had been more than a week since *The Fall,* which she had sketched on paper. To Wendell's delight, she had included the temperance lady in the drawing. Hannah smiled, remembering the preacher's laughter when he saw the depiction.

Pulling her coat closer and tightening the scarf around her head, she walked past the cockatiel cage.

Ezra was burning logs in firepots. "Gots ta keep da birdies warm; least dat be what Miz Bernadette says."

Hannah smiled at the sight. "You're doing a good job, Ezra."

"Preacher's in da barn, Miz Hanner."

She rewarded her friend with a smile. He understood her need to see Wendell.

Slowly opening the barn door, Hannah saw her beloved, standing at the last stall, pouring a cup of oats into the trough for his stallion. She knew he would be leaving soon. Sadness filled her heart at the thought, but time was a wastin' an daylight was a burnin' as old Ezra would say. The young girl pushed ahead, not willing to waste one moment that she could be with her suitor.

"Good morning, love."

His words warmed her heart in spite of the cold. "Good morning."

"I need to have a talk with you, Hannah."

He's leaving; I just know he's leaving. Moisture pooled in her eyes.

"Don't look so sad." Coming to join her, Wendell reached up, touching a curl that had escaped from her scarf.

"Let's go out behind the barn to the courting buggy. That will be a good place for our talk."

"The courting buggy?"

"Ezra didn't tell you about the courting buggy?"

She looked bewildered. "No."

"Back in the days of slavery, the slaves weren't allowed to court openly on this plantation. So Ezra came up with a plan."

"He did, did he?"

"Yessum, sho nuff."

Hannah buried her face in Wendell's shoulder, laughing at his rendition of Ezra's accent.

By this time, they had arrived at the buggy behind the barn. Hannah remembered thinking if the old buggy could speak, it could surely tell some interesting stories. "Is this the courting buggy?" She couldn't wait to hear about it.

"Sho nuff."

Removing leaves from the seat, Wendell held Hannah's hand, assisting her up. She wrapped herself tighter within the warmth of her coat. The wind blowing from the river held quite a sharp bite today.

Seating himself beside Hannah, Wendell pretended to lift invisible reins, clucking to the would be mule. "Now the story will begin. There was a time in the pre-war days when this plantation was abuzz with crop planting and harvesting. So much work was to be done, the plantation owner allowed no time for frivolous romancing."

"'Twas a shame, indeed, sir."

"'Twas, mam. Anyhow, Ezra came up with a plan to assist his people in nurturing their romantic inclinations."

"Do tell, sir."

"I'm a tryin', Miz Hanner."

She laughed, enjoying his telling of Ezra's plan. "Go on ahead, sir."

"Thank ya, mam. Well, anyway, Ezra parked the buggy by the old corncrib." Pointing into the distance, Hannah followed his direction, spotting the wooden structure, built off the ground with slatted sides.

She nodded.

"The young ones would pair off, taking their turn sitting side by side in the old buggy seat, shucking corn from the corncrib. Some of the corn was sent to the mansion for the owner's family. Some was left to dry in the crib, later being used to feed the animals. And so was the tale of the courting buggy."

"Was it only used during the corn harvest?"

"No, Hannah. From what Ezra says, many nights young couples could be seen shelling peas and snapping beans in the courting buggy. Guess they thought up many ways to keep it in use." With those words, he moved closer on the seat, pulling Hannah against his shoulder.

They sat together, both in their own thoughts. Hannah's mind wandered down a trail it wished not to explore. She lifted her head, staring into Wendell's endearing face. "You'll be leaving soon, won't you?"

"Yes, my dear. I shall leave as soon as Thanksgiving is over."

She relaxed, nestling again on his shoulder. Thanksgiving was still a little more than two weeks away. "I shall enjoy every day until you leave."

Gently taking her by the shoulders, Wendell turned Hannah toward him. "What would you think of being a pastor's wife, Hannah?"

She cast him a very mischievous look.

"I'm serious, Hannah. I want to know your heart."

"Do you think I would pass for a pastor's wife, Preacher?" The mischievous look was still very evident.

Cupping her chin, he brushed her nose with a quick kiss. "I think you'd make a fine pastor's wife—a mite exciting, but fine nonetheless."

"You wouldn't make me wear a tight bun and dress in black all the time?"

"I'd hope you'd not be in mourning if you were my wife."

Her smile was brilliant. "I'd not be mourning, Wendell Cunningham."

"Well then, will you?"

"Will I what?" Her teasing ways filled his heart with joy.

"All right." He moved to a kneeling position as best he could in the floor of the old courting buggy. "Miss Hannah Rose Baxter, would you be my wife?"

Her hands flying to her face, Hannah rose to her feet. "Wendell Cunningham, are you proposing to me?"

He stood, clasping her hands in his and looking into those beautiful green eyes, now mirroring the rays of the sun. "Yessum, I sho nuff am. What be yo ansa, mam?"

"Why I'd be right honored ta be yo wife, sir."

"Hannah, dear Hannah, you will be mine?"

"Well, I said yes, Preacher Man, and I don't recall stuttering."

Gently covering her lips with his own, Wendell imparted to her all the joy and warmth her acceptance had just brought him. Pausing, he reached into his coat pocket. "Something to match those beautiful eyes, eyes that have been in my memory since I met you."

Hannah gasped as he opened a drawstring pouch, removing a gold ring with an emerald stone. Wendell reached for her hand, reverently placing the ring on her finger and holding it as if to assure that it would stay there.

Hannah held her hand up, looking at the ring with pleasure. "It's beautiful, Wendell. Thank you." She decided to thank him quite properly with a kiss of her own.

An hour later, the two were still sitting in the courting buggy, sharing their dreams and plans.

"What be dis out hea, Wendell. Ya be a courtin' Miz Hanner in da courtin' buggy? Sho does ol Ezra real proud like." The old man's smile warmed their hearts all over again. Coming to stand by the two, Ezra looked up, shaking his head from side to side.

"She's gonna marry me, Ezra." Wendell lifted Hannah's hand, showing the ring with the small emerald stone.

"Sho nuff?"

"Sho nuff."

"Well, did ya ask her pappy fer her han in holy matrimony?"

"I asked for all of Miss Hannah, Ezra, not just her hand. Got the letter right here. Just got an answer from Mr. Baxter last week, giving his blessings."

"Well, glory be. Eliza's gonna cook a meal ta celebrate when she fines out."

"Celebrating is good, Ezra."

The old man walked back to his home, a smile still in place on his worn features. It seemed that he had fewer wrinkles since his son had returned. Ezra, Jr. and his wife had stayed for a week, celebrating the reunion. They had returned home but had plans to move back to Savannah.

Wendell turned serious. "Hannah, I need to give the parson at Rosewood an answer by Christmas."

"Rosewood might be your pastorate, Wendell?" The joy in her voice caused him to be taken aback.

"Yes, Rosewood is the church that has been offered to me."

"I do declare, Wendell Cunningham. On my way up to Savannah, I was thinking of what it would be like to be a pastor's wife in that home."

"I'm hoping your dreams included me."

"Now who else would they include, Preacher?"

"No one comes to mind."

"And my best friend will be living in Rosewood. Susannah is marrying Matthew Madison at Christmas, and I'm to be in their wedding."

"I knew that Susannah would be joining Matthew in Rosewood. I'll head back after Thanksgiving and start filling in for the parson. He wants me to take over the church as soon as possible. This will give us time to make the transition."

"So we can spend Christmas together in Laurel City?"

"Yes, mam."

She couldn't resist hugging him. "Wendell Cunningham, you make me so happy. I was afraid you would be disappearing and I'd never be able to find you on the trail."

"That's why I wanted to make you my own and put our heads together for a plan."

"Well, you've done a mighty fine job, right here in the courting buggy."

"When can we get married? How much longer are you committed to art school?"

"I'm finished in March, and wedding bells are ringing in my head."

"Could we have a March wedding, Hannah?"

"Yes, and if it is all right with you, I'd like to get married right here."

"In Savannah?" This was a surprise.

"Not just in Savannah, right here on this plantation where we have spent our times of romance." She hesitated. "If that's all right with you, of course."

"Hannah Baxter, you could ask for the moon, and I'd start climbing, trying to retrieve it. Anywhere you want to get married is fine with me."

"Are you sure I'll make a good pastor's wife?"

"Sure as I know the ocean has water in it." Tilting his head, he eyed her with a devious look. "Now you are a mite sassy and full of mischief, but the parishioners will just have to get used to it."

"What if they are expecting a tight-bunned woman with self-righteous ways? Won't they be disappointed?"

"They'll get over it when they see how much fun you can be."

"I don't know. Some church women look like their face would crack if they smiled."

"Well, my dear, we want to portray God in a different way. And besides, there are only a few women in the Rosewood church who would fall into that category. It is full of youth and vitality."

"Well, that's good to know."

"Now, come with me, and we'll share our news with Eliza. She told me to ask you to join us for dinner." Wendell helped Hannah alight, hugging her close against the cold.

"Is it already noon? Where did the time go?"

"Time flies fast in the courting buggy, doesn't it?"

"Yes, it does."

Hannah opened the door to Eliza's house. Eliza spotted her ring before Wendell and Hannah were seated at the table.

"What news do ya haf ta share with Eliza?" She stood there, kitchen towel in hand, with hands placed on her hips. "Won't be no dinner 'til ya spill da beans."

Wendell's grin spread across his face. "All right, Mama Eliza, Hannah's going to be my wife."

"Glory be." The kitchen towel went flying through the air as Eliza grabbed Hannah in a hug, dancing all over the kitchen. Her joy was overflowing.

"I sees ya heared da news, Eliza." Ezra was grinning from ear to ear. "Are we a gonna eat dinna taday, or da we haf ta wait fer supper?"

"Aw, sit yoseff down, Ezra. We's jes celebratin'."

Dinner was a happy occasion. As the dishes of food made their rounds, so did plans for the March wedding. Between mouthfuls of collard greens, fried slabs of sweet potatoes, and Eliza's special roast pork, everything was discussed from dresses to the wedding cake. It was truly a wonderful afternoon the four shared at the Perkins' home.

Wendell walked his bride-to-be to the back door of the mansion. "A March wedding will be fine with plenty of wildflowers in bloom." He closed his eyes. "Reminds me of you sitting on the spring grass in the meadow that day among the wildflowers. See you tomorrow, my betrothed."

"With pleasure, my beloved."

Hannah's mind was racing to her sketchpad as she climbed the stairs. Her first sketch was a self-portrait of her among the wildflowers, hair blowing in the wind, and showing those exposed ankles. She sketched Wendell coming into the meadow on his horse, pausing to watch her on the spring grass. Slowly she penciled her thoughts, *Love among the Wildflowers.* Now that was a fitting title.

Before evening shadows claimed the landscape of the De Ponte Plantation, Hannah Baxter was putting the finishing touches on her second sketch, *Courting Buggy Proposal.*

Finally satisfied that she had captured their true feelings on paper, Hannah closed her sketchpad. Her eyes kept going to the ring on her finger, Wendell's ring of love.

She barely heard the knock at her door. Tiptoeing over, she opened it. "Come in, Gabrielle."

"Wanted to say good night. I thought you might still be up."

The story of the courting buggy and the proposal was shared, with Gabrielle trying to squelch her shouts of glee at this late hour. "I'm so happy for you, Hannah." Her eyes took on a sad look. "Mother is busy with her matchmaking. We'll be leaving for our Thanksgiving holiday tomorrow. We've got days of travel ahead of us to reach the Chennault Plantation."

"Where is it located?"

"In Washington, Georgia."

"Sure wish you could have stayed."

"I wanted to, but you know how Mother is." Gabrielle had explained her predicament the day before. She hugged her friend before going off to her room.

Adding another log to the fire, Hannah curled up in bed, reliving every moment of her time in the courting buggy with Wendell. She would miss Gabrielle, but she looked forward to her time with the preacher.

Chapter 29

November flew by on frigid air. Thanksgiving morning Hannah arose, dressing in a beautiful crimson gown. She would be spending this day with Eliza, Ezra, and Wendell. She had enjoyed her time alone since the artist and his family had taken a holiday.

Hannah had hugged her friend good-bye two weeks ago, wishing she could erase the sadness in her eyes.

"Pray for me." It had been but a whisper from her friend.

"I shall."

Gabrielle's face had suddenly lit up. She touched Hannah's betrothal ring. "Enjoy your time with the preacher."

"I shall." And she had.

Today she would set out to get the most out of the day, for her betrothed would be leaving soon.

Finally satisfied that her hair was complimentary, Hannah exited the warm house, the cold pushing her forward.

Knocking on her friends' door, the warmth from Eliza's kitchen enveloped Hannah. "May I help you, Eliza?"

"Most of it done an ready, Miz Hanner. Ezra done an gots dem oysters out o da beds in da Savanny River. He's a roastin' em on a piece a tin over a firepit. He done an got Wendell out dere a heppin' him."

"That sounds wonderful, Eliza. What have you been cooking this morning?"

"I's been a makin' conebread dressin', an I gots some cranberry relish ta go wif it. We gonna have some pole beans, I done an put up myself; jarred em dis summer pass. Oh yeah, I made us up some noodles wif chicken. Made da noodle dough up yesterdy, cut it, dried it, and cooked it up dis mornin' wif a chicken. Ol Ezra rung his neck jes afore da break a dawn."

"Eliza, the chicken and noodles smell delicious."

The woman smiled at Hannah. "Well, we gots us some okry an tomaters ta go wif it all. I done an jarred it up from da summer garden."

Sitting around the table with her friends and her beloved, Hannah was at peace. This day was a day of blessings and feeling thankful, especially thankful for Wendell's love. His ring on her finger reminded her of his commitment.

"Eliza, this is surely the best cornbread dressing I've tasted."

"Miz Hanner, dat chicken was fat enuff ta season up da noodles an da dressin'."

Wendell reached for Hannah's hand. "We sure are thankful to have you as friends, Ezra, Mama Eliza."

"Preacher, we's glad ta share dis day wif da two of yous. An gonna be a sharin' Chrissmas wif my boy." The smile on Ezra's face beamed the very meaning of Thanksgiving.

On Friday, Hannah rushed about getting dressed for her day with Wendell Cunningham. Ezra was making a trip into Two Mules Junction, and Wendell would be accompanying him. He had invited Hannah to join them.

Descending the stairs, she reached for a cherry tart, rushing outdoors to meet the preacher.

Ezra and Wendell were in the new buggy ready and waiting.

"Good morning, my love." Taking her hand, helping her up into the wagon, Wendell gently caressed the ring that spoke of their devotion. The two shared an intimate smile, contentedly settling themselves on the wagon seat.

As Ezra turned onto the bumpy road leading to Two Mules Junction, Hannah remembered the roughness of the old wagon and was glad this new one rode more smoothly.

"I couldn't imagine a better way to spend the day than with you." Hannah snuggled closer to Wendell beneath the lap robe, her feet hugging the warming brick tightly.

"Our hearts are warm, if nothing else." His teeth were chattering as he lowered his head against the biting wind.

Finding a quilt under the seat, Hannah added its warmth to that of the lap robe. "Now that's better." The rest of the trip into Two Mules Junction was more comfortable.

Turning onto the main road of the small town, Ezra spoke from the front wagon seat. "We's in fer a sho taday. Would ya jes look yonder?"

Hannah and Wendell watched as Ezra edged closer, pulling the wagon to the side. It looked as if a ruckus was being played out, again, at the Watering Trough.

"Oh no, it's the Totems."

"Sho nuff, Miz Hanner. Dey be at it again."

"I had a run-in with that lady. Seems she thought I needed to be warned not to be around the saloon. I asked her what she was doing there." Wendell smiled with the remembrance. "Seems all these temperance women are the same."

"Speaking of temperance women, why, there with the spectacles is the woman from the Savannah Teetotalers. She must have moved over here since the saloon burned in Savannah." Hannah shook her head.

"I's remember her. Dats da day we gots mo than molasses." Ezra laughed, slapping his knee. "She's a comin' dis way. Musta spotted us. Lawd, hep us."

"Why, hello there, Preacher. How ya been a doin'?"

"Just fine, mam. How about yourself?"

"Well, I'm fair ta middlin', I reckon." Turning accusing eyes on Hannah, she looked back to Wendell. "I'd be a watchin' what compny I keep, Preacher."

"I'm in good company, mam."

"Well, let me fill you in, Preacher. That woman you be keepin' compny with, she's a brangin' shame ta whoever she's with."

"I'm proud to keep company with Miss Hannah. She's a fine lady; so fine, in fact, that I've asked her to be my wife."

The spectacled woman shook her head from side to side violently, causing her tight bun to shift ever so slightly. "Oh, Preacher. Ya better seek the Lord. Why that gal's been doin' the devil's work. Do ya know what kinda womern you been consortin' with? She's been out a ridin' one o those devilish bicycles, a showin' her ankles to passersby."

Wendell just grinned at the woman. "Is that so?"

"Why, she was a wearin' that split skirt ridin' habit . . . downright sinful, a devil's skirt I say. Saw it myself. The person who does these thangs ain't a gonna enter the pearly gates." She paused, pointing her finger in Wendell's face. "And I'm a sure of that."

Hannah secretly wondered how Wendell would handle this situation. She was afraid this incident would be repeated many times in their future. *Maybe I'm not the kind of cloth that a pastor's wife is cut from.*

Hannah could not believe the fire she saw in Wendell's eyes. "Mam, I don't believe God is going to ask your approval on who he lets into the pearly gates. We will all answer to his word, including you. Matter of fact, why didn't you try to help Miss Hannah when she fell from the bicycle?"

"Well, the Good Book says not to touch the unclean thing. And I'll be a tellin' ya now, Preacher, that gal and her wicked ways are unclean, and more'n that, she offends me in the worss kinda way. Jes downright ain't pleasin' to the good Lord above." She raised her finger, pointing toward the sky.

Hannah had held her peace long enough. She was determined to help Wendell out. "Mam, you are offended by my actions?"

"I sure am, you heathern womern."

"Well, your long tongue offends me, and if I had a sharp pair of shears, I'd cut it down to size."

The woman gave a loud harrumph, marching back across the street where Mrs. Totem was preachin' to Elijah and his friends. Hannah could hear her angry shouts from this distance, piercing the air in shrill shrieks.

"I'll be a burnin' this place down afore you know it, Lijah. I done had enough of the sin it brangs. We'll burn it ta the ground, jes like we did the Savanny Saloon."

All three of the wagon's occupants gasped. They couldn't believe their ears as the spectacled woman added her two cents' worth. "Yeah, Elijah, we'll burn it down. We prayed, and when it didn't happen, we put legs on our prayers."

Ezra's eyes were as round as saucers. "I ain't a believin' what I's hearin'."

Wendell's eyes showed alarm. "Should be an arrest before nightfall."

The temperance women were all standing on the front porch of the saloon, peering in the windows at the struggle going on within. They were shouting at Mrs. Totem. "You tell him, Myrtle. We here fer ya, Myrtle. You read him outta the big book, Myrtle." One began banging on the glass pane and jumping up and down on the boardwalk. "Brang him out here. Let's strang him up, Myrtle. We'll fix him."

"Sounds real Christian, doesn't it?" Wendell shook his head.

"Lookie there." Ezra was rising from his seat.

Coming out the door of the saloon was Mrs. Totem, her husband thrown across her shoulder like a sack of feed. The group of women of the temperance movement formed a line behind her, following her down the road singing off key. Their backs were straight, bustles swinging to the cadence they kept. Their buns didn't move a smidgen.

Ezra eased back down on the wagon seat. "Well, we sho nuff had us a show. Guess all good thangs gotta come to an end."

"It was sure worth the trip."

"Sho nuff, son, now what did we come fer?"

Wendell gave Ezra a secretive look. "You were going to pick up an extra saw blade while we were here, weren't you?"

"Dats right. I be headed to da tool shop."

Wendell and Hannah waited in the buggy while Ezra purchased the saw blade. Returning to the wagon, he drove back to the mercantile. "I be a waitin' right chere in da wagon while ya make yo purchase, Preacher."

Wendell jumped over the side of the wagon, not asking Hannah if she would like to accompany him. She thought it strange until he returned with a wrapped package in hand.

"For you, my dearest."

"Oh, Wendell, what have you done?"

Tearing the paper off, she exclaimed, "A box of Cadbury chocolates for me?"

"Yes, my dear. A fond memory to leave behind."

"This is a special gift, Wendell."

"Anything for my beloved."

Climbing beneath the lap robe, he drew her close, smiling into her green eyes.

The ride back to Savannah was filled with sweet remembrances of their times together at the De Ponte Plantation. Opening the box of chocolates, Wendell lifted one to the lips of his beloved.

Hannah savored the special treat, returning the favor. Time seemed to stand still, yet it passed too quickly.

As Ezra pulled the wagon up to the gate, Wendell spoke his thoughts. "It is fitting that we should marry here."

"Yes, it is. And we shall have a grand wedding outdoors. I think the peach orchard would be a wonderful place, with the lacy blossoms as a lovely backdrop, the gentle rolling hills embracing us, dressed in wildflowers."

"Anywhere you wish, Hannah. Just marry me. I can't wait to have you as my constant companion."

The thought brought tears to Hannah's eyes. She knew he was leaving. How could she make it without seeing his dear face every day? "When are you leaving?"

"In three days." He pulled her close, and she saw the struggle in his eyes, the loneliness he must already be feeling thinking of being without her.

She gently caressed his chin. "We shall enjoy these three days."

The three days passed much too quickly. Hannah stood outside in the cold, waving good-bye to Wendell, leaving atop his stallion. Their parting had been a long embrace and a sweet good-bye kiss in the barn. As they came out the door, Ezra and Eliza gave a final wave to their friend, quickly going back inside, where it was warm.

One more kiss and he had been on his way. Pulling away from her, Wendell looked forlorn and lost. Her heart felt his sadness, and she waved frantically, watching him ride down the drive, wishing he could stay. And then it was over. He shut the iron gates behind him, closing her off from his intended path, the path that would take him away from her.

She blew him a kiss, a kiss he would not see, for he was already making his way down the road alongside the river. *Go with God, my love.* The words followed him like a prayer as the young girl walked back inside to the warmth of the De Ponte kitchen. Her feet were numb from the cold. Her heart felt numb as well, having watched him riding out of her life. *But it is temporary,* thought the girl, looking ahead to her grand plans for the wedding.

That very night, Hannah was bent over her sketchpad, adding more sketches of her wedding gown. Undecided as to which one she would choose, she knew it would be a gown with simple, flowing lines, one that would be beautiful blowing in the March wind in the peach orchard.

Finally putting her pad away, she snuggled under her covers, watching the flames racing up the chimney. Thoughts of warm, spring weather, surrounded by the peach orchard in full dress, lured her into blissful sleep.

Hearing the carriage wheels coming up the drive, Hannah ran to her bedroom window, looking out. Two weeks had passed since Wendell had left, and the De Pontes were returning from their holiday.

Bernadette was sipping a cup of hot tea when Hannah entered the breakfast nook. "Oh, dahling, you won't believe the beautiful gowns I have ordered from a grand tailoring shop in Washington, near the plantation. The private boutique has the most fascinating winter colors from Paris."

"How exciting, Mrs. De Ponte. I hope you enjoyed your holiday."

"Yes, dahling, yes." And reaching for another sugar cookie, Bernadette made her way upstairs.

Mr. De Ponte came in the back door looking serious. "Good morning, Miss Hannah, Hilda."

"Good morning, sir. Da mizzus done went upstairs."

"She's tired from all the shopping. My wife studied the latest fashion plates for an entire day before choosing fabrics for her gowns. And then there were the fittings ... "

Although a faint smile appeared on his lips, Hannah thought the artist looked more worn out than his wife.

Jacques De Ponte lifted a newspaper in the air. "Well, President Grant has won a second term. Horace Greeley's wife died just before the election, and poor Mr. Greeley fell into madness and died the night before the electoral votes could be cast."

"That's terrible."

"Yes. I didn't agree with many of his radical thoughts, but you hate to see such tragedy. The article says that Greeley's wife was prone to depression and one of their daughters died of neglect as she doted on an infant son." Mr. De Ponte shook his head. He was a compassionate man, a man Hannah held in high esteem. How he had been trapped into a life with Miz Bernadette was more than the young girl could figure out.

She watched him make his way to the bottom of the stairs. "Good day, ladies. Oh, yes, I almost forgot. Susan B. Anthony has been arrested for casting her vote in the election." And then he mounted the stairs. Hannah could hear his murmur. "When will women be allowed the right to vote?" She imagined there would be no solace for the man making his way to the couple's bedchamber.

Gabrielle was the last one to come in. She ran to Hannah, embracing her. "I had to go say hello to Ezra and Eliza. I've missed them so. Hannah, Eliza's got a chicken stewing over the fire in the fireplace, and she wants us to come to supper, 'jes 'bout da edge o dark.'"

The girls laughed at Gabrielle's imitation of Eliza's words. "We'll talk later, Hannah. I have to write a letter." Making her way upstairs, Gabrielle sent a smile back to her friend, her eyes alight.

That evening, Hannah and Gabrielle sat around the fireplace hearth in the slave quarters, enjoying a bowl of stewed chicken. The warm, creamy broth filled with succulent chicken satisfied Hannah's hunger, leaving her content, except for missing her beau.

Gabrielle's tales of the Chennault Plantation helped to temporarily distract the young girl from thoughts of Wendell. The crackling fire created a cozy atmosphere for sharing the evening with friends.

Clapping her hands on her knees, Gabrielle De Ponte seemed anxious to share her news. "I had a most wonderful time at the plantation."

"Is that a romantic twinkle in your eye, Gabrielle?" Hannah accused.

"Well, Mr. Anthony Peabody has asked to be my suitor, and that suits me and Father just fine."

"Mr. Anthony Peabody, son of *the* Mr. Peabody, himself; *the* Mr. Peabody, owner of the Union Railroad?" Hannah's eyes were as round as saucers.

"Yes, mam." Gabrielle placed her hands on her hips, nodding with a smile.

"Well, I suppose your mother is happy?"

"Not really. She was expecting someone very snobbish and proper. Although this family is affluent, they are Bible-believing Christians and very humble."

"What does your mother think of Mr. Anthony Peabody?" Hannah asked.

"She's quite disappointed that the family takes their Christianity so seriously. Says that Anthony acts like a Bible-thumping peasant because he was sharing his faith with the orphans living near the plantation. He even gave a local inn money to cover Thanksgiving dinner for the entire orphanage."

"Praise be ta Jesus," Eliza shouted.

"I'm so happy for you, Gabrielle."

"Hannah, he's coming to Savannah with his father just before Christmas, but you'll be gone home." Her eyes danced with excitement.

"Miz Gabrielle, what kinda stories ya be a hearin'? Ol Eliza been wonderin' 'bout dat gold what's uppose a be up dat away; wanted to go huntin' fer it mysef."

Ezra swallowed a mouthful of the stew in a hurry, moving to the edge of his chair. "Sho nuff; we's a done an thought ta go a lookin' fer some a dat loss gold. They be a sayin' dat after a big rain, gold coins be a washin' up from da dirt near dat Cheennautt Plantation."

"I learned a lot about the plantation. Sure was a great history lesson just spending time there."

Ezra's chair tipped forward ever so slightly. "Tell us all, Miz Gabrielle. Ol Ezra be a wantin' ta hear da whole storey. It be a powerful great way ta spend da evening." The old man's smile was contagious. "Eliza, honey, could ya brang me another bowl o stew?"

"Miz Gabrielle, wait til I get da stew. I wants ta hear evry word."

Gabrielle nodded to her friend.

The sweet wife returned quickly with her husband's stew. "Was da place purty, likes day say, Miz Gabrielle?"

"Yes, Eliza, it had glowing pine wainscoting, eight fireplaces, and beautiful sitting porches overlooking magnificent gardens and rolling hills." Her eyes took on a faraway look, a telltale blush creeping onto her face. "The most romantic place I've ever been ... and with Anthony sitting beside me on the porch ... listening to the call of a whippoorwill ... " Gabrielle seemed to be in that place she was describing.

Shaking her head, she looked at her small audience. "You'll have to excuse me."

"Ya xcused, Miz Gabrielle, jes don't be too long a waitin' ta tell us mo." Ezra laughed, almost choking on his mouthful of chicken stew.

"We heard everything from the horse's mouth. Got the real story from the Chennault family; at least what they want to share."

Eliza and Ezra's eyes were glued to Gabrielle. Hannah could hardly control her own excitement. "Out with it, girl."

"Well, they say that Jefferson Davis, the president of the Confederate States, loaded two wagon trains with gold, silver, specie checks, and even gold floor sweepings from the Dahlonega mint during the last days of the war. The treasure train left Danville, Virginia, on April 6, 1865."

"Even da flo sweepin's, Miz Gabrielle?" Eliza shook her head.

"Yes, mam."

"What be dat speshee checks, Miz Gabrielle?"

"Ezra, that was paper money that could be redeemed for coins."

"All right now."

Gabrielle continued her story. "The Chennaults say that most of the money was given to soldiers returning home. Jefferson Davis was captured on May 10, just over a month after leaving Virginia."

"Sho nuff, I done an heared 'bout it. Somewheres down roun Irwinville, I believes."

"Yes, sir, he was captured in that small town right here in our state and the loot was all missing."

"Sho nuff." Shaking his head, Ezra stared into the flames dancing in the fireplace.

"On May 24, a group of Union bandits attacked the wagons that had stopped at the Chennault Plantation. More than $250,000 was lost and less than half of that was recovered, according to the Chennaults." Gabrielle's face turned mysterious, as if she knew a secret.

"Gabrielle, don't you be teasing us."

Her friend let out a sigh. "That is the real story we heard, Hannah. The Chennault family was set upon by a search party led by Union General Edward Wild." Her eyes took on a scary gleam, her words tumbling forth. "Wishing to recover the gold, the general tortured and arrested the Chennaults."

"I sho betcha dey could tell ya some storey."

"Yes, Ezra. It seems that General Wild thought the family was hiding the gold and he meant to have it. Their experience was horrific." Gabrielle looked as if she would take on the general by herself if she could get her hands on him.

"I's can jes emagine, Miz Gabrielle."

"Eliza, it was so bad that President Grant, who was a general at that time, removed General Wild from his command."

"That's a good thang."

"After the Chennaults were tortured, as if that wasn't enough, they were taken to Washington to be interrogated for a week."

"Do tell."

"Yes, mam, but they were proven innocent." Gabrielle paused, and rising from her chair, she continued with a raised eyebrow. "But one never knows for sure." She smiled, sadly shaking her head. "I am certain these people are innocent."

"Why, I heared Mr. Cheenault be a Methodist minister."

"Yes, you heard right, Ezra."

"And we know about them preachers, don't we?" It made Hannah think fondly of Wendell. *Wonder what he is doing right now?*

"We enjoyed our evening with you, but we'd best be going. It's getting late." Gabrielle led the way to the door.

"Yes, thank you for our supper." Hannah hugged her friends good night, following Gabrielle to the De Ponte mansion.

Lying in her warm bed, watching the flickering flames from the fireplace dance their own tune, Hannah let her mind roam. Allowing thoughts of Laurel City to lure her into her own dreams, she was looking forward to going home.

Wendell, I miss you so. Remembering her courting buggy proposal made her smile. She touched the emerald ring with her thumb, enjoying the feel of it on her finger. *I belong to him. Thank you, Lord.*

Chapter 30

December's chill brought frost. The top of the Savannah River was frozen, the ice keeping the big ships in port. The docks were still, awaiting a break in the cold temperatures. That day came at the end of the second week. The river continued its exporting business as if trying to make up for lost time. The sound of the riverboat whistles was a welcome sound.

Sitting at her window seat after dinner, Hannah was making a list of things to do for the wedding when she heard a knock at the door. "Come in."

"I know you are happy to be leaving on tomorrow's train, but I'm going to miss you, Hannah."

"I'll miss you terribly, Gabrielle. But I'll be back the second week of January."

"You promise?"

"Of course I promise. I'm finishing my art studies and getting married here. And don't you forget it."

Hope shone in the eyes of her friend. "I was just afraid you might go home and decide to get married there."

Hannah took her friend's hands in her own. "Gabrielle, I am coming back. Wendell and I have agreed that this is the place we want to get married. Most of our courtship was right here on this plantation. It will forever be our special place."

Gabrielle hugged her friend. "I don't want to lose you so soon. I know I'll have to let you go in March, but that will give me more time with you."

"Don't be sad. I'm coming back."

Gabrielle opened the door, retrieving a package from down the hall. "I want you to have your Christmas present early."

"Gabrielle, you don't have to do this."

"Yes, I do. Now open it, Hannah."

Tearing the paper, Hannah opened the package, removing a small music box. "Oh, Gabrielle, it's lovely." When she wound up the treasure, it played a melodious tune as a small horse turned in circles within the box.

"I know you love horses."

"This one reminds me of Wendell's stallion. Thank you, Gabrielle; I shall always cherish your gift."

"And I shall cherish you as a dear friend, Hannah." Tears were in her eyes as she hugged her friend and left the room.

Although it was sad to say good-bye to her friends, Hannah could not wait to board the train. Reticule in hand, she waved from her seat by the window, willing time to move forward. Her journey to her beloved stretched before her.

"All aboard." Those were happy words to the young girl's ears. Staring at the scenery she was passing through, her eyes became heavy.

The man sitting next to her reeked of garlic and onions. He was fast asleep with his head turned in her direction. Drool seeped from his mouth onto his suit. Unable to bear the sights and smells emanating from him, she had been staring out of the train window. Now she had a kink in her neck.

The porter must have noticed her grimace as she rubbed her neck. "May I hep ya, mam?"

"Could I take another seat, sir?" With the question, she surreptitiously looked over at the sleeping occupant in the seat next to her.

Following her gaze, the porter made a dour face. "Right dis way, mam. Sorry fer de inconvenance."

Hannah took her seat beside a sleeping lady. Turning to take a second look, she couldn't contain her glee. "Mrs. Baldwin?" She hoped it was Delia Baldwin.

"Yes... oh pardon me, miss." Delia Baldwin raised her head from the seat. Her eyes adjusting to the sight in front of her, she exclaimed, "Hannah Baxter. Oh my dear. How good to see you." She enfolded Hannah in a warm hug.

"I'm glad you could come to Laurel City for Christmas, Mrs. Baldwin."

"I wouldn't miss the birthing of my first grandchild for nothing in this world."

"Yes, I can't wait for the birthing of both Elizabeth and Katherine's babies. Isn't it exciting?"

"It is so exciting, my dear. And to think, my son is about to be a father." But the kind lady's eyes looked sad.

"Is something wrong, Mrs. Baldwin?"

"Well, dear, I suppose you haven't heard the news."

Hannah shook her head, afraid to hear what was about to be told.

"You didn't hear of the Great Fire in Boston?"

"No, mam. When?"

"Just last month, Hannah, November ninth. It was truly horrible." Her words were almost inaudible. "I lost my parents to the fire, dear."

"Oh, I am so sorry, Mrs. Baldwin." Hannah clutched her hand.

"Wyatt came up to help me settle the affairs of my father's business." Her voice cracked. "My parents had part-time living quarters at the shipping business, and as you know, they also lived with me." Her voice was now but a whisper. "My father wouldn't leave the premises. He was running from the harbor with buckets of water, trying to douse the flames. My dear mother was doing the same." She paused, daintily wiping her tears with a lace handkerchief, and then with a sigh, she began composing herself.

"How sad, Mrs. Baldwin."

"My parents never fully recovered from the inflammation in their lungs last winter. The smoke from the fire was just too much for them."

Hannah patted Delia Baldwin's arm. "So you are traveling alone?"

"Yes, dear. Wyatt had to return due to Katherine's delicate condition, and Josiah is studying at Harvard."

Hannah asked no more questions, but it was as if Mrs. Baldwin needed to talk. "The fire burned for twenty hours. Nearly everything was lost from Washington Street to Boston Harbor."

"Oh my."

"There had been an outbreak of horse influenza, so our men took the place of horses pulling the water wagons through the streets."

"It sounds just dreadful."

"The fire leapt from roof to roof. Fifty fire crews showed up, tossing wet blankets and carpets into the flames. You see, our roofs were too high to reach with the hoses." She paused, tilting her head to the side. "You know, we Bostonians must do everything in a grand way."

Hannah smiled.

"I'm afraid Boston has lost seven hundred and seventy six buildings. Remarkably, the Old South Meeting House was saved by a wet blanket brigade."

"I remember seeing that building when we visited Boston for Wyatt and Katherine's wedding."

"Yes, dear, that was a happy time. So glad my parents were part of the wedding, so glad." She stared out the window.

Hannah remained quiet, leaving Delia Baldwin with her own thoughts.

Snapping out of her sadness, the lady who was known for her impeccable manners and grace turned to Hannah. "Enough about me, dear. Now tell me about how you ended up on this train. I heard you were in art school in Savannah. I'm sure you're heading home for Christmas."

"Yes, mam."

"Then we shall have a grand time, birthing babies and sharing this wonderful holiday season. My parents are celebrating in another world, visiting the Christ we adore from below. I should be envious."

Talk turned to Hannah's wedding, and Delia Baldwin seemed enthused. "Maybe I'll still be in Laurel City in March. I just might make the journey to Savannah with the rest of the family."

"You are more than welcome to join us, Mrs. Baldwin."

She patted Hannah's hand. "We'll see, dear, we'll see."

Both women settled back for a nap, the clackety clack of the train putting them to sleep. Snuggling beneath blankets provided by the porter, they rested on their journey to beloved family and friends.

Before it seemed possible, the train was pulling into the Rosewood Station. Meals and conversations with Mrs. Baldwin blurred into one happy trip as the Rosewood church welcomed Hannah on her way into town. *What a beloved place.*

As they stood to exit the train, Hannah caught an even lovelier sight. There on the boardwalk, standing tall and painfully handsome, was the Reverend Wendell Cunningham. Hannah thought he seemed so at home in this setting, with his church nearby, the parsonage just waiting for her touch. Her fingers itched to pull back the curtains and peer out of the glass windows at the people on the street, people God was sending them to.

Mrs. Baldwin nudged her elbow. "You look mighty happy, dear."

"My suitor is waiting." Hannah pointed to the boardwalk.

"Enjoy every moment." And then Delia Baldwin descended the steps of the train, walking toward the open arms of her son.

With a quick hug, Dr. Wyatt Baldwin said good-bye to Hannah, tipping his hat to Wendell and rushing his mother to the doctor's buggy.

"I'm sure he doesn't want to leave my sister for long. And I am so glad to see you, Wendell Cunningham."

"Likewise, my darling." And right there on the sidewalk in Rosewood, the preacher picked up Miss Hannah Baxter and twirled her about for all the world to see.

Laughter erupted from Hannah.

Placing her on the ground, Wendell encircled her waist with a protective arm, guiding her to a bench on the boardwalk. "I'll retrieve your trunk, dear."

Hannah breathed deeply of the air. Barely cool, it invigorated her senses. She was glad to be sharing this wonderful time with her suitor.

A couple of women stepped up on the boardwalk. One peered down her nose at Hannah, the resemblance to the hateful woman of the Savannah Teetotalers causing her to catch her breath.

"I'd be a catchin' my breath too if'n I's seen a dancin' out here in broad daylight with a preacher no less."

Feeling her blood starting to boil, Hannah realized this was something she would likely have to learn to take in stride.

"Good day to you too, mam."

"Ain't a said nothin' 'bout it a bein' a good day."

"Well, this is the day the Lord has made, and he wants us to rejoice and be glad in it. Me and the preacher were just rejoicing a bit." Hannah cast the lady a sweet smile. Turning away, the lady's bun barely moved on her head, even with her exaggerated movements.

Her friend followed close behind. The second lady's murmur floated back to Hannah on the ill breeze that blew. "Don't seem fittin', what with the preacher a gettin' a gal like at. Reckon why he couldn't find a good un?"

"Maybe he feels sorry fer her. I's down in Laurel City at Paxton's store, and ol Mr. Rivers says she ain't right in the head. Maybe he jes feels sorry fer her."

"Ya gotcha a point there, Gassilda. Guess we'll jes have ta make do at the church. We probly gonna hafta take over the duties of the pastor's wife."

"Ya reckon?"

"Yeah, but I thank we'll do jes fine—jes fine an better."

The two walked over to the cracker barrel in front of the Rosewood General Store. Stopping beside one of the men sitting in a chair, Gassilda said, "It's done an pass time fer you ta come home, Wilburn. Get on up an let's go."

"All right, Gassilda, if I gotta go, I reckon I will." But Wilburn didn't move from his chair.

"Well shore ya gotta go. Cauz I sayed so."

The man rose from his chair. "All right, Gassilda. Jes be good an I'll foller along quiet like; if'n you be good, that is."

"Why o course, Wilburn. I got no cauz fer trouble taday. You seem like you's beehavin' when I walked up. You weren't playin' cards again, Wilburn, now was you?" The woman stopped in her tracks, wheeling around. This time, Hannah saw her tight bun move just a bit; not even enough you could prove it moved, but Hannah was sure it had. "Willlburrnn?" The screech became a scream until Hannah's ears felt as though they couldn't stand the pitch any longer.

Poor man.

"You better ainser me, Wilburn."

"Well, Gassilda, I, I ain't loss much taday a playin' cards. Jes two o them ol settin' hens o your'n and I's boun ta win em back if'n ya hadn't come up so soon like."

"Willlburrnn ... " And with that, Gassilda twisted the man's ear, leading him down the boardwalk and proceeding to make him follow the wagon she was driving. "Ya ain't a ridin' home with me, Wilburn." The words floated back from the driver's seat to the man following at a dead run to keep up with the wagon leaving town at a fast rate.

Wendell appeared at Hannah's side. "I reckon you've noticed we have our own Totem Chronicles playing out right here in Rosewood."

"Guess those cantankerous women are everywhere."

"So it seems." He placed her hand in the crook of his arm, a grin splitting his face. "You'll need to practice your new duties before March."

"With pleasure, my dear."

Having collected her trunk, Wendell Cunningham situated his betrothed in his new carriage.

"Nice ride." Hannah ran her hand over the leather seat.

"It's ours, dear. A gift from the church. They said I needed more than a stallion to look after the needs of the people."

"Sounds like they're planning to keep you."

"And I'm planning to keep you." Taking his place beside her, he brushed her lips as they exited town.

The sun was setting as the two made their way into Laurel City. Hannah breathed deeply. "There's no place like home."

Mr. Rivers was just leaving Paxton's General Store. Stepping off the boardwalk, his gaze met Hannah's smile. He squinted against the rays of the sun.

"Good evening, Mr. Rivers."

Shaking his head, the old man took another look at Hannah. Riding toward Laurel Oaks, she couldn't resist laughing aloud for his benefit. Turning to look at her critic, she saw him pointing at her.

Wendell took notice of the old man's actions. "Seemed to like it when you gave that silly laugh."

"Fits the message he's been touting around the pot belly stove." Hannah laughed.

"That's just one more thing I love about you."

"My ornery ways?"

"Your ability to overcome, your resilience. It will work well in the ministry."

Hannah tilted her head. "If I don't run all your parishioners off."

Wendell reached out, drawing Hannah near. "If you run 'um off, I guess he'll send us some more."

Hannah smiled up at him. It felt so right sitting beside Wendell, knowing this would soon be a way of life.

"Are you happy with pastoring Rosewood?" she asked.

"Yes, mam. Just can't wait to take a wife."

"Oh, sir, are you in the market for a wife? I reckon as how I could find ya one. Now, let's see." Hannah tapped her temple, like the temperance woman.

Wendell laughed so hard a fox nearby darted into the woods. "I'm sorry, mam, but I'm taken."

"And who's taken you, sir?"

"A lovely maiden with skin so fair and hair the color of sun-kissed honey."

Hannah scooted even closer to him on the carriage seat. "Sure is a nice ride, sir. I'd share your buggy any day."

"Miss Baxter, do you always address your minister in such a bold manner?"

"Heaven forbid." Laughing, she nearly fell off the seat. The carriage slowed to a crawl, stopping alongside the road.

Wendell put his finger to his lips. "Shh." He pointed to a tree just beyond the roadway. Peering into the distance, Hannah squinted. Finding nothing and turning back, her lips immediately were brushed by his.

"Just wanted an excuse for a private moment. This moment seemed so right."

"You don't need an excuse, Preacher." Her eyes teased him.

Wendell pulled her to him, holding her for a moment. She laid her head against his shoulder, for all the world wishing she would never have to move from this beloved spot.

Quiet surrounded them. Wendell lifted Hannah's head, peering closely into her eyes, alight with love in the moonlight. "Sealed with a kiss," he murmured, kissing her as if banishing all the days of separation. "Whew." Wendell shook his head. "Better move right along to Laurel Oaks."

Hannah rewarded him with a smile of contentment. "Wouldn't want the preacher to sin," she teased.

The cool air made for an enjoyable ride through the orange groves. Fruit, ripe for the taking, hung in golden pods from the trees. "It is so good to be home."

"Yes, it is," Wendell added. Hannah laced her arm through his, glad that he shared her love for Laurel City.

Coming up to the chapel, the two pulled into the yard. "It seems we have truly come home now." Wendell gazed into the night sky.

"Yes, it does." Staring at the steeple shining in the moonlight, Hannah saw it as a beacon of hope. "And to think the last time we were at this chapel together, I thought there was no hope for us, thought I'd never see you again."

"Isaac seemed to have taken possession that morning, but all's well that ends well, my dear." Reaching over, Wendell touched the tip of her nose before giving the reins a shake.

Candles lit up the windows of Laurel Oaks. Passing beneath the canopy of oaks, Hannah felt covered in all the love this place represented. Wendell pulled her closer. "Seems like Christmas. And I've already received my greatest gift."

Hannah lifted her hand in the moonlight, peering at the small emerald ring gracing her finger. "Likewise, sir, I am wearing mine; the token of our love."

Helping her alight, Wendell embraced her beneath the old oaks before escorting her to her family.

"Hannah, dear, how beautiful you look." Her mother wrapped her in a hug, refusing to let anyone else take their turn. "I'm so glad you're home; I've missed you so." Hannah noticed a small tear escaping her mother's eye.

"It's good to be home, Mother."

She reached for her father's hug as Wendell took his turn with his soon-to-be mother-in-law. "Welcome, Son."

Crowding around, everyone wanted to see Hannah's ring. "Your letter described it perfectly, dear."

"Mother, it matches my eyes."

"Oh, yuck." Blaine hadn't waited long to start his bantering.

"Aw, Blaine, can't ya say anything good to Hannah?" Turning to his sister, Blythe grabbed her in a bear hug. "I sure have missed you, Hannah."

Blaine was right behind him. "Me too."

Hugs and congratulations were given to the preacher and his betrothed; then everyone moved as one into the dining room.

"Hot chocolate and cookies, my dears."

"Oh, Mother, I've been craving your oatmeal cookies. Oh, you've made snickerdoodles too. Those are the preacher's favorite."

"I fed him snickadoodles." Little Beth laughed.

Wendell picked her up, hugging her tight. "You sure did, little one."

Ethan hadn't left Elizabeth's side since their arrival. Watching her for a moment, Hannah was sure she saw pain in her eyes. Her thoughts were interrupted by a shout from the front door.

"We're here. Where are y'all at?"

"Back in the dining room, Katherine. Come on back."

Hannah rose to meet her sister, who looked to be having just as much trouble moving about as Elizabeth. Neither did she miss the look passing between the two. When Katherine bent down, whispering in Elizabeth's ear, Hannah was barely able to make out the words. "Are you in labor too?"

The brief nod and the pain showing in her sisters' eyes alarmed Hannah. *How can they both be in labor at the same time?*

Joining everyone at the table for cookies and hot chocolate, Katherine and Wyatt conversed about their day at the office. "Mr. Rivers came by today. Says his wife's having trouble talking. Wanted some lozenges."

Katherine stirred extra cream into her hot chocolate, shaking her head.

"I know what you're thinking, Katherine. She's always had trouble talking around Mr. Rivers; can't get a word in edgewise."

"Something like that, Hannah." Her words seemed pained, her spoon stopping its circular motion. "Excuse me."

Wyatt was immediately helping his wife up from her chair. "What, my dear?" His face paled.

"Just help me to the sofa."

Mother and Hannah followed, as did Elizabeth. Everyone else let them have their privacy.

"We're here." Sara's voice rang from the front door. "Anybody home?" Sara peeked into the great room, removing her bonnet. "Not the both of you?"

From the girls' reclining positions with ottomans under their feet and the pain now showing on their faces, it was apparent they were in labor.

"I cannot have this child today. I must help you, Elizabeth."

Elizabeth's smile was forced. "I suppose the *twins* may have a mind all their own."

"Twins?" Katherine looked confused.

"I'm sure we'll call them twins if they are born the same day. Now imagine that!" Elizabeth chuckled.

Adeline Baxter smiled, placing cool cloths on her daughters' foreheads. "Looks like its going to be me and thee, Doctor."

Wyatt wiped his brow. "Looks like it. Mother will be here directly. Wanted to bring over some of the baby's quilts when she saw the pain in Katherine's eyes."

After knocking softly on the front door Mrs. Delia Baldwin entered, laden with an armload of clothing and bedding. "Oh my, we have two in such a fine state of affairs? How long have you been uncomfortable, my dears?"

Elizabeth was the first to respond. "About two hours."

Katherine winced and breathed deeply. "I felt my first pain just before coming over to see Hannah."

Wyatt held his wife's hand. "I do believe Elizabeth will deliver first, with this being her second baby."

"Good. I do want to assist."

"You are in no shape to assist, my dear." Wyatt rubbed his wife's head.

"The pains are still pretty far apart."

"Just rest, Katherine," Wyatt coaxed.

Delia Baldwin covered her daughter in law with a quilt. "Your mother and I can assist the doctor with you both."

Mrs. Baldwin's smile erased the sadness Hannah knew was filling her heart. *This is good for her.*

The evening progressed; midnight came and went with only soft moans coming from the sisters. The girls had been moved to their old rooms upstairs with their husbands keeping vigil. Adeline and Delia rested downstairs with Hannah and Sara keeping them company. Grandmam had been sent for.

Blaine and Blythe went to bed, Blaine complaining, "Hope they don't raise a ruckus havin' them babes."

The other men had retired to bed; Wendell having taken his leave after finishing his hot chocolate. Hannah already felt empty without him in the house. But her mind was busy thinking of her sisters' plights.

"I'm here, I'm here. Where are those girls?"

Hannah smiled at Grandmam's anxious greeting, running into her grandmother's embrace. "I intended to visit you early this morning, Hannah, just not this early." The grandfather clock in the corner chimed twice.

"They seem to be resting a little, Mama Elise. Wyatt believes Elizabeth will be ready soon."

"I suppose you've set the water to boil."

Delia Baldwin answered. "Water's bubbling, all the sheets are ready; tools have been boiled."

"Sounds like we're ready."

As if on cue, the doctor called from the threshold of the stairs. "Ladies, I'm in need of assistance."

Adeline Baxter was the first to rise. "Are you ready for the water, Wyatt?"

"Yes, quickly, please."

Although no panic was heard in his voice, all three matrons efficiently moved as one—two carrying the water and Grandmam following with the clean linens.

Hannah and Sara stayed a safe distance behind, peeking into the room. Both gave Elizabeth a quick peck on the cheek before leaving to check on Katherine.

Softly knocking on the door, they entered as Katherine called a weak greeting.

Both girls quickly joined their sister on her bed. "Katherine, are you all right?"

"Progressing quite nicely, my husband says." Her smile quickly faded. "Oh no, oh no, the baby is moving down. Please get Wyatt."

"What are we to do?" Hannah ran to Elizabeth's room. A loud cry rent the air.

The doctor smiled at the babe in his hands, passing it to Grandmam. "Quite healthy, I should say. Ethan, you have a fine son."

Hannah watched as Ethan reached for the child Grandmam was wrapping in a blanket. "My own son."

She waved frantically. "We are in need of the doctor across the hall please."

Wyatt's eyes grew large. "I'll be right there, Hannah." He was washing his hands with soap and water from the pitcher. "Mother, please help me into a clean smock."

Delia Baldwin was immediately at her son's side, assisting him and following him from the room. "My, but aren't we busy?"

The entourage made its way across the hall, leaving Elizabeth and Ethan to rest with their new baby boy. Hannah was the last to leave the room, kissing her sister and noticing the joy written across the faces of the new parents. She let her mind wander to thoughts of her and Wendell and their first child. Very quickly she pulled her attention back to the work at hand and took off across the hall.

"Oh, my, Wyatt, oh, my." Katherine was sitting up, thrashing her head from side to side.

"Darling, breathe deeply. It is supposed to help." But at the moment the doctor looked helpless. "Turn on your side, dear. Let me rub your back. I remember our patients experiencing some relief when you rubbed their backs."

Katherine turned on her side as if all her energy was spent. She froze. A shriek escaped her lips.

"Oh no, Kat, are you all right?" Sara asked.

"What can we do?" Hannah asked the doctor.

A frown creased Wyatt's moist brow. "The baby has moved down, but something doesn't seem right. Could I have a moment to check my wife, please?"

The girls left the room. Grandmam, Delia Baldwin, and Adeline Baxter followed.

"Let's have a cup of tea, dears. We may be in for a long night." Grandmam's words filled the quiet dining room. A scream traveled down the stairs.

Grandmam bowed her head in prayer. "Please give us grace and mercy with this, your child, Father." Silence was soon the only sound in the antebellum home.

After what seemed like an eternity, Wyatt stepped out of the room and came into the kitchen. "Please bring up some warm water. Katherine's not ready yet, but if we place warm cloths on her abdomen the muscles should relax and allow the baby to move on down."

"That sounds like a wonderful idea." Delia patted her son's back, rushing to assist Adeline and Grandmam with the water and cloths.

Pausing for a sip of tea that Hannah offered, Dr. Wyatt Baldwin raced back upstairs, taking them two at a time.

Joining him in the room, Hannah and Sara kissed their sister, heading back downstairs to wait and pray.

Hannah spoke first. "How have you and Tobiah been doing since I saw you in Savannah?"

"Just great, Hannah. We've got a little surprise."

"You're not having a baby, are you?"

"No, not anything so grand. We have added a very large room onto the cabin. We made it into a dining room and a bedroom."

"Well that sounds nice. I've always said you made enough money selling your sachets to the Yanks to build an entire house."

Sara laughed. "Well, it's paying off, Sis."

A piercing scream was followed by the soft wail of a child. Grandmam appeared on the stairs. "It's another boy; it's another boy. We've got ourselves another set of twin boys!" She ran down the stairs and back up, not knowing what to do with herself.

Hannah and Sara hugged each other, running upstairs hand in hand. Opening Katherine's door, the girls peeked in. Their sister was sitting up in bed. She smiled as she stroked the forehead of her baby boy.

The sight brought tears to Hannah's eyes. "Motherhood is the most beautiful thing I have ever seen."

"Yes, it is the most beautiful thing." Katherine kissed her son's cheek, her tears finding a path down his face.

Sara and Hannah came alongside their sister, placing their own delicate kisses on the little fellow's head. "They look so much alike."

"Well, Sara, Grandmam called them twins."

"We will leave you for the night." Sara grabbed Hannah's arm, exiting the room.

Ethan was in the hallway, holding onto Elizabeth and their son.

"What are you doing?" Hannah asked.

"Just going for a visit, Sister. Gotta introduce the twins to each other." Ethan and Elizabeth giggled. "Don't worry, I'm going right back to bed."

Blaine and Blythe appeared at the top of the stairs, visiting both the babies. "Glad to have another set of twins in the family." Blaine kissed each child on the head, pride beaming from his face.

"Handsome boys." Blythe was as proud as his brother.

So everyone finally settled in for the night. And what a night it had been. Only God could have arranged this special time for multiplying the Baxter family.

Chapter 31

The Baxter house was filled with preparations for Christmas. The new mothers had stayed a couple of days at Laurel Oaks, both returning home for their own Christmas preparations.

Delia Baldwin cared for Katherine and Little Wyatt Josiah Baldwin. Sara and Hannah were present to assist as well. And the same was true with Elizabeth; Grandmam lending more care to her eldest granddaughter since Delia Baldwin was on hand for Katherine. Adeline was in her element, running from Elizabeth's home to Katherine's.

And what wonderful days these were, pine boughs and Florida Holly filling every home with the sights and smells of Christmas. Tinkling bells, mistletoe, ribbons, and cinnamon candles graced the fireplace mantel at Laurel Oaks. The magnificent staircase, strewn with crimson ribbon and wreaths of pine, attested to the coming celebration. Small candles adorning the wreaths would be lit on Christmas Eve, along with the lighting of the tree.

Two more would receive presents this year. Gifts were mounting for Little Wyatt and Little Ethan.

"Can't wait to see these boots on the little fellows." Placing the packages under the tree, Grandpappy was proud of the boots he had commissioned Mr. Eaton to make. The great-grandfather had drawn a pattern, tracing the babies' feet on paper.

Hannah, busy stringing popcorn and berries for the tree, ran to answer the knock at the door. "I thought it must be you." Reaching up on tiptoe, she placed a peck on the cheek of her beloved.

Wendell pulled her into a quick embrace. "I love it when you answer the door; brings back memories."

Hannah looked into his eyes with a huge smile. "Those are very special memories. I remember when the cat had your tongue."

"Well, it ain't got it no more."

Hannah grabbed Wendell's hand, pulling him down the hall. "Supper's almost ready. Come into the great room and help me string popcorn for the tree."

"Gladly. Next year, we'll be stringing our own tree."

"That is a happy thought."

Grandpappy rose from the rocking chair by the hearth. "Good to see you, Wendell. How's the Rosewood pastorate?"

"Doing well. Can't wait to have my bride with me." He sat beside Hannah, helping her string the popcorn.

"It will work out fine, son. Three more months and you'll have your wish."

"Seems like an eternity."

Adeline Baxter appeared at the door of the great room. "Supper's ready."

Fried pork chops, rice, milk gravy, and black-eyed peas graced the table. Sara brought over a platter of fried cornbread.

"That cornbread looks mighty good."

"It's full of jalapeños. Hope your mouth can take the heat, Preacher."

Grandpappy blessed the food, and the dishes were passed around the table.

Blaine took three pieces of the cornbread.

The preacher took notice. "You must really like it, Blaine."

"Yeah, and I betcha cain't eat one. Betcha got one o them sissy mouths, you bein' off ridin' in the north country an all."

Wendell reached for a piece of the cornbread. Taking a bite, he followed with another. Hannah could see he was on fire but unwilling to reach for the sweet tea just yet.

She whispered instructions. "Don't eat it by itself, silly. Take a bite and then eat some peas or rice."

Wendell smiled, putting a large spoonful of peas in his mouth.

Blaine watched with a smirk.

Deliberately taking another large bite of the cornbread, the preacher followed with a spoonful of rice and milk gravy.

Blaine must have realized the preacher could take the heat better than he thought. "Mighty sissy way to eat cornbread."

Blaine stood up. "Forgot to bring the milk in. The cat'll be goin' for a swim, if I don't get it."

As soon as the back door slammed shut, Wendell downed every swallow of his tea. "Whew. That cornbread is hot. But delicious."

Everyone laughed at the preacher.

Tobiah reached for another piece of the crispy bread. "Took me a while to get used to it with the jalapeños, but it sure is good."

Blythe walked in the back door. "Elizabeth and Katherine said thank you for the meal."

"Wouldn't have it any other way." The Baxters were busy every day making extra food for the two families. With Christmas coming on, it just added to the festive feeling in the air.

"I'll take you to see the new babies after supper."

Hannah's offer brought a smile to Wendell's lips. "Can we walk through the orange grove?" She barely heard his whisper.

"Bad preacher, taking advantage of the sitchyachion." Wendell grinned at Hannah's use of Ezra's word.

The Christmas Eve program at the church had everyone laughing as they enjoyed cake and punch afterwards. Tilly Dawson's little girl had made everyone laugh until their sides hurt.

The little girl had told the Christmas story. She had recited her lines just fine at the last practice, which Sara and Hannah had held. However, by the night of the program, she had baby Moses in the manger, floating on the water while Mary took a bath nearby. Somehow, she had a big fish swallowing up baby Jesus and spitting him out in the lion's den, where the lions were fast asleep.

Seeing Blaine's look of satisfaction, Hannah began to put the pieces together. Walking over to her brother, she pulled him outside by the elbow.

"So, how did you pull it off, Blaine?"

He looked so smug, Hannah wanted to take him behind the woodshed herself. However, it made a funny sight as she looked up into his face, talking to him as if he were a three-year-old. "How did you do it?"

Blaine crossed his arms and laughed. "Well, she *is* quite fond of cinnamon drops."

"Blaine, you didn't." Looking over at Tilly's little girl standing nearby, Hannah could see her lips were red.

At that moment the girl looked up, adoration for Blaine showing on her cherub face. "Thank you, Bwaine. I wuv cinmin dwops."

"So how long did it take you to prepare her?"

"Oh, not so long. Not as long as it took you and Sara." The boy didn't even look ashamed. He actually looked rather proud of himself.

"You'd have never pulled this off if Elizabeth wasn't still recovering."

"Ya think I couldn't?"

"Elizabeth would have known."

"I don't know. You do remember the program with Isaac's mule, don't you?" His smirk was in place.

Hannah stood there shaking her head. "Won't you ever grow up, Blaine?"

"Cain't see no reason to."

Leaving the boy, Hannah walked back inside to find Wendell.

"Was it as you suspected?"

"Of course, Wendell. If mischief's around, you need look no further than Blaine."

"Walk with me to my carriage, *our* carriage, I should say." Wendell tucked her hand in his elbow.

"Must you leave, now?"

"It's a long ride to Rosewood, dear. I'll be back by noon tomorrow."

Hannah leaned into his shoulder. "Can't wait to see you again."

"I can't wait until we never have to part again."

"Three months, Wendell. Just three more months."

With a quick embrace, Wendell climbed into the carriage and was off to Rosewood. Hannah watched his dark silhouette leaving the chapel grounds, the steeple and outline of the church blending with the man and his carriage. Her heart was filled with peace and contentment. *Thank you, Lord.*

Wendell Cunningham held the reins loosely. The stallion and his mate were making their way down the moonlit path, pulling the carriage. They pulled in unison, the conveyance offering a smooth ride to the preacher whose thoughts were on the girl he was leaving behind.

He couldn't ask for a better mate than the one God had given him. A smile played at his lips as he thought of her spunk and enthusiasm. Miss Hannah Rose Baxter lived life to the fullest, enjoying every moment. He couldn't wait to share each of those moments with her.

Wendell's thoughts turned to Hannah's indignation for the self-righteous women in Savannah and again in Rosewood. Life sure would be interesting around the parsonage. As young as she was and probably due to her sound upbringing, she understood that being pious never helped the kingdom of God. It seemed she would declare all-out war on those who thought themselves better than others. The thought made him laugh aloud.

Even in the cool evening air, the preacher's heart was warmed by thoughts of his beloved. Driving up in the yard of the Rosewood parsonage, he could almost imagine her welcoming him home, pulling back the lace curtains and offering him a warm smile.

Unhitching his horses and putting the carriage away, he opened the back door of the parsonage, rushing to light a candle and start a fire in the cold fireplace.

Christmas Day 1872, the Baxters had two more family members in attendance. Babies' cries filled the antebellum home, adding to the excitement of the day. Adeline Baxter felt blessed beyond measure.

"Sara, stir the red-eye gravy, would you please?"

"Sure, Mother." Sara grinned at Hannah, who was adding more sugar to the sweet tea. "Can't keep her hands off those babies."

A knock sounded at the door, and Hannah tore off her apron, quickly tightening her hair combs and running to answer it. "Come in, Preacher Man."

"Why, yes, mam, I do believe I will." Removing his coat, he pulled Hannah into his welcoming arms. "I missed you last night at the parsonage. Could just imagine you pulling the curtains back, welcoming me home with that beautiful smile of yours."

Hannah's heart raced. "It's almost a reality, Wendell."

Hand in hand they walked down the hall. "*Almost* doesn't seem quite good enough today."

"Patience, Reverend, patience."

He rubbed his chin. "It is a virtue, isn't it?"

Walking into the great room, Hannah watched her mother trading Little Wyatt for Little Ethan. Beth joined her brother in her grandmother's lap. "She's nearly bursting with love for the little ones."

"Raised without love, I can understand how love chases away the loneliness."

Hannah squeezed her beau's hand a little tighter.

Wendell smiled a greeting to the family. "Looks like everyone's enjoying the little ones. Sure are fine-looking fellows."

The doctor and Ethan smiled, nodding their heads in assent.

Grandmam appeared at the doorway. "I do believe the food is ready."

After prayer, the group helped themselves from the overfilled buffet.

"It's so good to be home for Christmas. Mother and Grandmam's food is absolutely the best." Hannah took a little bit of most every dish.

"Hadn't had red-eye gravy in a blue moon." Wendell spooned an extra helping over his rice.

By the time the meal had ended, everyone gathered in the great room for an afternoon of enjoying the babies.

Blaine and Blythe came in from doing chores at dusk, each boy stopping to wash up before asking for a turn holding the babies.

Blaine looked intently into his nephew's face. "I'm gonna train you up right, Little Ethan."

"Don't you listen to him, son." Elizabeth pulled Blaine's ear.

Blythe held Little Wyatt, gently patting his back and rocking him in the same rocking chair his mother had used for him.

The great room was filled with love that Christmas Day. It was as if no one needed any gifts to celebrate. They had received so many blessings already.

Just before the lighting of the tree, Grandpappy told the Christmas story, then asked for everyone to offer thanks to God for a blessing received in 1872.

Delia Baldwin gave thanks for her grandson. And not a glimmer of sadness could be seen in the dear woman's eyes.

Tobiah's words were sincere. "I thank God that Sara is finally mine." Everyone in the room nodded their agreement, glad she was settled and with Tobiah.

It was Wendell's turn. Moisture showed in his eyes. "I'm so thankful to know I will be a part of this family, never had one of my own to speak of." Looking into Hannah's eyes and squeezing her hand, he gave thanks for his blessing. "I thank my God for allowing me the blessing of Miss Hannah Rose Baxter. I will be forever grateful."

Hannah reached up with her hankerchief, wiping a tear from her beloved's eye. "And I will be forever grateful for the gift of my preacher man."

Thanks were heard from everyone, and then the tree was lit and the candles on the stairway wreaths flamed bright and festive.

Gift passing ensued with shouts of delight around the room.

"This is the best Christmas I've ever had," Wendell whispered to Hannah. "It was always a sad, lonely time for me."

"You'll never be lonely again, my love. There's a scripture that says, 'God sets the lonely in families.'"

"I'm so glad he chose to put us together. Just think, if that sister of yours hadn't lost her wedding gown, we might have never met."

"Rue the day if she had not lost that gown." Hannah held her hand to her chest.

"Were you two talking about my lost wedding gown?"

"Yes, Elizabeth, it seems Wendell and I might have never met had you not lost it."

"Just goes to show you that when things look bad, God has a plan." Hannah's eldest sister's eyes twinkled as she reached to hug her.

"Thank God for even the things we don't understand. He is working all things for our good."

"That's right, Wendell. Keep on preaching. Looks like the Lord's giving you a fine wife, if you can keep her tamed down a bit." Elizabeth winked at her sister.

"I like her just the way she is. The parishioners will just have to get used to her."

Grandpappy's voice rang loud and clear, bursting forth with one Christmas carol and then another. Greg Baxter joined his father's baritone voice, as did the rest of the family.

Hannah tried to keep from laughing at Blaine and Blythe's croaky voices.

Looking over the group, Hannah couldn't imagine being happier anywhere else in the world. She would sketch this scene before bedtime. Wendell Cunningham indeed would have his new family . . . *the good Lord willing.*

The next few days, Hannah busily stitched her wedding gown with simple lines, attaching tiny pearls all over the bodice. Puffed sleeves, ending in pointed lace cuffs and boasting the same pearls, suited the young artist just fine.

Susannah came over every day to assist with the sewing. Hannah had helped her finish her own dress two days before Christmas. Hannah would wear her jade green gown when she stood up at Susannah's wedding.

Pulling the last stitch tight on the hem of her dress, Hannah held it back, knowing she was satisfied with her work. Mrs. Hattie had helped design this beautiful gown. She could almost see the dress blowing in the gentle breeze coming off the Savannah River.

The peach orchard would be dressed in blooms of lace for her March wedding. The vision brought a broad smile to the young girl's face.

"Thinking about your wedding, Hannah?"

"Oh, yes, Susannah. I just can't wait."

"Me either." The beautiful girl's eyes were alight with joy. "And I'm so glad we will both be living in Rosewood."

"Isn't God good to give us wonderful beaus and allow us to have our best friends living in the same town?"

"Yes, and attending the same church. We'll have fun, Hannah."

"I know. You'll have to help me *act* like a pastor's wife, Susannah. Don't encourage my comedic side too much."

"Well, God must like that side enough. He chose you for the job."

Hannah rose, placing her wedding gown over a high back chair. "Oh, I'm so happy for the both of us, Susannah."

The last day of the year, Susannah and Matthew stood in front of Grandpappy in the little chapel, repeating their wedding vows. Hannah thought her friend had never looked more beautiful.

"I now give to you Mr. and Mrs. Matthew Madison."

Mrs. Madison and Mrs. Frost wore happy smiles, sharing their children's joy. Back down the aisle the bride and groom went, now the couple they had longed to be.

After cake and punch, Susannah called good-bye to her friend. "I'll see you in Rosewood, Hannah." And with a wave of her hand, Hannah's childhood friend was gone, embarking on a new journey.

Hannah couldn't wait to begin hers.

January blew its frigid breath into Laurel City, but Hannah knew the temperatures were much colder in Georgia. Snuggling beneath her quilt, she was glad to be in Florida for a few more days.

Wendell came for his last visit to Laurel Oaks before her departure. At the end of the day, he waved good-bye. "I'll see you in Rosewood, my dear."

Hannah could hardly believe it was time to return to Savannah. But looking over all that had been accomplished, she knew the time was at hand. Her sisters' gowns, in shades of lavender and pink, were all finished, placed in the armoire for safekeeping until March.

"Mother, we'll use the Queen Anne's Lace blossoms for my wedding bouquet, surrounded by wildflowers. The girls can carry bouquets of wildflowers, and the peach orchard will furnish a beautiful setting."

"It all sounds so wonderful, my dear."

"Oh, Mother, you can't imagine how beautiful it will be with the sun almost setting and the gentle breeze blowing off the Savannah River." Closing her eyes, Hannah was all but standing in that orchard.

"Dear, I'm sure it will be beautiful." Her mother enfolded her in a hug. "My last daughter to marry, and, oh, I have missed you so. These few days have been a cherished blessing for me."

"Mother, I have enjoyed being here and planning the wedding."

"I shall miss you." Her mother reached up, pushing back a wisp of hair falling into Hannah's vision.

"I know you'll miss me, Mother, but isn't God good to give you two beautiful babies to fill your empty arms?"

"Why, yes, dear. He's making sure I won't be lonely again, isn't he?"

"Yes, mam, and he's making sure my Wendell will never be lonely as well."

"You'll see to that my dear, and oh, the joy you will bring him." Adeline Baxter traced her daughter's jawline. "Such a special child you are."

"I know, Mother. Father says the same thing to each of us."

"And it is true. Each of you are special in your own way."

And so another evening passed in the Baxter home, the last evening that Hannah would sleep in her bed as a single young lady. "I'll be married when I visit this place again." The words, spoken aloud, seemed to seal her joy. Snuggling beneath the quilt her mother had made, she sighed a deep sigh of contentment. Hannah Baxter would count the days until she became Mrs. Wendell Cunningham. *Hannah Rose Cunningham, now that sounds right nice.*

Chapter 32

Wendell paced the boardwalk in front of the train station, peering into the predawn darkness. Fog further hampered his vision, but the sound of a carriage rolling up made him quicken his step. Hat in hand, a broad smile lit his face as he recognized the Baxter carriage.

Pulling alongside the boardwalk, the Baxters hugged their youngest daughter good-bye and, after embracing Wendell, pulled back onto the road leading toward Laurel City.

"Bless them for allowing us some private time." Wendell pulled his pocket watch from his vest and replaced it. "And bless them for getting you here early."

"They left my trunk in front of the station."

"We've got time for a cup of coffee or tea. The Rosewood Bakery has the best pastries in town."

Pulling her coat tighter, Hannah welcomed Wendell's warmth as he placed his arm around her shoulders, leading her into the delightful place.

Seating her at a table, Wendell returned with coffee and peach and cherry pastries.

"These are wonderful."

"Yes, they are." Walking back up to the counter, Wendell ordered an extra half dozen for Hannah's trip.

"Oh my, but if I eat these, I'll not fit into my wedding gown."

"Your gown will fit just fine." Wendell took her hand in his.

The train whistle shattered the peaceful morning interlude.

Wendell clutched her hand a little tighter. "Can't believe it's time for you to go."

Hannah wished to remove the sadness in his eyes. She could almost feel the loneliness threatening to swallow him up at her departure. Tracing a pattern on the hand holding hers, she whispered, "The sooner I leave, the sooner our wedding will take place."

The mention of their wedding seemed to do the trick for Wendell. Pulling her hand to his lips, he kissed each finger in turn. Just when she thought a tear would escape, he looked into her eyes with a mischievous twinkle. "No more bicycle riding before our wedding. Promise me?"

"Well, I suppose I could refrain; at least I'll try."

"We better get you seated on the train, Hannah." A blast of cold air assaulted them at the door.

The chug of the engine belching black cinders in the air called to Hannah. The couple embraced just as Gassilda walked by. Turning back, craning her neck and giving them a huff, Hannah heard her murmur, "Don't know as our church can take such a wanton woman into our midst." Clucking her tongue and wagging her head from side to side, she sashayed down the boardwalk, tight bun unmoving.

"Never mind her, Hannah. It's just practice for later." Wendell laughed, wrapping her tighter in his embrace.

Hannah smiled, his words soothing her. She wanted to march down the boardwalk, behind Gassilda, sticking her tongue out all the while. *That would be childish,* she chided herself.

Wendell gazed deep into his beloved's eyes, savoring the moment. "Good-bye until March, my love." And then he brushed a gentle kiss against her lips. A kiss she could still feel. It had stayed with her all the way to the Savannah train station.

Wendell Cunningham returned to the parsonage feeling empty but looking forward to the day his beloved would join him here. Banking the fire in the fireplace, he situated himself in a comfortable armchair, propping his feet on the ottoman.

Closing his eyes, a vision of Hannah played out in front of him. He laughed aloud thinking of Gassilda and her pious ways. Hannah would be good for her; maybe she would teach those few self-righteous souls in his church how they ought to treat others. His musings were interrupted by a knock at the door.

The man standing before Wendell looked strangely familiar. "May I help you sir?"

"Your name Wendell Cunningham, Son?"

"Yes, sir, I'm the pastor of Rosewood Chapel."

"That's what they told me, Son."

Why does he keep calling me son? Wendell repeated his former offer, but the man just stood there nodding his head. It reminded him of his own behavior the first time he had seen Miss Hannah Baxter.

"Well, yes, Son, if you're Wendell Cunningham, I'd like to have a chat with you."

Wendell opened the door wide, closing it behind his guest. The gust of cold air disturbed the cozy warmth of the room.

"Would you like a cup of coffee, sir?" Wendell offered his guest.

The man rubbed his hands together. "It would warm me a bit, yes, thank you."

Retrieving a cup and filling it with the brew, Wendell thought to ask, "Cream or sugar?"

"Just black, Son, just black." The man smiled as Wendell handed him the cup of coffee. Taking a sip, he peered over his cup at Wendell. "Ever heard of Theodore Cunningham, Son?"

"Theodore, no, sir, I don't recall that name."

"Your granny never told you about me, Son?"

"No one by that name, sir." Wendell peered into the man's eyes, recognizing a resemblance to himself. He sat on the edge of his chair, his head tingling. *Surely this can't be. Well, the man would be old enough, but no, Granny said my father was dead. It couldn't be my father.* Just as Wendell had convinced himself, the man began to explain.

"Your mother died in childbirth, Son."

"Yes, sir."

"Your grandmother was a wicked woman, unless she changed, God rest her soul."

"Yes, sir." Wendell almost forgot to breathe.

"Well, Wendell Cunningham, I don't know what you have been told, but I am your father."

Running his fingers through his hair, Wendell wanted to believe this man. Yet he dared not hope this could be true. Confusion dulled his senses. "But how, where . . . "

"Son, I've searched for you all over five states. Sometimes I'd be mighty close to finding you, only to learn that your grandmother had whisked you away again."

"We did move around a lot. Never did understand why."

"When your mother died, I was grief stricken. She was a good woman. Don't know how she turned out so good, but she was a lovely creature, fragile and dainty—too dainty to make it through childbirth." The man before him sadly shook his head.

"So you are my father?" Wendell made the few strides to his father in record time. Suddenly everything made sense—the ploys of his grandmother and her wickedness.

"Yes, I am your father." The two men embraced, pulling back to stare into each others' eyes, and finding the truth there.

Wendell's tears ran down his face, tears of joy for the gift of a father and tears of sadness for all that had been lost.

"How did you find me, uh, Father?"

"Got a job with the railroad several years back, Son. Just got a transfer to Rosewood; never knew it was on the map."

"God in all his wisdom ordained us to be together after all these years, Father." Stepping forward, Wendell had to touch his father to make sure he was not dreaming.

Tears escaped Theodore Cunningham's eyes. "Amen. And to think that you're a preacher, why it does my heart good."

"I hope you'll be attending my church, Father."

"Wouldn't have it any other way."

"Where are you staying?"

"Just made arrangements at the boarding house. That's when I learned about the church and that you were the pastor. Couldn't believe how it all came together so easily."

"Well, after tonight, Father, I want you to stay with me."

Shock and unbelief showed in the man's eyes. "Oh, Son, I wouldn't want to impose. The railroad will pay for my room and board until I find a place to live."

"No bother, Father. I'm alone until March. You just missed my betrothed. She's on the train to Savannah to finish art school, and then we're getting married."

"How wonderful, Son. I'll be glad to join you, but only until March." Theodore Cunningham stared at his son, as if unable to comprehend what they had been blessed with. "I've been a believer for many years, been praying about finding you."

"Well, your prayers have been answered. God has given me a special gift. Always wanted a father."

"I thought about you every day of my life, Son. Went on to marry another lady, but she wasn't like your mother. Nagged all the time, right on up 'til her dying breath. Kinda reminded me of your granny."

"Well, I'm just glad you are here now, Father." Wendell patted him on the back.

"Me too, Son. I'll leave you to your day, and I'll be over this way tomorrow." Another embrace, and Wendell's father was out the door of the parsonage. The cold wind following his departure could not dampen the warmth rising in Wendell's heart. "Lord you are good."

Exiting the train, Hannah ran into Ezra's arms. Stepping up into the carriage, she exclaimed with glee as Eliza rose from the seat to wrap her in a hug. "Couldn't wait ta see ya, Miz Hanner."

"I'm so glad you came, Eliza. I've missed you. I brought you some oranges."

"Bless yo soul, Miz Hanner. I be enjoyin' mysef. Sho nuff."

It felt good to be in the company of her dear friends. The trip back to the plantation was filled with plans for the wedding. Eliza enjoyed learning every detail of who would be coming and how everything would take place.

Pulling up in the drive, Hannah felt happy. Gabrielle came bounding down the steps as they pulled around back. "Hannah, you're home. Oh, I simply must tell you everything about Anthony Peabody." Her face was aglow, and Hannah couldn't wait to join her.

Saying good-bye to Ezra and Eliza, the two girls bounded up the stairs with chunks of cheese, bread, ham, and pastries on a platter. Hannah knew they would talk until long after midnight.

"Oh, Hannah, Anthony is just the greatest."

"I'm so glad for you, Gabrielle. Isn't love grand?"

"Yes, it's the most wonderful feeling ever."

"Yes, it is. Now tell me everything."

And Gabrielle did tell Hannah every little detail about Anthony Peabody, from how he liked his toast burnt to how he got up every morning, walking the streets of Savannah to find someone in need that he could help.

"Your father must just love this man."

"Yes, he is so pleased. But if not for the Peabody name, Mother would be ashamed that he is my suitor. She's afraid he will be thought a needy soul because he associates so much with the disadvantaged.

The girls laughed and ate until they felt giddy.

Gabrielle's eyelids were drooping. "We had better go to bed, or we'll sleep until noon tomorrow."

"You're right, Gabrielle, but I've enjoyed our talk so much. Good night."

Gabrielle left Hannah's room, tiptoeing down the hall. Hannah prayed the floorboards wouldn't creak. It was well past two in the morning.

Hannah quickly fell into her old routine at art school, sketching and becoming even more proficient in the use of oils. Her paintings were proudly displayed alongside Jacques De Ponte's art work at the shows in the city.

With her work selling almost as well as the artiste's, she was busy every day, striving to fulfill the demand. Before she knew it, January had moved to February and the days were even colder.

Putting the finishing strokes of oil paint on canvas, depicting a garden scene, complete with Mrs. Bernadette's cockatiels, Hannah heard a skirmish in the hall.

The door of the studio flew wide open. Gabrielle ran in, her face flushed and fearful. "Hannah, you must come. Something terrible is about to happen."

Fear gripped Hannah's heart. Was it Ezra or Eliza or perhaps the artist or even Nellie? Quickly laying her paint brush aside, she asked, "What is it, Gabrielle?"

Gabrielle blurted out the reason for her concern. "Mr. Quantrail called out the Union soldier."

"*The* Union soldier, Gabrielle?" Hannah's mind raced, remembering the Union soldier that had fathered a child of Mr. Quantrail's wife. "The one, the one ... "

"Yes, Hannah, the one that Mrs. Quantrail had the babe for. He's called him out to a duel."

"Oh, no." Hannah had heard of duels but had never been a witness to one. Even though it sounded terrible, the girls couldn't resist trying to catch a glimpse of the action.

Grabbing their heavy coats, they were out the door in a flash. Spotting Ezra's buggy they ran, catching up with the conveyance, jumping aboard as if they had paid for a seat. Feeling the bump, Ezra and Eliza turned around, smiling.

Ezra pointed up ahead. "Dey's done an been a arguin' all mornin' so Adam Moses be a sayin'. Say he done an heared ol Mista Quantrail a callin' him out. I reckon as how dat soldier be a livin' nearby all dis time. Seems he be drunk an be a comin' ta take the mizzus away wif him."

Eliza pointed through the trees, whispering. "There they be."

"Sho nuff." Ezra nodded his head, pulling the wagon just out of sight a safe distance from the two.

They were already walking in opposite directions and counting. "Soon, dey be a turnin' round what ta face each other. Goodness sakes alive, somebody gonna be dead afore sundown." Both Ezra and his wife were praying.

Hannah and Gabrielle joined them. Before their eyes, the Union soldier hit the ground just as Mr. Quantrail turned around, drawing his gun. But he never shot it.

Ezra clapped his hands. "Looks like de soldier done an pass out. Sho nuff, guess his liquor got to 'im at jes da right time. Well glory be." Ezra laughed, and Eliza and the girls did too.

Walking over to the soldier, Mr. Quantrail gave his leg a kick. Placing his gun back in its holster, he shook his head and walked back to his house.

Looking up, Hannah pointed at Mrs. Quantrail, returning inside her home from her perch on the widow's walk.

The ride back to Ezra's barn was much more relaxed than the ride to the site of the duel. "Dey keeps on, an somebody gonna pay da price." Ezra's solemn words followed the girls back into the house.

"Let's have some hot cider, Hannah." Gabrielle was already pouring the liquid into a pot.

"Sure sounds good. I'm about to freeze my petticoats, staying out in that cold so long."

Hot cider, spiced just right with cinnamon, warmed the girls. The rest of the day was spent exchanging love stories about their beaus.

Hannah's letter from Wendell arrived the following day. She could scarcely believe what he wrote. Running to Gabrielle's bedroom, she couldn't wait to share the news. "Gabrielle, you won't believe it. Wendell's father found him."

"Where did he find him?"

"Right there in Rosewood. Oh, Gabrielle, do you see how good God is? Only he could put all these missing pieces together."

"What missing pieces, Hannah?"

"My sister lost her wedding gown, so my brother-in-law met Wendell, who found the gown. Then I met Wendell. He wanted to settle down and have a wife and be a pastor. The town of Rosewood wasn't even there yet, but God had it built and sent Theodore Cunningham all the way there to work for the railroad. He had been looking for his son for many years."

"Oh Hannah, I am so happy for you and the preacher. Now he doesn't have to be lonely while he's waiting for your hand in marriage."

"That's right. And Mr. Cunningham will live right there in Rosewood. Oh, Gabrielle, won't that be grand? Wendell says he is the nicest man." Hannah hugged the missive to her chest.

"Well, I sure hope he comes up for the wedding."

"Wendell says a team of wild horses couldn't keep his father from coming. The railroad has already granted him time off."

The wedding seemed even more real to Hannah with this wonderful news. She was so happy her father-in-law could be a part of this happy day.

February took wings. For the life of Hannah, she could not imagine where the days had gone.

Chapter 33

March winds were coming right on time, practicing for Hannah's wedding day. Listening to the sounds of the river, breathing in the smell of the fragrant garden below, the young girl knew she would miss this place, the place where she and Wendell had found true love.

But time marched on. New horizons awaited exploration. It was almost time for the next step on this exciting journey of life.

Final preparations were being made for the glorious day approaching. Packing a trunk for her parents to return to her new home in Rosewood, Hannah filled one for her honeymoon as well.

Beautiful gowns lay in her wedding trousseau trunk. Mrs. Bernadette De Ponte had treated Hannah to a shopping spree for nightgowns. And oh the beautiful silk creations they had chosen.

"Special for you, dahling." Touching the filmy beauties, Hannah remembered the lady's words. She blushed, thinking of Wendell's surprise and adoration on their honeymoon. The young girl pinched herself, telling herself this was real.

She was ready for the ceremony and for the much anticipated honeymoon. March 18, 1873, could never come soon enough.

The week before the wedding, Hannah leaned out of her upstairs window, reveling in the feel of the gentle breeze coming off the Savannah River. *It will be perfect,* she thought, envisioning her wedding gown blowing in that breeze.

Only a few days ago, she had visited the peach orchard, finding it fully decorated. Blooms of lace covered every branch for as far as the eye could see. The predusk time for the wedding would be perfect.

With pencil, Hannah sketched the orchard in all its glory, the sun's rays giving just the right hues, enhancing the lacey blossoms.

Coming back to the house, she had completed an oil painting of her wedding in the next two days, adding the preacher and herself, along with her sisters, brothers, and both Wendell's father and her own father in the wedding party, Grandpappy standing in front with his Bible open. Grandmam and Mother were painted in the scene, along with her friends, Ezra and Eliza and the artist and his wife. She added Delia Baldwin and the children in the family as well.

This would be her pride and joy and a great gift to her husband. *My husband,* she thought. And what a wonderful thought it was.

The week flew by, ushering in even more signs of spring. Birds now filled the front garden, covered in its beautiful spring foliage. The flowers were showing off their blossoms in a spectacular array of colors.

Ezra and Jacques De Ponte drove both the family carriages to the train, returning with the Baxter family. They were covered in cinders. Eliza brought out the soap and had them presentable by the time they were to meet Mr. and Mrs. De Ponte.

"My, but your gardens are lovely," Mother complimented Mrs. Bernadette De Ponte after the formal introductions.

"Why thank you, my dear. Can't take all the credit. The gardener tends the plants. Couldn't bear to get my nails chipped and dirty."

Adeline Baxter looked down at her own nails. They were cut close due to her time in the garden.

Jacques De Ponte picked up the conversation, showing his guests about and walking them through the art studio where Hannah's work stood on display. "These will all be sold very soon."

"Hannah, these oils are wonderful. I'm a proud father, my dear."

She came to stand by him, grabbing his arm. "Thank you, Father."

"Why Hannah, Grandpappy didn't know you could do such fine work in oil. But I'm not the least bit surprised."

Delia Baldwin coddled Little Wyatt, perusing Hannah's work. "No finer work is found in Boston, dear. You are quite an artist."

The whole family praised Hannah's work. It felt so good having them here in Savannah, being a part of her world. She was so glad they had chosen Savannah for their wedding place.

Just before sunset, the Baxters departed for their rooms at the Old Savannah Inn. That evening, Wendell arrived with Theodore Cunningham, proudly presenting his betrothed. "Father, meet my beloved."

Hannah's eyes misted with tears. The man in front of her was an older version of her preacher. She walked into his open arms.

Theodore Cunningham held her close. "I am so happy to have a daughter." He pulled her back, peering into her eyes. "And my, aren't you pretty. I can see why my son fell in love with you." He pulled her close again.

"Thank you, sir. I'll be honored to be your daughter."

The three walked through the peach orchard, sharing the story of Wendell and Hannah's romance here in Savannah, then showing him the courting buggy. At the end, they walked Wendell's father to the front of the house, showing him the spot where Isaac received his baptizing from the third floor.

"Serves the man right, Miss Hannah." Theodore Cunningham chuckled.

When his father retired to Ezra's house, Wendell and Hannah took a walk along the Savannah River, strolling arm in arm.

"Your father is easy to talk to. He is such a likable man."

"Yes, he is, Hannah. I'm glad you enjoy him."

She tickled his rib. "How could I not enjoy him? He reminds me of you."

"I can see why you couldn't resist him, then." Wendell laughed.

The two enjoyed their stroll, heading to their own private chambers for the night—Wendell to the Perkins' residence and Hannah to the De Ponte mansion. This would be their last night alone.

Rising early, Hannah went to her window seat. Watching the birds chase each other from branch to branch, she inhaled the sweet smell of roses from the garden below. Rising to view the Savannah River from her favorite perch, she breathed deeply of the air coming in her window.

Looking to the right, she saw her sisters and Gabrielle busily gathering wildflowers alongside Eliza. The kind woman had promised to find the best Queen Anne's Lace blossoms on the plantation and surround them with wildflowers matching the girls' bouquets.

Watching the group, Hannah was thankful for each of them. A touch of sadness flitted across her mind as she thought of Susannah. But she was returning to Rosewood, and her best friend would be waiting.

Looking to the heavens, Hannah felt the need to offer thanks. "Father, thank you for blessing me with a fine man, a wonderful family, and beautiful friends."

"Amen, sister." Wendell grinned at her from the other side of the hedge.

"Brother Preacher Man, don't you be calling me *sister.* And by the way, you're not supposed to see me today."

"My dear, I've already missed too many days seeing you. Eliza says to come back to her place for dinner. She'll be cooking up some of her finest." His bribe worked.

"I'll be there at noon." Hannah smiled to herself. *What a fine man. And he'll be mine before nightfall.* She could hardly wait to be off on the train for her honeymoon.

Gabrielle played softly on the flute as the wedding party took their places before Grandpappy. Her cousin, Larae De Ponte, had arrived just that morning. She stood beside Gabrielle's parents, noticing Blaine a little more than seemed necessary.

Hannah's family was so dear to her, even ornery Blaine. Soft rays of the setting sun placed a hallowed glow around the faces of the happy group.

The gentle breeze blew the skirts of the girls standing in a row. Hannah made her way toward her groom, this moment holding all the joy she had imagined.

Wisps of the curls Eliza had tediously fashioned blew their approval alongside the beautiful green eyes of the girl gazing at her beloved. His eyes returned all the love shining in her own.

Wildflowers, held by the girls and surrounding Hannah's bouquet of lacey blossoms, took Wendell's mind to another time and place. He could see his Hannah sitting amidst those wildflowers, soft rays of another sunset playing sweetly along the sunbeams glowing in her eyes.

And now she stood beside him, a vision in her simple dress with small pearls decorating her bodice and cuffs. *How did I ever deserve this, Lord? Me, just a simple boy raised by a mean woman. It had to be your love and mercy, Lord, and I thank you.*

Grandpappy opened his Bible, reading of love and awaking love. "The power of love is the strongest force God has made. For in it abides forgiveness, happiness, peace, and joy. Love is the fulfillment of every need we have in this life. For it is by love that we attend to the needs of our loved ones."

"You may join hands."

Hannah passed her bouquet to Gabrielle, facing Wendell as they joined both hands. He couldn't seem to take his eyes from hers.

"Will you, Wendell Cunningham, take Hannah Baxter to be your wife? Will you join yourself to her and her alone, placing her desires above yours for as long as you both shall live?"

"I, I will."

"Will you, Hannah Baxter, take Wendell Cunningham to be your husband, keeping him as your beloved, standing with him in everything this life has to offer for as long as you both shall live?"

"Yes, Grandpappy, I will."

"You may now exchange rings."

Blaine snickered as Wendell's hand shook, placing the ring on Hannah's finger. One curt look from his sister wiped the smirk from his face.

Grandpappy's voice floated through the orchard. "May the love you share grow through the years, and may you look back in fond memory, realizing that what you have today was only the beginning of greater things to come. May God add his blessings to this holy union." He nodded to Wendell. "You may kiss your bride."

The preacher took Hannah into his arms, just holding her against him as if she was the most treasured thing in his life. And she was. He didn't look up for a while. Finally he kissed her, and after embracing her again, they turned, facing the crowd.

Grandpappy called out loud and clear, "I present to you Hannah and the preacher."

Everyone laughed at Grandpappy's presentation. But it was a special thing that he did that day. Hannah was mighty proud to have her preacher.

Going back to the mansion, she quickly dressed in a traveling suit. Coming downstairs, she joined her family and friends, sharing the cake and punch Hilda had prepared.

Wendell rose from the table. "We thank you for sharing this day. My wife and I will be taking our leave now."

Everyone hugged the couple good-bye.

Wendell loaded the vis-à-vis carriage with Hannah's trunk and his saddlebag. Some habits were hard to break; the saddlebags had traveled with him through the years.

The De Pontes had insisted the couple take the vis-à-vis carriage for this first night of their honeymoon. Ezra sat proud as a peacock in the driver's seat. He would do the honors of dropping them off at the Majestic Oaks Hotel. Decorated with wildflowers, the spokes of the carriage turned in a wild profusion of color as Mr. and Mrs. Wendell Cunningham made their way down the plantation drive.

Turning onto the road, Hannah and Wendell watched as their family waved good-bye. Little Beth was blowing kisses, the "twin" baby boys nestled close within the arms of their fathers. It was a beautiful sight, enhanced by the very last rays of the setting sun.

Wendell and Hannah enjoyed the quiet ride. Romance was in the air. Little conversation was needed as they held each other.

Pulling up in front of the hotel, Ezra looked in the floor, mumbling to himself. "Where be da bags? I's sees da trunk and saddlebag what Mista Wendell put in, but I cain't fine dem obernight bags, Miz Hanner." Ezra looked beyond upset, peering under the seats on both sides of the carriage. "I done knows I's put em right chere."

"We do need our overnight bags." Hannah jolted upright. "Ezra, look no further. I remember Blaine leaving the side of the carriage and sneaking off to a nearby tree. That rascal."

"Ezra be right back. Don't ya be a worryin' yo purty head none, Miz Hanner. Ol Ezra gonna take care o Mista Blaine." The old man took off at a rapid pace, urging the horses forward. The flowers on the wheels of the carriage blurred into a dizzying collage as he sped around a corner, one wheel coming off the ground. Hannah and Wendell laughed as they made their way into the hotel. "Wouldn't want to be Blaine," Wendell said.

Settling themselves in their beautiful room, the newlyweds were just about to give up hope of the bags being found when a knock sounded at the door.

Hannah opened it. "Mam, someone left these bags for you. Said your brother was to blame after all."

"Yes, sir, thank you." The attendant flashed a bright smile at her happy face.

Opening the overnight bag, Hannah removed the gift she had prepared for her husband. She brought out the sketchpad, handing Wendell the sketches of their romance.

He had seen some of the drawings from the brush arbor meetings, but smiled looking at them again.

There before him was the sketch of him rowing the boat to the Seminole village. "I can see the love in my eyes for you. Could you see it this vividly?"

"I hoped so. There were times I doubted it after Isaac's interruption, but I sure lived with hope of that love being true."

Wendell pulled his wife to him, kissing her soundly. "It was always a love that was true. I just thought you preferred Isaac, but after the baptism from the third-floor window, you redeemed yourself, my dear."

Perusing the sketches, he came upon Hannah in the field of wildflowers. "This is a favorite of mine." He had to kiss her again.

She pointed to the next one. "What about that one?"

"Oh, so you put me in the garden with you. Nice."

Turning another page of the sketchpad, he read, "*Mo than Molasses.*" Wendell laughed at the temperance woman preaching him a sermon.

"Now that is a favorite as well." He was pointing to the sketch titled *I Love You More.* The roses he had picked for her that day lay on the seat, a perfect memory.

The last sketch was wrapped. Opening the framed print, there before him, in oil, was their wedding. "How, how?" He pointed at the painting, dumbfounded.

"Cat got your tongue, Preacher?"

"How… "

"I sketched and then painted the scene, adding the wedding party as I knew it would be. A larger version will be headed to the parsonage with my parents."

"My but you are a talented beauty, my dear. God must be smiling on this day that he has made you mine."

"He's not the only one smiling." Hannah put the sketches and painting aside. "I couldn't be happier with my preacher."

"And I couldn't be happier with the preacher's wife."

"You may see the day you don't think I'm the *proper* preacher's wife." She searched his eyes.

"Just like a wildflower, my dear, God planted you, picked you, and has placed you where he wants you to shine, spreading beauty everywhere you go."

"Thank you, Preacher Man, for that fine sermon."

"I'll be thanking you, mam, to oblige the preacher man with kisses."

And Hannah obliged the preacher that night.

Wrapped in their own world, they wiped the sleep from their eyes when Ezra knocked on the door the next morning. Jumping up from the bed, they dressed in a hurry.

"We've a train to catch to Charleston, my love. Can't wait to take you to the bridal suite at the Edward Rutledge House."

Hannah's eyes answered the love dancing in her beloved's eyes. The night had passed much too quickly for Hannah and the preacher.

Author Contact Information for Readers

Dear Reader,
I love hearing from you. Please take a moment to visit my Web site: RebeccaLorraineWalker.com. You may leave me an e-mail at inspiredpen@msn.com or at Lorraine@RebeccaLorraineWalker.com May you be blessed on your journey!
Blessings forevermore,
Lorraine

Be sure to read Rebecca Lorraine Walker's debut novel:
Love at Laurel Oaks: Laurel Oaks Trilogy • Book 1

and her second book in the trilogy:
Katherine's Heart: Laurel Oaks Trilogy • Book 2

listen|imagine|view|experience

AUDIO BOOK DOWNLOAD INCLUDED WITH THIS BOOK!

In your hands you hold a complete digital entertainment package. Besides purchasing the paper version of this book, this book includes a free download of the audio version of this book. Simply use the code listed below when visiting our website. Once downloaded to your computer, you can listen to the book through your computer's speakers, burn it to an audio CD or save the file to your portable music device (such as Apple's popular iPod) and listen on the go!

How to get your free audio book digital download:

1. Visit www.tatepublishing.com and click on the e|LIVE logo on the home page.
2. Enter the following coupon code: 26bc-f54c-f683-4984-9418-dee0-466b-712a
3. Download the audio book from your e|LIVE digital locker and begin enjoying your new digital entertainment package today!